PLAGUE

PLAGUE

Graham Masterton

First published in the UK in 1977 by W. H. Allen & Co. Ltd
This paperback edition first published in 2021 by Head of Zeus Ltd

9 7 5 3 1 2 4 6 8

A CIP catalogue record for this book is available from
the British Library.

ISBN (PB): 9781801101202
ISBN (E): 9781800243392

Typeset by Siliconchips Services Ltd UK

Printed and bound in Great Britain by
CPI Group (UK) Ltd, Croydon cro 4yy

MIX
Paper from
responsible sources
FSC
www.fsc.org
FSC® C171272

Head of Zeus Ltd
First Floor East
5–8 Hardwick Street
London EC1R 4RG.

www.headofzeus.com

Book One

The Quick

One

He was still half-asleep when the doorbell rang. The sound penetrated his head like someone dropping coins down a well. It rang again, long and urgent, and he opened his eyes and discovered it was morning.

'Just a minute!' he croaked, with a sleep-dry mouth. The doorbell wouldn't wait, though, and kept on calling him. He swung his legs out of bed, groped on the floor for his discarded bathrobe, and pushed his feet uncomfortably into his slippers.

He shuffled out into the hallway. Through the frosted glass front door he could see a short stocky figure in blue, leaning on the bellpush.

'Just a minute!' he called again. 'I'm coming!'

He unlocked the door and peered out. The brilliant Florida sunshine made him blink. The warm morning breeze was blowing the palms beside his driveway, and already the sky was rich and blue.

'You Dr. Petrie?' said the man abruptly. He was heavy-set, dressed in crumpled blue coveralls. He was holding his cap in his hand, and his face had the expression of an anxious pug-dog.

'That's right. What time is it?'

'I don't know,' said the man hoarsely. 'Maybe eight-thirty, nine. It's my kid. He's sick. I mean, real sick, and I think he's gonna die or something. You have to come.'

'Couldn't you call the hospital?'

'I did. They asked me what was wrong, and when I told them, they said to see a doctor. They said it didn't sound too serious. But it keeps on getting worse and worse, and I'm real worried.'

The man was twitchy and sweating and the dark rings under his eyes showed just how little sleep he'd had. Dr. Petrie scratched his stubbly chin, and then nodded. Last night's party had left him feeling as if someone had hit him in the face with a rubber hammer, but he recognized real anxiety when he saw it.

'Come in and sit down. I'll be two minutes.'

The man in the blue coveralls took a couple of steps into the hallway, but was too nervous to sit. Dr. Petrie went into the bedroom, threw off his bathrobe, and dressed hastily. He slipped his feet into sandals, ran a comb through his tousled brown hair, and then reached for his medical bag and car keys.

Outside in the hallway, the man had at last sat down, perched on the edge of a wooden trunk that Dr. Petrie used for storing old medical journals. The man was staring at the pattern on the tiled floor, with that strange dull look that Dr. Petrie had seen so many times before. *Why has this happened to me? Of all people, why has it happened to me?*

'Mr.—'

'Kelly. Dave Kelly. My son's name is David, too. Are we ready to leave?'

'All set. Do you want to come in my car?'

'Sure,' said Dave Kelly woodenly. 'I don't think I wanna drive any more today.'

Dr. Petrie slammed the glass front door behind them and they stepped out into the heat and the sun. His dark blue Lincoln Continental was parked in the driveway. At the kerb stood a battered red pickup which obviously belonged to Mr. Kelly. On the side it said *Speedy Motors Inc.*

They climbed into the car and Dr. Petrie turned on the air-conditioning. It was March, and by this time of morning the temperature was already building up to 75 degrees. All along the quiet palm-lined streets of the fashionable Miami suburb where Dr. Petrie lived and practiced, the neat and elegant houses had blinds drawn and shades down.

'Now,' said Dr. Petrie, twisting his lanky body in the seat to reverse the Lincoln out of the drive. 'While we're driving, I want you to tell me everything that's happened to your son. Symptoms, color, everything. Oh, and direct me, too.'

'I live downtown,' said Kelly, rubbing sweat from his eyes. 'Just off North West 20th Street.'

Dr. Petrie swung the car around, and they bounced over the sidewalk and into the street. He gunned the engine, and they flickered through the light and shade of Burlington Drive, heading south. The air-conditioning chilled the sweat on Mr. Kelly's face, and he began to tremble.

'What made you choose me?' asked Dr. Petrie. 'There have to be a hundred doctors living nearer.'

Mr. Kelly coughed. 'You was recommended. My brother-in-law, he's an attorney, he used to be a patient of yours. I called him and asked him for the best. I tell you, doc – I gotta have the best for that kid. If he's as bad as he looks, I gotta have the best.'

'How bad *does* he look?' Dr. Petrie swerved around a parked truck.

'Right now, when I left him, he didn't even open his eyes. He's white, like paper. He started to shake and shiver around ten or eleven last night. He came into the bedroom and asked for a glass of water. He looked yellow and sick right then, and I gave him water, and aspirin. Was that okay?'

Dr. Petrie nodded. 'They won't do any harm. How old is he?'

'David's just nine years old. Last Thanksgiving.'

Dr. Petrie turned on to 441 and drove swiftly and steadily south. He glanced at his gold wristwatch. It was a little after nine. Oh well, a good abrupt start to Monday morning. He looked at himself in the driving mirror and saw a clean-cut all-American doctor with hangover written all over his face.

Some of his more critical medical colleagues had sarcastically nicknamed Dr. Petrie 'Saint Leonard of the Geriatrics'. That was because his clientele was mainly elderly and exclusively rich – old widows with immense fortunes and skins tanned as brown as leather handbags. And it was also because of his uncomfortably saintly appearance – a look that gave you the feeling that he drew half of his healing talent from medical training, and the other half directly from God. It was to do with his tall, lean body; his clear and almost inspired blue eyes; his open, benign face – and it all contributed to his success.

The way Dr. Petrie saw it, rich old ladies needed medication just as much as anyone else, and if he could build up his income with a melting smile and a glossy clinic full of Muzak and tropical fish, then there wasn't anything medically or morally wrong. Besides, he thought, at least

I'm concerned enough to climb out of bed on a hot Monday morning to visit a sick kid whose father really needs me.

He just wished that he had been saintly enough not to drink eight vodkatinis last night at the golf club get-together.

'Who's with the boy now?' Dr. Petrie asked Mr. Kelly.

'His mother. She was supposed to work the late shift, but she stayed home.'

'Have you given him anything to eat or drink?'

'Just water. He was burning up one minute, and cold the next. His lips was dry, and his tongue was all furred up – I reckoned that water was probably the best.'

Dr. Petrie stopped for a red light and sat there drumming his fingers on the rim of the steering-wheel, thinking.

Mr. Kelly looked across at him, nervous and worried, and tried not to fidget. 'Does it sound like any kind of sickness you know?' he asked.

Dr. Petrie smiled. 'I can't tell you until I see the boy for myself. It could be any number of things. What about his motions?'

'His what?'

'His bowels. Are they loose, or what?'

Mr. Kelly nodded. 'That's it. Runny, like soup.'

They moved away from the lights, and Mr. Kelly gave directions.

After a couple of turns, they arrived at a busy intersection with a garage on the corner. The garage had three pumps and a greasy-looking concrete forecourt, and in the back were a broken-down truck and a heap of old fenders, jacks, wrenches, and rusted auto parts.

Mr. Kelly climbed out of the car. 'Follow me. We live up over the garage.'

Dr. Petrie took his medical bag and locked his Lincoln. He followed Mr. Kelly around the side of the garage, and they clanged together up a shaky fire-escape, to a cluttered balcony, and then into the Kelly's apartment. They stepped into the kitchen first. It was gloomy and smelled of sour milk.

'Gloria, I brought the doctor!' called Mr. Kelly. There was no answer. Mr. Kelly guided Dr. Petrie through into the dingy hallway. There was a broken-down umbrella stand, and plaques of vintage cars molded out of plastic. A grubby red pennant on the wall said 'Miami Beach'.

'This way,' said Kelly. He gently opened a door at the end of the hall and ushered Dr. Petrie inside.

The boy was lying on crumpled, sweat-stained sheets. There was a suffocating smell of diarrhea and urine, even though the window was open. The child was thin, and looked tall for his age. He had a short haircut that, with his terrible pallor, made him look like a concentration camp victim. His eyes were closed, but swollen and blue, like plums. His bony ribcage fluttered up and down, and every now and then his hands twitched. His mother had wrapped pieces of torn sheet around his middle, to act as a diaper.

'I'm Dr. Petrie,' Leonard said, resting his hand momentarily on the mother's shoulder. She was a small, curly-haired woman in her mid-forties. She was dressed in a tired pink wrap, and her make-up was still half-on and half-off, just as it was when her son's sickness had interrupted her the night before.

'I'm glad you could come,' she said tiredly. 'He's no better and no worse.'

Dr. Petrie opened his medical bag. 'I just want to make a

few tests. Blood pressure, respiration – that kind of thing. Would you like to wait outside while I do that?'

The mother stared at him with weary eyes. 'I been here all night. I don't see any call t'leave now.'

Dr. Petrie shrugged. 'Whatever you like. But you look as though you could do with a cup of coffee. Mr. Kelly – would you be kind enough to make us all a cup of coffee?'

'Surely,' said the father, who had been hovering nervously in the doorway.

Dr. Petrie sat by the bed on a rickety wooden chair and took the boy's pulse. It was weak and thready – worse than he would have expected.

The mother bit her lip and said, 'Is he going to be all right? He is going to be all right, aint he? Today's the day he was supposed to go to the Monkey Jungle.'

Dr. Petrie tried to smile. He lifted the boy's arm again, and checked his blood pressure. Far too high for comfort. The last time he had seen vital signs as poor as this, the patient had been dead of barbiturate poisoning within three hours. He lifted David's puffed-up eyelids, and shone his torch into the glassy eyes. Weak response. He pressed his stethoscope against the little chest and listened to the heartbeat. He could hear fluid on the lungs, too.

'David,' he said gently, close to the boy's ear. 'David, can you hear me?'

The boy's mouth twitched, and he seemed to stir, but that was all.

'He's so sick,' said Mrs. Kelly wretchedly. 'He's so *sick*.'

Dr. Petrie rested his hand on David's skinny arm. 'Mrs. Kelly,' he said. 'I'm going to have to have this boy rushed straight to hospital. Can I use your phone?'

Mrs. Kelly looked pale. 'Hospital? But we called the hospital, and they said just a doctor would be okay. Can't you *do* something for him?'

Dr. Petrie stood up. 'What did you tell the hospital? Did you say how bad he was?'

'Well, I said he was sick, and he had a fever, and he'd messed the bed up a couple of times.'

'And what did they say to that?'

'They said it sounded like he'd eaten something bad, and that I oughtta keep him warm, give him plenty to drink and nothing to eat, and call a doctor. But after that, he started getting worse. That's when Dave went out for you.'

'This boy has to be in hospital,' insisted Dr. Petrie. 'I mean *now*. Where's your phone?'

'In the lounge. Straight through there.'

On the way out, Dr. Petrie almost collided with Mr. Kelly, bringing a tin tray with three mugs of coffee on it. He smiled briefly, and took one of the mugs. While he dialed the hospital, he sipped the scalding black liquid and tried not to burn his mouth.

'Emergency unit? Hallo. Listen, this is Dr. Leonard Petrie here. I have a young boy, nine years old, seriously sick. I want to bring him in right away. I can't tell you now, but have a blood test ready. Sputum, too. Some kind of virus, I guess. I'm not sure. It could be something like cholera. Right. Oh, sure, I'll tell the parents. Give me five, ten minutes – I'll be right there.'

Mr. and Mrs. Kelly were waiting at the door. '*Cholera?*' Mr. Kelly said.

Dr. Petrie swallowed as much coffee as he could. 'It's *like* cholera,' he said, as reassuringly as possible, 'but it's not exactly that. I can't tell without a blood sample. Dr. Selmer will do that for me at the hospital. He's a good friend of mine. We play golf together at Normandy Shores.'

Mrs. Kelly couldn't take in what he was saying. 'Golf?' she asked vaguely.

Dr. Petrie went through into David's bedroom, and helped Mr. Kelly to dress the boy in a pair of clean pajamas. David shuddered and whispered to himself while they buttoned the jacket up, but that was the only sign of life. Dr. Petrie lifted David up in his arms, and carried him out down the fire-escape. Mr. Kelly followed with the medical bag.

'I sure hope he's going to be okay,' said Kelly. 'He was supposed to go on a school outing today. He'll be sorry he missed it. He didn't talk about nothing else, for weeks. "When I go to the Monkey Jungle..." every sentence.'

'Don't worry, Mr. Kelly. Once we get David to hospital, he's going to get the best treatment going.'

They were nearly at the bottom of the fire-escape when Dr. Petrie felt something go through David's body – a sigh, a vibration, a cough. He was a skilled doctor and he recognized it. The boy was dying. He needed to get him into a respirator as fast as he could, within the next two or three minutes, or that could be the end.

'Mr. Kelly,' he said tightly, 'we have to get the hell out of here!'

Mr. Kelly frowned. He said, 'What?' But when he saw Dr. Petrie clattering rapidly down the rest of the fire-escape and across to his car, he came running behind without a word.

'My car keys!' Dr. Petrie said quickly. 'Get them out of my pocket. No, the other side. That's right.'

Mr. Kelly, in his panic, dropped the keys on to the sidewalk, and they skated under the car. He knelt down laboriously and scrabbled beneath the Lincoln while his son weakened in Dr. Petrie's arms.

'Hurry – for Christ's sake!'

At last Mr. Kelly hooked the keys towards the gutter, picked them up and opened the car. Dr. Petrie laid David carefully on the back seat, and told Mr. Kelly to sit beside the boy and hold him, in case he rolled off. The hospital was five minutes away if you drove slow and sedate, but David didn't have that long.

The Lincoln's engine roared. They backed up a few feet, then swerved out into the street. Dr. Petrie crossed straight through a red light, sounding his horn and switching on his headlamps. He prayed that downtown Miami wouldn't be jammed up with early-morning traffic. Swinging the Lincoln across a protesting stream of cars, he drove south on South West 27th Avenue at nearly fifty miles an hour. He swerved from one lane to the other, desperately trying to work his way through the traffic, leaning on his horn and flashing his lights.

'How's David?' he shouted.

'I don't know – bad,' said the father. 'He looks kinda blue.'

Dr. Petrie could feel the sweat sliding down his armpits. He clenched his teeth as he drove, and thought of nothing at all but reaching the hospital on time.

He swung the Lincoln in a sharp, tire-howling turn, and in the distance he could see the white hospital building. They might make it yet.

But just at that moment, without warning, a huge green

refrigerated truck rolled across in front of them, and stopped, blocking the entire street. Dr. Petrie shouted, '*Shit!*' and jammed on the Lincoln's brakes.

He opened the car window and leaned out. The driver of the truck, a heavy-looking redneck in a greasy trucker's cap, was lighting himself a cigar prior to maneuvering his vehicle into a side entrance.

'Out of the goddamn way!' yelled Dr. Petrie. 'Get that truck out of the goddamn way!'

The truck driver tossed away a spent match and searched for another.

'What's the hurry, mac?' he called back. 'Don't get so worked up – you'll give yourself an ulcer.'

'I'm a doctor! I have a sick kid in this car! I have to get him to hospital!'

The driver shrugged. 'When they open the gates, I'll move out of your way. But I ain't shifting till I'm good and ready.'

'For God's sake!' shouted Dr. Petrie. 'I mean it. This kid is seriously ill!'

The truck driver blew smoke. 'I don't see no kid,' he remarked. He looked around to see if the gates were open yet, so that he could back the truck up.

Dr. Petrie had to close his eyes to control his fury. Then he spun the Lincoln on to the sidewalk, bouncing over the kerb, and drove around the truck's front fender. A hydrant scraped a long dent all the way down the Lincoln's wing, and Dr. Petrie felt the underside of the car jar against the concrete as he drove back on to the street on the other side of the truck.

Three more precious minutes passed before he pulled the car to a halt in front of the hospital's emergency unit. The orderlies were waiting for him with a trolley. He lifted David out of the back of the car like a loose-jointed marionette, and laid him gently down. The orderlies wheeled him off straight away.

Mr. Kelly leaned against the car. His face was drawn and sweaty. 'Jesus,' he whispered. 'I thought we'd never make it. Is he going to be all right?'

Dr. Petrie rested a hand on Mr. Kelly's shoulder. 'Don't you doubt it, Mr. Kelly. He's a very sick boy, but they know what they're doing in this place. They'll look after him.'

Mr. Kelly nodded. He was too exhausted to argue.

'If you want to wait in the waiting-room, Mr. Kelly – just go into the main entrance there and ask the receptionist. She'll tell you where it is. When I've talked to David's doctors, I'll come and let you know what's happening.'

Mr. Kelly nodded again. 'Thanks, doctor,' he said. 'You'll – make sure they look after Davey, won't you?'

'Of course.'

Dr. Petrie left Mr. Kelly to find his way to the waiting-room. He pushed through the swing doors outside the emergency unit, and walked down the long, cream-colored corridor until he reached the room he was looking for.

Through the windows, he could see his old friend Dr. Selmer talking to a group of doctors and nurses, and holding up various blood samples. Dr. Petrie rapped on the door.

'How's it going?' he asked, when Dr. Selmer came out. Anton Selmer was a short, gingery-haired man with a broad nose and plentiful freckles. He always put Dr. Petrie in mind of Mickey Rooney. He had a slight astigmatism, and wore heavy horn-rimmed eyeglasses.

Dr. Selmer, in his green surgical robes, pulled a face. 'Well, I don't know about this one, Leonard. I really can't say. We're making some blood and urine and sputum analyses right now. But I'm sure glad you brought him in.'

'Have you any clues at all?'

Dr. Selmer shrugged. What can I say? You were right when you said it looked a little like cholera, but it obviously isn't just cholera. The throat and the lungs are seriously infected, and there's swelling around the limbs and the joints. It may be some really rare kind of allergy, but it looks more like a contagious disease. A very virulent disease, too.'

Dr. Petrie rubbed his bristly chin.

'Say,' grinned Dr. Selmer. 'You look as though you've been celebrating something.'

Dr. Petrie gave him half a smile. 'Every divorced man is entitled to celebrate his good fortune once in a while,' he replied. 'Actually, it was the golf club party.'

'By the look of you, I'm not sorry I missed it. You look like death.'

A pretty dark-haired nurse came out of the emergency unit doors and both men watched her walk down the corridor with abstracted interest.

Dr. Petrie said, 'If it's contagious, we'd better see about inoculating the parents. And we'd better find out where he picked it up. Apart from that, I wouldn't mind a shot myself.'

'When we know what it is,' said Selmer, 'we'll inoculate everybody in sight. Jesus, we've just gotten rid of the winter 'flu epidemic. The last thing I want is an outbreak of cholera.'

'What a great way to start the week,' said Dr. Petrie. 'They don't even live in my district. The guy runs a garage on North West 20th.'

Dr. Selmer took off his green surgical cap. 'I always knew you were the guardian angel for the whole of Miami, Leonard. I can just see you up there on Judgement Day, sitting at God's right hand. Or maybe second from the right.'

Dr. Petrie grinned. 'One of these days, Anton, a bolt of lightning will strike you down for your unbelieving. You know, I bent my goddamn car on the way here. Some son of a bitch in a truck was blocking the street, and I had to drive over the sidewalk. Would you believe he just sat there and lit a cigar?'

Dr. Selmer raised his gingery eyebrows. 'It's the selfish society, Leonard. I'm all right, and screw you Charlie.' They started to walk together down the corridor. 'I guess that must have been when it happened,' Dr. Selmer said.

'When what happened?'

'When the boy died.'

Dr. Petrie stopped, and stared at him hard. 'You mean he's *dead*?'

Dr. Selmer took his arm. 'Leonard – I'm sorry. I thought you realized. He was dead on arrival. You better have your car cleaned out if he was sitting in the back. You wouldn't want to catch this thing yourself.'

Dr. Petrie nodded. He felt stunned. He saw a lot of death, but the death that visited his own clientele was the shadowy death of old age, of failing hearts and hardened arteries.

The people who died under Dr. Petrie's care were reconciled to their mortality. But young David Kelly was just nine years old, and today he was supposed to have gone to the Monkey Jungle.

'Anton,' said Dr. Petrie, 'I'll catch you later. I have to tell the father.'

'Okay,' said Dr. Selmer. 'But don't forget to tell both parents to come in for a check-up. I don't want this kind of disease spreading.'

Dr. Petrie walked quickly down the fluorescent-lit corridors to the waiting-room. Before he pushed open the door, he looked through the small circular window, and saw Mr. Kelly sitting hunched on a red plastic chair, smoking and trying to read yesterday's *Miami Herald*.

He didn't know what the hell he was going to say. How do you tell a man that his only son, his nine-year-old son, has just died?

Finally, he pushed open the door. Mr. Kelly looked up quickly, and there was questioning hope in his face.

'Did you see him?' Mr. Kelly asked. 'Is he okay?'

Dr. Petrie laid his hand on the man's shoulder and pressed him gently back into his seat. He sat down himself, and looked into Mr. Kelly's tired but optimistic eyes with all the sympathy and care he could muster. When he spoke, his voice was soft and quiet, expressing feeling that went far deeper than bedside manner.

'Mr. Kelly,' he said. 'I'm sorry to tell you that David is dead.'

Mr. Kelly's mouth formed a question, but the question was never spoken. He simply stared at Dr. Petrie as if he didn't know where he was, or what had happened. He was still sitting, still staring, as the tears began to fill his eyes and run down his cheeks.

Dr. Petrie stood up. 'Come on,' he said quietly. 'I'll drive you home.'

★

By the time he got back to his clinic, his assistant Esther had already arrived, opened his mail, and poured his fresh-squeezed orange juice into its tall frosted glass. She was sitting at her desk, her long legs self-consciously crossed and her skirt hiked high, typing with the hesitant delicacy of an effete woodpecker. After all, she didn't want to break her long scarlet nails. She was twenty-one – a tall bouffant blonde with glossy red lips and a gaspy little voice. She wore a crisp white jacket that was stretched out in front of her by heavy, enormous breasts, and she teetered around the clinic on silver stilettos.

For all her ritz, though, Esther was trained, cool and practical. Dr. Petrie had seen her comfort an old woman in pain, and he knew that words didn't come any warmer. Apart from that, he enjoyed Esther's hero-worship, and the suppressed rage of his medical colleagues whenever he attended a doctor's convention with her in tow.

'Good *morning*, doctor,' said Esther pertly, when he walked in. 'I looked for you in your bedroom, but you weren't around.'

'Disappointed?' he said, perching himself on the edge of her desk.

Esther pouted her shiny red lips. 'A little. You never know when Nurse Cinderella might get lucky and catch Dr. Charming's eye.'

Dr. Petrie grinned. 'Any calls?'

'Just two. Mrs. Vicincki wants to drop by at eleven. She says her ankle's giving her purgatory. And your wife.' Dr. Petrie stood up and took off his jacket. 'My ex-wife,' he corrected.

'Sorry. Your ex-wife. She said you'd have to pick your

daughter up tonight instead of tomorrow, because she's going to visit her mother in Fort Lauderdale.'

Dr. Petrie rubbed his eyes. 'I see. I don't suppose she said what time tonight.'

'Seven. Priscilla will be waiting for you.'

'Okay. What time's my first appointment?'

'In ten minutes. Mrs. Fairfax. All her records are on your table. There isn't much mail, so you should get through it all by then.'

Dr. Petrie looked mock-severe. 'You really have me organized, don't you?'

Esther made big blue eyes at him. 'Isn't that what clinical assistants are for?'

He patted her shoulder. 'I sometimes wonder,' he said. 'If you feel like making me some very strong black coffee, you may even find out.'

'Sure thing,' said Esther, and stood up. 'Just remember, though, that a girl can't wait for ever. Not even for Prince Valiant, M.D.'

Dr. Petrie went through to his clinic. It was built on the east side of the house – a large split-level room with one wide glass wall that overlooked a stone-flagged patio and Dr. Petrie's glittering blue swimming pool. The room was richly carpeted in cool deep green, and there were calm, mathematical modern paintings on every wall. By the fine gauzy drapes of the window stood a pale marble statue of a running horse.

Dr. Petrie sat in his big revolving armchair and picked at the mail on his desk. Usually, he went through it fast and systematically, but today his mind was thrown off. He sipped his orange juice and tried not to think about David

Kelly's flour-white face, and the anguished shivers of his grieving father.

There wasn't much mail, anyway. A couple of drug samples, a medical journal, and a letter from his attorney telling him that Margaret, his ex-wife, was declining to return his favorite landscape painting from the one-time marital home. He hadn't expected to get it back, anyway. Margaret considered that the home, and all of its contents, were fair pickings.

Esther came teetering in with his coffee. The way her breasts bounced and swayed under her white jacket, she couldn't be wearing a bra. Dr. Petrie wondered what she'd look like nude; but then decided that the real thing would probably spoil his fantasy.

She set the coffee down on his desk, and stared at him carefully. 'You don't seem yourself this morning.'

'Who do I seem like? Richard Chamberlain?'

'No, I don't mean that. I mean you don't look well.'

Dr. Petrie stirred Sweet'N Low into his coffee, and tapped the spoon carefully on the side of the cup.

'I'm worried,' he said. 'That's all.'

Esther looked at him seriously. 'Is there anything I can do?'

He raised his eyes. He gave a half smile, and then shook his head. 'I don't think so. It was what happened this morning. I was called out to help a young kid downtown. His father came all the way up here because I was recommended. He wanted the best, he said. But it was too late. The kid died on the way to hospital. He was only nine.'

'That's awful.'

Dr. Petrie rubbed the back of his neck tiredly. 'I know. It's awful. And that's all that I can say about it or do about it. I don't often feel inadequate, Esther, but I do right now.'

She gently laid her hand on him. 'If it helps any,' she said, 'you ought to think about the people you've saved.'

Just then, the phone bleeped. Esther picked it up, and said, 'Dr. Petrie's clinic – can I help you?' She listened, and nodded, and then handed the phone over. 'It's for you,' she said. 'It's Miss Murry.'

Dr. Petrie took the receiver. 'You don't have to look so disapproving,' he told Esther. 'You and me, we're like the dynamic duo – Batman and Robin. Inseparable.'

Esther collected his empty orange-juice glass and tidied up his mail. 'How can we be inseparable, if we've never been together?' she asked provocatively teasing him, and teetered back to her desk.

Adelaide Murry sounded out of breath. Dr. Petrie said, 'Hi. You sound breathless.'

'I am,' said the sweet little voice on the other end of the phone. 'I've just played three sets with the new pro.'

'Is he good?'

'He's not exactly Björn Borg, but he's better than his late unlamented predecessor. A bit heavy with the forearm smashes. Proving his virility, I shouldn't wonder.'

Dr. Petrie laughed. 'I used to like his late unlamented predecessor. He was the only tennis club pro I could ever beat.'

'Darling,' said Adelaide, 'the club *dog* could beat his late unlamented predecessor.'

'Well,' retorted Dr. Petrie, 'what's wrong with that? Listen – do you want me to pick you up at the club tonight?'

'Are you coming this way?'

'I have to pick up Priscilla.'

'*Tonight?* I thought it was tomorrow! Oh, darling – what about our elegant intelligent dinner-for-two on the Starlight Roof?'

Dr. Petrie took a deep breath. He knew that Adelaide wasn't crazy about Priscilla – maybe because Adelaide, at nineteen, was still just a little girl herself.

'We can eat at home,' said Dr. Petrie. 'That Polynesian place delivers. And champagne, too. How about that?'

Adelaide was sulking. 'It's hardly romantic. I feel like doing something *romantic*. Eating at home is so ghoulish. You have to wash your own dishes.'

Dr. Petrie ran his hands through his hair. 'Listen,' he said. 'I'll buy two candles, a single red rose, and a new Leonard Bernstein record. Is that romantic enough for you?'

Adelaide gave a deep mock sigh. 'I should have dated my Uncle Charlie. At least he knows how to twist. All right, darling. I surrender, as usual. What time will you get here?'

'Six-thirty. And listen – I love you.'

'I love you too. I just hope this phone isn't tapped. They'd report you to the medical council for suggestive conduct.'

Dr. Petrie shook his head in exasperation, and laid the phone down.

Esther was helping Mrs. Fairfax into the clinic. Mrs. Fairfax was the sole survivor of the Fairfax food family, who had made their millions out of early freeze-drying techniques. She was a slender old lady with a sharp, penetrating face and a violet rinse. She walked on two sticks, but she held herself upright, and Dr. Petrie knew from uncomfortable experience that she had a sharp tongue.

'Good morning, Mrs. Fairfax,' he said smoothly. 'Are you feeling well?'

Mrs. Fairfax sat herself laboriously down in one of Dr. Petrie's two white Italian armchairs. She propped her sticks against the glass-topped coffee table, and spread her elegant blue-flowered dress around her.

'If I were well, Dr. Petrie,' she said icily, 'I should not be here.'

Dr. Petrie left his desk and went to sit beside her in another armchair. He always preferred the informal touch. It made patients feel easier; it even made them feel healthier.

'Is your hip bothering you again?' he asked sympathetically.

Mrs. Fairfax gave a histrionic sigh. 'My *dear* doctor, there is absolutely nothing wrong with my hip. But there is a great deal wrong with my beach.'

Dr. Petrie frowned. He could see himself frowning in the large smokey mirror opposite his chair. He wondered if, despite his looks, he was beginning to get old.

'Your *beach*?' he enquired politely. He was used to the eccentricities of wealthy old widows.

'It's absolutely *disgusting*,' she said coldly. She brushed back her violet hair with a tanned, elegant claw. Today, her fingers were encrusted with sapphires, but Dr. Petrie knew that she had as many rings for every color of dress she ever wore.

'What's wrong with it?'

'What's *wrong* with it? I don't know how you can *ask*! Haven't you read the newspapers?'

Dr. Petrie shook his head. 'I haven't had much time recently for the *Miami Herald*.'

'Well you should make time,' said Mrs. Fairfax imperiously. 'It's been happening all along the South Beach. And now it's turned up on mine.'

Dr. Petrie tried to smile. 'I hate to appear ignorant,' he said. 'But *what* has turned up on yours?'

Mrs. Fairfax lifted her sharp, haughty profile in obvious distaste. In a quiet, cold voice, she said, 'Feces.'

Dr. Petrie leaned forward, 'I beg your pardon?'

Mrs. Fairfax turned his way with a look of frozen disdain. 'You're a doctor. You know what that means. I went down to my beach yesterday morning for a swim and I found it was soiled with feces.'

Dr. Petrie rubbed his chin. 'Was it – *much*?'

'The whole shoreline,' said Mrs. Fairfax. 'And the beaches next to mine, on both sides. I can't tell you – the smell is abominable.'

'Have you complained to the health people?'

'Of course I have. I spent most of yesterday on the telephone. I got through to some very junior official who told me that they were doing everything they could, and that they were going to try and clear the beaches with detergent. But it's really not good enough. It's there now, it smells revolting, and I want you to do something about it.'

Dr. Petrie stood up and went to the window. He felt sticky and tired, and the glittering pool outside looked very inviting.

'Mrs. Fairfax,' he said, 'I don't think there's very much I can do, apart from call City Hall, like you did. It's probably treated sewage brought in by the sea. I know it doesn't look or smell too good, but it's pretty harmless.'

Mrs. Fairfax snorted. 'You're absolutely right it doesn't

look too good. I have a beach party planned for tomorrow evening. What am I going to say to my guests – my doctor says it's harmless? I pay very high taxes to live on the ocean, Dr. Petrie, and I don't expect to have to swim in excrement.'

Dr. Petrie turned around and smiled. 'All right, Mrs. Fairfax. I promise that I'll call the health department this morning for you. I'm sure that it's one of those rare accidents, and if they say they're going to clear the beach with detergent, they probably will. They're pretty hot on things like that in Miami.'

Mrs. Fairfax shook her head. 'First it was oil and now it's sewage,' she said tetchily. 'I don't know whether I'm renting a beach or a city dump.'

Dr. Petrie helped her out of her armchair and gave her back her sticks. 'I promise I'll call this morning,' he repeated. 'If you hold on one moment, I'll get Esther to help you out.'

After Mrs. Fairfaix, he saw three more patients. Mrs. Vicincki, with her sprained ankle; old Mr. Dunlop, with his kidney complaint; and the younger of the two elderly Miss Grays, who was suffering from sunburn. As usual, he tried to be calm, comforting, and reassuringly efficient.

Just before one o'clock, he pressed the intercom for Esther.

'Yes, doctor?'

'Esther,' he said. 'What are you doing for lunch?'

'Nothing special. I was thinking of a diet cola and a cream cheese on rye.'

Dr. Petrie coughed. 'That sounds revolting. How about coming down to Mason's Bar with me and sinking a steak-and-lobster grill?'

'But doctor, my *figure*—'

'Your figure, Esther, is one of the natural wonders of the world. Now, do you want to come, or don't you?'

There was a bleep. Esther said, 'Hold on a moment, doctor. It's the outside phone.'

He waited for a few moments. Then Esther came back to him and said, 'It's Dr. Selmer, from the hospital.'

'Okay. First tell me whether you're coming to lunch, then put him on.'

'Dr. Selmer says it's urgent.'

'Lunch is urgent. Are you coming?'

Esther sighed. 'All right. If you insist on twisting my arm like that.'

Dr. Petrie picked up the outside phone and leaned back in his chair, propping his feet on the edge of his desk. He picked at a stray thread on his cotton slacks.

'Anton?'

'Oh, hi, Leonard,' said Dr. Selmer. 'I was just calling you about that kid you brought in this morning.'

'Did you find out what it was?'

'Well, we're not too sure yet. The blood and sputum tests haven't been completed, although there's obviously some kind of bacillus infection there. I had his parents in for a check-up this morning, and they seem okay, but I've asked their permission for a post-mortem.'

Dr. Petrie snapped the thread from his slacks. 'Have you any ideas what you're looking for?' he asked.

Dr. Selmer sounded uncertain. 'It could be tularemia. Did you notice any pet rabbits around the kid's place?'

'I don't think so. You really think it's that?'

'Dr. Bushart thinks so. He had a couple of cases out in California.'

'Sure, but that's California,' Dr. Petrie said. 'California has every weird bug and bacillus going. This is healthy, swamp-infested Florida.'

'We're checking up anyway,' said Dr. Selmer. 'Meanwhile, I shouldn't worry too much. If it was tularemia, the chances that you've picked it up are pretty remote. Just to be safe, though, I should give yourself a couple of shots of streptomycin.'

'Are you playing golf this weekend?' asked Dr. Petrie. 'I'm still short of a partner.'

'Why don't you teach that assistant of yours – what's her name – Esther. I'd sure like to see *her* swing!'

'Anton,' said Dr. Petrie, 'you have a very impure mind.'

There was a laugh from the other end of the phone. 'It's only because I never get to do anything impure with my body.'

Esther came into the room, signaling elaborately that she was ready for lunch.

Dr. Petrie said, 'Okay, Anton – I have to leave now. But let me know what you find out about the kid, will you? As soon as you know.'

'Sure thing,' said Dr. Selmer. 'And don't forget the shots. All I want right now is a golf partner down with rabbit disease.'

Dr. Petrie laughed. 'Who do you think I am? Bugs Bunny?'

It was a cool, cloudless evening. A fresh wind was blowing in from the Atlantic Ocean, and ruffling the dark blue surface of Biscayne Bay. As they drove across the North Bay Causeway over Treasure Island, a large red motor-launch furrowed the water, and seagulls twisted and spun in its wake.

Dr. Petrie was wearing a sky-blue sports shirt and white slacks belted with rope. He was feeling relaxed and calm, and he drove the Lincoln with one hand resting lightly on the wheel.

Beside him, Adelaide Murry was trying to put on lipstick in the sun-visor mirror. She was a tall, elegant girl, dressed in a low broderie-anglaise dress the color of buttermilk, which showed off her deep-tanned shoulders and her soft cleavage. Her brunette hair, streaked with subtle tints, was brushed back from her face in fashionable curls. She had unusual, asymmetrical features – a slight squint in her hazel eyes and pouting lips that made you think she was cross.

At the moment, she *was* cross.

'Do you have to drive over every pothole and bump?' she said, as her lipstick jolted up over her lip.

Dr. Petrie grinned. 'It's a hobby of mine,' he said cheerfully. 'It's called "Getting Your Girlfriend to Push Her Lipstick Up Her Nose".'

Adelaide patted her mouth with a pink tissue. 'You're such a laugh, aren't you. What time are we supposed to pick up Priscilla?'

Dr. Petrie checked his watch. 'Ten minutes. But I like to go a little early. Margaret has a habit of making her wait outside the house.'

'I don't know why you stand for it,' said Adelaide tartly, crossing her long brown legs.

Dr. Petrie shrugged.

'If I was you,' said Adelaide, 'I'd march right in there and beat the living shit out of Margaret. And that flea-bitten dog of hers.'

Dr. Petrie glanced across at Adelaide and smiled a resigned smile. 'If you'd paid out as much money as I have – just to get free from a wife you didn't want any more – then you'd be quite satisfied with paying your alimony, seeing your kid, and keeping your mouth shut,' he said gently.

Adelaide looked sulky. 'I still think you ought to break the door down and smash her into a pulp,' she said, with emphatic, youthful venom.

Dr. Petrie swung the Lincoln left into Collins Avenue. 'That's what I like about you,' he said. 'You're so shy and ladylike.'

He switched on the car radio. There was a burst of music, and then someone started talking about this year's unusual tides and weather conditions, and the strange flotsam and jetsam that was being washed up on the shores of the East Coast. A coastguard and a medical officer were discussing the appearance of unsavory bits and pieces around Barnes Sound and Old Rhodes Key.

'I'm not prepared right now to identify this washed-up material,' said the medical officer, 'but we have had complaints that it contains raw sewage, in the shape of sanitary napkins, fecal matter and diapers. We have no idea where the material is coming from, but we believe it to be a completely isolated incident.'

Adelaide promptly switched the car radio off. 'We're just about to have *dinner*,' she protested. 'The last thing I want to hear about is sewage.'

Dr. Petrie glanced in his mirror and pulled out to overtake

a slow-moving truck. 'One of my patients complained this morning. She said she went down for a swim, and found her whole beach smothered in shit.'

'Oh, Jesus,' said Adelaide, wrinkling up her nose.

Dr. Petrie grinned. 'It's pretty revolting, isn't it? Maybe we're learning that what the Bible said was right. Throw your sewage on to the waters, and it shall come back to you.'

'I don't think that's funny,' said Adelaide. 'This is supposed to be the great American resort. I make my living out of people coming down here and playing tennis and swimming and having a good time. Who's going to come down here to paddle in diapers and sanitary napkins?'

Dr. Petrie shrugged. 'Well, it hasn't killed anyone yet.'

'How do you know? They might have swum out there and sunk without trace.'

'Listen,' said Dr. Petrie, 'more people die from bad food in restaurants than ever die of pollution in the sea. You get uneducated kitchen staff who don't wash their hands, and before you know where you are, you've got yourself a king-size dose of hepatitis.'

'Leonard, darling,' said Adelaide, acidly, 'I wish you wouldn't play doctors *all* the time. For once, I wish I was cooking my own supper.'

Margaret Petrie lived in what their divorce attorneys called the marital residence out on North Miami Beach. Dr. Petrie said nothing at all as he piloted the Lincoln down the familiar streets, and up to the white ranch-style house with its stunted palms and its small, neatly-trimmed lawn. It was here, in this quiet suburb, that he had first set up in medical practice eight years ago. It was here that he had worked and struggled to woo the wealthier and more socially elevated sick.

It was here, too, that Margaret and he had gradually discovered that they no longer had anything in common but a marriage license. Uneasy affection had degenerated into impatience, bickering and intolerance. It had been a messy, well-publicized, and very expensive divorce.

As Dr. Petrie pulled the Lincoln into the kerb, he remembered what Margaret had shrieked at him, at the top of her voice, as he drove away for the last time. *'If you want to spend the rest of your life sticking your fingers up rich old ladies, then go away and don't come back!'*

That remark, he thought to himself, summed up everything that was wrong with their marriage. Margaret, from a well-heeled family of local Republicans, had never wanted for money or material possessions. His own deep and restless anxiety for wealth was something she couldn't understand at all. To her, the way that he pandered to rich old widows was a prostitution of his medical talents, and she had endlessly nagged him to give up Miami Beach and go north. 'Be *famous*,' she used to say, 'be *respected*.'

It only occurred to him much later that she really did hunger for fame. She had fantasies of being interviewed by *McCall's* and *Redbook* – the wonderful wife of the well-known doctor. What she really wanted him to do was discover penicillin or transplant hearts, and on the day that he had realized that, he had known for sure that their marriage could never work.

Priscilla, as usual, was waiting at the end of the drive, sitting on her suitcase. She was a small, serious girl of six.

She had long, honey-colored hair, and an oval, unpretty face.

Dr. Petrie got out of the car, glancing towards the house. He was sure that he saw a curtain twitch.

'Hallo, Prickles,' he said quietly.

She stood up, grave-faced, and he leaned over and kissed her. She smelled of her mother's perfume.

'I made a monster in school,' she said, blinking.

He picked up her case and stowed it away in the Lincoln's trunk. 'A monster? What kind of a monster?' Priscilla bit her lip. 'A cookie monster. Like in *Sesame Street*. It was blue and it had two ping-pong balls for its eyes and a furry face.'

'Did you bring it with you?'

Priscilla shook her head. 'Mommy didn't like it. Mommy doesn't like *Sesame Street*.'

Dr. Petrie opened the car door and pushed his seat forward so that Priscilla could climb into the back. Adelaide said, 'Hi, Prickles. How are you, darling?' and Priscilla replied, 'Okay, thanks.'

Dr. Petrie shut his door, started up the engine, and turned the Lincoln around.

'Did you have to wait out there long?' he asked Priscilla.

'Not long,' the child answered promptly. He knew that she never liked to let her mother down.

'What happened to the cookie monster?' he asked. 'Did Mommy throw it away?'

'It was a mistake,' said Prickles, with a serious expression. 'Cookie fell into the garbage pail by mistake, and must've gotten thrown away.'

'A mistake, huh?' said Dr. Petrie, and blew his horn

impatiently at an old man on a bicycle who was wavering around in front of him.

They had chicken and pineapple from the Polynesian restaurant, and then they sat around and watched television. It was late now, and the sky outside was dusky blue. Prickles had changed into her long pink nightdress, and she sat on the floor in front of the TV, brushing her doll's hair and tying it up with elastic bands.

Right in the middle of the last episode of the serial, the telephone bleeped. Dr. Petrie had his arm around Adelaide and his left leg hooked comfortably over the side of the settee, and he cursed under his breath.

'I should've been an ordinary public official,' he said, getting up. He set down his glass of chilled daiquiri, and padded in his socks across to the telephone table. 'At least ordinary public officials don't get old ladies calling them up in the middle of the evening, complaining about their surgical corsets. *Hallo?*'

It wasn't an old lady complaining about her surgical corset – it was Anton Selmer. He sounded oddly anxious and strained, as if he wasn't feeling well. As a rule, he liked to swap a few jokes when he called up, but tonight he was grave and quiet, and his voice was throaty with worry.

'Anton?' said Dr. Petrie. 'What's the matter? You sound upset.'

'I am upset. I just came back from the bacteriological lab.'

'So?'

'It's serious,' said Dr. Selmer. 'What that kid died of – it's really, genuinely serious.'

Dr. Petrie frowned. 'Did you finish the post-mortem?'

'We're still waiting for the last tests. But we've discovered enough to kick us straight in the teeth.'

'You mean it's not tularemia?'

'I wish it was. We found minor swellings in the joints and the groin area, and at first I thought they could have been symptoms of lymphogranuloma venereum, or some other kind of pyogenic infection. The kid had a lung condition, and we were working on the assumption that the swellings might have been associated with a general rundown of health brought on by influenza.'

Adelaide looked questioningly across the room. Prickles, busy with her doll's coiffure, didn't even notice. On the TV screen, the hero was mouthing something in garish color, a million light-years away from disease and infection and nine-year-old boys who died overnight.

'Well,' said Dr. Petrie, 'what do you think it is?'

Dr. Selmer said evasively, 'We carried out a pretty thorough examination. We took slides from the spleen, the liver, the lymph nodes and bone marrow. We also took sputum samples and blood samples, and we did bacteriological tests on all of them.'

'What did you find?' asked Petrie quietly.

'A bacillus,' answered Dr. Selmer. 'A bacillus that was present in tremendous numbers, and of terrific virulence. A real red-hot terror.'

'Have you identified it?'

'We have some tentative theories.'

'What kind of tentative theories?'

Dr. Selmer's voice was hardly audible. 'Leonard,' he said, 'this bacillus appears to be a form of *Pasteurella pestis*.'

'*What?* What did you say?'

He could hardly believe what Anton Selmer had told him. He felt a strange crawling sensation all over his skin, and for the first time in his medical career he felt literally unclean. He had dealt with terminal cancer patients, tuberculosis patients, Spanish influenza and even typhoid. But *this—*

Adelaide, seeing his drawn face, said, 'Leonard – what is it?'

He hardly heard her. She came over and he held her hand.

In a dry voice, he said to Anton Selmer, '*Plague?* Are you suggesting that it's *plague?*'

'I'm sorry, Leonard, but that's what it looks like. Only it's worse than plague. The bacterial samples we have here are not identical with any known profile of *Pasteurella pestis*. They certainly don't correspond with the 1920 records – which is the last time we had an outbreak of plague in Florida. The bacilli seem to have mutated or developed into something more virulent and faster-growing.'

Dr. Petrie looked at Prickles, squatting innocently in front of the television in her pink nightdress. Supposing he had picked it up himself, when he was carrying David Kelly? Supposing—

'Anton,' he said abruptly. 'Do you think *I* could have caught it?'

Dr. Selmer coughed. 'Right now,' he said, 'it's difficult for me to say. I'm still waiting for the sputum reports, and that will tell us whether the boy's throat and lungs were infected. You took the streptomycin shots, though, didn't you?'

'Sure. Right after you called me this morning.'

'Well, those should help. All antibiotics are useful in plague treatment. If you've come into contact with anyone for any length of time, I should make sure that they get shots too. I can get some serum flown in from the West Coast tonight, and we can all get ourselves vaccinated just in case.'

Dr. Petrie looked at Adelaide, and squeezed her hand reassuringly.

'Anton,' he said, 'what should I look for? What symptoms?'

'Leonard – I can't say. You'll just have to keep yourself under strict observation. If you have any swelling, or dizziness, or headache get in touch with me straight away. And cancel your clinic for three days. That's how long plague usually takes to develop.'

Dr. Petrie felt chilled. 'Anton,' he insisted, 'I have Adelaide and Priscilla with me. I had Esther around me all day. I went to a restaurant for lunch. And what about my patients?'

'I don't know, Leonard,' said Dr. Selmer tiredly. 'It depends on what kind of bacillus mutation we have here. Basically, plague comes in three recognized forms. There's bubonic plague, which is when you have buboes or swellings in the groin and axilla. Then there's pneumonic plague, when the bacilli are localized in the lungs – and septicemic plague, when the blood is infected.'

'And you don't know which one it is?'

'I'm not sure that it's any one of them. The way it looks right now, it could be a new strain of bacillus altogether. Some kind of super-plague.'

Dr. Petrie bit his lip. 'Do we know where the boy picked it up? Isn't it carried by fleas?'

Dr. Selmer sounded weary. 'I talked to the parents, but

they say he went out all day Sunday, and he could have been any place at all. He visited some friends, and then went swimming, and then he came home.'

'How about the friends?'

'Oh, we're having them checked. The police are out now, tracking down the last of them. We're taking this very seriously, Leonard. I believe we have to.'

'Do you think he might have come into contact with an infected rat, or a squirrel?'

'It's possible,' agreed Dr. Selmer. 'They've had three or four outbreaks in California and Colorado recently, and it seems like a few people got bitten by fleas from infected ground squirrels. That might have happened here, but we can't tell. The way it's transmitted depends on what type of plague it is.'

'What do you mean?'

'Well, bubonic plague is mostly carried by fleas which have bitten plague-ridden rodents, and then accidentally bite people. It isn't a human disease at all, and humans only get caught up in the cycle by mistake. But that doesn't make it any less fatal, and the trouble is that a flea which has been infected in October can still pass on plague the following March. What's more, plague can spread to domestic rats and mice.'

Dr. Petrie frowned. 'But can't one person pass it straight on to another?'

'With bubonic plague, that's difficult,' said Dr. Selmer. 'It doesn't spread easily from man to man.'

'How about the other plagues? Surely pneumonic plague is catching?'

Dr. Selmer said, 'Yes, it is. If you're suffering from

pneumonic plague, you only have to cough in someone's face, and they'll almost certainly catch it. It's the sputum. Plague bacilli can stay alive in dried sputum for up to three months.'

'Oh, God,' said Dr. Petrie. 'Listen – when will you get your final results?'

'Two or three hours, the lab people say. As soon as I know for sure, I'll warn City Hall and all the health people.'

Dr. Petrie nodded. 'Okay, Anton. Keep me in touch, won't you? And don't forget to take some streptomycin yourself.'

'Are you kidding? We're walking around here in masks and gloves and flea-proof clothing. It's going to have to be a pretty damned smart bacillus to get through to us.'

Dr. Petrie laid the phone down. Adelaide was looking at him anxiously. On the floor, Prickles was tucking her doll in for the night underneath the armchair, and singing her a lullaby in a small, high voice.

'Did I hear you say plague?' asked Adelaide.

'That's right. That boy I picked up this morning, the one who died. He was infected with some kind of mutated plague bacillus. They're trying to pinpoint it now.'

'Is it dangerous?'

Dr. Petrie went across and picked up his drink. He took a long, icy swallow of chilled white rum, and briefly closed his eyes.

'All diseases are dangerous, if they're not treated promptly and properly. I've taken a couple of shots of antibiotics myself, but I think you and Prickles ought to have the same. Plague will kill you if it's left untreated, but these days it's pretty much under control.'

'Are you sure? I mean—'

Dr. Petrie shrugged. 'I can't be sure until the experts are sure. But I wasn't close to that boy for very long, and the chances are that I probably haven't caught it.'

Adelaide sat down. She watched Prickles playing for a while, and then said, 'I just find it so hard to believe. I thought plague was one of those things they had in Europe, in the Middle Ages. It just seems so weird.'

Dr. Petrie sat on the arm of the settee opposite. Unconsciously, he felt he ought to keep his distance. There was something about the word *Plague* that made him think of infection and putrescence and teeming bacteria, and until he knew for certain he was clean and clear, he didn't feel like breathing too closely in Adelaide's direction.

He sipped his drink. 'I was reading about it the other day, in a medical journal. We've had plague in America since the turn of the century. We've still got it – particularly in the west. They had to lift the ban on DDT not long ago, so that they could disinfect rats' nests and ground squirrels' burrows. Don't look so worried. It's just one of these things that sounds more frightening than it really is.'

Adelaide looked up, and gave him a twitchy smile. 'Plague. The Black Death. Who's frightened?' she said softly.

Prickles was shaking her doll. 'Dolly,' she said crossly, 'are you feeling giddy again?'

Dr. Petrie smiled. 'Is dolly feeling sick, too?' he asked. 'Maybe she needs a good night's sleep, like you.'

Prickles shook her head seriously. 'Oh, no. Dolly's not tired. Dolly doesn't feel like going to bed yet. Dolly's just feeling giddy.'

Dr. Petrie looked at his little daughter closely. Her hair was drawn back in a pony-tail, and her profile was just like his. When she grew up, and lost some of that six-year-old chubbiness, she would probably be pretty. Margaret, when he had first married her, had been one of the prettiest girls on the North Beach.

'Well,' he said, 'if dolly's feeling giddy, perhaps dolly would like some nice streptomycin.'

Prickles frowned. 'No, dolly doesn't want any of that. Dolly doesn't like it. She's just feeling giddy, like Mommy.'

Dr. Petrie stared at Prickles intently. 'What did you say?' he asked her. He said it so sharply that she looked up at him with her mouth open, as if she'd done something wrong.

He knelt on the floor beside her. 'I'm not angry, darling,' he said. 'But did you say that Mommy was giddy?'

Prickles nodded. 'Mommy went swimming, and when she came back she said she felt sick, and the next day she was giddy.'

Dr. Petrie leaned back against the settee. The creeping sensation of anxiety was spreading all over him.

Adelaide, her face pale, said, 'Leonard... you don't think that Margaret...?'

Dr. Petrie stood up. 'I don't know,' he said hoarsely. 'What worries me is how many *other* people have caught it. I think I'd better get down to the hospital and find out what's going on.'

'Is Mommy all right?' said Prickles, frowning.

Dr. Petrie forced a smile, and laid a gentle hand on his daughter's pony-tail.

'Yes, honey. Mommy's all right. Now – don't you think it's time that dolly went to bed?'

Prickles sighed. 'I suppose so. She *has* been very giddy today. Do all dollies get giddy? All the dollies in Miami?'

Dr. Petrie picked Prickles up in his arms, and held her close against him. The doll was made of lurid pink plastic, with a shock of brassy blonde nylon hair. He examined it closely, and then pronounced his diagnosis.

'I think that dolly's going to get better. And I *don't* think that all the dollies in Miami will get giddy. At least—'

He couldn't help noticing Adelaide's anxious, attractive face.

'At least I hope not,' he finished quietly, and laid his daughter down.

It was nearly midnight when the black and white police patrol car turned the corner from Washington Avenue into Dade Boulevard, cruising up the warm, deserted streets at a watchful speed. At the wheel, in his neat-pressed shirtsleeves, sat 24-year-old Officer Herb Stone – a thin-faced cop with a dark six o'clock shadow and a pointed nose. Beside him, eating a hot dog out of a pressed cardboard tray, sat his buddy, 26-year-old Officer Francis Poletto, a chunky, tough-looking young police athlete with a face like a pug.

'I almost broke my ass laughing,' Poletto was saying, with his mouth full. 'The guy gets on the water-skis, the boat starts up, and the next thing I know, they're pulling him right across the bay *underwater*. He climbs out, coughing and spluttering, and he says, "Well, that's great for a start – now teach me how to do it on the surface!" Laugh? I broke my ass.'

Herb Stone grinned politely, and left it at that. He liked Poletto, and there were a couple of times when he'd been glad of Poletto's rough-house style arrest. But Stone was quiet and academic, and hoped to make it through to detective school, and promotion.

Poletto, on the other hand, liked to keep in touch with the streets, and the tough cookies who hung around the beaches. He was hard and dedicated and had once shot a hippie in the left arm.

They stopped at a red light, and waited at the empty junction. Crickets chirruped in the grass, and palms rustled drily in the soft night air. Herb Stone whistled tunelessly under his breath. Poletto munched. The radio said something indistinct about a traffic violation on Tamiami Trail.

Just as they were about to move off, a second-hand silver Pontiac came swerving across the junction in front of them, bouncing unsteadily on its springs, and roared off down Alton Road. Stone looked at Poletto and Poletto looked at Stone.

'Let's go,' said Poletto, screwing up his cardboard hot-dog tray. 'This might be the only action we get all night.'

Herb Stone switched on the siren, and the police car squealed and skittered around the corner and bellowed off after the speeding Pontiac. They saw its crimson tail-lights vanishing down Alton Road in the direction of MacArthur Causeway, swaying erratically from one side of the road to the other.

'Drunk,' snarled Poletto. 'Drunk as a fucking skunk.'

Herb Stone, tense and sweating, closed the gap between the speeding Pontiac and the warbling, flashing police car. In a few seconds, they were close enough to see the dark shape of the driver, hunched over his wheel. Herb tried to nudge the police car up alongside the Pontiac and force him over, but the Pontiac slewed from kerb to kerb, tires squealing and suspension banging at every turn.

Suddenly, the Pontiac driver slammed on his brakes. Herb, dazzled by the red glare of the fugitive's tail-lights, went for his brake-pedal and missed it. The black and white police car smashed noisily into the back of the silver Pontiac, knocking it sideways into the kerb. Herb stamped on the brakes and stopped savagely.

'You're supposed to chase him,' said Poletto bluntly. 'Not smash the ass off him.'

The two officers climbed out of their car and walked across to the Pontiac. Poletto unbuttoned his top pocket and took out his notebook.

'Okay, Charlie,' he snapped. 'What's all this, *Death Race 2000?*'

The driver didn't answer. He was middle-aged, with rimless glasses, and he was sitting upright in his seat like a wax dummy. His face was a ghastly and noticeable white.

Herb stepped up closer and saw that his eyes were closed. He had gray, close-cropped hair and a check working man's shirt. He looked respectable, even staid. He was shivering.

'Do you think he's okay?' asked Herb uncertainly. 'He doesn't look too well to me.'

Poletto shrugged. 'Herb – if you'd drunk as much as this guy, you wouldn't look too well, neither. Okay, Charlie, out of the car.'

The man didn't open his eyes, or stir, or say anything. He just sat there shaking, pale and beaded with perspiration.

'Come on, wise guy,' ordered Poletto, and wrenched open the dented car door. He was about to reach in, but he stopped himself. He pulled a contorted face and said, '*Jesus H. Christ.*'

'What's wrong?' said Herb. Then, before Poletto could answer, he smelled it for himself. It was so rank that he almost felt sick.

'I think he's ill. Frank,' said Herb. 'Get an ambulance, will you, and the wreck squad, and I'll pull him out of there.'

Poletto screwed up his nose. 'Rather you than me, buddy boy. That guy smells like a goddamned drain.' Poletto went across to the police car, reached inside and picked up the mike. Herb heard him calling for an ambulance. Taking a deep breath he pushed open the Pontiac's door as wide as he could, and tried to get his hands under the driver's armpits. The man murmured and mumbled, and feebly pushed Herb away. But then he sagged and collapsed, and Herb dragged his heavy body out of the diarrhea-filled driving seat, and laid him on the road.

The man whispered something. Poletto, coming back from the police car, said, 'What's he chirping about? Is he sick, or what?'

'I don't know,' said Herb. He knelt on the road beside the feverish driver, and put his face as close as he could to the sick man's mouth. He never did understand what the man was trying to say, but he remembered the spittle that touched his cheek as the man's lips whispered those last, incomprehensible words.

In the distance, they heard the ambulance siren. Herb lifted the man's head from the concrete road and said gently, 'Don't worry, mac. You're going to be all right. They'll take you away, and you're going to be fine.'

★

Dr. Petrie reached the hospital a little after twelve. He was surprised to see that the casualty reception area was crowded with ambulances and police cars, and even a couple of Press cars. All the lights were on inside the building, and people were running backwards and forwards with medical trolleys and blankets.

He parked the Lincoln on the road and walked across to the hospital doors. A shirt-sleeved policeman said, 'Sorry, friend. This is off limits.'

Dr. Petrie reached into his white linen jacket and produced his identity card. 'I'm a doctor. I came down here to see Anton Selmer. He's in charge of emergency. Say – what goes on here?'

The policeman examined the identity card suspiciously. 'Are you sure you're a doctor? You don't look like a doctor.'

Dr. Petrie raised his eyebrows. 'What's a doctor supposed to look like? Marcus Welby, MD?'

The policeman shrugged, a little embarrassed, and handed the card back. 'I guess it's okay,' he said, ungraciously. 'Seems like they've got some kind of epidemic around here. They just told me to keep people out. Through there.'

'I know the way,' Petrie said, and pushed through the swing doors into the brightly-lit hospital corridors.

There was obviously some kind of panic in progress. The corridors were lined with trolleys, all waiting to collect patients from the ambulance bay; and there were nurses and doctors everywhere, bustling around with medical report sheets, diagnostic kits and bundles of sheets and robes and plastic gloves.

He reached Dr. Selmer's office and rapped on the door. A nurse answered it, wearing a cap and mask, her forehead glistening with perspiration.

'Yes? What is it?'

'I'm Dr. Leonard Petrie. I came to see Dr. Selmer. I thought I could help.'

'Just hold on there. Don't come inside. He won't be a moment.'

Dr. Petrie was about to say something else, but the door was shut firmly in his face. He shrugged, and leaned up against the corridor wall to wait for Dr. Selmer. As he stood there, a medical trolley was rushed past, with a young woman lying on it. Her face was deathly white, and she was shivering and trembling. A young doctor came hurrying in the other direction, calling out for a nurse to bring him some blankets and antibiotics.

It was ten minutes before Anton Selmer appeared. He came out into the corridor, freckled and ginger and worn out. He managed a weak smile as he pulled off his cap and mask, and let out a long, exhausted sigh.

'Hi, Leonard. Glad you could make it.'

Dr. Petrie inclined his head towards the door of the emergency ward. 'How long have you been in there?'

'All day,' said Anton Selmer, rubbing his eyes. 'It looks like it'll be all night, too.'

'Is it the plague?'

Dr. Selmer scratched his head tiredly. 'We've had twenty-eight more cases since eight o'clock. They're picking them up all over the place. We've had a bar tender, a supermarket

manager, two cops and four ambulance crew. We've even
had a hooker. They come from all over town. Most from the
south – Coral Gables and South Miami. But two or three
from Hialeah, and some from the Beach.'

Dr. Petrie stepped back to let a trolley rattle past. 'What
about treatment? Are they responding?'

Dr. Selmer didn't look up. 'Five of them are dead already.
Two were dead on arrival. We've tried streptomycin,
tetracyclines and chloramphenicol. We even tried aureo-
mycin, in case the bacilli were resistant to streptomycin. I've
brought in plague antigens from Tampa, and I'm having
serums made up from avirulent strains flown in right now
from Los Angeles.'

'And?'

Dr. Selmer's voice was unsteady with emotion. 'It's not
going to work, Leonard. It's not going to work at all.'

Dr. Petrie frowned. 'What do you mean – not going to
work?'

'Just that, Leonard. The plague is not responding to
the normal methods of treatment. Not sulfonamide, not
anything. I guess it's because it's some kind of mutation.
It's totally resistant to antibiotics, and it's even resistant to
heat.'

'What about the antigens?'

Dr. Selmer took out a handkerchief and wiped his
forehead. Then he blew his nose loudly. 'They slow it up,
that's all. Usually, they cut the mortality rate. You can save
two out of three. But with this plague, they hardly help at
all. Whatever we do, Leonard, they're dying just the same.'

Dr. Petrie leaned back against the wall. He tried not to
think of Prickles and Adelaide. The corridor was bright

and clinical and smelled of disinfectant. Outside, through the constantly swinging doors, he could see the red flash of ambulance lights, and the clatter and shuffle of trolleys. He heard someone shouting and moaning, and someone else trying to argue in a high, persistent voice.

'Have you told the health people?' he asked quietly.

Dr. Selmer nodded. 'I told them around half-past nine. They didn't really believe me at first. Wanted proof. So I brought Jackson and Firenza down here, and let them see for themselves.'

'What are they going to do?'

'Wait and see. Firenza said he thought it was probably an isolated outbreak.'

'*Wait and see?* Are you kidding? What makes him think it isn't going to spread around the whole damn city?'

Dr. Selmer shrugged. 'Precedent. The worst outbreak in American history was New Orleans, in 1920, when eleven people died. Firenza doesn't believe that we're going to lose more than twelve.'

'Didn't you tell him you'd lost five already? Jesus, Anton, this thing is far worse than bubonic plague. Doesn't he understand that?'

Dr. Selmer pulled his surgical cap on again. He looked at Leonard Petrie with his pale, worn-out eyes, and when he spoke his voice seemed hollow with tiredness.

'I think he understands that, yes. But he's like everyone else. They watch Dr. Kildare and Ben Casey, and they don't believe that American medicine can ever be licked. They don't understand that we can make mistakes. Officially, we're not allowed to. Officially we're not even permitted to be baffled.'

PLAGUE

Dr. Petrie looked serious. 'Anton,' he said, 'how bad is it really?'

Before Dr. Selmer could answer, his nurse came out of the emergency ward door and said, 'Doctor, he's almost gone. I think you'd better come.'

'There's a mask and a gown spare, Leonard,' Dr. Selmer said. 'Come inside and you can see for yourself how bad it really is.'

They pushed their way into the emergency ward. Dr. Petrie tugged on a tight surgical cap and laced a mask over his nose and mouth. The nurse helped him put on green rubbers and a long gown. She gave him transparent latex gloves, and he pulled them on to his hands as he followed Selmer into the glare of the surgical lamps.

It was the middle-aged man that Herb Stone and Francis Poletto had picked up in Alton Road. His face was drawn and lividly pale, and his eyes were rolled back into his head so that only the whites were showing. Beside the couch, on the luminous dials of the diagnostic equipment, his respiration, heartbeat and blood pressure were slowly subsiding.

The nurse said, 'His breathing is failing. Dr. Selmer. We can't keep him much longer.'

Dr. Selmer, helpless, stood at the end of the couch and watched the man gradually die.

'This is how bad it really is,' he said to Dr. Petrie, in a hushed voice. 'This man's wife told us that he felt sick just after lunch. By the evening, it had gotten so bad that he decided to go and look up his doctor. He was on his way there when he was picked up by the cops for drunk driving. He wasn't drunk, of course. He was dying of plague. Twelve hours from first symptoms to death.'

Dr. Petrie saw the pulse-rate drop and drop and drop. The luminous ribbon of the cardiac counter was barely nudged by the man's weakening heart.

'Is his wife here?' Dr. Petrie asked.

Selmer nodded. 'We're keeping every relative and friend in the waiting-room, under observation. The way this plague seems to develop, you show your first symptoms three or four hours after you've been exposed to it. We had a young girl brought in about three-and-a-half hours ago, and her father's showing the first signs. Dizziness, sickness, diarrhea, shivering. It's the fastest infectious disease I've ever seen.'

Dr. Petrie said nothing as the man on the couch died. Whoever he was, whatever he did, his forty-five years of life and memory and experience dwindled to nothing at all, and vanished on that hard, uncompromising bed.

Dr. Selmer motioned to the nurse and they drew a sheet over his face and disconnected the diagnostic equipment. One of the doctors called for a porter from the mortuary.

'Poor guy,' said Dr. Petrie, 'He never even knew what it was.'

Dr. Selmer turned away. Though an emergency ward doctor he was torn apart by losing his patients. He was skillful and talented and he never lost his enthusiasm for other people's survival. What was happening here today was, for him, relentless and unstoppable agony.

'There's one consolation,' said Dr. Selmer hoarsely. 'It looks as though we're not going to get it ourselves.'

'We're not? I always thought doctors and nurses were first-line casualties with plague.'

'Maybe they are. But it was nine o'clock this morning

when you came into contact with David Kelly, wasn't it? And are you sick yet? I came into closer contact than you, and I'm okay. Perhaps we're going to get lucky, and stay alive.'

'I still think you ought to call Firenza. Tell him again how bad this is.'

Dr. Selmer shrugged. 'It's not that he doesn't believe me. It's his reputation. I don't think he wants to be known as the health official with the highest mortality rate in the history of Florida.'

'That's absurd,' said Dr. Petrie.

'You think so? Go and talk to him yourself. Meanwhile, you can do me a favor.'

'What's that?'

'Tell this guy's wife that he's gone. Her name's Haskins. She's waiting by the water fountain, just down the corridor.'

Dr. Petrie lowered his head. Then he said, 'Okay,' and went back to the wash-up room to take off his mask and robe. He glanced at himself in the mirror as he straightened his jacket, and thought that he looked tall, tired, handsome and helpless. Maybe Margaret had been right all along. Maybe it *was* futile, caring for rich and hypochondriac old ladies. Maybe his real work was here, in the thick of the blood and the pain, the failing hearts and the teeming bacteria.

He opened the door and peered down the crowded corridor. Mrs. Haskins was standing on her own – a gray-haired woman in a cheap brown print dress, holding a plastic carrier bag with her husband's clothes and shoes in it. She seemed oblivious to the bustle of medics and porters, as more and more sick people were wheeled swiftly into the hospital. Outside, as the doors swung open, the ambulance sirens echoed through the warm night streets of Miami. Mrs. Haskins, alone by the water fountain, waited patiently.

Dr. Petrie walked across, and took her arm. She looked up at him, her eyes pink with tiredness and suppressed tears.

'Mrs. Haskins?'

'Yes, sir. Is George all right?'

Dr. Petrie bit his lip. In a few short words, he was going to destroy this woman's whole world. He almost felt like saying nothing at all, prolonging her suspense. At least she would believe her husband was still alive. At least she would have some hope.

'George was very sick,' said Dr. Petrie softly.

She nodded. 'I know. He was taken bad right after his lunch. He took his swim in the morning, and then he came back and was taken real bad.'

'He took a swim? Where?'

'Where he always does. Off the beach.'

Dr. Petrie looked at the woman's weary, work-lined face. First it was David Kelly, and he'd taken a swim. Then it was Margaret, and she'd taken a swim. Now it was George Haskins. And all along the beaches, raw sewage was floating in from the Atlantic Ocean. Poisonous, virulent, and seething with diseased bacteria.

'Mrs. Haskins,' he said simply, 'I'm sorry to tell you that George is dead.'

Mrs. Haskins stared at him. 'I beg your pardon?' she said.

'George died, about five minutes ago.'

She frowned, and then looked down at her carrier bag. 'But he can't have. I've got all his clothes in here.'

'I'm sorry, Mrs. Haskins. It's true.'

She shook her head. 'No, that's all right,' she said, with an attempt at brightness. 'I'll just wait here.'

'Mrs. Haskins—'

He was interrupted by the public address system. *'Dr. Petrie, telephone please. Dr. Leonard Petrie, telephone.'* He held Mrs. Haskins' hand. 'I'll be right back,' he told her. 'You just wait there, and I'll be right back.'

Mrs. Haskins smiled blandly, and agreed to wait.

Dr. Petrie pushed his way past trolleys and anaesthetic cylinders, nurses and porters, and made his way to the phone outside the emergency ward. He picked it up and said, 'This is Dr. Petrie. You have a call for me?'

'Hold on, doctor,' said the telephonist. 'Okay, ma'am, you're through now.'

Dr. Petrie said, 'Adelaide?'

Adelaide sounded jumpy and frantic. 'Leonard? Oh God, Leonard, something awful has happened! I've been trying to call you for the past twenty minutes, but the hospital lines were all tied up.'

'What is it? Is it Prickles? Is she sick?'

'No, it's not that. It was Margaret. She knocked at the door, and I opened it up, thinking it was you. She came straight in, like she was drunk or something, and she pulled Prickles out of bed and carried her off.'

'She *what*?'

'She carried her off, Leonard,' said Adelaide miserably, bursting into tears. 'I tried to stop her, but I couldn't. Oh God, Leonard, I'm so sorry. I tried to stop her.'

'You say she was drunk?'

'She seemed like it. She was swaying around and cursing. It was awful.'

Dr. Petrie rested his head against the wall. 'Okay, Adelaide, don't worry. I'll get right back there. I shouldn't think she's taken Prickles far. Just stay there, and I'll get back in ten minutes.'

He laid down the phone. Dr. Selmer was standing right behind him.

'You're not going home?' asked Dr. Selmer. 'I'm sorry, but I came to look for you, and I couldn't help overhearing.'

'Anton, I have to. My wife has taken my little girl.'

'Leonard, I need you here. You have to talk to Firenza. Please. I can't get away myself.'

Dr. Petrie shook his head. 'Anton – I can't. I think that Margaret has the plague. I have to go get Prickles back, Anton. I can't just leave her. Look—' he checked his watch '—just give me two hours, and I'll come right back here. I promise.'

Dr. Selmer looked desperate. 'Leonard, it's Firenza. You have to convince him. If we don't put this whole city into quarantine – well, God knows what's going to happen. I spoke to him just now. He still refuses. He says that until we find out what's causing this epidemic, there's no medical justification for sealing the city off.'

'We *do* know what's causing it,' said Dr. Petrie.

'We do?'

'I think so. It's the sewage that's been washed up on the beaches. Every one of the people I've come across with plague went swimming – either yesterday, or today.'

Dr. Selmer dropped his hands in resignation. 'Then we have to close the beaches,' he said. 'Go see Firenza, tell him what you think, and insist that he closes the beaches.'

Dr. Petrie looked at his watch again. He had just seen

a man die from the plague; he knew how short a time it took. If Margaret was already in the dizzy, drunken stage, she may only have a couple of hours left – three or four at the most. Supposing she died when Prickles was with her? Supposing she was driving her car?

'Anton,' he said desperately. 'Just two hours. Please. No one goes swimming at night, anyway.'

Dr. Selmer wiped his brow with the back of his hand. 'Go on, then,' he said softly. 'I can't stop you.'

'Anton, it's my daughter.'

Dr. Selmer nodded, and looked at Mrs. Haskins, waiting, shocked and patient, by the water fountain, and the white shivering people who were being wheeled in through the hospital's double doors.

'Sure. It's *your* daughter, and *her* husband, and *his* son, and *my* uncle. Everybody belongs to somebody, Leonard. I'm just disappointed, that's all. No matter how people criticized you, I didn't think you were that kind of a doctor.'

Leonard Petrie rubbed the back of his neck. The muscles were knotted and tense, and he could feel the beginnings of a pounding headache.

Dr. Selmer watched him, saying nothing, waiting for him to make up his mind.

Finally, Dr. Petrie sighed. 'All right, Anton. You win. Where does Firenza live?'

'Out by the university on South West 48th Street. The number's here.'

Dr. Petrie took the creased card and tucked it in his pocket. 'I'll be right back when I've seen him. Then I must go and look for Prickles. You understand that?'

Dr. Selmer nodded and laid a hand on his shoulder.

'I won't forget this, Leonard. Just talk sense into those bastards, that's all. I'll catch you later.'

Dr. Petrie was about to leave when he noticed Mrs. Haskins.

'Anton,' he said quietly. 'She still doesn't believe it. Tell her, for Christ's sake, or she's going to stand by that fountain all night.'

Dr. Selmer nodded. Then Dr. Petrie turned, and walked quickly down the hospital corridor, out through the double doors, and into the humid tropical night. By the clock over the hospital's main entrance, it was just past one-thirty. He slung his jacket in the back of his car, started the engine, and squealed off south.

He made a conscious effort to wipe any thoughts of Prickles out of his mind as he drove. There were too many giddy dollies in this city to think about just one of them, no matter how dearly he loved her, no matter how much it hurt to leave her to whatever fate she faced.

Two

Ivor Glantz stalked fiercely across his New York apartment, plucked the stopper out of the whiskey decanter, and splashed himself a more-than-generous glassful. He swallowed it like medicine, grimacing at every gulp, and then, with heavily suppressed fury, he set the glass quietly and evenly back on the table.

His attorney, Manny Friedman, stood watching this performance with respectful distaste.

'Ivor,' he said, in his persistent, nasal voice. 'Ivor, you'll kill yourself.'

Ivor Glantz looked at him and said nothing. He walked across to the floor-to-ceiling window, and parted the expensive translucent drapes. Sixteen floors below, on this gray and rainy Tuesday, the four o'clock traffic was beginning to congest the junction of First Avenue, measled with yellow taxis and teeming with people. Glantz let the drape fall back, and turned to face his attorney with exasperation and badly-concealed ill grace.

'You smart-ass,' he growled. 'You unctious, greasy, half-circumcized smart-ass.'

Manny Friedman frowned nervously. He was clutching his briefcase in front of him like a protective shield.

'Ivor,' he said uncertainly, 'it's a question of legal technique.'

'*Technique?*' snapped Glantz. 'You tell the jury what a short-tempered tyrannical bastard I am, and that's supposed to be *technique?*'

Manny Friedman licked his lips. 'Ivor, I *explained* it. I explained that we had to admit your past mistakes before the defense could get their teeth into them and make a meal out of the whole thing. What we're trying to say is that you're human, and you've made mistakes, but that *now*, in spite of everything, you've been misjudged, and taken advantage of.'

Ivor Glantz sat down heavily in one of the huge off-white armchairs. 'Oh, sure,' he said sarcastically. 'Well, you certainly made a good job of that. Now they think I'm a cross between Caligula and Adolf Hitler. I've been misjudged? And taken advantage of? What the hell kind of a performance is that?'

'Ivor, listen to me—'

'I *won't* listen!' snapped Glantz. 'I think I've listened to your half-assed advice long enough! This is *my* court case, and we'll run it the way *I* want it! Just because that Finnish bastard has lived a life of one hundred percent purity, that's supposed to give him the right to steal my research? It's not *my* fault the guy's a virgin, is it? That's *my* fucking patent, and he's infringed it. That's all there is to it!'

Manny Friedman swallowed hard. He sat down, still clutching his briefcase.

'Ivor,' he said. 'For one moment, just for one second, please listen.'

Ivor Glantz sniffed. 'What do you want me to do now?

Confess that I'm a homosexual, so the jury won't think I'm having an incestuous relationship with my daughter?' He paused, looking the discomfited Manny up and down. 'Come on, stop looking so goddamned nervous!'

'It's all a question of credibility,' said Friedman earnestly. 'You're a scientist, and a good scientist, but you also have a checkered kind of a past.'

'Because I argued with those stuffed shirts at Princeton, and told DuPonts to go fuck themselves? That's a checkered past?'

Friedman winced. 'To a jury, Ivor, yes. What we've been trying to do today is to show that you're an honest American Joe, with a particular talent for bacteriological research, and that in spite of your mistakes you've been trying to make good. All of a sudden, you find out how to mutate bacilli with radioactive rays – the greatest discovery of your whole life, the discovery that's going to make it big – and what happens? Some foreign schmuck steps in and claims that it's his idea, and that you're some kind of a quack.'

Ivor rubbed his eyes tiredly. 'Manny,' he said, with immense and laborious patience, 'I am not just an honest American Joe. I am the best-paid, best-known, most successful research bacteriologist in the entire American continent. Manny, just look around you. Is this the kind of place your honest American Joe lives in? Concorde Tower? Stop playing Perry Masonstein and treat this whole thing with *reality*!'

Manny shrugged. 'You're looking at it through the wrong end of the telescope, Ivor. We don't want the jury to think you're some kind of fat plutocrat, parking your backside on medical patents for your own financial benefit.'

'*I discovered it!*' protested Glantz. 'Why the hell *shouldn't* I get the financial benefit?'

Manny flapped his hands like two neurotic doves. 'There's no reason at all, Ivor. No reason at *all*. Except that any wealthy executive with any kind of capitalistic sympathies never *serves* on a jury. The people you get on juries are threadbare working-class mugs whose employers won't say their services are indispensable. Juries don't like people with bulging wallets.'

Ivor Glantz shook his head impatiently. 'That's bullshit, Manny.'

'That's where you're *wrong*,' said Manny. 'The way things are going, the jury is more likely to feel sympathetic towards Forward than they are towards you. Forward is a proud, dedicated man who's worked his way up from a working-class background. He's scored one or two minor successes in pharmacology and bacterial study. Not as spectacular as you, Ivor, but steady, reliable stuff. If you want to win against a man like that, you've got to come down off that stack of dollars and make out you're Thomas Edison, slaving away in a shed. You've got to make the jury believe that Forward stole this idea from a plain and hard-working American worthy. Ivor, in cases of patent infringement, you have to look *deserving*, as well as right.'

Glantz slumped down in his chair. 'I'm beginning to wish that patents were never invented.'

Manny opened his briefcase and began to shuffle green and yellow papers. 'Well, maybe you do,' he said, in his plangent Bronx voice. 'But if you keep hold of this one, it will make you rich. I mean, *really* rich. Not just rich rich.'

Ivor Glantz watched his attorney rustling through

sheaves of flimsy legal paper with mounting distaste. He had never liked litigation, but right now he had about as much say in the matter as a man who leaps off the Empire State Building has in whether he hits the ground or not. He took a cigar out of the breast pocket of his tight gray suit, and clipped the end with a gold cutter. He lit up, and began to puff out cloud after cloud of pungent blue smoke.

Glantz was not a handsome or friendly-looking man. He was almost bald except for a frieze of neatly-oiled curls around the back of his neck. His face was apishly coarse while his bright, near-together eyes were as sharp as his tongue.

He smoked some more, and drummed his fingers on the arm of the chair. He hadn't even had time to get used to his new apartment – one of thirty luxurious new condos in Concorde Tower. He had wanted to spend this month settling in, rearranging the paintings and the furniture, and sorting out his stacks of books. His stepdaughter Esmeralda, who shared the condo with him, had already shuffled the bedrooms and the sitting-room into some kind of shape, but Glantz felt the need to move things around himself.

It was all Sergei Forward's fault. When Ivor Glantz had returned six weeks ago from an extended lecture tour of South and Central America, explaining his new bacteriological techniques to major universities, he had been tired and irritable and aching for rest. But then he had picked up *Scientific American* to find a lengthy and colorful article by Sergei Forward on how *he*, the great Finnish research bacteriologist, had discovered how to mutate various bacilli with Uranium-235.

Glantz had had no choice at all but to sue, and right now,

the case of the mutated bacilli was a minor *cause célèbre* in the Federal District courts.

Manny Friedman sniffed, and then took out a crisp white handkerchief and blew his nose like the second bassoon in the Boston Pops.

'Tomorrow,' he said, 'we start proving what a two-hundred-percent clean cut, hard-working American fellow you are. We also emphasize the privations of your background – how hard it was to get to the top.'

Ivor Glantz stared. 'Privations?' he said. 'What do you mean – *privations?*'

'Your parents had to work for a living, didn't they? That's a privation.'

'My father, as you well know, was president of the Glantz and Howell Banking Trust. That's not exactly your roach-ridden corner store.'

Manny looked philosophic. 'Well, maybe it's not. But we'll try and play that down. Let's just say that you worked your way to the top through your own efforts, and despite some hard luck and bad knocks, you made it.' Ivor stood up, and walked across to the far wall. He carefully straightened a large abstract canvas, and stepped back to make sure it was hanging true.

'Manny, you're wasting your time. Just go in there tomorrow and show the jury the absolute, indisputable truth. Sergei Forward is a cheap no-hoper who thought he could filch his way to medical fame by cadging my discovery. Tell the jury something they'll understand. Tell them he's just as much a thief as the guy who steals apples from the A. & P.'

Manny rubbed his nose. 'I don't know whether that's the

right approach, Ivor. Most of the people you get in juries these days are so poor that stealing apples from the A. & P. is nothing. They do it themselves, all the time.'

The door chime rang. Ivor went across and opened it, and in came Esmeralda, piled high with marketing bags and with a long French loaf tucked under her arm. She kissed him lightly on the cheek.

'Hi, pa. Hi, Manny. Tonight, we eat French. Clams gratinées, baby lamb with fresh beans, and hot garlic bread.'

Manny, rising up from his chair, dropped a pile of papers on to the carpet. 'I'm afraid I can't eat garlic,' he blushed. 'It gives me heartburn.'

Ivor came over and patted him on the back. 'That's okay, Manny. You're not invited to dinner anyway.' Esmeralda walked through the sitting-room and into the kitchen. She dumped her parcels and her loaf of bread, and came back in. 'He can stay if he wants to. I bought enough for three.'

Ivor sucked his cigar and shook his head. 'I've had enough of attorneys for one day. I would just like to spend an evening in the quiet and charming company of my daughter.'

'It's quite okay,' Manny said. 'My sister is coming around tonight, and she cooks a beautiful fish pie.'

'That's wonderful for you. Es – do you want a drink? I'll just show Manny out.'

'Brandy-soda,' called Esmeralda, disappearing into one of the bedrooms, 'I'm just going to change into something more comfortable. See you soon, Manny. Come for dinner next time.'

Ivor showed Manny to the door.

'There's just one thing,' said Manny, laying his hand on

Ivor's sleeve. 'When we go in there tomorrow, I want you to understand that you mustn't show any signs of bitterness, or revenge. I want you to act magnanimous. Like, Forward's made a mistake, but you're willing to forgive and forget – provided he drops his claim to the process. If you're all sour grapes and spit, the jury won't like you. Will you do that for me?'

Ivor stared at him, poker-faced.

'*Please?*' said Manny.

Ivor nodded. 'Okay. Tomorrow, it's all sweetness and light. Do you want me to wear the wings, and the halo?'

Manny shook his head. 'A smile should be quite enough.'

'Okay.'

Without another word, Manny turned on his heel and made off towards the elevator. Ivor thoughtfully shut the door, and walked back into the sitting-room to fix himself another Scotch, and a brandy-soda for Esmeralda. He sat down with a heavy sigh, and wondered if all men of fifty-two felt as old and used-up as he did.

Esmeralda came back in, dressed in a long turquoise silk negligee. It had a wide, floppy collar, pleated sleeves, and yards and yards of floating train. She was a tall, pale girl, with an exquisitely beautiful face; the kind of haunting eyes that *fin-de-siècle* artists gave to their decadent dryads. Her hair was long and curly and very black, and she wore a thin turquoise headband. As she walked past the windows that made up two walls of the high, rectangular room, the pearly afternoon light shone through the silk of her negligee and gave her stepfather a shadowy outline of high pointed breasts and flat stomach.

'Bad day at Black Rock?' she asked, picking up her drink, and sipping it.

He shrugged. 'Courts were made for lawyers, not people. This is the fifth day, and so far we haven't got any place at all.'

She sat down, in a cloud of turquoise, in the opposite chair.

'Never mind. It will soon be over. You'll see.'

He swallowed Scotch. 'That's why I love you. You're such an optimist.'

There was a short silence. Esmeralda looked at him over the rim of her glass.

'My optimism?' she said. 'Or my body?'

Ivor grunted in amusement. 'I guess it's both. Seems like, these days, I've had more of the former than the latter.'

'Are you saying that man cannot live by optimism alone?'

'I don't want to force you. I don't want to make you feel obliged.'

She gave him a calm, almost supercilious smile. 'No man ever could. You know that.'

'I hope so,' he said, crossing his legs. 'I mean, the gallery, and this place – you mustn't feel you have to pay me back.'

She didn't look up. She was twisting a gold and cornelian ring around her finger. 'I feel *grateful*,' she said. 'You can never stop me feeling that. You know, I looked around the gallery today, and it's so perfect, and it's all because of you. You're a very beautiful man, pa. I mean that.'

He pulled a face. 'Your mother didn't think so.'

'My mother didn't know shit from sauerkraut.'

He laughed, despite himself. 'Don't say that. That's my former wife you're talking about.'

Esmeralda stood up, and walked around the apartment with her bluey-green train floating around her. She wore gold rings on her toes, which Ivor always thought was incredibly erotic.

'Do you think this place is too sombre?' she asked.

He looked around. The sitting-room was decorated in creams and grape colors, with muted abstract paintings on the two inner walls. The furniture was all mirrors and maple.

'It has to be sombre,' he said. 'When you pay $185,000 for seven rooms, and $1,100 a month carrying charges – that's sombre.'

She came over and looked at him. Then she knelt down beside his chair, holding her brandy in one hand, and stroked the back of his wrist with one finger. He looked back at her, expressionless, seeking some kind of emotional flicker. She smiled.

'I'd like to say thank you,' she said softly.

'You don't have to.'

'But I would.'

She took his hand, and stood up.

'Come on,' she said, tugging him.

He thought for a moment. Then, without a word, he laid down his drink, and followed her. They walked across the soft, silent carpet to the main bedroom.

On the wide, tapestry-covered bed, she sat him down and undressed him. First his shoes, then his short black silk socks. He started to loosen his own necktie, but she wouldn't let him, and picked at the knot herself with her long dark-red fingernails.

Soon he was naked. His body was white and plump.

There was gray wiry hair around his nipples, and his legs were thin and stick-like. He lay there, bald and old and unprepossessing, with his eyes closed. He knew what he looked like, but he also knew that when his eyes were shut, and the reality of age and unfitness were blocked out, there was a warm world of fantasy waiting that was more than nourished by Esmeralda's arousing treats.

Like a great blue-green moth, she mounted him. Her hand sought his hardened penis, and guided it up between her wide-parted thighs. She eased herself back on him, and she sighed a distant, muted sigh, as strange as the cry of some satisfied bird. Ivor kept his eyes tight shut, and said nothing.

Time passed. The apartment was quiet, except for the smooth rustle of Esmeralda's negligee, and their tense and excited breathing. Then Esmeralda started to tremble and shake. She sat in her stepfather's lap with her hands clenched tight against her breasts, feeling the deep, dark ripples of her own orgasm.

They lay side by side in silence for nearly half-an-hour. Ivor felt himself drifting into a curious sleep, and awoke after five minutes with a headache, and a metallic taste in his mouth. He sat up, and reached for his black silk bathrobe.

Esmeralda, her negligee spread romantically around her, opened her dark eyes and grinned.

'We're a strange pair, you and I,' she said, as Ivor walked across to the mirror.

He raised his head and examined her for a few moments in the glass. Somehow, she seemed less beautiful when her face was transposed by a mirror. But that didn't make him love her any the less. He loved her more than any possession he had ever had. Almost as much as his work, and far more than her mother. To fuck a daughter after fucking her mother is like buying your first new car, after you've had second-hand models all your life.

He brushed his few curls flat, splashed on some aftershave, and turned back to his stepdaughter with a serious face.

'I guess we are. Strange, I mean. Sometimes I can't believe it's really happening.'

'Isn't that the way with everything wonderful?'

Ivor nodded. 'It is. But it's the same with terrible things, too. When something truly terrible happens, you can never believe it's for real. You keep smacking yourself and hoping that you'll wake up.'

Esmeralda stretched luxuriously. 'Pa,' she said. 'What in the whole world could possibly happen to us that's *terrible*?'

On the floor above, in apartment 110, a tall man of sixty years old sat in a large Victorian spoonback chair, in almost total darkness. The heavy drapes were drawn over the windows, and the condominium was rank with cigarette smoke. The man had a handsome but heavily wrinkled face, a white mane of leonine hair, and he was dressed in a light blue nylon jersey jumpsuit that was absurdly young for his age. He held his cigarette in a long ivory holder, and the ribbon of blue smoke rose rapidly up to the ceiling.

He had been watching home movies. An expensive projector on the small inlaid table beside him had just run through, and the stray end of the film was still flicking against the spool. On the far wall of the sitting-room was a blank movie screen – an incongruously modern intrusion in an apartment that was crowded with antiques.

The man seemed to be paralyzed, or frozen. His eyes were focused into some remote distance, and he let his cigarette burn away without lifting it once to his lips. His name was Herbert Gaines, and he had once been Hollywood's hottest new property.

If you ever saw *The Romantics* or *Incident at Vicksburg*, you'd remember the face. Or at least a smoother and younger version of it – a version that remained confident, and open, and bright. Herbert Gaines had just been watching that face, and those movies, for the thousandth time. It no longer hurt, but on the other hand it no longer anaesthetized the present, either.

The door from the bedroom opened, and a diagonal slice of light lit up the ageing actor, in his antique chair, like a movie spot. A young man of twenty-two, with denim shorts and bare feet, his chest decorated with tattoos of eagles, came padding into the sitting-room. He was drying his short-cropped hair with a yellow towel.

The young man looked at the blank screen. 'Have you finished sulking yet?' he asked. 'Or are you going to watch the other one as well?'

Herbert Gaines didn't answer, but there was a subtle change in his expression. His attention was no longer fixed on the faded memories of 1936, but on the present, and on the careless intrusion of his lover, Nicholas.

The young man came and stood between Gaines and the blank screen. A rectangle of white light illuminated his tight denim shorts, with their suggestive bulge, and the fine plume of hair that curled over the top of them. Herbert Gaines closed his eyes.

'I don't know why you're sulking,' said Nicholas. 'I never said anything unpleasant.'

Gaines opened his eyes again. He reached over and switched off the projector, and as he did so, a long column of ash fell on the pale blue jumpsuit.

'You're so *sensitive*,' Nicholas went on. 'This is supposed to be an open, man-to-man relationship. Least, that's what you called it when it first began. But all we do these days is argue, and fight, and then you go off in a sulk and play those terrible old movies of yours.'

Gaines' mouth turned down at the corners in bitterness. But he still refrained from answering.

'I sometimes think you *want* to fight,' said Nicholas. 'I sometimes think you take umbrage on purpose, just to get me upset. Well, it won't work, Herbert, it won't. I'm not the vicious kind. But damn it all, I'm the kind that gets tired of fights.'

Herbert Gaines listened to this, and then took the burned-out cigarette from his ivory holder and replaced it with a fresh one. He lit up, watching Nicholas with one limpid eye.

'When you're tired of fighting me, Nick,' he said, in a rich, hoarse, cancerous voice, 'then you're tired of loving me.'

Nicholas finished rubbing his hair and threw his towel on the floor. Herbert Gaines smoked listlessly, with his holder clenched between his teeth.

Nicholas paced from one end of the room to the other. Then he stopped beside Gaines' chair – tense and exasperated.

'You won't understand, will you? You're too busy

wallowing in forty-year-old memories and uneasy nostalgia. Why don't you try looking outside yourself for a change? Open up the drapes, and realize what year it is? Christ, Herbert, I wasn't even *born* when you made those movies!'

Herbert Gaines looked up. 'You were there though,' he said, in his throaty voice.

Nicholas was about to say something else, but he stopped and looked quizzical. 'What do you mean?'

'Precisely what I say. You were there. Haven't you seen yourself?'

'Seen myself? I don't—'

Herbert Gaines put down the cigarette holder and laboriously got out of his chair. Nicholas watched him uneasily as he walked across to the bookshelves, and took down a large *Film Pictorial Annual* for 1938. The old man put the book on his desk, and opened it out. Then he beckoned Nicholas over.

'Look,' he said, pointing with his pale, elegant finger to a large black-and-white photograph. 'Who does that remind you of?'

Nicholas took a cursory glance. 'It's you. It says so, underneath. "Herbert Gaines plays young Captain Dashfoot in *Incident at Vicksburg*".'

'Cretin,' said Herbert Gaines. He gripped Nicholas by the back of the neck, and forced him over to the large gilt Victorian pub mirror that hung on the wall beside the desk. Then he lifted the open book and held it up beside Nicholas' face.

'Well,' said Nicholas. 'I guess there's a kind of passing resemblance. But we're not exactly the Wrigley Doublemint twins, are we?'

Herbert Gaines let him go, and tossed the annual back on the desk.

'You don't think so? You don't even know. The first time I saw you, down in the Village, I felt a sensation like I'd never felt before. At first, I couldn't understand it. I stared and stared at you, and still I couldn't grasp what it was that made me stare. Then I saw myself in a bookstore window. I saw *myself*. And I realized what it was about you that attracted me so much. You, Nicholas, are the spitting image of me, when I was in movies.'

Nicholas looked uncertain. 'That's not why you like me, though, is it? I mean – that's not the only reason?'

Herbert Gaines walked carefully back to his chair, and sat down. It looked as if his jumpsuit was filled with nothing more substantial than bent coat-hangers and odd bones. When he was comfortable, he fixed his gaze on Nicholas again – those deep, disturbing eyes – and he spoke in grave, sonorous tones.

'Nicholas,' he said, 'I love you.'

Nicholas scratched the back of his neck in embarrassment. 'I know that, Herbert, but—'

'But nothing,' said Herbert. 'I love you. Does it matter why?'

Nicholas lowered his eyes. 'I guess not. It was just that I wondered if you loved me because I was me, or because, well...'

'Because what?'

'Well, because I was *you*. I mean – is it *me* you love, or your old self?'

There was an uncomfortable silence. Then, unexpectedly, Herbert Gaines nodded. 'Yes,' he said. 'It is me that I love.

You are the personification of what I once was, and what I could be once more, if they would give me a chance. That, and that alone, is why I love you.'

Nicholas stood there, biting his lip. He watched Herbert Gaines for a while, but Herbert didn't look back. The old actor sat in his Victorian chair, smoking steadily and staring at the floor.

'Well, fuck you,' said Nicholas.

Herbert Gaines said nothing.

'Do you think I can take that?' said Nicholas, his eyes filling with tears. 'Do you think I can just stand here and take that? What do you think I am? Just one of your goddamned celluloid images? Just one of your old movies? Well, fuck you, Herbert Gaines!'

Gaines shrugged. 'Please yourself, dear boy.'

Nicholas wiped his eyes with his arm. 'Oh, that's great, that is. That's just too fucking neat for words. You spend your whole time sulking and moping like an over-age Shirley Temple, and when I tell you the truth about it, you come out with a charmer like that. Well, I can tell you here and now – I'm packing.'

'Packing?' said Gaines. 'What for?'

Nicholas bent forward and hissed the words at him. 'To leave you, my withered darling, that's what for.'

Herbert caught his wrist. His mouth twitched for a moment as he searched for the words. 'You leave me, you young bastard, and I'll break your neck.'

Nicholas pulled himself away. 'You might have been a muscle boy in 1936, but there's not much chunk left on the old bones now, is there, Herbert?'

He turned and walked towards the bedroom. Herbert

Gaines, with a curiously intense expression on his face, heaved himself out of his chair and went after him. Hobbling as quickly as he could, he caught up with Nicholas in the doorway, and snatched at his arm.

Nicholas shook himself free. 'Herbert, it's no fucking *use!*'

Herbert clutched his young lover again. 'You're not leaving, Nicky. Not really.'

Nicholas turned away. 'What do you want me to do? Stay here and listen to your ramblings about the good old days for the rest of my life, and how fucking wonderful I am because I look just like you used to look, in one of those two dreary old pictures of yours? Jesus, Herbert, I don't know which is more boring – you or your second-rate movies.'

Herbert slapped him, quite hard, across the face. Nicholas stared at him, more in surprise than in pain. A red bruise spread across his left cheek. He lifted his hand and dabbed it.

Without a word, Nicholas punched Herbert in the stomach. Herbert gasped, and collided with the doorjamb. Nicholas hit him again, with his open hand, and he fell to the floor with his nose bleeding.

Herbert didn't cry out, didn't even raise a hand to protect himself. Viciously and systematically, Nicholas punched him in the face and chest, lifting him up each time he dropped to the floor by tugging his pale blue jumpsuit. There were speckles and splashes of blood down the front, and Herbert's face was a mass of bruises.

Finally, with his rage exhausted, Nicholas let him fall on to the pink Wilton carpet, and stumbled unsteadily into the bedroom. He collapsed on to the bed, and lay there panting and sobbing, his legs curled up in a foetal crouch.

After a few minutes, he became aware that Herbert was standing at his bedside, his white hair awry, his jumpsuit dark with blood. Herbert reached out with a wrinkled and trembling hand and touched his bare shoulder. Nicholas recoiled.

'Nick,' whispered Herbert Gaines. 'Nicky.'

Nicholas turned his face away.

'Nicky, listen,' said Herbert thickly.

Nicholas shook his head.

'Nicky, you still haven't punished me enough.'

Nicholas turned, and lifted his head. The handsome, wrinkled face was swollen and red. The bony shoulders were bowed.

'Not *enough*?' said Nicholas, unbelievingly.

Herbert Gaines, the one-time movie hero, dropped to his knees. 'I have sinned against myself,' he said hoarsely. 'I have grown old, and unappealing. You must punish me.'

Nicholas sat up. He took Herbert's hand in his, and gripped it tight. 'Herbert, you mustn't say things like that. Nobody can help themselves from growing old. And anyway, what's sixty? It's when you get to ninety-five that you've got to start worrying!'

Herbert wiped blood from his chin. 'Sixty is older than twenty. Nick. It's all my fault. I threw my youth away. Two movies, too much money too fast. They offered me $25,000 for my third picture. I was high on my own conceit. I said $100,000 or nothing.'

'And?'

'You know what happened. I got nothing. I was young

and headstrong, and I wouldn't give in. Don't you think that's worthy of punishment?'

Nicholas rested his head in his hands. He felt tired and depressed, and he didn't know what possible words of comfort he could give. He was a one-time art student, a one-time merchant seaman, and articulating his sympathies didn't come easy.

'Nicky,' said Herbert Gaines, 'you must hit me.'

Nicholas shook his head. 'No, Herbert, I can't.'

'But you must! It's the only way! The past must punish the future!'

Nicholas stood up, and walked over to a painting of a Chinese mandarin on the other side of the room. He looked ancient, and inscrutable, and deeply wise. The youth gazed at his calmness, and wondered how it was possible to live the kind of life where you could smile as calmly and benignly as that, even once.

'Nicky,' whispered Herbert Gaines again.

'What is it, Herbert?'

'I want you to kill me.'

Nicholas almost smiled. 'No, Herbert, I can't.'

'The police needn't know. You could drown me in the bath. An unfortunate accident. Only – I couldn't do it myself. I'm a Catholic. It isn't easy to want to die, and to be afraid of it.'

Nicholas turned around. He stared at this pathetic, blood-smattered figure, and he shook his head once again.

'I can't kill you, Herbert. You're indestructible. You're in movies, aren't you? Two magnificent movies. It doesn't matter if your body is dead, does it? Every time those movies play, you'll come back to life again.'

'Nicky,' said Herbert wretchedly, 'I need to be punished.'

'You *are* being punished,' said Nicholas, quietly. 'Every day of your miserable life, you're being punished. You don't need me to do it. Only one thing will ever let you off the hook, Herbert, and that's the end of civilization. When there are no more people to go to the movies, and the last picture-house closes down, that's when you get your freedom.'

Herbert lowered his head. In a scarcely audible voice he said, 'If that's true, Nicky, then I pray God that civilization comes to an end before I do.'

Nicholas walked back and rested his hand on Herbert's shoulder.

'The way things are going these days, God might even grant your wish. Now, let's go and get you cleaned up, hey?'

Across the hallway, in apartment 109, Kenneth Garunisch was the only person in Concorde Tower who was concerned about the plague. He was sitting at his cluttered desk, trying to fix his necktie, watch television, and talk to his union attorneys on the telephone, all at the same time. He spoke with the steady relentlessness that had earned him the nickname of 'Bulldozer', and he was angry.

'This thing broke out last night, Matty. How come they only told me this morning? Because I have a *right* to know, that's why! What do you mean, emergency? I don't care what they call it.'

Through the open hatch in the sitting-room wall, he could see his wife, Gay, in the kitchen, fixing cocktail snacks with their black maid, Beth. She was warbling *Strangers in the Night* as she popped little curled-up anchovy fillets on to crackers and cream cheese. Beth, silent and fat, was peeling prawns.

'You'd *better* believe it.' Garunisch said, in his hectoring voice. 'I got a call from two of my guys at the hospital. Plague, that's what they got. The Black Death.'

He put his hand over the receiver and sighed. He was a short, stocky, bullet-headed man with an iron-gray crew-cut. His eyes were pale and uncompromising, and there was a prickly roll of fat at the back of his neck. He spoke with a monotonous harshness, like the retreating sea dragging pebbles down the beach. He was Germanic and hard-bitten, and he was president of the Medical Workers' Union – a union he had started himself in 1934, with four other hospital porters from Bellevue – and which was now a powerful, nut-cracking international with a billion-dollar fund and a two and a half million membership.

'You hear that? *Plague.* They don't know what kind, and they've got people dying like flies. So how come I only found out this morning?'

Gay stuck her heavily-lacquered blue-rinsed curls through the serving hatch.

'What did you say, Ken? Did you say something?'

Kenneth waved her away. 'I was talking to Matty. They got some kind of plague in Miami. Can you believe that?'

Gay, with her head still stuck through the hatch, blinked her eyes as if she was trying to work out whether she could believe it or not. Finally, she said, 'What's plague?'

Kenneth ignored her. His attorney was asking him what he intended doing about Miami.

'What do you *think* I'm going to do? I want to protect

my members. If my members have to handle people with plague, they're gonna catch it themselves, right?'

His attorney guessed that was right.

'In which case,' went on Garunisch, 'I suggest you call the health department down at Miami and tell them it's double time or nothing, and all hospital workers got the right to refuse to handle plague cases, without penalization, recrimination, or loss of benefits.'

His attorney was silent for a while. Then the lawyer suggested that under the circumstances, union action might be construed as taking immoral and unfair advantage of a medical emergency.

'Listen,' grated Garunisch, 'you just get on to that telephone to Florida, and you tell those health folk that if they want my members to risk their lives, they're gonna have to pay for it. I don't want no arguments, and I don't want no fuss. Now do it.'

He clamped the receiver back on the phone, and shook his head. 'Immoral and unfair advantage,' he repeated, sarcastically. 'You get some underpaid Cuban hospital porter to risk his life, and you don't expect to pay him no more? Immoral and unfair advantage, my ass.'

Gay popped her head through the hatch again. 'Did you say something, Ken?'

Garunisch stood up and walked over to the kitchen, tying up his necktie as he went. It was a very lurid necktie, with purple flowers and greenish spots. It had been an expensive gift from Gay.

'Was that something serious, dear?' said Gay, rinsing her hands. 'You look awful sore.'

Garunisch reached over to pilfer a smoked-salmon canapé. 'It's just the usual,' he said, with his mouth full. 'They got some kind of epidemic down in Florida, just like the Spanish influenza, and they're expecting the porters and the drivers to handle the patients without any compensation for extra health risk.'

'That's *awful*,' said Gay. She was a small, busty woman with wide-apart eyes. 'Supposing they caught it? Supposing their *children* caught it?'

Garunisch looked around the expensive, glossy Colonial kitchen, with its antique-style tables and chairs. It still gave him a sense of justice and satisfaction, this condominium. For the first time in his life, he owned a luxurious home, decorated just the way that he and Gay had wanted, and he could turn around to all those capitalist palookas who had tried to crush him, and grind him and his union out of existence, and he could raise two rigid fingers.

'That's right,' he said absent-mindedly. 'Supposing their children caught it.'

Gay said, 'Beth, haven't you finished those prawns yet? We still have the fondant frosting to make.'

Beth peeled as quickly as her fat fingers would allow. 'I don't have too many more now, Mrs. Garunisch. Just as soon as I'm through, I'll make that frosting.'

'Well!' said Gay Garunisch, turning back to her husband. There was a pleased little smile on her face. 'Our first social event at Concorde Tower! Isn't it exciting?' Kenneth looked up. He was miles away. 'It's terrific, Gay. I just wish we didn't have this plague business hanging over our heads. It really kind of worries me.'

'It's not hanging over *my* head,' said Gay. 'I don't even know what it is.'

Garunisch took another canapé, and pushed it into his mouth whole. 'Plague is a deadly epidemic disease,' he mumbled, spitting out crumbs. 'They used to have it back in the Middle Ages. These days, it's pretty much under control. But, you know, people can die when they get it, and that's serious. The news said that thirty or forty people were already dead.'

Gay Garunisch was taking off her apron. 'Thirty or forty's not many,' she said, looking for the pepper. 'Why, more people die in a single plane crash.'

Garunisch looked at her patiently for a moment. He loved her, but he sometimes wondered how she could be so totally impervious to everything that went on around her. She lived in her own self-contained world of cocktail parties and celebrity luncheons, and the real events of America escaped her attention.

'Plane crashes,' he said, very gently, so that he didn't sound sarcastic, 'are not catching.'

The doorbell rang. The chimes were a copy of the bells of Amory Baptist Church, which used to ring outside Mrs. Garunisch's home when she was a little girl. Beth looked up from her prawn-peeling, but Kenneth moved to get it.

He opened the door with a fixed grin on his face, and welcomed his first visitors. It was Mr. and Mrs. Victor Blaufoot, from the apartment above theirs. They had met in the elevator just the other day, and Kenneth, in an expansive mood after successful overtime talks, had invited the Blaufoots along to their condo-warming.

'Mr. Bloofer, isn't it?' said Garunisch, showing them in. 'Would you like something to drink?'

'Blaufoot,' corrected the guest. He was neat and small, in a shiny blue mohair suit, with gold-rim spectacles, and a large nose. Mrs. Blaufoot was even smaller, in a dark green dress and a fur stole.

Kenneth Garunisch laughed. 'I'm sorry. I'm usually terrific with names. This is my wife, Gay.'

There was a lot of handshaking and uncomfortable laughter. Then they all stood there and looked at each other.

'I hope we're not early,' said Mrs. Blaufoot. 'The truth is, we don't have very far to come.'

They all laughed some more.

'You've certainly made your place look different,' said Mr. Blaufoot, looking around. 'I don't think that any of the other apartments have been done like this. It's – it's – well, it's very different.'

'It's a genuine replica,' smiled Gay Garunisch, pleased. 'It's just like the old Colonial farmhouse at Trenter's Bend, Massachusetts. Right down to the patterns on the drapes.'

Mrs. Blaufoot laughed nervously. 'You must be the only people on First Avenue with an authentic early-American farmhouse.'

Kenneth Garunisch, grinning, put his arm around his wife. 'We were thinking of having ourselves a farm, too, but they don't allow cows in the lobby.'

They all laughed.

Kenneth fixed some drinks, and they perched themselves around the sitting-room on the early-American rockers and upright reproduction Windsors.

'You're in unions, aren't you, Mr. Garunisch?' asked Victor Blaufoot politely. 'The Medical Workers, if I recall.'

'That's right,' nodded Garunisch. 'It's not the biggest union around, but I guess you could say that after the Teamsters, it has one of the hardest clouts. When we get up to defend our members' interests, Mr. Bloofer, there aint many people who don't tremble in their shoes.'

Victor Blaufoot smiled uncomfortably. 'No, I'm sure. I've heard a lot about you. Myself, I'm in diamonds.'

Gay Garunisch looked interested. 'Diamonds, huh? The girl's best friend? Can you get me a diamond tiara, at wholesale?'

Mr. Blaufoot stared for a moment, then looked embarrassed. 'I regret not, Mrs. Garunisch. It's not exactly a jeweler's. It's more of a brokerage.'

Gay's smile stayed on her face, but she was obviously confused. 'Brokerage?' she asked.

'That's correct. I buy uncut stones from South Africa, and sell them in New York.'

'Oh,' said Gay Garunisch. 'So you don't have tiaras?'

Mr. Blaufoot shook his head.

There was another long silence, and they all sipped their drinks and smiled at each other. Then, to Kenneth Garunisch's relief, the telephone rang. He reached over and picked it up. Everyone else watched him because there was nothing else to do.

'Garunisch. Oh, hi, Matty. What news? Did you get through?'

There was obviously a long explanation on the other end of the phone.

'You what?' said Garunisch. 'You couldn't reach him? That's ridiculous! Didn't you tell the switchboard who you were? You did? And they still didn't—? Get back on there and try him again. Yes, now! And call me back when you've spoken!'

He slammed the phone down angrily. 'Would you believe that?' he grated. 'That was my chief attorney. He's been trying to call up the health people down at Miami for twenty minutes, and they can't find the guy in charge. They can't find him – can you believe that?'

'I heard about Miami on the news,' said Mrs. Blaufoot. She looked like an old, unsteady pigeon. 'I understand they have an epidemic down there.'

'They sure do,' said Garunisch. 'They have an epidemic, and it's already knocked off thirty or forty people, and my members are having to deal with it. That's what I'm trying to sort out now.'

'Excuse me,' said Mr. Blaufoot, 'but what exactly are you trying to sort out?'

Garunisch opened his wooden Colonial cigarette box and took out a cigarette. He didn't offer them around. He lit up, and tossed the spent match into an ashtray.

'Pay, mainly,' he said. 'My members are having to drive and carry people infected with this disease, and I want to make sure they're properly compensated. I also want to make sure they have a choice of whether they want to do the job or not, without penalties.'

'Surely it's an emergency,' said Mr. Blaufoot, looking concerned. 'Does pay matter so much, when there are people's lives at risk?'

'My *members*' lives are at risk,' replied Garunisch. 'I

believe that every man who willingly risks his life at work should be paid for taking that risk, and that he should also have the choice of whether he wants to take the risk or not.'

Mrs. Blaufoot held her husband's hand. 'Supposing none of your members wants to take the risk? What happens then?'

Garunisch shrugged. 'That's one of those bridges we'll have to cross when we come to it.'

Victor Blaufoot spread his hands, appalled. 'But what if it were your own sick child, and a hospital worker refused to carry him into hospital, because he was not getting paid enough, or because he didn't choose to? What then?'

Kenneth Garunisch blew out smoke. He had heard all these soft-headed emotional arguments a million times before, and they cut no ice with him.

'Listen, Mr. Bloofer – everyone is somebody's child, and my members have parents and families as well. They're entitled to danger money, and that's as far as it goes. Before you start shedding tears for the patients, think of the kids whose fathers and mothers have to treat those patients. Everyone has their rights in this kind of situation, and those rights have to be respected.'

Victor Blaufoot frowned. 'I see. Everyone has rights, except the sick and the needy.'

'I didn't say that,' snapped Garunisch. 'I said everyone has rights, and I mean everyone.'

'But what if it was your own child? Answer me that.'

Garunisch was about to say something, then bit his tongue and stopped himself. He said quietly, 'I don't have any children.'

Victor Blaufoot nodded. 'I thought not. You talk and

behave like a man with no children. Men with no children have nothing to lose, Mr. Garunisch, and with respect, that makes their bravery very hollow. I know you think that I'm an emotional old fool. I can see it on your face. But I have a daughter in Florida, and I'm worried about her.'

Kenneth Garunisch crushed out his cigarette and stood up. 'Okay, Mr. Bloofer, Mrs. Bloofer, I'm sorry. I didn't mean to upset you. I didn't realize you were personally involved.'

Mrs. Blaufoot looked up at him. A frail old lady staring pointedly at the heavyweight union boss. 'Would it have mattered if you *had* realized?' she asked. 'Would it have changed, one iota, what you have asked your people to do?'

Garunisch shook his head. 'No, Mrs. Bloofer, it wouldn't.'

Gay Garunisch, sensing unpleasantness, said brightly, 'Would anyone like something to eat? We have some hot spiced sausage, and some Southern fried chicken.' Nobody answered. 'Hold the food,' Garunisch said. 'Wait till some more people arrive. I don't think Mr. and Mrs. Bloofer are very hungry.'

'I could use another drink,' said Mr. Blaufoot, holding up his empty glass. 'Please.'

The doorbell chimed. Kenneth Garunisch collected Mr. Blaufoot's glass, and then went over to answer it. It was Dick Bortolotti, one of his union officials – a young blue-chinned Italian with suits that always reminded Kenneth of the Mafia.

'Dick?' he said. 'What's wrong?'

Bortolotti stepped in, and closed the door.

'I know you're having your party, Ken, and I don't want to spoil your fun. But there's big trouble down in Miami, and we can't get through.'

'What do you mean?'

'It's this epidemic. It says on TV that it's getting worse – spreading. They won't even say how many people are dead, because they can't keep count.'

A muscle in Garunisch's cheek began to twitch. 'Go on,' he said in a whisper. 'What else?'

'The hospital phones are jammed solid. I can't get through to any of our organizers for love nor money.'

The telephone began to ring, and Garunisch knew it would be Matty, with the same story.

He held himself in close control. 'Who do we have at Fort Lauderdale? Maybe they could drive down and take a look-see.'

'I had a call from Copes, out at Tampa. He said the Miami health people were being really cagey and uptight. They keep insisting it's nothing too serious, and that they've gotten it under control, but the evidence sure doesn't point that way. I think it's a bad one, Ken. I mean, it sounds like a real bad one.'

Garunisch bowed his head. He was thinking, fast and hard. If there was an epidemic in Florida, his members were going to be right in the front line, and he was responsible for them.

Eventually, he looked up. 'Okay, Dick. You'd better come in. Grab yourself a drink and something to eat, while I try to talk to those health department dummies down at Miami. Maybe I can get some sense out of this situation.'

Garunisch turned back to his guests. 'Sorry about the interruption, folks, but it seems like some urgent union business has just come between me and my fun again. Just enjoy yourselves, and I'll join you in a moment.'

Victor Blaufoot looked round. 'Is it the plague? Have you heard any news?'

Kenneth Garunisch smiled. 'Don't concern yourself about that plague, Mr. Bloofer. Everything about the plague is well under control.'

Edgar Paston first heard about the plague on the radio of his seven-year-old Mercury station wagon. He was driving back to Elizabeth, New Jersey, after picking up fifteen boxes of canned peaches from his wholesaler. It was growing dark, and he had just switched on his headlights.

The radio newscaster was saying, 'Unconfirmed reports from Miami say that nearly forty people have fallen victim to an inexplicable epidemic disease. Health authorities say that the epidemic is well under control, and have warned Miami residents not to panic or react prematurely to what health chief Donald Firenza called "an unfortunate but containable outbreak".

'Hospitals and police are working overtime to cope with suspected sufferers, and Miami Police Department have reported that nine of the epidemic victims are police officers who were called out to assist with casualties. Specialists have been unable so far to identify the disease, but Mr. Firenza has likened it to Spanish influenza.

'The mayor of Miami, John Becker, has sent personal messages of condolence to the families of the dead, and has called for a speedy containment of what he described as "this tragic mishap".

'We'll have more reports about the epidemic later, but

meanwhile here's the weather report for New York and Jersey City...'

Paston switched the radio off. He reached across to the glove box, and found a peanut bar. Tearing the wrapper off with his teeth, he began to chew. He hadn't eaten since early this morning, when he had stopped for a cheese Woppa just outside Elizabeth.

Edgar Paston was the owner and manager of Elizabeth's Save-U Supermart. He had bought the premises ten years ago, at an auction, when they were nothing more than a dilapidated tire-fitting works on the outskirts of town. He had taken a risk, because in those days, zoning laws still prevented any residential development in that part of Elizabeth. Business, at first, had been hard, and the family ate cheap vegetable soup and corn biscuits at night, even though they served hams and chickens by day.

A new housing policy changed all that, and overnight the area was designated suitable for a new suburb. The Save-U Supermart attracted more and more customers as houses and streets went up all around it. What had once been a wilderness of truck stops and rough fields became a thriving cluster of chalet-style suburban houses, with neat gardens and kids on scooters. Now Edgar Paston had a healthy yearly profit, a four-bedroomed chalet, and two cars.

To look at, he was a supermarket manager and nothing else. Thirty-nine years old, with thinning hair, thick-lensed spectacles, a five o'clock shadow and a taste for plaid short-sleeved shirts.

He finished the peanut bar and tucked the wrapper in his shirt pocket. He never littered. It was eight-fifteen. He would be back at the store in twenty minutes. That would just give him time to unload the peaches, lock everything up, and go home for his dinner. Today was his wife, Tammy's, half-day at the telephone company, and that meant a good hot supper with fresh-baked bread.

Soon the wide lighted window of Save-U Supermart appeared at the end of the block, and Edgar swung the station wagon off the road, over the car park, and pulled up outside. He switched off the engine, and wearily climbed out.

He opened the Mercury's tailgate, dragged out one of the boxes of peaches, and walked quickly across to the supermarket entrance, and inside. The lights were bright in there, and he blinked. His assistant, Gerry, was standing by the cash desk chewing a pencil.

Edgar put down the box. 'What's the matter?' he said, half-stern and half-joking. 'Your mother not feeding you enough?'

Gerry, a thin and serious boy of sixteen with a beaky nose and short blond hair, looked worried.

'Hi, Mr. Paston. It's those kids again. They came in about ten minutes ago, and they're up to something, but I don't know what. I daren't leave the cash desk, and they've been down by the freezers for quite a while.'

Paston peered down the length of the store, past the shelves filled with cereals and cookies and baby-foods. There were only a few late shoppers left now, trundling their carts around and picking up TV dinners and canned drinks. The freezers, where he kept the meat and the beer, were down at the far end.

'Hold on, Gerry. I'll go and take a look.'

When he reached the end of the supermarket, he saw exactly what was going on. Four or five teenage boys in denims and black leather jackets were sitting around on the floor, drinking beer from a six-pack they had taken from the fridge.

'Okay,' said Edgar sharply. 'What the hell's happening here?'

The kids looked at him, and then looked at each other. A couple of them giggled.

'Come on, get your butts out of here, or I'll call the cops.'

None of the kids moved. One of them took a mouthful of beer and sprayed it in the air, and the rest of them laughed.

'All right,' said Edgar. 'I've warned you before. If that's the way you want it.'

He turned away, and walked towards the telephone on the wall. He was just about to pick it up, when one of the boys called out, 'Paston!'

He looked round. He had seen this kid before. He was tall for his age, with a tight black jacket decorated with zippers. He had a thin, foxy face, and greased-back hair.

'Are you talking to me?' said Edgar, putting the phone back on the hook.

'That's right, Paston,' said the kid. He came up closer and stood only a couple of feet away, his thumbs in his belt, chewing a large wad of gum with quick, noisy chews.

'It's *Mr.* Paston to you,' said Edgar calmly.

The kid nodded. 'That's okay, *Mr.* Paston. And it's *Mr.* McManus to *you*.'

Edgar adjusted his glasses. 'Are you going to leave the store now, or do I have to call the cops and get you thrown out?'

McManus chewed, and looked Edgar up and down. 'Is that the way you talk to all your customers, Mr. Paston? It seems to me that me and my friends, we're just ordinary, law-abiding customers, and there aint nothing you can do to get us out of here.'

Edgar swallowed. The rest of the gang had now picked themselves up off the floor, and were lounging behind McManus in what they obviously considered were cool and threatening poses. One of them started cleaning his fingernails with a long-bladed knife.

'You took beer,' said Edgar quietly. 'You took beer and you drank it.'

McManus raised his eyebrows. 'Is there any law says you can't consume food and drink on the premises, provided you pay for it when you leave?'

'Yes, there is. Until you've paid for it, the stuff belongs to me, and if you drink it, that's theft. Now, you've got ten seconds to get the hell out.'

McManus didn't move. 'If you're saying I'm a thief, Mr. Paston, you'd better call yourself a cop and prove it.'

Edgar looked around the loutish faces of McManus and his gang, and then nodded.

'Okay,' he said tightly, and picked up the phone. The gang watched him with remote curiosity.

He spoke to the police, and then laid the phone down again.

'They said a couple of minutes,' he announced.

McManus shrugged. 'Seems to me they take longer every time,' he said, and his cronies all giggled.

It wasn't long before they heard the sound of a siren outside, and the crunch of car doors being slammed. Edgar looked towards the front of the store, and saw two police hats bobbing towards him behind one of the rows of shelves. Round the corner by the dog-food came Officer Marowitz, and his partner Officer Trent. They were big, weatherbeaten local patrolmen, and Edgar knew them well.

'Hi, Mr. Paston,' said Marowitz. He had a broad, swarthy face and a drooping mustache. 'Looks like you got Shark trouble.'

'Wit-ty,' sneered one of the kids.

Marowitz ignored him. 'McManus,' he snapped. 'Have you been bothering my friend Mr. Paston?'

McManus grinned a foxy grin. 'Mr. Paston here says I'm a thief. I drank some beer in the store, and he says I stole it. Look, I got my money all ready to pay, and he says I stole it.'

Marowitz sniffed. 'Do you want to bring a charge, Mr. Paston?'

McManus said, 'I didn't steal it, man. The money's here. I was thirsty, and I opened a couple of cans, that's all.'

'You shut your mouth, McManus. Do you want to bring a charge, Mr. Paston?' Marowitz repeated.

Edgar Paston bit his lip, and then sighed. 'I guess not. Just get them out of here.'

Marowitz shrugged. 'It's up to you, Mr. Paston. If you want to bring a charge, you can do so.'

Edgar shook his head. 'For a few mouthfuls of beer, it isn't worth it. But if there's any more trouble, McManus, I know your face and I'm going to have the law on your tail so fast you won't know what's hit you.'

McManus grinned, and saluted. 'Jawohl, mein Führer,' he mocked.

Marowitz closed his notebook. 'All right, you guys – scram. Next time you won't be so lucky.'

Giggling and larking about, McManus and his gang shuffled out of the store, and then amused themselves for a few minutes by pressing their faces against the glass of the window, pulling grotesque faces.

'They're only kids,' said Marowitz. 'Weren't you the same when you were a kid, Mr. Paston?'

Edgar looked up at him. 'No,' he said quietly. 'I wasn't.'

Marowitz grinned. 'Well, don't you worry. Different strokes for different folks. You have to remember these kids have got nothing to do in the evening around here. There's no dance halls, no movies, and most of them are banned from the hamburger joints. It's natural they're going to raise a little hell.'

Edgar picked up the beer-cans that were strewn on the floor, and went to fetch a damp cloth to wipe up the mess.

'You wouldn't happen to have one of those cans of beer going spare, would you?' Marowitz asked.

Edgar stared at him. Marowitz said, grinning, 'It gets kind of dry, patrolling around all evening.'

Edgar reached into the refrigerator and took out a six-pack of Old Milwaukee. He handed it over, and said flatly, 'That's one dollar and eighty-five cents. You can pay at the desk.'

Marowitz took the pack without a word. He muttered to Trent, 'Come on, we got more friendly places to visit,' and walked out. Just by the cash desk, he banged his money down in front of Gerry, and called out loudly, 'Support your local police department!'

Edgar watched them drive away, and then went out into

the car park to fetch the rest of his canned peaches. The night was growing cooler now, and there was a soft wind from the east. A couple of trucks bellowed past on their way to Jersey City, and one or two cars, but mostly the roads were empty and silent.

He didn't realize what had happened at first. But when he reached into the back of the car, he noticed how low down it seemed to be. He frowned, and looked around the side. All four tires had been slashed into black ribbons, and the Mercury was resting on its wheel hubs.

Edgar stood there for a while, feeling utter frustration and despair. Then he slammed the tailgate angrily shut, locked it, and walked back to the supermarket.

Gerry was just counting up the day's takings. 'What's wrong, Mr. Paston?' he asked.

'Someone slashed my tires. I'll have to take the pick-up. Let's get this place closed down for the night, and leave it at that.'

'Do you think it was Shark McManus?'

'Is that what they call him? Shark?'

'I guess it was after *Jaws*. He's a kind of a wild kid.'

Edgar almost laughed. 'Wild? He's a goddamned maniac. I mean, what kind of a person goes around stealing beer and slashing tires? What the hell's it all *for*?'

Gerry shrugged. 'I don't know, Mr. Paston. I guess they get kind of frustrated.'

'Oh yeah? Well, I wish they wouldn't take their half-baked frustrations out on me.'

He went to check the cold shelves and the meat, to make sure that everything was kept at the right temperature for overnight storage. Then he swept up the rubbish, while Gerry restocked some of the canned goods. He did everything quickly and superficially, because he wanted to get home. He could always get up early and clean the place more thoroughly tomorrow.

He was almost finished when he thought he heard a tap on the store window. He looked up, frowning. There was another tap, louder. Then, right in front of his eyes, the huge plate-glass window smashed, and half-a-hundred-weight of glass dropped to the sidewalk with a shattering, pealing sound.

Edgar ran to the front of the store and stared out into the night. It was silent, and dark. The wind blew fitfully into the store, making price tags flap on the shelves. He crunched across the sea of broken glass, still staring, still searching.

In the distance, he thought he heard someone laugh. It could have been a dog barking, or a car starting up. But the sound of it was enough to make him shiver.

Three

Miami was always quiet in the small hours of the morning, but tonight that silence seemed to be sultry and threatening. As Dr. Leonard Petrie drove through echoing and deserted streets, he sensed in the air the beginning of something new and frightening and strange.

Two or three cars and an ambulance passed him as he drove downtown. Out on the expressway, lines of traffic still shuttled backwards and forwards from the airport, and trucks and cars still traveled up and down US 1, heading north for Fort Lauderdale or south for the Keys. It could have been any night of any year in Miami. The radio was playing country music from Nashville, and the hotels along the Beach glittered with light.

Dr. Petrie swung the Lincoln left on West Flagler and 17th. For the first time, he saw the spreading effects of the plague. There were four or five bodies lying on the sidewalk, sprawled-out and motionless in the light of a store window. They looked as if they were fast asleep.

He drew the Lincoln into the kerb, and got out to take a look. It was a family. A father – middle-aged, with a small mustache; a middle-aged mother; and two small boys, aged about eight and ten. It was so unbelievably odd to see them here, on this warm and normal night, lying dead and pale on the sidewalk, that Dr. Petrie was moved to prod the father's body with his toe, to see if he were sleeping.

The father's hand slipped across his silent chest, and rested on the concrete.

A police car came cruising up 17th in the opposite direction, and Dr. Petrie quickly stepped across the sidewalk to flag it down.

The cop was wearing orange sunglasses, even though it was night-time, and a handkerchief over his mouth, bandit-style.

'I'm a doctor,' Petrie said. 'I came around the block and saw those people. They're all dead, I'm afraid. I guess it's the plague.'

The patrolman nodded. 'We're getting cases all over. Six or seven cops down with it already. Okay, doctor. I'll call headquarters and notify them about the dead people. Between you and me, though, I don't think they got enough ambulances to cope. It won't be long before it's garbage trucks.'

'Garbage trucks?' said Dr. Petrie. He was appalled. He looked back across the street, and the family was lying there, pale and still. The children must have died first, and the mother and father died while trying to nurse them. 'You mean—'

The cop said, 'They don't have enough ambulances, doctor. It's either that, or we leave them to rot in the streets.'

Dr. Petrie rubbed his face tiredly. 'Have you seen many like this?' he asked the cop.

'A couple of dozen maybe.'

'And what are you supposed to do about them?'

The cop shrugged. His radio was blurting something about a traffic accident on the West Expressway. 'We have to report them, that's all. Those are the orders. Report them, but don't touch them.'

'And that's all? No orders to stop people using the beaches, or leaving the city?'

The cop shook his head.

Dr. Petrie stood beside the police car for a moment, thinking. Then he said, 'Thanks,' and walked back to his Lincoln. He climbed in, gunned the engine, and drove off in the direction of Donald Firenza's house.

The more he heard about the health chief's inactivity, the more worried and angry he grew. If one cop had seen two dozen cases, there must be at least a hundred sick people in the whole city, and that meant a plague epidemic of unprecedented scale. He drove fast and badly, but the streets were deserted, and it only took him five minutes to get out to Coral Gables.

He had no trouble in picking out Donald Firenza's house. There were cars parked all the way up the street, including a television truck and a blue and white police car, and every window was alight. He pulled his Lincoln on to the sidewalk and switched off the engine. Over the soft rustling of palm trees and the chirrup of insects, he could hear voices raised in argument.

He was greeted at the door by a fat uniformed cop with a red sweaty face.

'I'm a doctor,' Petrie said. 'I just came up from the hospital. Is Mr. Firenza home?'

The cop scrutinized Dr. Petrie's ID card. He was monotonously chewing gum. 'Guess Mr. Firenza's pretty tied up right now, but you can ask. Go ahead inside.'

Dr. Petrie stepped through the door. The house was crowded with newspaper reporters and television cameramen, all lounging around with cardboard cups of coffee and cans of beer. It was one of those houses that in normal circumstances was guaranteed to make Dr. Petrie wince. There were coach lamps and sculptured carpets, wrought-iron banisters and paintings of horses leaping through the foamy sea. On one wall was a print of a small girl with enormous eyes, out of which two fat sparkling tears were dropping.

In the pink-decorated sitting-room, Petrie found Donald Firenza, sitting back in a large plastic-covered easy chair, talking to a young reporter from the *Miami Herald* and a bald man in a bright sport shirt from UPI. Dr. Petrie recognized a couple of friends from the city health department at the back of the room, and he nodded to them briefly. Tonight was not a night for smiles.

'Mr. Firenza?' he said crisply. 'I'm Dr. Leonard Petrie. I just came from Dr. Selmer, down at the hospital.'

Mr. Firenza looked up. He was right in the middle of saying, '—all the epidemic deaths we've suffered so far have been tragic, but unfortunately they've been unavoidable—' He didn't look at all pleased at being interrupted.

'Can it wait?' he said. He was a small, pale-faced, curly-headed man wearing a green turtle-neck sweater.

'I don't think so,' said Dr. Petrie.

The UPI man turned around in his chair. 'Is it something to do with the epidemic? Is it getting worse?'

Dr. Petrie didn't look at him. 'I came to talk to Mr. Firenza, not to the press.'

'What's the latest death-toll?' persisted the man from UPI. 'Has it gone above twelve yet?'

Dr. Petrie ignored him. 'Mr. Firenza,' he said. 'I'd appreciate a private word.'

Mr. Firenza sighed, and stood up. 'Excuse me, you guys,' he said to the two reporters. 'I'll be right back.'

He led Dr. Petrie through the throng of police, health department officials and newsmen to a small study at the back of the house. He closed the door behind them and shut out the babble of conversation and argument.

'Sit down,' said Mr. Firenza. 'We've met before, haven't we?'

Dr. Petrie sat down, and nodded. 'Two or three times, at health department meetings. Maybe at dinners once or twice. Perhaps we should've gotten better acquainted.'

Firenza reached for a large briar pipe and proceeded to stack it with rough-cut tobacco. 'I want to tell you here and now that I'm very proud of the way that Miami's doctors are rallying to help,' he said.

'Thank you.'

'However – I don't really think that you picked the subtlest way of breaking into a press conference,' Firenza went on. 'I've just been trying to convince our friends from the papers that this epidemic is containable and isolated.'

'Do they believe you?'

Firenza looked at Dr. Petrie curiously. 'Of course they believe me. Why shouldn't they?'

Dr. Petrie coughed. 'Because it's not true.'

Firenza pushed some more tobacco into his pipe, and then laughed. 'You've been talking to Dr. Selmer, haven't you? I know he thinks this is the end of the world, and that we're all going to get stricken down. I had to remind him that this is Miami, which has more qualified doctors per square inch than almost any other city in the continental United States, and that we have both the finance and the resources to cope with any kind of epidemic.'

'Is that your considered opinion, or is that the story you're telling the press?' Dr. Petrie asked.

'It's both.'

'Have you been down to the hospital within the last hour?'

'No, of course not. I've been up here. This is where we're doing all the planning and the organization. I get constant reports from all over, and the police and the hospitals are keeping me up to date with every new case.'

'So you know how many people have died?'

Firenza looked at him narrowly. 'Yes, I do,' he said, in a slow voice. 'What are you getting at?'

'I'm not getting at anything. If you know how many people have died, how come this city isn't already in quarantine? When I drove here, I saw people lying dead on the sidewalks.'

Firenza struck a match and began to light his pipe. 'There are more people lying dead on the sidewalks in New York City, my friend, and they don't even *have* an epidemic there.'

Dr. Petrie frowned. 'Mr. Firenza,' he said, 'that is completely irrelevant. We have a serious epidemic disease on our hands right here in Miami, and it's up to us to do something about it.'

Firenza crossed his little legs. 'We *are* doing something about it, doctor. We have all the medical people on call that we need. But you don't think that a medical officer can only concern himself with medicine, do you? It's just as important for me to protect Miami's interests as a city as it is for me to protect the health of its citizens.'

Dr. Petrie stared at him. 'You mean – what you're telling the press – it's all to protect the city's *business?*'

'Partly. It has to be. You think I want panic in the streets? What we have here is a very tragic, very unfortunate incident. But it's no more than an incident. The last thing we want is for people to get hysterical.'

Dr. Petrie looked up. 'In other words, you don't want them to cancel their holidays?'

Firenza caught the tone of his voice. 'Look here, Dr. Petrie, I don't quite know why you're here, but I have a serious job to do and I don't appreciate sarcasm.'

'Dr. Selmer has a serious job to do, too. He has to stand there and watch people die.'

'He's getting all the back-up he needs. What more does he want?'

'He wants to be sure that this epidemic doesn't spread. We have a general idea of how it started. All that raw sewage that's been piling up on the beaches in the past couple of days has polluted the water and the sand. Somehow, the plague bacillus has been developing inside the sewage, and anyone who's gone down on the beach or swum in the ocean has caught it.'

Firenza puffed his pipe. 'You've got proof?' he said shortly.

'I don't think it needs proof. Every plague victim we've come across went swimming over the weekend or early yesterday morning.'

'That doesn't mean anything. Sixty percent of the population goes swimming over the weekend.'

'Yes – but mostly in private pools. All the victims went for a swim in the ocean.'

'I still find that hard to believe, Dr. Petrie. We've had raw sewage wash up on the beaches a couple of times before, and each time it's proved neutral.'

'Have you tested *this* sewage?'

'The health department didn't consider it necessary,' Firenza replied firmly.

Dr. Petrie stared at him. 'Mr. Firenza,' he said, 'am I hearing things? We have a dozen people dead of plague down at the hospital, and thirty or forty, maybe more people sick. We have beaches ankle-deep in sewage. Don't you think that, between the two, there's just the *shadow* of a probable link?'

Firenza shrugged. 'You're a doctor. You ought to know the danger of jumping to conclusions.'

Dr. Petrie sucked in his breath in exasperation. 'Mr. Firenza, I came here to ask you to close down the beaches. Not ask – *insist*. We have some kind of disease on our hands that's spreading faster than any disease we've ever come across before. People are dying within three to four hours of first catching it. Unless you want the whole population of Miami dead or dying within a couple of days, I suggest you act pretty fast.'

'Oh, you do, do you?' sneered Firenza. 'And just how do you suggest that I shut down twenty miles of beach without setting off the biggest hysterical exodus in American history?'

Dr. Petrie stood up. He was very tired, and he was angry. 'I think it's far better to set off an hysterical exodus of living people, than it is to shovel them up unhysterically when they're dead.'

Firenza almost grinned. 'Dr. Petrie,' he said. 'You have a fine turn of phrase. Unfortunately, you're reacting like all of your breed when you're faced with genuine diseases instead of old people's hypochondriac complaints. Real diseases frighten the pants off you. For once, you've got to do some real medical work, instead of prescribing sugar pills and syrup for rich and bad-tempered old ladies. Come on – admit it – you're scared.'

Dr. Petrie's face was strained with suppressed fury.

'Yes,' he said, in a shaking voice. 'I'm scared. I'm scared of a disease that kills people off like bugs down a drain, and I'm scared of you.'

Firenza stood up, too. He was nearly a foot shorter than Dr. Petrie.

'I suggest you go get yourself some rest,' said Firenza. 'In the light of day, the whole thing is going to look a lot less scary. I'm not saying that the situation isn't serious. It is, and I'm treating it as a medical emergency. But that's no reason to disturb the whole city, to cause unnecessary distress and anxiety, and to kill off the proceeds from a vacation season that's only just started. If we quarantine this city, Dr. Petrie, we'll destroy our business-folk, and our ordinary men and women, just as surely as if they'd gotten sick.'

Petrie looked at him for a long while, then slowly shook his head.

Mr. Firenza said, 'I promise you, and I promise Dr. Selmer, that if this epidemic gets any worse by tomorrow noon, I'll bring in the Dade County Health Department, and seek some federal help if we need it. Now – is that to your satisfaction?'

There was a long, awkward silence. Dr. Petrie opened the door of the study. 'I don't know what to say to you, Mr. Firenza. If you won't listen, you won't listen. Maybe I should go straight to the mayor.'

'The mayor's in Washington, for two days.'

'But he knows about the epidemic, surely?'

He's heard about it, on the news. He called me, and I told him it was all under control, and to stay put. All I can say, Dr. Petrie, is that it's up to the men of healing like you and Dr. Selmer to prove me right.'

Dr. Petrie turned away. 'If it didn't mean a terrible loss of life,' he said bitterly, 'I'd do anything to prove you wrong.'

He called Dr. Selmer from the phone-booth on the corner of the street, and told him what had happened. Selmer sounded frayed and worried, and on the point of collapse.

'Doesn't he have *any* idea how bad it is?' asked Anton Selmer. 'I've had fifteen more deaths since you left. I've had three nurses and two doctors down with it, and it won't be long before I get it myself.'

'Of course you won't. Just like you said, you and I are probably immune. Maybe it was contact with David that did it, or maybe we're just lucky.'

'I need to be lucky, if Firenza won't close the beaches.'

'I'm sorry, Anton. I did try. He's still telling the press that it's containable and localized, and that we're all going to wake up in the morning and discover it was nothing more than a nasty dream.'

'Jesus Christ.'

'I'm going after Prickles now,' Dr. Petrie said. 'I don't know where Margaret's taken her, but maybe if she's sick she's gone home. It shouldn't take long.'

'Will you come back here, just as soon as you can? I need every bit of help I can get. Joe Mamiya is making some tests on the bacillus, but it's going to take him a long time to come up with anything positive.'

'Anton – I'll be as quick as I can.'

Dr. Petrie put the phone back in its cradle, and went back to his car. On the far sidewalk, he saw a man shuffling and staggering along, leaning against parked cars for support. The man suddenly stopped, and his head jerked back. Then he dropped to his knees, and fell face-first on to the concrete. He lay there muttering and twitching, his cheeks bruised and pale, his right leg nervously shuddering.

Dr. Petrie walked across the road and knelt down beside him.

'I'm a doctor,' he said. 'Do you feel bad?'

The man turned his bloodshot eyes upwards to look at him. 'I'm dying,' he muttered hoarsely. 'I got that disease, and I'm dying.'

'Do you want anything? A drink maybe?'

The man closed his eyes.

Dr. Petrie stayed beside him for a few minutes, then the man opened his eyes again.

'It hurts so bad,' he whispered. 'It hurts me in my guts. In my balls. It's like someone's eating me up alive.'

'Don't worry. The pain will soon be over.'

'I'm dying, doc.'

'Leonard, my name's Leonard.'

The man, his face pressed against the rough sidewalk, tried to smile. There was a cold wreath of sweat around his forehead, and his face was now a ghastly white.

'Leonard...' he whispered.

Dr. Petrie took out his handkerchief and wiped the man's forehead. He turned him over, and tried to make him as comfortable as he could. He checked the pulse, and the rate of respiration, and it was quite obvious there was nothing he could do. The man would be dead in a matter of minutes.

The man opened his eyes one last time. He looked up at the night sky as if it was something he had never seen before, and then he turned his gaze back to Dr. Petrie. He stared at him for a long time, and then, in a small, quiet voice, he said, 'Leonard?'

Dr. Petrie said gently, 'Don't try to talk. Just lie still.'

'Thank you, Leonard.'

'You've got nothing to thank me for. Now, stay still. It won't hurt so bad if you're still.'

The man reached out with cold sweaty fingers and took Dr. Petrie's hand in his. He attempted a squeeze of friendship.

'Thanks for – thanks for—'

Dr. Petrie was going to answer, but it was too late. The man was dead. He released his hand, and stood up. He thought about going back to Firenza's house, and telling the police that the body was lying here, but then he considered that the police had enough bodies to pick up, and that they'd spot this one soon enough. Maybe it was better for his freshly-dead acquaintance to spend a last night in the open, under the night sky, than be shoveled straight away into the back of a garbage truck.

He went back to the Lincoln, climbed in and slammed the door. He felt physically and morally drained. For a moment, he held up his hands in front of him, and imagined they were teeming with infected bacilli. The enemy was invisible and endlessly malevolent, and so far there was no way of fighting back.

Dr. Petrie released the brake, and turned the car east. There was no future in thinking things like that. Right now, it was Prickles he wanted. A safe, healthy, and happy Prickles.

He joined the North-South Expressway and drove up towards North Miami Beach at nearly seventy miles an hour. The ocean was turning pale misty blue on his right, and the sky was growing lighter. The clock in the car reminded him that it was nearly dawn, and that he hadn't slept all night. There was hardly any other traffic at all, and several times he had to pull out to overtake abandoned cars.

It was almost light by the time he pulled up outside the white ranch-style house with the stunted palms. He shut the car door with a bang and strode across the lawn. There were no lights in the house, but Margaret's cream-colored Cutlass was parked in the car port. He went up to the frosted-glass front door and rang the bell.

There was no answer. He rang again and again, and shouted, 'Margaret! Margaret – are you in there? Margaret, it's Len!'

He tried to peer in through the sitting-room window, but it was too dark to make anything out. He went around the side of the house and tried the side door, but it was locked and bolted. He banged on it a couple of times and shouted his wife's name, but again there was no reply.

Dr. Petrie was just walking back across the lawn towards his car when he turned and saw a bedroom curtain move upstairs. The window opened and Prickles leaned out.

'Daddy,' she called, with a serious frown.

'Prickles! Listen, give me a couple of minutes and I'll get you out of there.'

'I didn't want to go but Mommy said I had to. Daddy, I'm *frightened*. Mommy says she's sick. Daddy, I'm real frightened.'

Dr. Petrie was still standing there when the front door opened. It was Margaret. She was very pale, and she was wearing a red flowery wrap. It gave him an odd sensation to see her there, because she was at once so familiar and so hostile. There was the same bird's-wing sweep of dark hair; the same wide-apart eyes; the same tight mouth; the same long angular nose. But there was something else as well – a blank stare of bitter resentment and dislike.

'Margaret?' said Dr. Petrie, walking back across the lawn towards her. 'Are you all right? Prickles said you were sick.'

Margaret attempted a smile.

'I have been unwell, Leonard. If that interests you.'

Dr. Petrie pointed up to the bedroom window. 'Why did you take her back? I thought you were going to Fort Lauderdale to see your mother.'

Margaret was holding the door so tight that her knuckles were white.

'So you care about her when it suits you,' she said slurrily.

'Look Margaret – are you sick, or what? What's the matter with you?'

'I'm fine, now. I was a little under the weather, but I'm fine.'

'You don't look fine. You look terrible.'

Margaret laughed, humorlessly. 'You don't look so good yourself. Now, why don't you just get out of here and leave us alone.'

Dr. Petrie went right up to the door. But before he could push his way in, Margaret closed it, and latched the security chain. She peered at him through the four-inch gap that was left, like a suspicious animal in its darkened den.

He tried to force the door, but it wouldn't budge.

'Margaret,' he warned. 'Open this door.'

'You're not coming in, Leonard. I won't let you. Just go away and leave us alone.'

'Margaret, you're sick. You don't know what you're saying. You could have the plague. There are people dying in the streets. I've seen them.'

'Go away, Leonard! We can manage without you!'

Dr. Petrie slammed his shoulder against the door. The security chain was wrenched in its screws, but it stayed firm.

'Margaret – you're *sick*! For Christ's sake, think of Prickles! If you're sick, then she's going to get sick, and that could mean that both of you *die*!'

Margaret tried to close the door completely, but Dr. Petrie kept his foot jammed in it, and wouldn't let her.

He was so busy trying to wrench the door open that he didn't hear the car stop in the road, or see the two men walking slowly across the lawn towards him. It was only when Margaret looked up, and the cop said, 'Okay, Superman, what's going on here?' that he realized what was happening.

The policemen looked tired and hard-faced. One of them was standing a little way back, with his hand on the butt of his gun. The other was right up behind him, with his arms akimbo. They both wore sunglasses, and they both had knotted handkerchiefs around their necks, ready to pull over their nose and mouth in case of plague duty.

Dr. Petrie pushed back his hair from his forehead. He knew how disreputable he must look after a whole night without sleep. He said weakly, 'This is my house. I mean, this *was* my house.'

'This *was* your house?' said the cop. 'What's that supposed to mean?'

'This *was* my house and this lady *was* my wife. We were having a slight argument. That's all.'

The cop strained his eyes to see Margaret standing in the shadows of the hall.

'Is this true, ma'am?'

Margaret sounded so different that Dr. Petrie could hardly believe it was the same person. Instead of speaking harshly and bitterly, she was like a pathetic little girl, all weak and heartbroken and begging for sympathy.

'I was only trying to reason with him, officer. He went crazy. Look, he broke the door. He went absolutely crazy. He said he was going to beat me up, and take my little girl away.'

Dr. Petrie stared in amazement. 'But – this is preposterous – I was—'

The cop reached down, and calmly attached a handcuff to Dr. Petrie's wrist. 'I have to advise you of your rights,' he said. 'You have the right to remain silent, you have the right to—'

'I didn't *do* anything!' snapped Dr. Petrie. 'My wife came around to my place and took my little girl without my permission. Now she's sick with the plague and she won't let me take my daughter back. For God's sake, look at her! She's sick with the plague! If you take me away, my daughter's going to catch it and die! Don't you understand that?'

The second cop was opening the police car doors.

The first cop said, 'Listen, sir, we've all had a very trying time recently with this epidemic. You know what I mean? I picked up a guy for breaking in a TV store just half-an-hour ago. He said his old granny was dying of sickness, and he wanted to make her last hours happy by letting her watch TV. It's an emergency situation. Lots of people are trying to take advantage of it. Now, let's go, huh?'

Dr. Petrie said, 'I don't suppose it would make any difference if I told you I was a doctor?'

The cop pushed him into the car and sat down beside him. The second cop settled himself down behind the steering wheel, and pulled away from the kerb, siren whooping and lights ablaze.

'You're a doctor, huh?' answered the cop, after a while. 'Well, maybe you ought to be out there healing some of these sick people, instead of bothering your ex-wife.'

Dr. Petrie said nothing. The police car squealed on to the North-South Expressway, and sped downtown.

They took his money, his keys and his necktie, and locked him in an open-barred cell with two black looters and a drunk. He was exhausted, and he lay on the rough gray blanket of his bed, and slept without dreams for four hours.

It was eleven o'clock when he woke up, feeling cramped

and sore but slightly more human. The drunk had gone, and the two negroes were left by themselves, murmuring quietly to each other.

He sat up, and rubbed his face. There was a small basin in the corner of the cell, and he splashed cold water over himself, and wiped himself dry with his handkerchief.

He went to the bars and looked out, but there was no sign of anyone. Nothing but a gray-painted corridor, and a smell of body odor and carbolic soap. He turned around to the blacks.

'What do you have to do to get some service around here?'

The blacks stared at him briefly, and then went back to their conversation.

'I'm a doctor,' Petrie insisted, 'and I want to get out of here.'

The blacks stared at him again. One of them grinned, and shook his head.

'They don't let nobody out today, man. It's emergency regulations. Anyway, if things don't get much better out there on the streets, maybe you safer where you at.'

Dr. Petrie nodded. 'You're probably right. But what do I have to do to get some attention?'

The other black said, 'This ain't the Doral-on-the-Ocean, man. This is the Slammer-in-the-City.'

They both laughed, then resumed their talk.

Dr. Petrie went to the bars and shouted, '*Guard!*'

The blacks stopped talking again and watched him.

He waited for a while, and then shouted, '*Guard! Guard! Let me out of here!*'

A few more minutes passed, and then a young policeman

with rimless spectacles came down the corridor jangling a bunch of keys.

'You Dr. Petrie?' he asked.

'That's right. I want to see my lawyer.'

'You don't have to. You're free to leave.'

The guard unlocked the cell, and Dr. Petrie stepped out. One of the blacks said, 'So long, honky, have a nice day,' and the other laughed.

Dr. Petrie was ushered back to the police station desk, where the two arresting officers had brought him that morning. Adelaide was there, with dark rings under her eyes. She was still wearing the buttermilk-colored dress in which he had picked her up last night.

'Leonard – are you all right? Oh God, I was so worried.'

She came up and held him close, and he was so relieved to feel her and see her that he felt tears prickling in his eyes.

The desk sergeant said, 'When you've quite finished the love tableau, would you mind signing for these personal possessions?'

Dr. Petrie signed. 'Listen,' he told Adelaide, as he tied his necktie, 'I have to get back to the hospital. I promised Dr. Selmer.'

'It was Dr. Selmer who told me you were missing,' Adelaide said. He called at the house to see if you were there. When I said you weren't, he called the police, and they found out that you were here. I came straight over.'

'Have they closed the beaches yet?' he asked her, as they walked out of the tinted glass doors of the police station into the brilliant mid-morning sunlight.

'Not yet. The news says that it's serious, this plague, but that people mustn't get too worried. But it doesn't make sense. What the newspapers are saying, and the TV, it doesn't seem to tie up at all. I've seen people sick in the streets, and yet they keep saying there's nothing wrong.'

Dr. Petrie looked around. The sky was its usual imperturbable blue, flecked with shadowy white clouds. But the city was quiet. There were only a few cars, and they seemed to be rolling around the city streets in a strange dream. Some of them were piled high with possessions – chairs, tables and mattresses – and it was obvious that the few people who had realized what was going on were getting out as quick as they could.

The sidewalks – usually crowded with shoppers and tourists – were almost empty. People who needed to go for food or drink were hurrying back to their cars and avoiding strangers like—

Like the plague, thought Dr. Petrie bitterly.

'Have you seen any bodies?' he asked Adelaide.

She shook her head. 'I've heard though,' she said quietly. 'I caught a taxi, and the taxi driver said he'd seen people lying on the ground, dead.'

'I saw a whole family last night,' Dr. Petrie said. 'It was awful. They were just lying on the sidewalk. I can't understand how Donald Firenza has kept this under wraps for so long.'

'Are you going back to the hospital?' Adelaide asked.

'I have to.'

'Do you want me to come with you?'

He shook his head. 'It's too risky. The hospital is full of infection. I don't know why on earth I haven't caught the plague yet but Dr. Selmer reckons that a few people could be immune. Maybe I'm one of them.'

Adelaide held his arm. '*Maybe?* Leonard – what if you go

to the hospital and – well, what if I never see you again?'
She looked away.

'Adelaide, I'm a doctor. This city is dying around us. Look
at it. Have you ever seen downtown Miami as quiet as this
on a Tuesday lunchtime? I have to find out what's going on,
and I have to help.'

'Leonard, I'm not leaving you. Not again. I've just spent
the most frightening night of my life, waiting for you to
come back, and I'm not going to let it happen again.'

A cab was parked at the corner. The driver, a squat
middle-aged man in a straw hat, was calmly smoking a
cigar and sunning himself as he leaned against the trunk.

Dr. Petrie walked over, holding Adelaide's hand, and said,
'Will you take me to the hospital?'

The taxi driver looked him up and down. 'You sick?' he
asked.

'No, I'm a doctor.'

The man reached behind him and opened the door.
'That'll be forty bucks,' he said, without taking the cigar
out of his mouth.

'*Forty bucks?* What are you talking about? That's a two-
dollar ride at the most.'

The taxi driver slammed the door shut again. 'That's the
price. Forty bucks or no trip.'

Dr. Petrie said firmly, 'Come on, Adelaide. We'll find
ourselves a cab driver with some goddamned morality.'

The taxi driver was unfazed. 'Mister,' he said, 'you can
search all day. All the moral cab drivers have taken their
taxis and headed north. So has anyone else who's realized
what the hell's going on in this town.'

Dr. Petrie reached for his wallet and peeled off three

ten-dollar bills. 'Here's thirty. Take me down to the hospital, and you'll get the other ten. But don't think for one moment that I enjoy paying money to a flake like you.'

The taxi driver tucked the cash in his shirt pocket, and opened the car door. They climbed in, and the driver performed a wide U-turn, and drove them downtown to the hospital.

'I seen fifty, sixty people dead in the streets,' said the driver conversationally, puffing on his cigar. 'I came out for my roster this morning, and I couldn't believe it. You know what they said on the radio? It's a kind of an influenza, and that it's all going to be over by the end of the week. Nothing to get excited about. You think fifty or sixty stiffs is nothing to get excited about?'

'I'm surprised you didn't leave town along with the rest of your buddies,' said Adelaide tartly.

'Why should I?' said the cab driver, turning the car towards the hospital. 'I can make a few bucks here in the city. I've lived here all my life. Look – there's another stiff on the sidewalk – right there.'

They looked, and saw the body of a woman in a blue-and-green dress lying on the concrete sidewalk outside a delicatessen. Her basket of groceries had spilled all over the pavement, and her arms were drawn up underneath her like a sick child.

The delicatessen proprietor was standing in his doorway staring at her, but what struck Dr. Petrie more than anything else was the attitude of the few passers-by. They stepped over the sprawling woman as if she and her shopping were quite invisible.

Dr. Petrie said, 'Don't slow down. I have to get to the hospital as soon as I can.'

Adelaide was pale. 'Leonard,' she said. 'That woman.'

Dr. Petrie looked away. 'There's nothing we can do. She's probably dead already.'

The taxi driver puffed his cigar. 'You bet she's dead. I hear tell they got so many stiffs in the streets, they're going to start collecting them with garbage trucks.'

Adelaide looked shocked. 'Yes,' Dr. Petrie said, 'I heard that too.'

Dr. Selmer was waiting for him in his private office. The corridors outside were jammed with medical trolleys, and the weeping and wailing relatives of the dead were adding to the confusion of amateur ambulance drivers and local doctors who had been brought in to console the sick. All that was left to give was consolation. In spite of every kind of antibiotic treatment, people who caught the plague were dying with the inevitability of mayflies.

'Firenza was on the phone about an hour ago,' said Anton Selmer, leaning back wearily in his large leather chair, and resting his feet on his cluttered desk. 'He's agreed to close the beaches.'

'What's the death toll?' asked Dr. Petrie, taking off his jacket and rolling up his sleeves.

'About a hundred and twenty so far. That's with this hospital and all the others. Add to that another thirty who may be lying dead in their apartments or in the streets, and you've probably got yourself a reasonably accurate figure.'

'The city's real quiet. I thought it would have been more.'

Dr. Selmer shook his sandy head. 'Don't worry, Leonard. It *will* be more before the day's over. Every one of those dead people came into contact with seven or eight or maybe even more live people, and every one of those live people, right now, is incubating the plague bacillus.'

'What about quarantine? Did Firenza mention that?'

'He said that he's talking to Becker, when the mayor flies back from Washington this afternoon. Between them, they're going to decide what emergency action they ought to take.'

Dr. Petrie heaved a sigh. 'For the first time in five years, I feel like smoking a cigarette.'

Anton Selmer pushed a wooden box across the desk. 'Have one,' he said. 'It might even be your last.'

Adelaide knocked on the door and came in. She had been down in the ladies' room, washing her face and repairing her make-up. She looked pale and tense, and her hands were trembling.

'Hallo, Adelaide,' Anton Selmer said. 'Take a seat. Can I fix you a drink? I have some fine medicinal whiskey.'

'Please.'

'Leonard?'

'I'll take a beer. The way this city's going, I'm not sure how long it's going to be before we taste cold beer again.' Selmer fixed the drinks. 'I wish I knew how this city *was* going, Leonard. It seems to be impossible to get any straight information. Either the newspapers are blind and deaf, or else they're following a deliberate policy of keeping this thing quiet. It's the same with the TV channels. They all keep saying that the epidemic is isolated, and that it's containable, and that it won't spread. But, Jesus Christ, you only have to come here to the hospital, or walk out into the streets, and you can see that something's wrong. We have a major epidemic on our hands, Leonard, and yet everybody in charge of anything seems to be smiling and waving and making out it's nothing worse than a slight head cold.'

Adelaide said, 'Doesn't the government know? What about the federal health people? Surely they've been informed? Even if they haven't, they must be worried.'

Dr. Petrie pulled the ring of his flip-top can, and took a freezing mouthful of beer. He stood up and walked across to the window. Through the Venetian blinds, he could see the sparse streets of downtown Miami, and the afternoon sun on the white buildings opposite. High in the sky, a long horse's-tail of cirrus cloud was curled by the wind.

'Maybe they do know,' he said. 'Maybe they're helping to keep the whole thing quiet. I haven't heard any airplanes coming out from the airport this morning, Anton.'

'Oh, *that*,' said Dr. Selmer. 'As a precautionary measure, the baggage handlers at Miami International Airport have suddenly decided to go on strike, which means all Miami flights are being diverted to Palm Beach or Tampa.'

'That's convenient. Maybe Firenza does take this plague more seriously than we think. What about boats?'

Dr. Selmer shrugged. 'I don't know, but I guess they're working the same kind of stunt there.'

'But why no official quarantine?' frowned Dr. Petrie. 'I know this thing has spread in just a few hours, but surely there's somebody around with enough *nous* to seal the city off for a while, even if Firenza won't do it.'

'Don't ask me,' said Dr. Selmer. 'The official line is perfectly straightforward. We have a minor epidemic of something akin to Spanish influenza which we expect to have run its course by the end of the week. I've seen it on the television, and I've read it in the paper. Here.'

He leafed through a stack of letters and manila files, and produced the morning's paper. The main headline read: *Twenty Die In Influenza Outbreak*.

'That's incredible,' Adelaide said. 'There are people lying around in the streets dead. Why don't they print the truth?'

Dr. Petrie shuffled through the newspaper until he found the telephone number of its city desk. Without a word, he picked up Dr. Selmer's phone, and dialed. He waited while it rang, and Adelaide and Anton watched him in tense anticipation.

The girl on the newspaper's switchboard answered, and Dr. Petrie asked for the city desk.

There was a long pause, and then finally he was switched through. A nasal, surly sub-editor answered. 'Can I help you?'

'Maybe you can. My name is Dr. Leonard Petrie and I'm down at the hospital here with Dr. Anton Selmer. Look, I've just seen your morning edition and it doesn't seem to bear any relation to what we know to be the real facts.'

'I see.'

'What we have here is a form of *Pasteurella pestis*, which is the medical name for plague. It's very virulent, and very dangerous, and so far as we know to date, almost a hundred and fifty people have died. By the end of the day, it could be five or six times that figure.'

There was a silence. The sub-editor coughed, and then said, 'Well, Dr. Petrie. Your theory is very interesting.'

'What are you talking about? These are *facts*! I've seen dead people on the streets myself!'

'Oh, sure.'

'Aren't you interested? Isn't this newsworthy? Or have

you gotten so goddamned deadened to violence that when a hundred and fifty Miami residents die of the plague, it only rates two lines on the inside page?'

'I am not deadened to violence, Dr. Petrie. I am simply doing my job.'

Dr. Petrie frowned. 'I wish I knew what your job was. So far, it seems to amount to out-and-out misrepresentation.'

'I resent that, Dr. Petrie.'

'Oh you do, huh? Well, I resent a newspaper that deliberately obscures the truth.'

The sub-editor sighed. 'Dr. Petrie, we're not dummies. We know what's going on, and so does City Hall and the County Health Department and the US Disease Control people in Washington.'

'Well, there isn't much evidence of it.'

'Of course not. We've already been briefed along with all of the other media that we have to play this thing right down. No screams, no shouts.'

'No *facts*?' said Dr. Petrie, incredulous.

The sub-editor sighed again. 'Dr. Petrie, do you have any idea what would happen if the majority of people in Miami became aware that plague was loose in the city? Panic, looting, robbery, violence – the city would die overnight. Apart from that, people carrying plague would spread over the surrounding countryside faster than you could say epidemic. It's not the way we usually do things, this play-down policy, but in this particular case we felt obliged to agree.'

Dr. Petrie was silent.

'The city health people have known about the plague since Friday of last week,' the sub-editor continued. 'A young baby in Hialeah went down with it, and died. The doctors did a routine test, and passed the information to Mr. Firenza. He went straight to the federal health authorities, they sought higher sanction, and the government decided that fewer people would be exposed to risk if they kept it quiet.'

Dr. Petrie said, 'You *can't* keep it quiet! The rumors are going around already. Have you seen US 1 and the North-South Expressway? People are beginning to drive out of Miami like rats out of a sinking ship.'

The sub-editor coughed. 'They won't get far.'

'What do you mean?'

'Well, you're not supposed to know this, doctor, but you're bound to find out sooner or later. Every route out of Miami is sealed off. The whole city has been in the bag since about midnight last night. The National Guard have orders to stop and detain anyone trying to leave or enter the city limits.'

'And what about people who insist?'

'They're detained along with the rest of them.'

Dr. Petrie rubbed the back of his neck. 'I don't know what to say,' he said wearily. 'I guess you've told me all there is to know.'

'I just hope you see what we're doing in the right light,' said the sub-editor, with unexpected sincerity. 'I mean, we love this city, and we're real worried about this plague, but if we let the pig out of the sack, this whole place is going to be ripped apart in five minutes flat. Especially when people realize that they can't escape.'

Dr. Petrie nodded. 'Yes,' he said, 'I should think you're right.' Then he laid the phone back down, and sat there for two or three minutes with his head in his hands.

'Well?' said Adelaide. 'What was all that about? Don't keep us in suspense.'

He took her hand, and squeezed it. 'It appears that we have been taken for mugs. Donald Firenza and his health department have known about the plague since Friday. As soon as they identified it, they sought advice from the federal government, which is probably the real reason that Becker is in Washington. The federal government has covertly sealed off Miami during the night, and is arresting and detaining anyone who tries to get in or out.' Dr. Selmer said, open-mouthed, 'They *knew*? They knew about the plague all along and they didn't warn us?'

'I guess they realized that warnings were futile. This plague kills people so fast, the whole population might have contracted it by now. All they want to do is stop it spreading.'

'But what are they doing about it? Are they trying to find an antidote? What are they doing about *us*? They can't just seal off a whole city and let it die.'

Dr. Petrie drummed his fingers on the edge of Dr. Selmer's desk.

'No,' he said softly. 'I don't suppose they can.'

Throughout the afternoon, and into the evening, it became clear that the plague was spreading through Miami and the suburbs like a brushfire on a dry day. Dr. Petrie and Dr. Selmer tried several times to get through to Washington, and to Donald Firenza, but the telephone switchboards were constantly busy. They were aware that four of their plague victims had been telephone operators, so it was likely that the exchange was seriously undermanned.

They worked hour after hour in the bald fluorescent light of the emergency ward, sweating in their flea-proof clothing, comforting the dying and easing the pain of the sick. Dr. Petrie saw an old woman of ninety-six die in feverish agony; a young boy of five shuddering and breathing his last painful breaths; a twenty-five-year-old wife die with her unborn baby still inside her.

Ambulances and private cars still jammed the hospital forecourt, bringing more and more people to the wards, even though the regular ambulance drivers had almost all sickened and died. Nurses made makeshift beds from folded blankets, and laid the whispering, white, dying people down in the corridors.

During a break in his work, Dr. Petrie stood in one of those corridors and looked around him. It was like a scene from a strange war, or some whispering asylum. He rubbed the sweat from his eyes and went back to his latest patient.

Dr. Selmer looked up from giving a streptomycin shot to a young teenage girl with red hair. 'What's it like out there?' he said hoarsely. 'Are they still coming in?'

Leonard Petrie nodded. 'They're still coming in, all right. How many do you reckon now?'

Dr. Selmer shrugged. 'If all the hospitals are coping with the same amount of patients – well, six or seven hundred. Maybe more than a thousand. Maybe even more than that.'

Dr. Petrie shook his head. 'It's like hell,' he said. 'It's like being in hell.'

'Sure. Would you take a look at Dr. Parkes? He doesn't seem too well.'

Dr. Parkes was an elderly physician who used to have a practice out at Opa-Locka. Dr. Petrie had met him a few times on the golf course, and liked him. Now, across the crowded emergency ward, he could see Dr. Parkes wiping his forehead unsteadily, and taking off his spectacles.

'Dr. Parkes?' he said, pushing his way past two part-time trolley porters.

Dr. Parkes reached out and leaned against him. 'I'm all right,' he said quietly. 'I just need a moment's rest.'

'Dr. Parkes, do you want a shot?'

'No, no,' said the gray-haired old man. 'Don't you worry about me. I'll be all right. I'm just tired.'

Dr. Petrie shrugged. 'Well, if you say so. You're the doctor.'

Dr. Parkes smiled. Then he turned away from Dr. Petrie, and immediately collapsed, falling face-first into a tray of surgical instruments, and scattering them all over the floor.

'Nurse!' Dr. Petrie shouted. 'Give me a hand with Dr. Parkes!'

They lifted the old man on to a bed, and Dr. Petrie loosened the pale blue necktie from his wrinkled throat. The elderly doctor was breathing heavily and irregularly, and it was obvious that he was close to death.

'Dr. Parkes,' said Dr. Petrie, taking his hand.

Dr. Parkes opened his pale eyes, and gave a soft and rueful look. 'I thought I was too old to get sick,' he said quietly.

'You'll make it,' said Dr. Petrie. 'Maybe you're just tired, like you said.'

Dr. Parkes shook his head. 'You can't kid me, Petrie. Here – lift up my left hand for me, would you?'

Dr. Petrie lifted the old man's liver-spotted hand. There was a heavy gold ring on it, embossed with the symbol of a snake and a staff, the classical sign of medical healing.

'My mother gave me that ring,' whispered Dr. Parkes. 'She was sure I was going to be famous. She's been dead a long time now, bless her heart. But I want you – I want you to take the ring – and see if it brings you more luck than me.'

'I can't do that.'

'Yes you can,' breathed Dr. Parkes. 'You can do it to please an old man.'

Dr. Petrie tugged the ring from Dr. Parkes' finger, and pushed it uncertainly on to his own hand.

Dr. Parkes smiled. 'It suits you, son. It suits you.'

He was still smiling when he died. Dr. Petrie covered his face with a paper towel. They had long since run out of sheets.

Anton Selmer came across, patting the sweat from his face. 'Is he dead?' he asked, unnecessarily. Dr. Petrie nodded.

'I think I'm becoming immune,' said Dr. Selmer. 'Even if I'm not immune to the plague, I'm immune to watching my friends die. I don't even want to think how many good doctors and nurses we've lost here today.'

Dr. Petrie fingered the ring. 'It makes you wonder whether it's worth it. Whether we should just leave all this, and get the hell out.'

Dr. Selmer tied a fresh mask around his face. 'If there was any place to get the hell out *to*,' he said, 'I'd go. I think we have to face the fact that we're caught like rats in a barrel.'

The ward doors swung open again, and they turned to see what fresh victims were being wheeled in. This time, it looked like something different. A young dark-haired boy of nineteen was lying on the medical trolley, with his right side soaked in blood. He was moaning and whimpering, and when the amateur ambulance attendants tried to ease him on to a bed, he screamed out loud.

Dr. Selmer and Dr. Petrie helped to make him comfortable. Dr. Selmer gave him a quick shot of painkiller, while Dr. Petrie cut away the boy's stained plaid shirt with scissors.

'Look at this,' said Dr. Petrie. He pointed to the fat, ugly wound in the boy's side. 'This is a gunshot wound.'

Dr. Selmer leaned over the boy, and wiped the dirt and sweat from his face with a tissue. There was asphalt embedded in the youth's cheeks, as if he had fallen on a sidewalk or roadway.

'What happened, kid?' said Dr. Selmer. 'Did someone shoot you?'

The boy gritted his teeth, and nodded. With his face a little cleaner, he looked like the sort of average kid you see working behind the counter at a hamburger joint, or delivering lunchtime sandwiches for a delicatessen.

'Who shot you, kid?' asked Dr. Selmer, coaxingly. 'Come on – it might help us to make you better. If we know what kind of gun it was, we can find the slug faster.' The boy took a deep whimpering breath, tried to talk, and then burst into tears. Dr. Selmer stroked his forehead, and spoke soothingly and softly to him, like a mother talking to a child.

'Come on, kid, you're going to be all right. Tell me who shot you, kid. Tell me who shot you.'

The boy turned his head, his eyes squeezed tight shut. 'We was – we was going to get out—' he panted. 'Me and my friend – we heard there was plague – and we was going to get out—'

'What happened?'

'We – we took his dad's old – Buick. We drove up as far as – the turnpike – and they – they sent us back.'

'*Who* sent you back, kid?' asked Dr. Selmer.

'National – Guardsmen – sent us – back – said we couldn't – leave—'

'So what did you do?'

The boy was biting his tongue so hard that blood was running down his chin. He shook his head desperately, as if he was trying to erase the memory of something that he never wanted to think about again.

'What did you do?' Dr. Selmer repeated. 'Did they shoot you?'

'My friend – said – we ought to make a – break – said – they wouldn't really shoot us. So we – put the gas – down and – tried to get – through. They – they blew off – his whole – they blew off his – they blew off his head—'

Dr. Petrie laid his arm on Dr. Selmer's shoulder.

'Leave the kid alone, Anton. We might have guessed they were going to keep us in the hard way. It's either die here or else die on the city limits.'

Dr. Selmer nodded bitterly. He called one of his assistants to see to the boy's bullet-wound, and then he went through to the scrub-up room to wash. Dr. Petrie came with him.

'I've been on the emergency wards for a long time,' said Dr. Selmer, drying his hands. 'And if there's one thing that constantly amazes me, it's how totally callous we Americans can be to each other. Over the past ten years, I've had people brought in here who were found bleeding in the street, while dozens of passers-by walked around them. I've had women who were raped or beaten-up, while crowds just stood around and watched. And now this. We may be two hundred years old, Leonard, but if you ask me we're still a nation of strangers.'

Dr. Petrie was combing his hair. 'Would you do any different, if you had the federal government's problem? Wouldn't you seal off the city?'

'Maybe not. But at least I would let us unlucky rats, caught in our barrel, know what the hell was going on. So far as we know, and so far as the rest of the country knows, this is just a mild outbreak of Spanish influenza.'

Dr. Petrie said, 'Has it occurred to you that this might be germ warfare? That the Russians might have started this disease?'

Dr. Selmer laughed wryly. 'The Russians didn't need to, did they? We've done a good enough job of it on our own. I don't know where all this sewage came from, but I'm ninety-nine-per-cent convinced that you're right. The shit of sophisticated society has come to visit upon us the wrath of an offended and polluted ocean. What a way to go. Poisoned by our own crap!'

Dr. Petrie said, 'You're tired, Anton. Go take a rest.'

Dr. Selmer shook his head. 'The rate this plague is spreading, the whole city is going to be dead by Thursday. If I went to sleep I'd miss half of it.'

'Anton, you're exhausted. For your own sake, rest.'

'Maybe later. Right now, I could do with some coffee.'

They left the emergency ward and went out into the corridor, stepping over sick and dying people wrapped up in red regulation blankets. A couple of thin and desperate voices called out to the doctors but there was nothing they could do except say, 'It won't be long now, friend. Please be patient,' and leave it at that.

No treatment could arrest the course of the plague, and most of these people would have done better to stay at home, and die in their own beds. Dr. Petrie found there were tears in his eyes.

A cop came slowly down the corridor towards them, wearing a bandit neckerchief around his nose and mouth.

'Excuse me, doctors,' he called. 'Excuse me!'

'What's wrong, officer?'

The cop stepped carefully over an old man who was wheezing and coughing as the plague bacillus clogged his lungs.

'It's the Chief of Police, sir. He's been taken real bad.'

Dr. Selmer looked at him, without moving. 'So?'

The cop seemed confused. 'Well, sir, he's sick. I thought that maybe someone could come out and take a look at him.'

'What's wrong with him?' Dr. Selmer asked. 'Is it the same as these people here?'

The cop nodded. He was only a young kid, thought Dr. Petrie. Twenty, twenty-one. His eyes were callow and uncertain as they looked out from between his bandit mask and his police cap.

'Well, then,' said Dr. Selmer, 'don't you think that if I could cure these people here, I'd have done it?'

'I guess so, doctor, but—'

'But nothing, officer, I'm afraid. I can't save your Chief of Police any more than I can save these folk. Keep him comfortable, and dispose of the body as quickly as you can when he dies.'

The cop seemed stunned. He looked around him for a moment at the huddled shapes of the dead and dying, and

Dr. Petrie was surprised to find himself feeling sorry for a policeman. He touched the cop's arm and said, 'I should get out of here now, son. This place is thick with the plague, and if you hang around too long, there's a danger you'll catch it yourself.'

The cop paused for a while, then nodded again and stepped his way back along the corridor.

'Plague is a great leveler,' said Dr. Selmer hoarsely. 'Chief of Police or not, that's the end of him.'

'You're in a philosophical mood today, Anton.'

Dr. Selmer pushed the elevator button and waited while the numbers blinked downward to the ground floor. 'I think I'm entitled to be,' he replied bluntly.

Adelaide was still waiting in Dr. Selmer's office. She had been trying to call Washington on the phone all afternoon, but it was unrelentingly busy. She made them a couple of cups of instant coffee, and they took off their shoes and relaxed.

'Is it still bad?' she asked. She sat beside Leonard, stroking his forehead, and he loved the touch and the fragrance of her. It almost made the carnage of the wards seem like a half-forgotten nightmare, and nothing more.

'Worse,' put in Dr. Selmer. 'But I guess it can't go on for ever. Sooner or later, the people who keep on bringing people to the hospital will get sick themselves, and that will be the end of that.'

Dr. Petrie rubbed his eyes. 'This whole damned city is dying and we can't do a thing about it.'

Adelaide said, 'I had a priest in here a little while ago.'

'What was he doing?' asked Dr. Petrie. 'Hiding from the vengeance of the Lord?'

'No,' said Adelaide, brushing her brunette curls away from her forehead. 'He seemed to think that America was getting no more than it deserved. He really felt that we were getting our just desserts for everything. For mistreating the Indians, for inventing the motor car, for suppressing the blacks, for destroying the environment.'

Dr. Petrie sipped his coffee. 'I don't suppose he was willing to intercede with God, and get this whole thing stopped?'

Adelaide shook her head. 'If you ask me, the Church will be delighted. If this doesn't turn a few more millions into true believers, I don't know what will.'

The office phone rang. Dr. Selmer answered it, then passed it over. 'It's for you, Leonard, Sister Maloney from the emergency ward.'

Sister Maloney spoke to Dr. Petrie in her careful Irish accent, 'We have a patient down here who is asking for you by name, doctor.'

'By name? Do you know who she is?'

'I'm afraid not, sir. She's very sick. I think you'd better come down quickly if you want to see her alive.'

'I'll be right there.' He put down the phone, swallowed the rest of his coffee, and collected his green mask and gown.

'Leonard,' said Adelaide. 'Is anything wrong?'

'Sister Maloney says a woman is calling for me. She's probably one of my regular patients. Why don't you stay here and force Anton to drink another cup of coffee? At least it'll keep him out of the ward for five more minutes.'

Dr. Selmer chuckled. 'Alone at last, Adelaide! Now we can pursue that affair I keep meaning to have with you.'

Dr. Petrie closed the office door behind him and walked

quickly down to the elevators. There was a strange bustling whisper throughout the hospital, a sound he had never heard before – like a thousand people murmuring their prayers under their breath. He was alone in the elevator, and he leaned tiredly against the wall as it sank downwards to the ground floor.

The elevator doors slid open, and he was back in hell. The corridors were crowded with moaning, crying people. There were people lying white-faced and shuddering against the walls; people coughing and weeping; people hunched silently on the floor.

The plague had taken both the rich and the poor. There were elderly widows, tanned by years of Florida sun, dying in their diamonds and their pearls. There were waitresses and mechanics, shop assistants and chauffeurs, hotel managers and wealthy executives. Anyone who had swum in the polluted ocean was dying; and anyone who had talked to them or touched them was dying, too.

Dr. Petrie, grim-faced, stepped carefully through the plague victims, and pushed open the door of the emergency ward. Sister Maloney, wearing a big white surgical gown and a surgical mask, was waiting for him.

'Where is she? Is she still alive?'

'Only just, doctor, I'm afraid. It won't be many minutes now.'

Dr. Petrie put on his gown and mask, and followed Sister Maloney into the crowded ward. He had to squeeze his way past the bedside of a 24-year-old policeman called Herb Stone, who was now in the final stages of sickness. His face was gray, and he was muttering incoherently.

Sister Maloney, forging through the patients like a great

white ship, brought Dr. Petrie at last to a bed in the corner. A woman was lying on it with dark circles under her eyes, clutching a soiled blanket and shaking with uncontrollable spasms.

Dr. Petrie leaned forward and looked at her closely. He felt a long, slow, dropping feeling in his stomach. The woman opened her eyes and blinked at him through the glare of the ward's fluorescent light. 'Leonard,' she whispered. 'I knew you'd come.'

'Hallo, Margaret,' he said quietly. 'Are you feeling bad?'

She nodded, and tried to swallow. 'I'd sure like a drink of water.'

'Sister? Could you get me one please?' Dr. Petrie asked.

Sister Maloney steamed off for him, and Dr. Petrie turned back to his former wife.

'Where's Prickles?' he asked. 'Is she safe?'

Margaret nodded again. 'I left her with Mrs. Henschel, next door. She's all right, Leonard. She didn't catch anything.'

'You can't be sure.'

Margaret looked at him for a while. 'No,' she whispered. 'I can't be sure.'

'Is there anything you want me to do? Are you comfortable?'

'It hurts a little. Not much.'

He reached out and took her hand. He could hardly believe that, less than two years ago, he had lain side by side in bed with this same woman, that he had kissed her and argued with her, and that he had actually given her a child. He remembered her in court, in her severe black suit. He remembered her on the day that he had walked out, red-eyed and crying by the front door. He remembered how she had looked on the day they were married.

'Leonard,' she said, stroking the back of his hand.

'Yes, Margaret?'

'Did you ever love me?'

Dr. Petrie turned away and stared for a long time at the wall.

'You can't ask me that, Margaret. Not now.'

'Why?'

'Because I would probably lie. Or worse than that, I might even tell you the truth.'

'That you did love me, or that you didn't?'

He felt her pulse. She was fading fast. She was being taken away from him like a Polaroid photo in reverse, each detail gradually melting back to blank, unexposed, featureless film.

'How do you feel now?' he asked her.

'You're changing the subject.'

'No, I'm not. I'm trying to treat you like a doctor treats a patient.'

'Leonard, didn't you ever love me? I mean – really, really love me?'

He didn't answer. He looked at her dying, and held her hand, but he didn't answer. He didn't know at that moment what the true answer was.

'Leonard,' she said, 'kiss me.'

'What?'

'Kiss me, Leonard.'

He saw that she was almost dead. Her eyes were glazing, and she could barely summon the breath to speak. Her head was slowly sinking towards the rough blanket on which she lay, and even the shudders of plague had subsided in her muscles.

There was no time to decide whether to kiss her. Instead, he pulled the blanket over her face.

Sister Maloney, busy with a sick boy, said, 'Has she gone, Dr. Petrie?'

Dr. Petrie nodded. 'Yes, sister. She's gone.'

As he passed by, Sister Maloney laid a hand on his sleeve. Her sympathetic green eyes showed above her surgical mask.

'Was she someone you knew rather well, Dr. Petrie?'

Dr. Petrie took a deep breath, and looked around him. 'No, sister, she wasn't. I didn't know her well at all.' It was not a callous denial, it was the truth. There were parts of Margaret he had understood thoroughly, and hated – but there was so much, he realized now, that he had not known at all.

Afterwards, as he walked back down the crowded corridor towards the elevators, he felt oddly calm and numb. He didn't feel happy; he had never, in his bitterest moments, wished Margaret dead. But now the problem had been taken out of his hands by chance, and by *Pasteurella pestis*. He was free at last.

A nurse came up to him and touched his arm. She was a small, pretty colored girl. He had seen her around the emergency wards before, and even toyed with the idea of asking her out for a drink.

'Doctor Petrie?' she said.

He looked at her. 'Yes, nurse?'

She lowered her eyes. 'I don't know how to say this. It sounds ridiculous.'

He looked at her steadily. Like every nurse in the hospital, she had been working for hours without a break, and all around her, she had seen doctors and interns and sisters dying on their feet. She was tired, and her black face was glossy with perspiration.

'Why not try me?' he asked huskily.

'Well,' she said, 'I heard a rumor.'

'What kind of a rumor?'

'My brother's friend works for the Miami Fire Department. It seems like he told my brother they've been given special orders. The firemen, I mean. They've been told to get ready for some big blazes.'

Dr. Petrie felt a cold sensation sliding down his spine.

'Some big blazes?' he said. 'What did he mean by that?'

'I don't know, doctor,' said the nurse. She still didn't look up, and her voice was barely audible. 'I guess they mean to burn the city.'

Dr. Petrie let the words sink in. *I guess they mean to burn the city.* It was a medieval way of dealing with an epidemic, but then, all things considered, they were faced with a medieval situation. For the first time in a hundred years, they had a raging disease on their hands that modern medical treatments could neither suppress nor deflect.

He reached out and gently lifted the nurse's chin. 'I'm not going to pretend I don't believe you,' he said, 'because I've seen enough of this administration's tactics to believe it could be true. You might as well know that Miami has been thrown to the wolves. The city is surrounded by National Guardsmen, and there's no way out.'

She held his hand for a moment, and then nodded. 'I guessed they would do that,' she said simply.

They stepped back for a moment while a medical trolley

was pushed between them, carrying a shivering middle-aged woman in a soiled white summer coat.

'Well,' said the colored nurse. 'I suppose I'd better get back to work.'

Dr. Petrie said, as she turned, 'You could try to escape, you know. You could run away.'

She looked back. 'Run away? You mean, right out of Miami?'

'That's right. Right out of Miami.'

'But there are people here who need me. How could I leave my patients?'

'Nurse,' said Dr. Petrie, 'you know and I know that they're all going to die anyway. You don't think that anything you can do will prevent that?'

'No, I don't,' she said, without hesitating. 'But it's my duty to stay with them, and do whatever I can. It's only human.'

Dr. Petrie said, 'You know that you'll die yourself, don't you?'

She nodded.

He didn't say anything else – just looked at her, and thought what a waste it was. She was young and she was black and she was pretty, and she had everything in the world to stay alive for. Now, because of some crass and destructive official bungling, she was going to die.

'Doctor,' she said quietly, 'I know what you're thinking.'

He looked away, but she stepped up to him again and laid her hand on his arm.

'Doctor, we're all human here. We're nothing special – just ordinary people. I want to stay because that's my choice, but maybe you want to go. Doctor, you don't have to seek my approval to do that. You only have to walk right out of here, and take your chance.'

'I have a daughter,' he said, in a trembling voice.

The nurse smiled, and shook her head. 'There's no reason to make excuses. Not to me, nor anyone. Just go, Doctor Petrie.'

He bit his lip, then turned away to the elevators. The last he saw of the colored nurse was her forgiving, resigned and understanding face, as the elevator doors closed between them. There are some people, he thought, whose devotion makes everything else around them seem tawdry and irrelevant.

Dr. Selmer was fast asleep on the couch when Dr. Petrie returned to the office. Adelaide was sitting beside him reading a medical magazine and yawning.

'That didn't take long,' she said.

He sat down next to her and rubbed his eyes. 'It was Margaret,' he said wearily. 'She just died, about five minutes ago.'

Adelaide slowly put down her magazine. 'Margaret?' she said, shocked.

'She's dead, Adelaide. She had the plague.'

She reached over and grasped his wrist. 'Oh, Leonard. Oh, God – I'm sorry. I know that we wished all kinds of things on her. But not this.'

Dr. Petrie sighed. 'There's nothing we can do. She caught it, and she died. It doesn't matter what we wished or didn't wish.'

'What about Prickles? Has she got it too?'

'I don't know. Margaret said she hadn't. She left her with the woman next door when they took her into hospital.'

Adelaide frowned. She could see what Leonard was thinking. He was exhausted, and the past forty-eight hours seemed to have bent and aged him. He was suddenly faced with a choice – to shoulder the responsibility of saving what he had left; or to close his eyes to his own loves and feelings, and plunge himself into a medical battle that he knew was utterly hopeless.

'Leonard,' she said softly, 'I know that you're a doctor, and whether you can cure people or not, you still have to do your best.'

He didn't answer. He merely said, 'Is there any more coffee?'

She held his wrist harder. 'Leonard, if you want to stay here, I'll understand. But if you want to make a break for it, I'll understand that, too. I want to be with you, that's all.'

Dr. Petrie leaned over and kissed her cheek. She turned her face, and kissed him on the mouth. There was passion in their kiss, but there was also a kind of exploration and communication. Lips touching each other, tongues touching each other, questioning and asking.

At last, he said, 'A nurse downstairs told me they were going to burn the city. She heard it from a fireman.' Adelaide stared. 'They're going to do *what*?'

'The plague is obviously out of hand. They're thinking of burning the city.'

'Who is?'

'I don't know. Firenza, the Disease Control Center, the county health chief. What does it matter?'

'But that's *insane*. They can't set fire to the whole of Miami!'

Dr. Petrie stood up. 'They can, honey, and they probably will. Now, how about that coffee?'

Adelaide stood up, too. 'Leonard – damn the coffee! If

this city's going to burn, I'm not going to burn along with it! You think I'm going to stand here passively making cups of coffee while the whole place goes up in flames? You're out of your mind!'

Dr. Petrie held her shoulders and calmed her down. 'Don't *panic*, Adelaide, for God's sake. It's probably nothing more than a contingency plan, that's all. Whenever there's a plague, you have to burn clothing and blankets and bodies, just to stop further infection. Look – we don't even know what's really happening. We have no idea how many people have died, or whether the plague is spreading or not.'

Adelaide looked straight into his eyes. 'Leonard,' she said, 'I don't care. I just think we ought to get the hell out of here before they put a match to us.'

'Even if I decide to stay?'

'You *can't* decide to stay!'

Dr. Petrie turned away. 'That girl downstairs – the one who told me they were going to burn Miami – *she's* staying. She wants to stand by her patients.'

'This is *her* hospital,' persisted Adelaide. 'It's her *job* to stay. What about Prickles? Are you just going to leave her out there, and cross your fingers that she won't get sick – or burned – or raped by some maniac?'

'*Adelaide!*' shouted Dr. Petrie.

'For Christ's sake, Leonard, this is not the time to play at heroes!' retorted Adelaide. 'These people don't *need* you! They're all going to die, aren't they? What's the *use* of staying, Leonard?'

Dr. Petrie turned around, clenching and unclenching his fists. He stared at Adelaide, with her fierce brown eyes, and her brunette curls, and that disturbing, angry, beautiful face.

'The use—' he began, uncertainly. 'The use is—'

'The use is *what*?' interrupted Adelaide hotly. 'You can't cure them, so what are you going to do for them? Make sure that the last thing they see on earth is your benign and self-sacrificing mug? Leonard, for Christ's sake, you're not Albert Schweitzer!'

Dr. Petrie was about to answer, but changed his mind. He simply said: 'No, honey, I know I'm not Albert Schweitzer.'

'Then let's *go*,' said Adelaide. 'Let's just get out of here while we can.'

Dr. Petrie nodded. 'I was going to go anyway. I guess I just needed someone to persuade me. I just don't feel very proud of myself.'

Adelaide sighed. 'Leonard, it's not a question of pride. It's purely a matter of survival.'

Dr. Petrie sat down heavily, with his face in his hands.

She knelt down in front of him, and took his hands away. 'You don't have to justify what you do. There doesn't have to be a reason. It's the same with everything. Why did we fall in love? Why do I want to cling on to you so much?'

'I'm not a great sheltering tree, you know,' said Dr. Petrie. 'I don't even know if I'm a great sheltering man. I feel like a goddamned broken reed at the moment.'

Anton Selmer, asleep on the couch, grunted and whispered something. Dr. Petrie gently laid Adelaide's hands aside, and walked over to look at him. The stocky, red-headed doctor looked pale and sweaty. Petrie lifted his wrist and checked his pulse.

'Is he all right?' asked Adelaide.

He counted the pulse-rate and respiration-rate. Under his probing, long-fingered hands, Dr. Selmer didn't even stir.

'I think he's okay,' Dr. Petrie said at last. 'But he's totally exhausted. He needs all the rest he can get.'

'Are you going to wake him, and tell him we're leaving?'

'I'll try.'

Dr. Petrie shook Dr. Selmer's shoulder. The sleeping doctor licked his lips, and stirred. Dr. Petrie shook him again.

'Anton – wake up. It's Leonard.'

Finally, Dr. Selmer opened his eyes. They were bloodshot from lack of sleep, and his mind was completely fuddled. 'Leonard... what's going on? I was dreaming we were playing golf.'

'Was I winning?'

'Like hell you were. You were three strokes down. What's going on?'

Dr. Petrie said awkwardly, 'We've come to a decision, Adelaide and I.'

Adelaide interrupted, 'We're leaving.'

'*Leaving?*' Dr. Selmer sat up. 'I don't understand.'

Dr. Petrie shrugged. 'We're going to try and make a break. I want to see if I can rescue Prickles, and then maybe we can get through the quarantine cordon and find ourselves a remote place to stay until this whole thing's over.'

'But supposing you spread the disease beyond Miami? Jesus, Leonard, this thing could wipe out the whole damned United States!'

'That's why we want to go some place remote,' said Dr. Petrie. 'We can keep ourselves under observation until we're sure that we're clear.'

'The National Guard will kill you,' said Dr. Selmer. 'You saw what happened to that boy downstairs.'

'They'll kill us either way,' said Dr. Petrie. 'The rumor's going around that they're going to burn the city down.'

Dr. Selmer shook his head. 'I don't know what to say. I'm a doctor, and so are you. How can we leave this place?'

Leonard Petrie couldn't answer that. He didn't know what the answer was. He only knew that all his instinct and personality were telling him now that it was important for him to survive. He completely accepted a doctor's responsibilities to care for his patients, yet he was unable to invest any belief in a hopeless situation. To him, it was like moths flying into the windshields of speeding cars.

He knelt down beside Dr. Selmer's settee, and said, 'Anton, I'm not running out. I just don't believe that it's worth sticking around here any longer. We're not doing anyone any good. Least of all ourselves.'

Dr. Selmer looked thoughtful. 'Well,' he said, 'I can't prevent you from going. I won't say I'm not disappointed.'

'Will you come along with us?'

Dr. Selmer shook his head. 'No, Leonard. That's my emergency ward down there, and I have to stay whether I like it or not.' He got up from the settee. 'I do feel disappointed, Leonard, but that doesn't mean I don't wish you luck.'

Dr. Petrie got up from his knees. Dr. Selmer gave him a small, rueful grin. 'I can't hold you back, Leonard. Maybe it's right that you should be the one to go. Someone has to get out of here and tell the people of this country what's happening. Now, if I were you, I'd get my lady out of here as quick as I could, and high-tail it for the city limits before dawn.'

Dr. Petrie checked his watch. It was already 11:47. 'Okay, Anton,' he said gently. 'But do me a favor, will you?'

'If you promise to keep on playing such a lousy game of golf in my dreams, I'll do you any favor you want.'

'Look after yourself. If they start burning the city, do your best to get out. When this is all over, I want you and me to meet up, and have ourselves a couple of drinks at the club, and drown the memory of this goddamned plague for ever.'

Dr. Selmer scratched the back of his gingery neck. 'I think you've got yourself a deal there, Leonard.'

The two men clasped hands for a long moment, and then Dr. Petrie took Adelaide by the arm, and led her out into the corridor. As he closed the door behind him, Dr. Selmer called out, 'Please, Leonard – take care.'

Dr. Petrie nodded, and closed the office door behind him for the last time.

They pushed their way along the crowded hospital corridors as quickly as they could. Adelaide kept a handkerchief over her nose and mouth, and Dr. Petrie steered her clear of obvious plague cases. There was a background of low muttering and whispering, occasionally interrupted by cries of pain or anguish. People sat and lay everywhere, huddled in corners too sick to move, or gradually dying on their trolleys. The stench of dead bodies was almost too much to bear.

Two patients, nearly dead themselves, watched with glazed eyes as a doctor, gasping and shuddering with his own plague, tried to inject them with painkilling drugs. In the night outside, the streets echoed with the never-ending wail of sirens.

They broke out of the hospital doors and into the warm, neon-lit hospital forecourt. The place was still cluttered with ambulances, but there was noticeably less activity than there had been before. Dr. Petrie's car was still at Margaret's. By now it had probably been stolen, commandeered or towed away. But there was a whole hospital car park round the side of the building, and they were bound to find a car with its ignition keys left inside.

Adelaide said, 'My God, it's gotten so much worse. Look – there's a couple of bodies over there, by the hospital entrance.'

Dr. Petrie took her arm. 'Don't worry about that. Let's just get the hell out.'

They half-ran, half-walked round to the side of the hospital. The car park was dark, and shadowed from the street lights by the fourteen-story bulk of the hospital tower. Dr. Petrie said: 'You take the first row of cars, I'll take the second. Try the driver's door, and see if it opens. If it does, check for keys.'

As swiftly and silently as they could, they went from one car to the other, trying the door-handles. By the time Dr. Petrie had tugged at his twelfth car, he was beginning to wonder if the staff of this particular hospital weren't security-conscious to a fault. Then Adelaide hissed, 'I've got one!'

She was opening the door of a bronze Gran Torino. Dr. Petrie skirted around the back of the car that he had been trying to open, and crossed the space in between the rows of parked vehicles. The moment he stepped into the open, a rough voice shouted, 'Hold it right there, buddy!'

He froze, with his hands above his head. A stocky shadow disengaged itself from all the other shadows, and started to walk towards him. In a thin slanting beam of light from one of the hospital windows, Dr. Petrie saw a solid, middle-aged security guard, with a navy-blue uniform, a face as hard as a concrete post, and a revolver.

'I'm a doctor,' Petrie said.

The security guard came up close, and shone a torch in Dr. Petrie's face. 'Then how come you're trying to steal yourself a car?'

'Someone took mine. I have an emergency.'

'You got ID?'

'Sure. It's in my top pocket. Here – I'll get it out for you.'

'Don't you move a muscle.'

The security guard came forward, reached into Dr. Petrie's inside pocket, then tried to open the papers with one hand. As he did so, Dr. Petrie grabbed the man's gun wrist, and tried to twist the revolver out of his grasp.

Forcing the guard's arm around in a circle, he jammed his leg behind the man's calf, and pushed him. The man fell backwards on to the tarmac, jarring his knee – but he still kept his grip on the gun.

Dr. Petrie pressed the guard's wrist against the ground, and then trod on it, hard. At last, the fingers opened, and Dr. Petrie snatched the revolver away from him.

The guard cried, 'Don't shoot.' He raised his arms protectively over his face. 'I got a wife with a bad leg.'

Dr. Petrie said, 'I'm not going to hurt you, you dumb ox. Just get up and get the hell out of here.'

The guard got to his feet, and dusted himself off. 'You won't get far, you know,' he said, stepping cautiously backwards. 'They got the cops on the lookout for bums like you. All I have to do is call them up, and they've got your number.'

Petrie waved the gun in his direction again. The guard said, 'Hey – I didn't mean it serious. I was joking! You go right ahead.'

Adelaide was watching, tense and fearful, from a few feet away, holding the door of the Gran Torino. Dr. Petrie looked at her, and couldn't see her eyes, only the dark brunette curls of her hair. The guard was shuffling away from them, step by step, holding his hands out in front of him.

As if in a dream, Dr. Petrie fired the revolver twice. The guard yelped like a small dog, and started running away across the car park. Dr. Petrie lifted the revolver in both hands, held it steadily, and fired again. He missed. He fired once again, and the bullet sang mournfully off the fender of a parked car.

Dr. Petrie lowered the gun, and peered into the darkness.

'He got away,' he said, as the smoke drifted away across the car park.

'You might have killed him,' Adelaide gasped. 'You meant to.' She sounded very frightened.

Dr. Petrie put the revolver in his pocket.

'Yes,' he said. 'I meant to. But I didn't.'

They drove out of the car park in silence, and out into the plague-ridden streets of Miami.

They switched on the car radio. It was now just past midnight, into the early hours of Wednesday morning. What they heard on the news and what they saw as they drove through the dark broken streets of the city were so different as to be totally bizarre.

The calm, rich voice of the mayor, John Becker, was reassuring citizens throughout Florida and the United States that the breakdown in communication between Miami and the outside world was 'purely temporary and technical, and in the best interests of all concerned.'

Dr. Petrie glanced across at Adelaide, and shook his head. She smiled him a tight little smile.

Mayor Becker went on, 'This epidemic, which is still awaiting medical analysis, is proving a little more difficult to control than we had originally hoped, and for the protection of residents and folks on vacation, we've had to restrict some of the highway traffic through the city. But we can assure you that there's nothing to worry about, provided you follow a simple safety code and remain at home whenever possible.'

It was while he was saying this that, without warning, the city lights of Miami began to go out. Most of the downtown office buildings and stores were already in darkness, but now the street lights flickered out, and everything electrical dimmed and died. Like stars obscured by the passing of a murky cloud, the bright subtropical city with its glittering strip of hotels and its garish downtown streets, was gradually overtaken by a shadowy gloom, as dark and threatening as a primitive jungle.

'I expect it's the power station,' Dr. Petrie said. 'They've got the plague.'

He switched on the car's headlights. The streets seemed wrecked and deserted. Store windows were smashed, and there was garbage and junk strewn all over. Despite the threat of summary shooting, the looters had obviously been out in force. As they turned north on to 95, they saw a small group of blacks running furtively through the shadows with television sets, stereo equipment and records.

Abandoned cars – some with their dead drivers still

sitting in them – cluttered the highway. From the height of the expressway, Dr. Petrie and Adelaide could see small fires burning all over Miami in the tropical darkness, and a few buildings uncertainly lit by emergency generators. The whole city echoed with the endless warbling of police and fire sirens, and the crack of spasmodic shooting.

In just over four days, from the first signs of plague in Hialeah, Miami had collapsed into pandemonium. It was like an old painting of hell with lurid flames and demonic shadows; and above everything was the terrible wail of sirens, the smashing of glass and the ceaseless blast of car horns, pressed down by the weight of their dead owners.

Dr. Petrie opened the car window and slowed down for a while, listening and looking in cold disbelief.

'It's like the end of the world,' whispered Adelaide. 'My God, Leonard, it's like the end of the world.'

The stench of burning and the inhuman sounds of a dying city filled the car, and Dr. Petrie wound up the window again. He felt exhausted beyond anything he had ever known before. He had to open his eyes wide to clear them and focus them, and even then he found it difficult to drive through the debris and jetsam that strewed the highway.

They were almost level with Gratigny Drive when he had to pull the Torino up short. The road was entirely blocked by two burning cars. One of them, a Riviera, was already blackened and smoldering, but the other, a Cadillac, still had its tires ablaze, like a fiery chariot from Heaven.

Dr. Petrie opened his car door and got out. The heat was oily and fierce. Shielding his eyes, he went as close to the wrecks as he could, and to his horror, he saw a woman still sitting in the Cadillac – her face was roasted raw, but she was lifting her smoking arm up and down, trying to call out. A lurch of nausea made his empty stomach turn over, and he had to look away.

Adelaide called out, 'What is it? Can we get past?'

Dr. Petrie shouted back, '*Stay there! Just stay there!*'

He took the security guard's revolver out of his pocket, held it tight in both hands, and hoped to God that he wouldn't miss. He inched as close to the blazing car as he could, and then fired. The woman jerked sharply back into her ruined seat as if he had kicked her. She disappeared in a torrent of rubbery smoke.

Dr. Petrie climbed back into the Gran Torino.

'Was there someone in there?' Adelaide asked quietly.

He nodded, and laid the gun on the parcel shelf. For some reason, the killing seemed to have purged something within him; to have quelled his broken nerves. Maybe it was because, for the first time since Mr. Kelly had woken him up on Monday morning, he had been able to act, to do something positive.

'Honey – I'm going to have to ram my way through there,' he said. He twisted around in his seat, and backed the car up thirty or forty yards. He stopped. 'All you have to do is hold tight.'

He licked his lips. Then he shifted the car into 2, and stamped on the gas. The back tires screeched and slithered as they fought for traction on the concrete, and then the Torino bellowed forward – straight towards the two smoking wrecks.

There was a heavy smash, and for a moment Petrie thought the car was going to roll over. But he forced his foot harder on the gas, and their car gradually shoved the black carcass of the Riviera, its buckled hubs scraping and shuddering on the road, right to the edge of the expressway. Then Dr. Petrie backed up a foot or two, turned the wheel, and drove the Gran Torino over broken glass and oil and litter until they were clear. The car gave one last snaking skid, and they were driving north again.

'Are you all right?' asked Dr. Petrie.

Adelaide brushed back her hair. 'I bruised my knee when we collided, but that's all. I'm okay.'

Dr. Petrie checked his watch. 'Another two or three minutes, and we'll be there. Then we can try and get out of this godforsaken place.'

They drove without talking for a moment or two, and then Adelaide said, 'Was it a man or a woman?'

Dr. Petrie frowned. 'Was what a man or a woman?'

'In that burning car. I just wondered.'

He rubbed at his left eye. The road was dark and confusing, and he had to swerve to avoid an abandoned police car.

'It was a woman,' he said baldly. 'Does it make any difference?'

'I don't know. I got the feeling you needed to kill someone.'

He glanced across at her. 'What made you think that?'

'It was the way you fired at that security man. He wasn't doing anything. He was just doing his job. Somehow, you looked as though you really needed to kill him.'

She was right, but Dr. Petrie could no more analyze his reactions than she could. It was connected with his present sense of helplessness as a doctor, with the need to protest, however ridiculously, against the outrage that was sweeping through his city. 'I don't know,' he said. 'I guess I'm just tired and frustrated.'

They didn't say anything more until they had driven through the dark suburbs of North Miami Beach up to Dr. Petrie's former house. He pulled the Gran Torino up to the kerbside, and climbed out. With Adelaide he walked across the grass to the house next door. It was a pink Spanish-style ranchette, called El Hensch, and owned by the Henschels. There was a bright gas-light burning in the living-room, so Dr. Petrie assumed his erstwhile neighbors were at home. He rang the doorbell, and it played *The Yellow Rose of Texas.*

The frosted-glass door opened half-an-inch. Dr. Petrie saw one bespectacled eye and the muzzle of a .38 revolver.

'Who's that?' said David Henschel. 'You get along out of here before I put a hole through ya.'

'Mr. Henschel,' said Dr. Petrie. 'It's me. Leonard Petrie. Used to live next door – remember? I've come for Prickles.'

There was a pause, then Dr. Petrie heard Gloria Henschel saying, 'David – open the goddamned door, will ya? It's Dr. Petrie. I seen him through the upstairs window.'

After a lot of rattling of chains and locks, the door was opened. Dr. Petrie took Adelaide by the arm and stepped inside. Mr. Henschel, a fat, fiftyish man with a check shirt and a pot belly, opened the living-room door for them.

On the living-room table was a butane camping lamp. It made the room seem like a dazzling religious grotto. Prickles was lying on the red velvet-style settee, with her thumb in her mouth, and her long honey-colored hair tied back with a pink ribbon. She was holding a worn-out teddy bear with a peculiarly manic smile on its face, and she was wearing a red dressing-gown and one red slipper.

Dr. Petrie knelt down on the floor beside her, very quietly, and watched her sleeping. Her cheeks were flushed, but she didn't look as if she had contracted plague. He ran the tip of his finger down the middle of her forehead, and down the small curve of her nose. Adelaide came up behind him, and put her arm around him.

He looked up. 'She's beautiful, isn't she?' he said, shaking his head – a proud father who couldn't believe that his luck was real.

Mrs. Henschel came into the room in a dazzling yellow bathrobe and pink-rinsed hair in curlers. She looked like a giant canary.

'Dr. Petrie,' she crooned. 'Well, it's been a long time. Have you come to stay awhile? You know you're welcome.'

Dr. Petrie looked at his watch. It was 12:35. 'I'm sorry, Gloria,' he said. 'I've come to collect Prickles, and then we're getting out of here.'

Mr. Henschel frowned, 'Getting out? You mean, leaving town?'

'Sure. Don't you know how bad it is?'

'How bad what is?'

Dr. Petrie felt like a time-traveler who has accidentally stepped into the past.

'The plague. The epidemic. The whole of Miami is sick with plague.'

Mr. Henschel looked suspicious. 'Plague?' he said. 'You mean – like sickness? I heard on the television there was 'flu, and that forty or fifty people was dead, but that's all.

We haven't been out of the house today, this is my week off work.'

'Is that all they've been saying on television?' Adelaide asked. 'Forty or fifty dead?'

'Sure. They said it wasn't nothing to worry about.'

Dr. Petrie sat down on the edge of the settee where Prickles slept. 'I'll tell you how much it is to worry about,' he told them. 'Margaret died of this sickness just an hour or two ago, and she's just one of thousands.'

While the Henschels stood there, barely able to grasp what he was telling them, he explained the raw facts about the plague, and how long it was going to be before fire or bacilli were going to destroy the Miami way of life for ever.

As he spoke, he saw the growing desperation and terror in their faces, and he understood for the first time why nobody from City Hall or Washington had considered it prudent to let them know before.

'I'll get my rifle,' said David Henschel, his voice unsteady. 'I'll get my rifle and I'll blast my way out of this town, even if I die trying.'

'Mr. Henschel,' said Dr. Petrie, as the old man went for the door.

'What is it?'

'I'm afraid you probably will.'

'I probably will what?'

'Die trying.'

Mr. Henschel stared at him balefully for a moment, and then without a word, went off to fetch his gun.

Four

Kenneth Garunisch eased himself back into his big Colonial armchair and took a swig from his ice-cold beer. Pulling his necktie loose, he propped his feet up on the Colonial coffee table. It had been a hard, long night, and he felt as if he had been beaten up by three Polish muggers in a Turkish bath.

The lavatory flushed, and Dick Bortolotti came out, wiping his hands on a towel.

'Is there any of that beer going spare?' he asked, coughing.

'There's a six-pack in the icebox,' growled Garunisch. 'I couldn't face any breakfast.'

'What time is it?'

Garunisch peered at his watch. 'Five-forty-five.'

Bortolotti came back with a beer and sat down next to him. There was a large-scale map of Florida and Georgia on the coffee table, and it was marked in several places with red felt-tip pen. During the night, Garunisch, apart from the US Disease Control Center and the federal government, had been one of the best-informed people on the spread of the unstoppable plague. His members in hospitals all the way up the East Coast had been reporting outbreaks as they happened, and although he didn't yet know that Miami had been completely sealed off by National Guardsmen, he *did* know that the hospital system there had virtually collapsed.

'What are they saying on the television news?' asked Bortolotti.

'They're still making out that it's swine 'flu or Spanish 'flu or some other kind of 'flu. But they're having to fess up that it's getting worse. They can't hold the lid on this thing for ever.'

'Did you try your guy at *The Daily News*?'

'I just came off the phone. He says there's a hundred-percent media cooperation with the federal government. It's not as voluntary as it looks, though. The White House is apparently ready to do some kind of deal over their interpretation of secrets bill. If the press and the TV boys play ball, the government will ease off their legislation.'

Dick Bortolotti swallowed beer, and grinned wryly. 'Sounds just like the politicians I know and love.'

Kenneth Garunisch opened his cigarette box and lit a cigarette. 'Don't worry about it. The most important thing is protecting our members. Apart from that, I think we can squeeze some future guarantees and emergency pay scales out of the health people. This may be a serious situation, but it's an illness that brings nobody any good.'

'You kidding?' Bortolotti asked.

Garunisch blew smoke noisily, and nodded. 'I'm kidding that this whole goddamned business doesn't bother me, because it sure as hell does. But there's no future in being squeamish. If we can't force some favorable negotiations out of this little baby, then we don't deserve to be wearing long pants. Take a look at this map.'

Dick Bortolotti leaned forward.

'This thing is spreading like shit on a shoe,' said Garunisch. 'Here's the first reported outbreak – in Hialeah, on Friday. By Tuesday afternoon, they're counting the dead in hundreds. By Tuesday evening, they've stopped counting the dead because there are too many. The last I heard was four a.m., and the whole of Miami has packed up. No power, no police, no nothing.'

'Any of our members still alive?'

Garunisch shrugged. 'It's hard to tell. I had Evans call Grabowsky, but his home phone isn't answering, and we can't get through to the hospital. If you ask me, Dick, this epidemic is a whole lot worse than anyone knows. We've had reports of outbreaks down as far as Bahia Honda, and we've had them *here*, at Fort Lauderdale, and *here*, at Fort Pierce, and about fifteen minutes ago I heard that there are suspects at Jacksonville.'

'So? What's your conclusion?'

'My conclusion has got to be very simple,' he said, wiping his lips with the back of his hand. 'I take out my measuring rule and I discover that the distance between Miami and Jacksonville is approximately 300 miles. I divide 300 miles by four days and I learn that this plague is traveling northwards up the East Coast at a rate of 75 miles a day. Maybe faster. This means that if it continues spreading over the next couple of weeks in the same way that it's been spreading up till now, it'll be *here*.'

'Here?' said Bortolotti, frowning at the map.

'*Here*, dummy!' snapped Garunisch. 'Here in New York City! They're already dropping dead in the goddamned streets in Miami! Imagine what's going to happen if it starts infecting people *here*!'

Bortolotti blinked. 'Jesus,' he said. 'That would be murder. Nothing short of murder.'

'You bet your ass it'd be murder,' Garunisch stood up and walked across to the window. A dirty dawn was just making itself felt over the East River, and he lifted the embroidered net curtains and stared out at it. Then he turned around.

'And do you know *whose* murder?' he said. 'Not the fucking federal government's murder. Not the kiss-my-butt President of the United States. Oh, no. *They're* okay. They have their private doctors and their quarantined quarters, and if the worst comes to the worst, they can always fly off and leave us to stew in our own germs. Dick – if anyone's going to get murdered in this epidemic it's the members of the Medical Workers' Union. Our members. Our boys. And what do you think the federal government is doing about it, right now, right this minute?'

'Fuck all, I should guess,' said Bortolotti.

Garunisch wrinkled up his nose. 'Don't swear, Dick, it doesn't suit you.'

Bortolotti said, 'But I'm *annoyed*, Ken. I'm just as annoyed as you.'

Garunisch, in a burst of temper, threw his half-full can of beer across the living-room. It splashed against the wall and rolled under a fat Colonial settee.

'*Nobody* is as annoyed as I am! *Nobody!* This half-assed administration is using my members as cattle-fodder, and it's going to *stop*!'

Dick Bortolotti coughed. 'What are you going to do, Ken?'

'I want the legal department round here right now. Get them out of bed if you have to. I want Edgar and Cholnik round here too. This government may have gotten the press to play patsy, but they're not doing it to me. Unless we get assurances on protection and pay, we're coming out. Today.'

Dick Bortolotti put down his can of beer. 'Ken,' he said uncertainly, 'wouldn't that kind of make matters worse? I mean, if this plague's spreading at 75 miles a day, and our members go out for a couple of days, well that's 150 miles, and maybe a whole lot more, just because they weren't there to slow it down.'

Kenneth Garunisch stepped up to his aide and patted him, a little too briskly for comfort, on the cheeks.

'You're quite the little Einstein, aren't you Dick? Yes, that's exactly what would happen. And if this tight-assed government have any sense at all, they won't argue for five minutes. We're just about to see the biggest pay and benefits deal that any union ever negotiated, Dick.'

It was five hours later before Herbert Gaines woke up. To help himself sleep, he had drunk half a bottle of Napoleon brandy, and his mouth was furred and dry. He slept in a long kimono of black silk, decorated with dragons, with a hair net to keep his white leonine mane from getting mussed up on the pillow. He opened his eyes just a fraction, and reached across the bed to make sure that Nicky was still there.

Nicky, of course, was. He was rude, bitchy and defiant to Herbert, but he never forgot that he was comfortably ensconced in a luxury condominium in Concorde Tower, and it would take more than an argument, no matter how brutal or vicious, to winkle him out. He lay naked and seraphic, his hands raised on either side of his head, his soft and hefty penis resting on his thigh.

Herbert raised himself on one bony elbow, leaned over, and kissed that penis with showy reverence. Then he swung his legs out of bed, and went to fix himself a blender full of mixed vegetable juice.

He was slicing up tomatoes and green peppers when the doorbell chimed. He frowned up at the early-American wall-clock, and muttered 'Who the hell...?'

He was still trying to figure out which of his less couth friends would dare to disturb him before noon when the doorbell chimed again, and someone hammered on the door. Herbert Gaines sighed crossly, and tugged off his hair net. He walked quickly through the dark, heavily-curtained living-room and up the three steps to the door.

'Who is it?' he called.

There was no reply.

He bent down and put his eye to the peep-hole, but whoever was out there must have had his hand across it.

Herbert called, 'I can't let you in until I see who you are!'

The hand was removed. Herbert squinted out, and saw a stocky, well-groomed man in a respectable gray mohair suit.

'Well,' said Herbert. 'What do you want?'

The well-groomed man gave a smile. A radiant, politician's smile. 'My name's Jack Gross,' he said. 'I was wondering if you could spare me a few minutes of your time, Mr. Gaines.'

'Do I *know* you?' asked Herbert irritably. Shouting always made him hoarse, and there was still enough of the actor left in him to worry about protecting his voice. 'You should do. Do you read *Time* magazine?'

'Sure, for the showbiz section.'

'Well, if you have last week's edition, you'll see something about me in the politics section. Go and look. I can wait.'

Herbert sighed again. 'Look here, Mr—'

'Gross, Jack Gross.'

'This is very *early* for me, Mr. Gross. At this time of the morning, I am still rescuing myself from the little death. Even if you are who you say you are, I can't help feeling that a few minutes of my time would be a ridiculous waste of *yours*.'

Jack Gross, seen through the peep-hole in the door, smiled his radiant smile again. 'I'm sure it won't be, Mr. Gaines. All I want to do is make you an interesting offer.'

Herbert Gaines stood up, away from the peep-hole, and rubbed his eyes. Until noon, and until he'd ingested a pint of cold vegetable juice and a large plain gin, his brain never seemed to function at all. But he supposed it was going to be easier to invite this grinning Mr. Gross inside, than go through the complicated hassle of getting him to go away.

'Mr. Gaines?' persisted Mr. Gross.

'Very well,' said Herbert, and opened the security locks. He turned away from the door, haughtily winding himself in his long black kimono, as Jack Gross stepped inside.

Jack Gross respectfully removed his hat, and peered into the stale, unventilated gloom. 'I've never been in Concorde Tower before. Quite a place you have here.'

'It's adequate,' said Herbert. 'I trust you don't mind if I finish preparing my breakfast.'

'Not at all,' said Jack Gross, affably. 'You just go right ahead.'

Herbert Gaines shuffled back into the kitchen and picked up his slicing knife. Jack Gross followed him, peeping as discreetly as he could into bedrooms and down corridors.

Herbert sliced vegetables while Jack Gross perched

himself on a kitchen stool, balanced his hat on his knee, and started to talk. Gross spoke directly and fast, but his eyes flickered around the room as he talked, taking in the authentic antiques, the genuine butcher's table and the expensive built-in ovens and ranges. Even the view through the kitchen window, a misty panorama of Gabriel's Park and downtown Manhattan, was worth more money than most people ever accumulated in their whole lives.

'Mr. Gaines,' he said, in his brusque, cheerful voice, 'you're still something of a hero to most people.'

Herbert looked at him balefully. 'Do you think I don't know that? Down in Atlanta, people still stand up in the movies and cheer at Captain Dashfoot. A thirty-year-old picture, and they *cheer*.'

Jack Gross kept smiling. 'We know that. That's why I've come around to see you this morning.'

'Well, fire away, Mr. Gross. I may look as if I'm fixing breakfast, but I assure you that I'm agog.'

Jack Gross said, 'Thank you.' Then he fixed his smile into a serious, sincere expression and continued, 'It's a question of public sympathy, if you see what I mean.'

'No. Spell it out for me.'

'Well, it's like this. A politician and an actor have got more in common than most people would like to think. Look at Ronald Reagan. Look at Shirley Temple Black. They didn't have to go through the hard graft of building themselves a sympathetic image in the public eye because they had it already, through movies. All they had to do was convince the public that they were serious, identify themselves with a clear-cut political line, and they were made.'

Herbert Gaines dropped peppers, tomatoes, celeriac

and sliced apple into his blender. 'Are you trying to suggest something, Mr. Gross?'

Jack Gross smiled warmly. 'My people are, Mr. Gaines.'

'And who, exactly, are *your people*?'

Jack Gross looked almost embarrassed. 'Well, Mr. Gaines, let's say that my people are political realists. They come mainly from the staunch right wing of the Republican party, and also from industry and finance. They're not, though, what you'd call the old guard. I guess the easiest way of describing us would be to say that we are the young, committed right.'

Herbert Gaines raised an eyebrow. '*How* right?' he asked. 'Right of Ford?'

'Certainly.'

'In other words,' Herbert said, 'you're the Green Berets of the Grand Old Party?'

Jack Gross grinned. 'You could say that, Mr. Gaines. That's a nice turn of phrase.'

Herbert Gaines left his blender and moved closer to Jack Gross.

'Mr. Gross,' he said steadily, 'I've been a Republican all my voting life. I used to go around with pals of Duke Wayne, and I've come out now and again and said my piece about pinko thinking and moral standards. I have letters of admiration from the Daughters of the American Revolution, and I contribute to veterans' charities and several other conservative causes.'

Jack Gross didn't flinch. 'We know all that, Mr. Gaines. We have a dossier.'

Herbert Gaines stood straight, and nodded. 'I'm sure you do, Mr. Gross. But there is one thing that your dossier obviously omits to mention.'

'What's that, Mr. Gaines?'

'I am not a politician, Mr. Gross, and I never want to be. I have a patriotic duty to my country, but I also have a private and personal duty to my art.'

'Your *art*?'

Herbert Gaines lifted his gaunt, withered head.

'Yes, Mr. Gross, my art. I am – I *was* – one of the finest movie actors that ever crossed the screen. I made two pictures and both pictures are classics. Even today, after three decades, people still applaud out loud when they see them. Mr. Gross, I have an abiding duty to those people. It is my task in life to make sure that those magical images I created in my youth stay fresh. If I come out now, like a skeleton out of a closet, and try to whip up political support on the strength of those images, my whole life's achievement would be destroyed. Who could ever look at Captain Dashfoot again, after seeing me, as I am today, talking about busing and housing and economic tariffs?'

Jack Gross still smiled. 'Mr. Gaines,' he said gently, 'we don't want you to talk about anything like that. We want you to talk about plague.'

Herbert Gaines frowned. 'I beg your pardon?'

'Plague, Mr. Gaines. The ancient scourge of nations. The Black Death.'

'I don't understand.'

'Have you heard the news?'

'I haven't had *breakfast* yet, for God's sake.'

'Well,' Jack Gross explained, 'there's a serious epidemic down in Florida. The government and the press have been keeping it tightly under wraps, saying it's an isolated outbreak of swine 'flu, but we know better. It's a highly dangerous, highly virulent strain of plague. The whole of Miami is afflicted, and there's talk of razing the whole city to the ground. It's also broken out in Fort Lauderdale, Jacksonville, Brunswick and Charleston.'

'Is this some sort of joke?'

Jack Gross shook his head. 'It's not a joke, Mr. Gaines. It's the most disastrous result of this administration's mismanagement we've ever experienced. The US Disease Control Center have failed to contain the outbreak, and the government is so terrified that they don't know what to do next. They're too frightened even to tell the nation what's really going on.'

'But—'

Jack Gross raised his hand. 'It's the chance my people have been waiting for, Mr. Gaines. It's the chance to show up these weak-kneed liberals for what they really are. It's the chance to make the GOP a pure and concerted and effective machine again.'

Herbert Gaines ran his hand through his white hair. 'And you want me to help you? Is that it?'

'We want you as our figurehead. Captain Dashfoot to the rescue.'

Herbert Gaines found himself a kitchen stool and sat down. He was thoughtful and grim-faced.

'Mr. Gross,' he asked, after a few moments, 'is this epidemic really serious?'

Jack Gross nodded. 'As far as we can tell, between six and seven thousand people are dead, and many more are dying.'

Herbert Gaines looked up. 'So there must be great fear and panic in those places? In Florida and Georgia?'

'There is. The police and the National Guard have cordoned off the Florida state line, as far as they can. And no one, but no one, is allowed out.'

Herbert Gaines got up from his stool and walked across to the kitchen window. He stared out at Gabriel's Park for a while, then he said, 'Mr. Gross, you're asking me to do something that conflicts with my sensitivities.'

'I'm sorry, Mr. Gaines. I don't get you.'

The old movie actor turned around. 'If there's an epidemic in the south, and people are dying, then the last thing I want to do is make political capital out of it. It's against my nature to advance myself through the fear and suffering of others. I have made terrible personal mistakes in my life, Mr. Gross, and I have been fortunate or *unfortunate* enough not to have been punished for them. I don't intend to add callousness and exploitation to my list of sins.'

Jack Gross smiled. 'Well, I understand your objections. But there's no reason why they should stand in your way. You have to see this thing in its historical context. A chance like this may never happen again.'

'A chance like *what*? A chance to put the squeeze on the public's uncertainty and fear? A chance to sweep into power on a tide of dead bodies? I'm not interested, Mr. Gross.'

Jack Gross sighed. 'I really think you're being oversensitive, Mr. Gaines.'

Herbert returned to his blender, and mixed his vegetables into a reddish-green froth. He poured the juice into a tall glass of crushed ice, and sipped it. He didn't look at Jack Gross, and was obviously waiting for him to go.

Jack Gross stared at the floor. 'I didn't want to do this, Mr. Gaines,' he said softly.

Herbert Gaines patted his lips with a Kleenex. 'Do what?' he said impatiently.

'Exert pressure.'

'Don't make me laugh,' said Herbert Gaines. 'What possible pressure could you exert on me?'

Jack Gross shrugged, still staring at the floor. 'There's always Nicky,' he said.

'What do you mean by that?'

Jack Gross was silent. He just smiled.

'*What do you mean by that?*' Herbert snapped.

Jack Gross looked up. 'I mean that our patriotic duty sometimes has to come before our personal opinions – and that it *always* has to come before our personal pleasures.'

'Is that a threat? By God, you'd better not threaten me, Mr. Jack Gross.'

Jack Gross took his hat off his knee and parked it neatly on his head.

'I'll make myself plain, Mr. Gaines. We need you, and we need you now. If you don't oblige us with your assistance, then some friends of ours will have to pay you a visit. Those friends of ours come from Chicago, Mr. Gaines, where the stockyards are, and they've had a lifetime of experience with stud bulls like Nicky. When those stud bulls won't behave, they take their stockman's knives, the sharp ones with the hooked blades, and they castrate them.'

Jack Gross said all this with the same radiant smile on his face with which he had first walked in. At the kitchen door, he turned and said, 'Think about it, Mr. Gaines. I'll be in touch.'

Then he let himself out of the apartment, and closed the door behind him.

Herbert Gaines, pale-faced, went slowly into the bedroom, and stared for a long while at Nicky, sleeping peacefully on the satin sheets. 'Oh, God...' he murmured, with a shiver and went back into the living-room to find the brandy.

At two-thirty, just before the court hearing *Glantz vs Forward* went back for its afternoon session, the news finally hit the streets that Florida and parts of Georgia were stricken with plague.

The New York Post brought out a special edition with a front-page photograph of Miami's ruined Civic Center, and a banner headline saying SUPER-PLAGUE SWEEPS SOUTH, THOUSANDS DIE. A kind of nervous ripple went through the city, and the lunchtime bars stayed crowded until well after three as New Yorkers watched the special half-hourly TV reports on the effects of the epidemic.

The President, looking tired but, trying to sound optimistic, explained in a special interview that 'everything humanly possible has been done to contain the outbreak.' He announced that the entire state of Florida was quarantined until further notice, and that ocean bathing was prohibited all the way from Cape Fear to Key West.

'It appears on first examination that a possible source of the plague bacillus is pollution of the ocean by raw sewage, although where this sewage is coming from, and how such an unusual and virulent bacillus could have developed within it, are still mysteries. This year's unusual climatic conditions, in which the currents in the ocean are running counter-clockwise, may be a contributing factor.'

The President wound up by saying that he intended to pray for the sick and the dying, and that the best medical brains in the country were working on antidotes.

Ivor Glantz, sitting with his attorney Manny Friedman in a dark and busy Wall Street bar, watched the President fade from the TV screen next to the bottles of Jack Daniel's, and shook his head.

'You know what that means?' he said seriously.

'Sure,' said Manny Friedman, rustling impatiently through a sheaf of pink legal papers. 'It means the end of civilization as we know it. Now, can we please go over these patents?'

'It means,' said Ivor, 'that they haven't yet found a way to cure it. If they could cure it, or contain it, they'd say so. But they can't. You see what the paper says? "Super-plague". Ordinary plague responds to sulfonamides or Haffkine antiserum, but this one evidently doesn't.'

'Ivor,' interrupted Manny impatiently, 'today is the most crucial day of all. Can we just concentrate on *your* bugs, and leave the President's bugs alone?'

Ivor checked his watch. 'We'd better get back to court anyway. But I'd sure like to know a little more about this plague. Do you realize – this could be an entirely new disease? Some new strain of bacillus, totally unknown?'

They collected their things together and went out into the humid afternoon street. Manny hailed a cab, and they drove through heavy traffic towards the courthouse. Ivor, sweating in his dark, too-tight suit, mopped his forehead with a clean handkerchief.

The cab driver, a big-nosed Czech in a cloth cap and horn-rimmed spectacles, was rapping about the plague.

'If you ask me,' he said, swerving imperturbably across three lanes of traffic, 'if you ask me it's the Soviets.'

'How do you make that out?' asked Ivor. 'Are you a buddy of Kosygin?'

The cab driver laughed. 'You gotta be kidding. If you ask me, the Soviets is responsible for half the troubles this country's got. They bought our wheat, correct? Well, they bought our wheat so that they could trade good American grain for worthless roubles, right? I mean, what good's a rouble to anyone? Grain – that's different. You can offload a loaf of bread any place.'

Ivor grinned. 'You wouldn't be Polish by any chance?' he asked.

'Am I *hell*,' said the cab driver.

The courtroom, dusty and badly-lit, looked as if a burglar had just rifled it. Sheaves of paper spilled on to the floor, and volume after volume of legal books and evidence, files and clippings lay scattered all over the attorneys' desks. It was the debris of a four-day hearing.

Ivor Glantz and Manny Friedman pushed open the swing doors and went to their places. Across the court, a thin, blue-suited figure with a gray crewcut, Sergei Forward the Finnish-born bacteriologist, was consulting with his lawyer. He was a calm polite man with a meticulous accent and a way of leaning forward when he spoke, like a near-sighted stork investigating an appetizing grub. He didn't look up when Glantz and Friedman came in.

By three o'clock, the courtroom was filled. There was a high burble of conversation – more intense than this morning. News of the Florida plague had spread, and every science journal and bacteriological expert in the place was discussing it. To them, it was the hottest medical story in years.

Esmeralda, severe and elegant in a pale pink 1930s suit, her curls tucked into a pink turban hat with a diamond brooch and a feather, came into the courtroom just before the judge. She sat down behind her stepfather, in a heady cloud of Chant d'Arômes, and touched his shoulder.

'Have you heard about the plague?' she whispered. 'Isn't that awful?'

'I heard over lunch,' Ivor whispered back. 'I'm only guessing, but I'd say it's even worse than they're pretending.'

'The Army have sealed off Pensacola and Mobile,' said Esmeralda. 'I just heard it on the car radio. They say that people are dying at the rate of two thousand a day.'

At that moment, Judge Secombe came into the courtroom, and they all stood. When he had sat down and put on his spectacles, Sergei Forward's attorney raised his hand to make an application.

'My client respectfully wishes to apply for adjournment, your honor. While he appreciates the serious consequences of this action for infringement of patent, he believes he can make a material contribution to the government research work to find an antidote for the plague that we now hear is threatening our southern states. Mr. Forward is sure that Mr. Glantz will not stand in his way in this crucial emergency, and he hopes that Mr. Glantz will perhaps also wish to join in the government research work.'

Manny Friedman swore under his breath.

'What does he mean,' Ivor Glantz asked. 'He can't do this.'

Manny Friedman said, 'He can and he has. Unless you agree to an adjournment, you're going to look like a self-centered schmuck who puts his own money-making before the good of America. He's got you, right by the balls.'

Ivor frowned. 'But why does he want an adjournment? What for?'

Manny shrugged. 'Don't ask me. Whatever he's up to, I don't like it.'

Judge Secombe called for Manny Friedman's attention. 'Mr. Friedman,' he said, 'does your client have any strong feelings about an adjournment?'

Manny Friedman stood up. 'My client appreciates Mr. Forward's devotion to public service, your honor, but does not regard an adjournment necessary. This action can only take one more day at most, and twenty-four hours is hardly likely to make any material difference to Mr. Forward's research. Perhaps I can remind the bench that most of the great breakthroughs in bacteriology only came after years of intensive labor – including the process claimed by my client under this present action.'

Sergei Forward's attorney protested. 'Your honor, we believe that twenty-four hours – even *four* hours – could be vital. This plague has infected an entire state in a week. People are dying right now, even as we speak.'

Manny Friedman glanced down at Ivor Glantz, who shrugged helplessly. Then he looked at the press table, where reporters from *The New York Times*, *The Daily News* and Associated Press sat with their pens poised, eager for any story that would tie up with the plague. He could see the headlines now. 'No Mercy Adjournment, Insists Litigating Scientist.'

Manny said quietly, 'Very well. We will agree to an adjournment until the present national crisis has passed.'

Judge Secombe said, 'Adjourned *sine die*,' and rose. The court rose, too, and people began to shuffle out.

While Manny Friedman busied himself gathering his papers, Ivor Glantz sat still, his head in his hands. Esmeralda came and sat next to him, and stroked his few sparse curls.

'Papa,' she said. 'It's not the end of the world.'

He grunted. Then he smiled warmly, and took her hand. 'Don't mind me,' he said. 'I'm disappointed, that's all.'

'Don't worry,' she reassured him. 'As soon as the plague is over, you can apply for the hearing to continue.'

Ivor rubbed his eyes tiredly. 'The way this plague's spreading, that could be *never*. If it goes on like this, we'll all be six feet underground by the time this action gets heard.'

'You don't think it's *that* serious, do you?'

He shrugged. 'I don't know. What disturbs me is that they don't have any way to cure it. We're all so used to living in a society that protects us with drugs and medicines that when we're exposed to something really deadly, we don't take proper precautions.'

'Come on, Ivor,' Manny Friedman said. 'This whole thing will fade away in two weeks, just like swine 'flu did. One minute it's panic stations, the next minute everybody's saying, "Plague? what plague? *I* never heard of no plague!"'

Friedman led the way out of the courtroom. 'What will you do now?' he asked over his shoulder. 'Do you want to see if you can bring the action forward to a specific date?'

Ivor shook his head. 'I don't know yet. This thing has cost me a goddamned mint as it is. I have five corporations wetting their pants to buy this process, and until I can clear it through the courts, I'm fucked.'

Outside the courthouse, in the humid afternoon sun, they

met Sergei Forward and his attorney. Forward came up to Ivor with his hand extended, and a watery smile on his lean, Nordic features.

'I hope there are no tough feelings,' he said.

Ivor ignored the Finn's hand, and pulled a face.

'It *is* our patriotic duty, you know – as Americans,' Forward added.

Ivor turned and stared at him. 'You've been an American for precisely four months,' he said sarcastically. 'When I need lessons in patriotism from you, I'll pack my case and go live in Russia.'

Manny Friedman took Ivor's arm. 'Come on, Ivor, don't get involved in a fight. He's up to something, and there's no point in losing your cool until you know what it is.'

Ivor shouted angrily, 'No half-baked Finnish quack is going to—'

'Yes, he is,' insisted Friedman, and pulled Ivor away. 'I'm your attorney, and when I say leave off, I say it for your own good.'

Esmeralda, following close behind, said, 'He's right, papa. Let's just have a drink and forget about it.'

Ivor surrendered, and took his stepdaughter's hand. 'Okay, Es. You win. I could do with a quart of Scotch right now.'

They walked around the block to the meter where Esmeralda's Skylark was parked. Manny climbed into the back, and Esmeralda herself was about to get in when someone called, 'Miss Baxter!'

Esmeralda turned. A tall, good-looking young man in a pale suit was waving to her across the street. 'Are you calling *me*?' she asked.

The young man dodged a passing cab, and came across the street. He was a little out of breath. He had dark, slightly Italian looks, with black curly hair, a straight nose, and a firmly-cleft chin.

'I hope you don't mind, Miss Baxter,' he said, 'but I've been wanting to meet you for some time. You are the Esmeralda Baxter who runs Esmeralda's gallery, aren't you?'

Esmeralda looked puzzled. 'That's right, I am. But should I know you? I don't recall your face.'

The young man grinned. 'Oh – I'm sorry. My name's Charles Thurston. Charles Thurston III, actually, but my father and my grandfather were so undistinguished that nobody gets confused. I write books on art. Maybe you saw my book on Man Ray.'

Esmeralda blushed slightly. 'I'm afraid I didn't. Listen – do you want to make an appointment to see me? I'm pretty tied up right now.'

'Can I call you at the gallery?'

'Well, sure.'

Unexpectedly, Charles Thurston III lifted Esmeralda's hand and kissed it. 'You know something,' he said. 'I'm sure you and I will get along like a house on fire.' Afterwards, as they drove back to Concorde Tower, Ivor said caustically, 'Did you see the way he kissed your hand? Goddamned almost swallowed it. Maybe kids these days don't get enough to eat.'

'Oh, papa,' Esmeralda protested. 'He's not a *kid*. In fact I think he's rather gracious.'

In the plush quietness of their condominium, Mr. and Mrs. Victor Blaufoot tried again and again to call their daughter Rebecca in Florida. Each time, the lines were busy. After five hours of dialing, Mrs. Blaufoot went and sat at one end of the shot-silk settee, fiddling restlessly with her large diamond engagement ring, and biting her lips in endless nervousness.

Mr. Blaufoot came up and put his arm gently around her shoulders. 'The lines,' he said, 'they're bound to be busy. It's a crisis. But don't worry. If she's in trouble, she'll find some way to let us know. She always has, hasn't she? Always, when there's a problem.'

Mrs. Blaufoot suddenly started to weep. Her tears dropped on the rug.

'But what if she's *dead*?' she cried miserably. 'What if she's caught that plague, and she's *dead*? How could she call us then?'

At five-twenty, Kenneth Garunisch announced on television that the Medical Workers' Union were coming out on strike, after the failure of negotiations with the federal government for emergency pay increases during the plague crisis. There would be no porters, no hospital cleaners, no janitors, no administration assistants, no sanitation engineers, no ambulance maintenance men, no electricians, no pharmacy assistants.

The government insisted that to pay emergency rates would be to surrender to 'heinous moral blackmail' and that it would create 'a disturbing and destructive precedent.'

On the six o'clock news, an outbreak of possible plague was reported at Newport News, and the ban on sea bathing was extended northwards to Delaware Bay. Residents of cities and towns along the eastern seaboard were urged to remain calm, and not to take hasty or ill-considered action. All airlines reported heavy bookings for westbound flights, and the Highway Patrol said that traffic through the Alleghenies was well above seasonal norms.

Quiet fear began to spread throughout the eastern states, but nobody knew quite how bad the plague was, or what to do about it, because the press and television were still keeping a low profile. Nobody knew that four hundred people – men, women and children – had been shot dead by the Army and National Guardsmen while trying to escape from quarantined areas.

Edgar Paston ate a quiet dinner at his home in Elizabeth, New Jersey. His wife Tammy had come home from the telephone company half-an-hour early, and had made a chocolate pudding. Edgar sat at the round table with its red check tablecloth, silently spooning the pudding into his mouth, and thinking.

'You're awful quiet,' said Tammy, bustling into the dining room in her apron. She was a short, big-breasted woman of 33, with wiry blonde hair and plump cheeks.

'I was thinking,' said Edgar.

'You're not still worried about those kids?'

He sighed, chasing the last spoonful of chocolate around his bowl. 'No, I guess I've reconciled myself to that. I was thinking about this epidemic, this plague.'

'What about it? It's miles away! I mean – how far is Georgia from New Jersey?'

'I don't know. Eight hundred miles, I guess.'

'Well, then.'

Edgar Paston laid down his spoon and pushed his plate

away. 'It's eight hundred miles away *today*, Tam – but how long is it going to take to get *here*? I mean, I'm kind of worried.'

Tammy took his plate away, and flapped some crumbs off the table with her apron. She kissed him loudly on the forehead.

'The television said it wasn't going to spread too far, and that nobody should worry about it, or panic. If the television says that, well…'

Edgar pushed his chair neatly under the table, and followed Tammy into the kitchen to help with the washing up.

'I guess you're right,' he said. 'They don't usually put anything on the television unless it's true. All the same, I think we ought to have some kind of emergency plan, in case the plague does spread.'

Tammy stacked the dishes in the dishwasher while Edgar rinsed them under the tap. Their kitchen was simple and modern, and decorated in candy-apple red. On the wall was a color print of fall tints in the Catskills, and a wrought-iron profile of President Eisenhower.

'Emergency plan?' asked Tammy. 'Eddie – I don't think we have to. You remember the last time we had an emergency plan, during Cuba? You spent the whole weekend digging a hole in the garden for an atom shelter!'

Edgar laughed at the memory of it. 'I guess you're right, Tam. I guess I made a fool of myself over that.'

After they had washed and wiped the dishes, they went into their yellow-decorated living-room and joined their children, 10-year-old Marvin and 14-year-old Chrissie.

Both children were watching television. Edgar asked, 'Is there any more news about the plague?'

Chrissie said, 'Nothing much, dad. They said they had some people in isolation at Newport News, but they didn't know if they were sick with the plague.'

'Newport News? I though they only had the plague in Georgia.'

'Well,' she shrugged, 'that's what they said. They're going to have another speech by the President later.'

Edgar frowned. 'That doesn't sound too healthy. I just hope the darned thing doesn't spread up this way.'

'Dad – what's plague?' Marvin said.

Edgar Paston blinked. 'Plague? Well, it's a kind of disease. You know, a real serious disease, that you can die of.'

'Sure, Dad. But what's it like?'

Edgar Paston looked at Tammy, but Tammy knew as little about it as he did.

'I don't know. Why don't you look it up in your Children's Encyclopedia? It cost me five dollars a month for three centuries, you might as well use it.'

Edgar watched television until seven o'clock, then roused himself to go and close the store. Gerry was in charge at the moment, but Edgar always liked to check the final day's takings himself, and make sure that everything was locked up. He kissed Tammy at the front door, and went out into the cool darkness to fetch his car.

A cricket was chirruping on the front lawn. He climbed into his Mercury wagon, and switched on the lights. Tammy waved from the front door. He drove down the road, and round the corner to the junction where the Save-U Supermart stood.

He didn't realize that anything was wrong until he pulled up outside. He saw Gerry inside the brightly-lit store, bending over for some reason. Then, as he climbed out of the wagon, he saw what had happened. He ran heavily across the car park and into the supermarket, panting with exertion and alarm.

Gerry had a red bruise on his left eye. 'I'm sorry, Mr. Paston, I did try to stop them. But they held me down, and they hit me. I'm just trying to clear up.'

Edgar looked around his store in frantic horror. Every shelf in the entire store had been cleared of groceries, and every can and packet and bag had been tossed on to the floor. Thousands of dollars' worth of flour and candies and nuts and cake-mixes and household goods had been spilled and trampled on.

He walked the length of the supermarket in a stunned dream of despair. A few customers still stood around, embarrassed and silent. As Edgar walked, he trod on fruit and broken glass, cornmeal and crumpled packets. Gerry, dabbing his bruised eye, followed behind.

'What happened here?' Edgar said hoarsely, when he got to the freezer cabinet. Though he could see for himself.

'They – er – they pissed in it,' said Gerry. 'I'm sorry, Mr. Paston. I did try my level best to stop them.'

Edgar stood still and cast his gaze over the whole wrecked store. The new store-front window, which had been installed first thing that morning, had been cracked. Displays and signs costing hundreds of dollars had been torn down and smashed. Honey and molasses oozed from cracked jars, the contents of cereal boxes were strewn everywhere.

'Who was it?' asked Edgar quietly. 'McManus?'

Gerry looked at the floor. 'They said they'd kill me if I told. I'm sorry, Mr. Paston. I'm so sorry.'

Edgar laid a hand on the boy's shoulder. 'I understand. Well, I guess we'd better call the cops.'

'I would have called them myself, sir, but after yesterday I didn't know whether they'd like it.'

Edgar shook his head. 'It's not a question of whether they *like* it. It's their job.' He went to the wall phone, and picked it up.

He was in the middle of dialing when he heard someone laughing outside the store. A raucous, mocking laugh. He paused, and then laid the telephone receiver down again. Quickly, making sure that he didn't tread in any debris, he made his way towards the cash desk, searching in his pants pocket for his keys.

Gerry called, 'Mr. Paston—' but he ignored the boy, and ducked low behind the counter. He lifted his keys, examined them closely, and picked the right one. Then he unlocked the drawer under the till, and took out a .38 revolver.

Holding the pistol behind his back, he stalked slowly towards the front of the store. He eased open the glass door, and looked out into the breezy night. Across the car park, close to his station wagon, he saw a huddled group of kids. They were laughing and hooting and horsing around, and he knew damned well who they were.

He shouted, 'McManus! Shark McManus!'

The kids went quiet, and looked in his direction. He raised the .38 in his right hand, supporting his wrist with his left, and squinted down the barrel. The kids were all close together, and they presented an easy target.

Edgar, his voice tight, shouted again, 'McManus! Stand forward, McManus, and get what's coming to you!'

The kids evidently didn't realize that Edgar was holding a

gun, because they started laughing again, and jeering. Edgar aimed carefully at the tallest figure in the group, and let out his breath. He fired, and the pistol kicked in his hand. There was a flat, echoing bang. One of the kids fell to the ground, without a sound. The rest of them suddenly scattered.

Edgar, holding his gun raised up, walked slowly across the car park to the fallen youth. The boy was sprawled on his stomach, and there was a wide pool of glistening blood around his head. Edgar hunkered down and examined him. The bullet had hit him in the back of the skull, and must have killed him instantly.

He looked around. The car park was silent.

Gerry, walking on tippy-toes for some reason, came up behind him.

'Mr. Paston—' he breathed.

'What is it, Gerry?'

'Mr. Paston, you shouldn't have!'

Edgar stood up. 'Shouldn't have? Did you see what these scum did to my store? These are *scum*, Gerry, and don't you forget it! He tried to destroy my way of life, and the only way I could answer that was to try and destroy his! Don't you forget that, Gerry!'

Edgar was shaking. He still had the gun in his hand, but he didn't know what to do with it.

'Mr. Paston,' said Gerry, miserably. 'This isn't Shark McManus. This isn't his gang.'

Edgar felt cold. He looked down at the boy's body lying on the concrete. The blood kept spreading, and there was no way to mop it up and return it to his veins.

'I don't understand you. He was laughing. They were all laughing.'

'They come around here quite often,' Gerry said. 'They don't mean no harm. I know one or two of them. They come around to the store after meetings, and buy candy.'

'Meetings?' said Edgar numbly. 'What meetings?'

'Boy Scout meetings, Mr. Paston. They're Boy Scouts.'

Edgar stared down at the body. 'Boy Scouts,' he whispered, 'Well – what – I mean – *Boy Scouts*?'

He was still standing by the body when the black and white police car came howling into the car park, lights flashing, and squealed to a stop beside them. The doors opened, and Officers Trent and Marowitz came briskly across the concrete.

They looked down at the body. Marowitz said briskly, 'Is he dead? Has anyone checked?'

Edgar said, 'He's dead all right. I got him in the head.'

He lifted his pistol, and handed it silently to Officer Marowitz.

'It appears he's a Boy Scout,' explained Edgar. 'I thought he was a vandal, and I shot him by mistake.'

Officer Marowitz looked hard at Edgar for a moment, then at the boy's body.

'You shot and killed *a Boy Scout* by mistake?'

'That's what I said.'

'In that case,' said Officer Marowitz, with a humorless grin, 'I had better advise you of your rights. You're under arrest, Mr. Paston, for suspected homicide.'

'Yes,' said Edgar. He stepped around the body, and walked towards the police car of his own accord.

Book Two

The Dead

One

They had been driving for ten minutes when Adelaide, in the back of the car, said, 'Look!'

Dr. Petrie had already seen the first distant flickers in his rear-view mirror, but they could have been anything – a burning car, or an isolated house on fire. Now, when he slowed the Torino and turned around in his seat, he could see that the whole southern horizon was growing red with flame, and that the city of Miami was ablaze from stern to stern, like a gigantic ocean liner burning on a rippling ocean of sparks.

'*Miami*,' whispered Mr. Henschel, sitting next to Dr. Petrie, his rifle in his lap. '*That's the whole damned city of Miami.*'

'Do you think they did it on purpose?' Adelaide said.

Dr. Petrie speeded up, heading north on nothing but marker lights. 'I guess they might have done,' he said. 'More likely it was looters and arsonists and untended fires.'

They were all very tired. It was well past one o'clock, and the night was into its weariest and longest hours. Prickles was still fast asleep, in Mrs. Henschel's arms, but the rest of them were too tense and too worried to rest.

'I suppose you realize we might have taken the plague with us,' remarked Adelaide. 'I mean, for all we know, one of *us* might be infected.'

Dr. Petrie nodded, his face illuminated green from the dials on the instrument panel.

'That's possible, but I think it's unlikely. I've been exposed to the plague more than any of you, and I haven't caught it. Maybe I'm just immune. From what we've seen of the plague so far, it strikes very quickly. If we haven't had it yet, I don't think we're going to get it now.'

'Please God,' muttered Mr. Henschel.

'Yes,' said Dr. Petrie, 'please God.'

They drove in silence for a while. It was early Wednesday morning, before the news of the plague had officially been released by the news media, and all their car radio could tell them was that Spanish or swine 'flu was 'still causing some fatalities in Miami and southern Florida.' When the radio said that, Dr. Petrie looked up at his mirror. He saw the huge columns of fire that distantly leaped and roared from the hotels along Miami Beach, and wondered, not for the first time in his life, how politicians and newsmen could possibly get away with what they did and said.

He was still pondering on this when Mr. Henschel pointed up ahead. 'I see lights,' he said tensely. 'Looks like there's a roadblock up there.'

Dr. Petrie slowed down, and they all peered anxiously into the night. Half a mile up the road, they saw the bright glow of spotlights, and a cluster of cars and trucks.

'Where is this?' asked Adelaide.

'Looks like Hallandale,' said Dr. Petrie. 'They must've pulled the roadblocks back a bit.'

'What are you going to do?' said Mr. Henschel. 'If they stop you, you're finished. They won't let you past.'

By now, they had almost reached the roadblock. It was

the National Guard, and they had obstructed the highway with trucks and signs. As they approached in their car, a guardsman in combat fatigue stepped forward with his hand raised. Dr. Petrie slowed down and stopped.

The guardsman stayed well away from them. He was carrying a sub-machine gun, and he obviously intended to use it if life got a little difficult. He was only about nineteen or twenty years old, and his thin face was shadowed by his heavy helmet.

'Sorry, folks!' he called out. 'You'll have to turn back!'

Dr. Petrie said, 'I'm a doctor. I have ID. All these people are clear of disease.'

The guardsman shook his head. 'Sorry, sir. We have orders not to let anyone through under any circumstances.'

'But I'm a doctor,' persisted Dr. Petrie. He held out his identity papers and waved them. 'I have to get through on urgent business.'

The National Guardsman stepped forward a couple of paces and peered at the papers. Then he stepped back again, and said, 'Just hold on a moment. I'll get some confirmation.'

They waited for more than five minutes before the young guardsman came back with an officer. The officer was a tough, grizzle-haired veteran who was obviously enjoying his new-found responsibilities.

'Hi,' called Dr. Petrie. 'My name's Dr. Leonard Petrie.'

The officer took a look at their car, and walked around it. Then said, 'My apologies, doctor, but you'll have to go back.'

'Back where? The whole of Miami's on fire.'

'I don't know where, doctor, but I'm afraid that's the order. You have to turn back.'

Dr. Petrie paused for a while. He looked at the officer and

the guardsman, standing twenty feet away on the spotlit highway, and then he turned and looked at Mr. Henschel.

'David,' he said, using his neighbor's Christian name for the first time ever, 'do you think you can take the boy?'

'Quick?' asked Mr. Henschel, almost without moving his lips.

Dr. Petrie nodded. 'I'll turn, and drive around them. Take the boy first because he's got the most fire-power. Then the officer.'

Quite casually, Mr. Henschel chambered a round and pushed the bolt of his rifle forward.

'Ready when you are,' he said.

Dr. Petrie leaned out of the car window. 'We're just leaving,' he said to the guardsmen. 'We've decided to turn back.'

Adelaide whispered, 'Leonard – please don't kill them. Look at him – he's only a boy.'

Dr. Petrie turned and looked at her. 'Adelaide, we have to. If we don't we're all washed up. There's no other way of getting through. Now just sit still and keep your head down.'

Dr. Petrie released the handbrake, and slowly turned the Gran Torino around. As he did so, Mr. Henschel lifted his rifle and rested it across Dr. Petrie's shoulders, aiming out of the driver's window towards the two National Guardsmen.

'Now,' said Dr. Petrie quietly, as he swung the car around in a tight curve. 'They're off balance – now!'

As the car screeched around them, the guardsmen turned to follow its progress, and as it curved behind them they were momentarily left unprotected, with their weapons pointing the opposite way. Mr. Henschel squeezed off one shot, then another, then another. Dr. Petrie felt the rifle jolt against his shoulders, and one of the spent cartridges rolled into his lap. He kept the car turning in a circle, faster and faster, and as the two guardsmen crumpled to the ground, he forced his foot down on the gas, and steered the Torino straight for the wooden bar that obstructed the road.

With a heavy clang, the car toppled the barrier and skidded off northwards into the night. They heard four or five isolated shots being fired in their direction, but after a few minutes there was nothing but the sound of the car, and the wind that rushed past the open windows.

'Guess they're pretty thin on the ground,' said Mr. Henschel. 'Otherwise they'd have chased us something rotten.'

Dr. Petrie wiped his sweating forehead against his sleeve. 'Nice shooting, David. I think you got us all out of trouble there.'

Adelaide said, her voice quavering, 'We may be forced to do it, Leonard, but we don't have to call it *nice*.'

Dr. Petrie didn't answer for a while. Then he said, 'I'm sorry Adelaide, but I think we must all be quite clear what we're up against. Until we get clear of the quarantine area, we're going to be treated like diseased rats. Their orders are quite explicit. Don't let anyone through, and if anyone tries to get through, kill them.'

'What do you mean?' Adelaide asked.

Dr. Petrie glanced around. 'I mean quite simply that if we want to survive, we're going to have to behave the way *they're* behaving. We have to be vicious, and we have to be quick. Don't worry – they won't have the slightest compunction about shooting us.'

Mr. Henschel was reloading his rifle, 'You're right, Leonard. It's them or us'n. And I don't care what anyone says – I don't want it to be *them*, if that's the odds.'

The shooting had woken up Prickles. She started to cry for her mother, and they drove in painful silence for a while until Mrs. Henschel calmed her down.

'Mommy's gone for a little vacation,' she murmured soothingly. 'But look – Daddy's here. Daddy's going to look after you now.'

Adelaide said, 'Oh, God. You know, if anyone had told me last week that this was going to happen, I wouldn't have believed them. God, it's like a nightmare.'

Leonard remained silent. It was one thing to explain to the others the need for crude survival, it was quite another to have to actually carry it out. To coldly be prepared to kill.

They were approaching the outskirts of Fort Lauderdale, and so far they had seen no other traffic, and no sign of National Guardsmen. Dr. Petrie, with nothing but marker lights to steer by, had to strain his eyes into the darkness to see if there were any obstructions on the road, and his head was beginning to pound. Adelaide passed him a can of warm Coke from the back seat, and he swigged it as he drove.

The power supply was out at Fort Lauderdale, too. The town was dark and deserted. Abandoned and burned-out cars were strewn all over the streets, and here and there they could make out huddled bodies lying on the sidewalks and in store entrances. A few dim and flickering lights still burned in private houses and hotel rooms, like the lamps of cave dwellers in a primitive and hostile age, but the town was overwhelmingly silent, and from as far away as Route 1 they could hear the sound of the Atlantic surf.

Not far from the beach they saw a large building on fire, with dim gray smoke rising into the velvety night sky. Mr. Henschel guessed it was the Holiday Inn Oceanside. There were no sirens, no fire tenders, and no one seemed to be attempting to put the blaze out.

Like travelers through a strange dream, they drove up North Atlantic Boulevard close to the ocean. Through the darkness, they could see the white breakers of the polluted sea. They were all exhausted, and they said very little. Prickles had gone back to sleep, and was snoring slightly. Mrs. Henschel said it sounded as if she had a cold.

'Just so long as she didn't catch plague from Margaret,' said Adelaide. 'That would be great, wouldn't it? Margaret getting her revenge from beyond the grave.'

'*Adelaide*,' said Dr. Petrie coldly. 'She's dead and that's that.'

Adelaide was silent for a while. Then she said, 'Okay, I'm sorry.'

Just before dawn, they stopped the car by the side of Route 1 near Palm Bay. They laid out blankets on the ground, underneath a scrubby grove of palm trees, and slept.

As Dr. Petrie lay there, feeling the hard stones of the dry soil under his blanket, he heard insects chirp, and the occasional swish of a passing car. The plague had left many survivors, but those who had somehow managed to avoid infection were trying to get out of Florida as fast as they could. What none of them yet knew was that plague was breaking out all along the coast of Georgia and the Carolinas, as tides and currents washed a thick black ooze of raw sewage on to the beaches.

He had two hours of restless dozing, filled with weird

and terrifying dreams. The sky was light when he opened his eyes. Mr. and Mrs. Henschel, Adelaide and Prickles were all still asleep. Dr. Petrie lifted himself on one elbow, rubbing his aching eyes, and looked around.

They had company. Beside the car were two unshaven National Guardsmen in uniform and helmets, their eyes hidden behind mirror sunglasses. They were both carrying automatic weapons, and neither looked in the mood for friendly banter.

'How do,' said one of them laconically. He was chewing gum in ceaseless circles.

Dr. Petrie nudged Adelaide, who was lying snuggled up against him. She stirred, and opened her eyes.

The guardsman stepped forward, and looked around their makeshift encampment. 'You folks travelin' north?' Dr. Petrie didn't answer. Mr. and Mrs. Henschel had woken up now, and they blinked across at him in silent bewilderment.

'It's kind of inadvisable – travelin' north,' said the guardsman, pacing around them.

'Is there a regulation against it?' asked Dr. Petrie.

The guardsman chewed gum for a while. 'Nope,' he said eventually. 'I don't reckon there's no regulation against it.'

'But it's inadvisable?'

'Yep. That's the word. Inadvisable.'

'Well… what do you advise us to do instead?'

The man shrugged. 'It aint up to me to advise you to do nothing. What you do is entirely your decision. Is this your car?'

'It belongs to a friend.'

'You able to prove that?'

'I don't think so. He's dead. He died of the plague two days ago.'

The guardsman walked slowly back to where his friend was standing.

'Any of you folks sick, or infected?'

'I don't believe so.'

'How about that little girl? She don't look too bright.'

'She has a cold, that's all. A summer cold.'

'Is that right?'

'I'm a doctor. I should know.'

'You're a doctor, huh? How come you aint helpin' out someplace, 'stead of sleepin' rough?'

Dr. Petrie said, 'I was helping in a hospital in Miami. Last night, it was burned to the ground, along with the rest of the city. There isn't much I can do there now.'

The men were not interested.

'Nope,' said the one with the gum, 'I guess there aint.'

There was a long, awkward silence. Mr. Henschel eventually asked, 'Are you going to let us leave, or do we have to stay here all day?'

'You can leave if you like,' said the guardsman.

'But you don't recommend northwards?'

'Nope.'

'Are the highways blocked off? Is that what's happening?'

Both men nodded. 'The entire state of Florida is in quarantine, friend. You can drive north if you feel like wastin' your time, but I can tell you here and now there aint nobody gets through the state line alive or dead.'

'That must include you,' said Dr. Petrie.

The guardsman shook his head. 'No way, doctor. Every National Guardsman has been immunized.'

Dr. Petrie frowned. 'Immunized? What do you mean?'

The guardsman mimed a syringe being squeezed into his arm. 'The jab. Ninety-eight percent effective, the doc said.'

Dr. Petrie looked across at Adelaide, and she raised her eyebrows.

'I don't quite know how to say this,' Dr. Petrie said to the National Guardsmen.

'You don't quite know how to say *what*?'

'Well, whatever they've injected you with, it's useless. There *is* no way of immunizing yourself against this plague.'

The guardsman placidly chewed gum, and said nothing.

'Have you tried to get back across the state line yet?' asked Dr. Petrie.

'Nope. This is our first turn of duty.'

Dr. Petrie stood up, and brushed down his clothes. 'Well, I'm sorry to say it's going to be your *last* turn of duty, as well. There is absolutely no way that you can be protected against this disease. We know it's a type of pneumonic plague, but we don't know how it's transmitted, and we don't have the remotest idea how to cure it.'

'Are you pulling my leg?' said the guardsman, frowning.

'I wish I was. I think you've been conned. They needed someone to keep law and order around here, to stop things going completely berserk, and so they let you think that you were immune. You're *not*, and that's all there is to it.'

'He's joshing,' said the other National Guardsman. 'Don't you take no mind of him, Cal, because he's sure as hell joshing.'

'I can show you my medical papers.' He reached into his back pants pocket, and took out his ID. He held it up, and waved it.

'Don't you take one step nearer,' said the National Guardsman, raising his automatic weapon.

Even afterwards, Dr. Petrie couldn't work out what happened next. It was too quick, too illogical and too spontaneous. He didn't see David Henschel go for his rifle, but he guessed that was what happened. The guardsman suddenly swung round and fired a deafening burst of automatic fire towards the trees, and Mr. Henschel said 'Ah!' and fell to the hard ground with a heavy thud like a sack of flour. Two or three bullets caught Mrs. Henschel, and she rolled over, screaming.

Dr. Petrie, instinctively trying to protect Prickles, ducked forward and wrestled the machine-gun from the guardsman's hands. The other guardsman lifted his gun, but Dr. Petrie caught the first soldier around the neck, and pulled him up against himself as a human shield.

He waved the automatic rifle in the other guardsman's direction, and snapped, '*Drop it!* Drop it, and put up your hands!'

The man hesitated, and then slowly laid his weapon down on the ground. Mrs. Henschel was moaning loudly, while Adelaide bent over her, trying to see if she could help. Prickles stood by herself, still in her red dressing-gown, and howled.

'Turn around!' Dr. Petrie shouted hoarsely. 'Put your hands on your head!'

The guardsman did as he was told. Then Dr. Petrie pushed the first guardsman away from him, and ordered him to do the same. The two of them stood side by side in the road, their hands on top of their heads, and Dr. Petrie stepped forward and picked up the other automatic weapon.

'Now,' Dr. Petrie said, 'if you don't help me, I'm going to blow your heads off. Where's your first aid kit?'

One of the guardsmen said, 'I've got one right here, in my pack.'

'Put your hand in your pack slowly, lift the kit out in plain view, and lay it on the ground.'

The man did as he was told. Dr. Petrie went across and picked it up, keeping the machine-gun trained carefully on his captives. Then he backed up, and knelt down beside Mrs. Henschel. He handed the gun to Adelaide, and told her to shoot without hesitation if either guardsman moved.

Mrs. Henschel was bad. One bullet had hit her in the chest and pierced her left lung. Every time she breathed, bloody bubbles trickled from her dress. Another bullet had hit her in the ear, and the side of her head was sticky with gore. The pain was by now so intense that the poor woman had passed out.

Working as quickly as he could, he dabbed the wounds reasonably clean, and bandaged them with lint.

Prickles was standing close by, watching her father, quiet and red-eyed. She said, 'Is Mrs. Henschel dead, daddy?'

Dr. Petrie tried to smile. 'No, honey, Mrs. Henschel just hurt herself. Don't you worry – she's going to be fine.'

Prickles pointed to Mr. Henschel, curled up in a stain of blood. 'What about him? Is he going to be fine?'

Dr. Petrie sighed heavily and said, 'Mr. Henschel's gone to heaven, I'm afraid. He's dead.'

'Will he come back?' the child demanded.

Dr. Petrie stood up, and took the gun back from Adelaide. He ruffled Prickles' hair. 'No, baby, he won't come back. But wherever he's gone, I'm sure he's going to be real happy.'

'Is he an angel now? With wings?'

Adelaide looked at Leonard with sad eyes. He answered, 'Yes, I expect so. With wings.'

They cleared up their blankets and their few belongings and stowed them in the car. While Dr. Petrie kept the guardsmen covered, Adelaide dressed Prickles in a short blue dress, and sandals. She herself changed into a white T-shirt and jeans, and unpacked a green plaid shirt and white slacks for Dr. Petrie.

When they were ready to leave. Dr. Petrie went over to Mrs. Henschel. She was conscious again, and she was groaning under her breath. He knelt down beside her, and laid a hand on her forehead.

'How do you feel?' he asked her.

'Bad,' she croaked. 'Real bad.'

'Do you think you can travel?'

She coughed up blood, and tried to shake her head. 'Just leave us be,' she said hoarsely. 'You go on and leave us be.'

'Mrs. Henschel – we have to get you to a hospital, if there are any hospitals left.'

She groaned, and shook her head again. 'Just leave us. Dave'll look after me, won't you, Dave?'

Dr. Petrie bit his lip, and looked across at David Henschel's body.

'Mrs. Henschel,' he said gently, 'I can't leave you here to die.'

She coughed more blood. 'Die?' she said. 'Who said anything about dying?'

'You have to realize that you need attention. Dave – doesn't she need attention?'

He paused, and then he said, 'There – Dave says you need attention, too.'

Mrs. Henschel opened her eyes. 'Let me see him,' she said. 'Are you there, Dave? Are you there?'

She tried to raise herself, but then she started coughing, until the blood was splattering the hard ground in front of her.

'I don't feel so good,' she said. 'Just give me a minute.'

She lay back and they waited. The breeze rustled the grove of palms, and the National Guardsmen shuffled their feet uncomfortably on the roadside. The sky was clear blue, and if it hadn't been for the silence and the strange absence of traffic, you would have thought it was a day just like any other.

Later, Dr. Petrie remembered that moment more clearly than almost all others – waiting by the roadside near Palm Bay for Mrs. Henschel to die.

She went without a sound, sliding easily into death. Dr. Petrie thought she was sleeping at first, but then he saw that she had stopped breathing, and that her right hand was slowly opening like a white flower with crumpled petals.

He stood up, and walked around to face the National Guardsmen, pointing his gun straight at them. He was scruffy and unshaven, with dark rings under his eyes, and his clothes still had the creases of the suitcase on them. His hair was ruffled in the morning breeze.

'I ought to kill you,' he told the men. 'I ought to waste you here and now.'

The one who was chewing gum looked up. 'Guess that's your privilege,' he said. 'Seeing as *you've* got the gun.'

Dr. Petrie cocked the weapon and raised the barrel. For

a moment, he was almost tempted to shoot them, but the moment didn't last long. His angry bitterness of the previous night had faded with the sun, and he was beginning to see that they were all, soldiers included, tangled up in a situation they could neither control nor understand.

'Just for safety,' he said, 'I want you to walk down the road a couple of hundred yards. Then we're going to drive off.'

The other guardsman said, 'What about our guns? We aint gonna last long without our guns. Can't you leave them behind?'

Dr. Petrie shrugged. 'You're not going to last long anyway. What I said about those immunization jabs was true. Now, start walking.'

He told Adelaide and Prickles to get into the car. He tossed the automatic weapons on the back seat, and climbed in himself. He started the engine, and they moved off northwards up Route 1, leaving the two guardsmen standing in the road watching them go.

The day was hot and clear. There were one or two other cars on the road, but they kept away from each other, staring suspiciously from their tightly-closed windows. Just outside Melbourne, there were a few hitch-hikers trying disconsolately to pick up lifts, but there were too many bodies lying around the sidewalks and verges to suggest that anyone around there might have escaped infection. It only took one drop of spittle, one breath, to pass the plague on, and Dr. Petrie wasn't prepared to risk the lives of those he loved talking to anyone if he could avoid it.

In the center of Melbourne itself the police and the National Guard had set up another roadblock. He drove cautiously up to it and stopped.

A heavy-built cop walked up to the car and said, 'Sorry, sir, you're going to have to turn around.'

Dr. Petrie nodded. There was nothing else he could do. There were seven or eight cops and guardsmen surrounding the barricade, and there was no hope at all of forcing a way through there alive. He backed the Gran Torino up, turned it around, and drove southwards again.

They were hungry and thirsty, and the day was growing hotter. The car's air-conditioning was faltering, and the interior was becoming unbearably stuffy. Prickles, lying in Adelaide's arms, looked flushed and sweaty, and Dr. Petrie checked her pulse regularly as he drove. It was probably nothing more than a cold or 'flu, but he couldn't be sure. Her lips were dry, and she was finding it more and more difficult to breathe.

There was no sign of the two National Guardsmen as they drove back past Palm Bay. Not far from the grove of trees where they had spent the early hours of the morning, Dr. Petrie took a right turn inland, and drove down the dusty, deserted road until he reached Interstate 95. Then he turned north again until he crossed Highway 192, and turned even further inland, towards St. Cloud and Lake Tohopekaliga. This time, they came across no road blocks and no troops, but there were signs of the plague everywhere. Bodies lay by the road, smothered in flies, and cars and trucks were abandoned at every junction and layby.

Around lunchtime, they found a deserted McDonald's. Dr. Petrie parked outside, and left Adelaide and Prickles in the car while he scouted around with his automatic weapon. There were two bodies in the yard at the back, both crawling with flies, but apart from that the place was empty. They went inside and sat down.

Petrie lifted the counter and went in search of baked beans, milk, cheese and soft drinks. 'The ice cream's melted,' he said, 'but if you don't mind *drinking* it, you're welcome.'

Prickles was still hot, but she managed to eat a few cold baked beans and drink some milk. Dr. Petrie ate quickly and hungrily, keeping his eye on the empty highway and the surrounding buildings.

'Well,' he said after a while, wiping his mouth. 'It's not exactly the Starlight Roof, but it's nutritious.'

Adelaide gave a tight, humorless smile.

'Is anything wrong? You don't look too happy.'

She waited until she had finished her mouthful of cheese. 'I'm not, if you must know.'

'Why not? Come on, Adelaide, we've had a hard time of it, but that's no reason to give in. If we stick together, we'll get out of this okay, don't you worry.'

'Well,' she said, casting her eyes down. 'I don't think so.'

Dr. Petrie stared at her. 'What do you mean?' he asked. 'I don't understand.'

She looked up. 'You might as well know,' she told him. 'I think that Prickles has the plague. I think we're going to have to leave her behind.'

Prickles blinked listlessly. Her face was crimson with heat and fever, and she was obviously sick.

Dr. Petrie burst out, 'That's impossible. You don't know what you're suggesting.'

Adelaide reached out and held his wrist. 'Leonard,' she

said, 'I know it sounds harsh, but it's a question of survival. Like you said before. *My* survival, and *your* survival. If Prickles has the plague, we could *all* die. At least if we find some way of making her comfortable, and leaving her behind, then we could live.'

'That's crazy,' he said. 'You're out of your mind. Prickles is my daughter.'

'Yours and Margaret's daughter.'

He leaned forward. 'Is that it? Is that why you want me to leave her behind? Because she's Margaret's daughter!'

'Oh Leonard, I didn't mean that. I just mean that if we really have to be fierce, the way you said, then we have to be completely fierce. With ourselves, as well as with other people.'

Dr. Petrie didn't know what to say. He stroked Prickles' sticky little forehead, and gave her another spoonful of baked beans.

'Leonard,' insisted Adelaide, 'I don't want to see you die, and I don't want to die myself.'

Dr. Petrie said slowly, 'If you had plague, honey, I wouldn't leave you behind. I won't leave Prickles behind, either.'

Adelaide sighed, and tapped her fingernails on the formica tabletop. 'In that case, I'm going alone. I'm sorry, Leonard. I love you. But I love life better than lost causes.'

Dr. Petrie wiped his forehead with the back of his wrist.

'I can't stop you,' he said hoarsely. 'I love you, too, as a matter of fact.'

'But you love Prickles more?'

He looked at her. He said, 'Don't try and measure my love, Adelaide. It won't work. I've told you I love you, and you should know how much. If you want to leave, I won't stand in your way, but I can't say that I'm glad to see you go. Just be realistic, that's all. Prickles is a six-year-old girl, and she's my daughter, and no father worthy of the name would leave her to die on her own.'

Prickles looked from Adelaide to Dr. Petrie and back again.

'Am I going to die, too?' she asked.

Dr. Petrie put his arm around her. 'Of course not, honey. We're just talking stupid.'

'I don't think we are,' said Adelaide. 'Listen, Leonard. I'm not cold-hearted and I'm not a bitch, but I *beg* you. Leonard, I love you. I don't know what else I can say. I love you and I want to see you live.'

'Will I be an angel?' said Prickles.

'No, baby, you won't,' Leonard Petrie said.

He stood up, and collected his automatic weapon. Adelaide stayed where she was, picking at the few remnants of cheese and pickle on her plate.

'You're welcome to come along,' he said softly. 'I don't seriously think that Prickles has the plague, and I would like to have you with us.'

Adelaide pouted. 'You wouldn't think she had it, would you? You're her dear devoted daddy.'

Dr. Petrie didn't answer. He took Prickles by the hand and led her outside to the car. It was past noon now, and the heat rippled off the concrete car park in heavy waves. They climbed into the car, and Dr. Petrie started the engine. Adelaide stayed where she was, sitting inside the plate-glass window of McDonald's, her face hidden from view.

He waited, engine turning over, for five minutes. Adelaide stayed at the table, not moving. Prickles said, 'Isn't Adelaide coming, daddy?'

Dr. Petrie wiped the sweat from his face. 'No,' he told her. 'I guess not.'

He released the brake, and moved off across the car park and up to the highway. He slowed down, and took one last look in the mirror. Adelaide was still inside the hamburger bar, head bent, not even looking their way. He licked his lips, turned on to the highway, and put his foot down on the gas.

They passed Walt Disney World. It was silent and dead – a fairy-tale land that had been stricken by pestilence. The two of them, father and child, wandered around it for almost twenty minutes, looking at the turrets and towers and silent streets. A warm breeze blew from the west, making flags flutter, and waste paper dance across the empty sidewalks. Most grotesque and incongruous of all, a man in a Mickey Mouse head lay dead on the ground, still smiling cheerfully, still bright-eyed and round-eared and happy.

'Why is Mickey Mouse lying down?' Prickles demanded.

He took her back to the car.

Adelaide spent nearly an hour preparing herself for her solitary escape from Florida. Around the back of McDonald's, she found an abandoned Delta 88 with the keys still in it, and a tankful of gas. She drove it around to the front, opened the trunk, and packed it with cans of franks and beans. She also took a couple of McDonald's coveralls that she found hanging in a closet, in case she needed a change of clothes.

She was almost ready to leave when she lifted her head and listened. At first she couldn't be sure – but then the distant sound became increasingly more raucous and distinct. Half-muffled by the wind, it was the faint ripsaw noise of approaching motorcycles.

Hurriedly, she packed away the last of her provisions. The motorcycle noise grew louder and louder, and soon it was clear that there were five or six of them, and they were traveling fast. She climbed into the car, and turned the key. The starter whinnied, but the motor wouldn't fire. She kept trying, jamming her foot down on the gas pedal, turning the key until at last the starter motor moaned in protest.

The rippling sound of the bikes was so near now that she could hear it even with the car windows closed. Sweat was streaming down her face. Until the motor started, the car's air-conditioning wouldn't work, and she was sitting in a ninety-degree Turkish bath with PVC seats.

The first of the motorcycles came roaring around the curve in the road. It was a massive chopper, with extended forks, and it was ridden by a muscular Hells Angel with dark glasses, wild hair, and a metal-studded jacket. Adelaide opened the car door, jumped quickly out, and made a run for McDonald's.

The Hells Angel swung his bike around the car park in a wide, bellowing circle, followed by four others in formation. Adelaide pushed her way through the front door of the hamburger bar, and tried to shut it. The catch was broken. Desperately, whimpering under her breath, she tried to slide a heavy table across the restaurant and block the doorway.

Outside, the Hells Angels parked their cycles, switched off their engines, and casually dismounted. They peeled off their jackets, took off their helmets, and then started to walk slowly towards the hamburger bar.

Adelaide tippy-toed hurriedly to the other end of the kitchen and tried the restaurant's back door. It was open. She tugged it ajar, and looked out. She saw the bodies that Dr. Petrie had seen, smothered in flies, but apart from that the back yard looked clear. Behind her, she heard the front door of the restaurant bang open.

Holding her breath, she stepped into the back yard and softly closed the door behind her. Then she crossed the yard as quickly as she could, and went through the gate into the car park at the rear of the buildings. She looked left and right, but there was no one around.

She was just about to circle around the back and see if she could find another car when one of the Hells Angels, a tall bearded blonde in nothing but filthy jeans and motorcycle boots hung with chains, came running around the corner in front of her.

Adelaide's heart bumped. She turned around and started to run away, her hair flying behind her, along the length of the strip's back yards.

She was almost at the end, and just about to turn the corner, when another Hells Angel emerged in front of her. Ginger-haired, muscular, in a sweat-stained purple T-shirt. She turned, and tried to run across the car park towards the back of some distant houses.

Her vision jolted as she ran. Glaring sunlight, concrete, abandoned cars. And behind her, the heavy loping of two silent men, and the chink-chunk of their chains and their boots. She saw far-away palms and white peaceful-looking homes.

It was the blonde who caught her. For a split-second, she could hear him panting up beside her, and then his hard hand snatched her shoulder, and she tripped and fell sideways on to the hot concrete. He grabbed her arms, dragged her on to her feet, and held her tight. They stared at each other, sweating and panting.

When the blonde had caught his breath, he licked his lips and said, 'Oats at last, Trumbo. Real good oats at last. What's your name, honey?'

Adelaide didn't answer. Her lungs felt scorched from running, and her arm was stinging where she had fallen.

'Silent type, huh?' he said. 'Well, don't you worry, because that's the way we like 'em. Aint that correct, Trumbo?'

The ginger-haired Trumbo, still gasping for breath, nodded and grunted in agreement. They started to walk her back to McDonald's. The other three Angels were waiting for them at the back gate, shading their eyes against the harsh sunlight. Adelaide's legs went mechanically one in front of the other.

The Hells Angels' leader applauded Adelaide as his two cohorts brought her in.

'A nice piece of meat there, gentlemen. I couldn't've picked it better myself.'

He came forward and inspected her appreciatively. 'You got a name?' he said mildly.

'Adelaide.'

'That's pretty. I'm the Captain. That's Trumbo there, and the gentleman holding your arm is Fritz. These others are Okey and Sbarbaro. We're a kind of a team, if you understand what I mean.'

Adelaide didn't answer.

The Captain said, 'I hope you don't think we're imposing or nothing. I mean, we'd hate to cause you any kind of inconvenience.'

Adelaide looked at him. She tried to speak boldly, but she felt terrified. 'Will you let me go, please?' she said, in a high voice.

'Let you *go*?' the Captain said, frowning. 'Do you think that's a very good idea?'

'I would like to go,' said Adelaide quietly. 'If you don't mind.'

The Captain shook his head like a worried welfare officer. 'It aint as *easy* as all that,' he said thoughtfully. 'Y'see, this disease business, well, it's really changed the way things are. Because the cops have had to help out with the sick people, well, they've all caught this disease business themselves, and now there aint too many cops left. That means that folks like us, who *didn't* have to help out, we're left alive. We're left in charge.'

'I just want to go,' Adelaide repeated. She started to cry.

The Captain gently laid his hand on her shoulder.

'Please don't upset yourself,' he said. 'We're going to let you go, all right, but you must realize that we want you to exercise your rights.'

One of the Angels started giggling. The Captain glared at him with mock-disapproval.

'Everyone has rights, my dear,' went on the Captain, in a soothing voice. 'You have the right to say that, *yes*, you would like to entertain us gentlemen, or that, *no*, you wouldn't like to.'

Adelaide felt tears sliding down her cheeks. 'What – what's supposed to happen – if I don't?'

The Captain stared. 'The question don't never arise. They all says *yes*.'

Adelaide stopped weeping and looked at him. A long

silent moment passed them by, and miles away they heard the sporadic crackle of rifles.

Finally, she said, 'I don't care what they all say. *I* say no.'

The Captain nodded equably. 'Okay, then,' he said. 'If that's what you want. It's your privilege.'

He snapped his fingers and it all happened with the well-rehearsed speed and proficient brutality of long practice. Trumbo and the Norseman marched her into the restaurant again, through the kitchen, and pushed her against the wall of the hamburger bar. She stood there, wild-eyed and panting. Then the Captain stepped forward, very close, and grasped the top of her white T-shirt. She could see the necklace of sweat along his upper lip, and smell his heavy, ox-like odor. His hands were hard and powerful, with big death's-head rings on the middle fingers.

'Last word?' he said gently.

Adelaide closed her eyes. It was going to happen, one way or another, and neither *yes* nor *no* were going to make any difference. The Captain said, 'Okay,' and ripped her T-shirt apart with three savage tugs, baring her breasts.

She tried to protect herself with her hands, but he forced them away, and roughly pulled and squeezed her breasts and nipples.

'Oh God,' she begged him. 'Please don't, please don't.'

He seized the top of her jeans, and tore them open. She tried to twist away from him, but Okey and Trumbo took hold of her arms, and pinned her against the formica wall while the Captain jerked them down.

When she was completely naked, they stood around and touched her and grinned. All she could do was stare at them, and whimper. It wasn't even worth screaming.

She was alone with these animals in a world where no one could hear her, no one could protect her, and no one cared.

The Captain casually unzipped his jeans, and prized his penis out. It was stiff and swollen, and he held it in his hand in front of her.

'Are you ready for the Captain's Special?' he asked her softly.

They pushed her face-down on to one of the tables. Her breasts were pressed against the sticky formica, and her legs were held wide apart. She stared at the floor, at the mosaic pattern of red-and-white, and tried to detach her mind from what was happening and think about something else altogether, like her childhood in Maine, or her mother's kindly face...

He forced himself into her. He seemed enormous, and it hurt so much that she bit her tongue. His hard hands were gripping her thighs, pulling her on to him, and she couldn't do anything but twist and turn and keep her teeth tightly clenched together.

They all raped her, one after the other, and it took an hour and a half. After an hour they didn't even have to hold her down, because she lay there gripping the table-top of her own accord, dulled to everything that they were doing to her. She didn't even hear them leave when it was all over, and she lay on the table until it began to grow dark, her body red and sore, her eyes swollen with unshed tears.

One by one the bikes started up, and roared off northwestwards into the gathering night.

A little after midnight, in the first few moments of Thursday morning, Dr. Petrie and Prickles crossed the Suwannee River on 75, not thirty miles away from the

Georgia state line. It was a black, cloudy night, like the suffocating inside of a soft velvet bag, and the Torino's air-conditioning had packed up altogether. They drove with the windows open wide, feeling the damp night draft blowing in on their faces.

They had had no trouble with roadblocks or National Guard since they had left Disney World. Through Clermont, Gainesville and Lake City they had seen nothing but deserted houses, corpses covered in black flies, and burning cars. If anyone had been left alive in this part of Florida, they were long gone.

Prickles was still pale and sweaty, but her pulse seemed to have normalized, and her breathing was easier, too. Dr. Petrie was still determined that her condition was nothing more than summer 'flu. The hurt, if she died now, would be more than he could bear.

He checked his rear-view mirror regularly to see if Adelaide might be following. Just outside Clermont, he had seen a bunch of bikers way behind, but they had turned off west towards Groveland, long before he had got a good look at them. He kept the National Guard automatic rifle propped up on the seat next to him, in case they were ambushed by looters or Hells Angels or even by police, but north Florida was more like a graveyard than a jungle.

It took him forty-five minutes, driving on marker lights alone, to reach the state line. He saw the floodlights before he saw anything else. Two miles ahead, the highway was illuminated by batteries of powerful lamps, and the surrounding trees and brush were swept by searchlights and torches. It was the National Guard again, imposing their doomed quarantine on a dead state.

He pulled the car over to the side of the road, switched off the engine, and rubbed his eyes. Crossing the state line was going to be a hell of a lot harder than he had expected. By now, he conjectured, all the National Guard contingents which had been ordered to prevent a northward exodus of plague-carrying Floridians must have been pulled back to the border. Florida, with only two dozen major roads connecting it to the main body of continental America, was an easy limb to amputate.

'Prickles,' he whispered softly, 'try and get some sleep. I think we're going to have to wait until morning before we go any further.'

Prickles was almost asleep already, but he had been keeping her awake in case they ran into trouble. All the way from Lake City, he had been singing her nursery songs and half-remembered rhymes, just to keep her alert. He was surprised how many he remembered.

Prickles, sucking her thumb, said sleepily, 'Sing the song about the blanket lady.'

Dr. Petrie coughed. His mouth was dry, and he felt exhausted. 'No, baby, that's enough for tonight.'

'Please, Daddy.'

Dr. Petrie sighed. Then in a hoarse, off-key voice, he began to sing,

> 'There was an old woman tossed up in a blanket
> Seventeen times as high as the moon;
> Where she was going I could not but ask it,
> For in her hand she carried a broom.
> "Old woman, old woman, old woman," quoth I;
> "O whither, O whither, O whither, so high?"

*"To sweep the cobwebs from the sky
And I'll be with you by-and-by!"'*

Prickles smiled. Her eyelids dropped. In a few moments, she was fast asleep, her breathing quiet and regular. As a last check, Dr. Petrie gently lifted her wrist and timed her pulse. It was normal.

He closed the car windows, leaving only a small gap for ventilation, and settled down to get some rest himself. His neck muscles creaked with tiredness, and he felt unbearably cramped. But after five minutes of restless shifting around, his eyes began to close, and in ten minutes he was asleep, his head bowed over the steering-wheel like a man in prayer.

He was awakened four hours later by a cool dawn breeze flowing into the car. He lifted his head, and blinked. He felt as if his back was clamped in irons, and one of his feet was completely numb. He looked across at Prickles, who was still soundly sleeping, and then he checked his surroundings in the gray first light of another day.

They were closer to the state line than he had guessed, and he could see the barricades across the highway a mile or so in the distance. It was too hazy to see how many National Guardsmen there were around, but he guessed they'd be out in force.

He climbed out of the car and stretched. Then he opened the trunk and took out some of their provisions – some Kraft cheese, a packet of crackers, and a can of orange juice. He looked pensively for a moment at some of Adelaide's tennis rackets and shoes strewn hurriedly in the back, but then he closed the trunk and pushed Adelaide out of his thoughts. He had spent the whole of yesterday afternoon worrying about her, and wondering if he ought to go back, but there seemed to be something about the plague that was destroying normal values and normal sentimentality. Perhaps there was too much death around to think about love.

Dr. Petrie nudged Prickles awake, and she yawned and shook her head like a small puppy. They sat in silence, sipping orange juice and eating crackers, and he looked at her, his daughter, and considered what kind of a world he had brought her into. In less than an hour, they were going to try and cross the state line, and that meant that both of them could be shot dead.

'Have you had enough?' he asked her, as she finished her juice.

'I wish I had some toast,' she said, looking at him seriously.

He gave her a small grin. 'So do I,' he told her. 'In fact, I'd do anything for a piece of toast.'

He packed everything away, brushed the crumbs from his crumpled slacks, and then walked along the highway a short distance to see if he could work out how to evade the quarantine barrier. He shaded his eyes against the early sun, but it was impossible to distinguish any signs of life around the National Guard trucks and jeeps and barbed wire. As far as he could make out, the best thing to do would be to leave the Torino where it was, and try to skirt around the barricade to the east, on foot.

Then they could pick up Route 41, and commandeer another car. It would take most of the morning, particularly at Prickles' pace, but it was better than trying to force their way through the barrier in a show of dangerous heroics. Even National Guardsmen shot straight sometimes.

Dr. Petrie went back to the Torino, started it up, and drove it off the side of the highway into a sparse clump of palms. He slung his gun over his shoulder, quickly filled a bag with cans of orange juice and food, and knelt down beside the car to lace up Prickles' walking shoes.

'Do we *have* to walk?' she asked plaintively. She was looking much better than yesterday, but she was still pale.

'I'm afraid so. You don't want to end up as an angel, do you?'

'No. I don't like angels.'

Keeping to the side of the highway, they began to walk northwards towards the state line. The clouds were gradually fading, and the day was growing hot. A tall man and a small girl, side by side. Their feet crunched over the rough fill beside the road, and Dr. Petrie had to stop a couple of times to winkle stones out of Prickles' shoes.

He was about to leave the highway and strike off northeast when he heard the distant sound of a car, coming up behind them from the south. He turned, and strained his eyes. The sun flashed off a windshield, and the noise came closer. He took Prickles' hand and pulled her as fast as he could, across the gravel and stones, and together they crouched down behind a stack of rusty oil-drums that someone had left beside the road years ago. He put his finger across his lips to tell her to keep quiet.

The car wasn't approaching very fast, but the driver obviously meant to go straight up to the state line barricade, and try to get through. Dr. Petrie wanted to see what would happen – how many National Guardsmen would come out to stop it, and what kind of firepower they had.

It was only when the car came near and had flashed past

their hiding place that he realized who was driving it. It was a dusty Delta 88, and behind the wheel was Adelaide.

'*Adelaide!*' he shouted, and scrambled out from behind the oil-drums, waving his arms. '*Adelaide!*'

She neither heard nor saw him. She kept on driving towards the barricade, and as she approached it, he saw her red brake lights flare. She had pulled up right next to a National Guard truck, and was waiting there.

Dr. Petrie bit his lip, watching anxiously. Minutes passed, and no National Guardsmen emerged from the truck, nor from any of the makeshift command posts that had been set up around it. He saw Adelaide get out of the car and look around.

Five minutes went by, and he understood then what had happened. He walked quickly back to the oil-drums and collected Prickles. Then, picking her up in his arms, he jogged as fast as he could back to the hidden Torino. He climbed in, started the car up, and swung back on to the highway in a cloud of white dust.

He drove the mile up to the barricade and stopped. Adelaide was still standing there, looking around in a strangely dazed way, supporting herself against the side of her car.

He got out, and walked across to her.

She turned. Her face was bruised, and her lips were swollen. Her hair was mussed up and filthy. She was dressed in nothing but a red coverall with McDonald's embroidered on the pocket. Her eyes stared at him as if she was having difficulty focusing.

'Adelaide?' he said quietly.

He came nearer, and held out his arms towards her. She kept on staring at him like a stranger.

'Adelaide? It's me – Leonard.'

She said nothing.

'Adelaide – what's happened?'

She lowered her eyes. Tears dropped down her cheeks, and stained her red coveralls with damp.

'Oh, Leonard,' she choked. 'Oh, Leonard, I'm sorry.'

He took her arm. She was shivering, in spite of the heat, and she couldn't seem to stop.

'Sorry? Adelaide – what's happened to you? Who's made you like this?'

'I'm sorry, Leonard,' she wept. 'Oh, Leonard, I'm so sorry.'

He said, 'Adelaide—' But then she clung to him, and cried in great desperate, agonized gasps. She tugged at his sleeves, at his wrists, and wound his shirt in her hands, shaking and trembling with anguish. He couldn't do anything else but hold her, and soothe her, while Prickles sat in the car and watched them both with a concerned frown.

The National Guardsmen were all very young, and they were all dead. The plague had touched them all during the night, and they lay where they had been infected by it. In their bunks, beside their truck, in their command posts.

Dr. Petrie kept Adelaide and Prickles well away while he checked over the barricade and its twenty corpses, and he wound a scarf around his own nose and mouth in case he wasn't as resistant to plague as Anton Selmer had suggested. The whole place was buzzing with glistening flies, and stank of diarrhea and death.

Beside one young guardsman, he found an open wallet with a photograph of a smiling woman who must have been the boy's mother. But this was not a war – the mothers didn't wait at home, fondly smiling, while their sons died on the battlefield. If the mother lived in Florida, she was probably dead, too. Plague did not discriminate.

When he had finished his cursory check of the command post, Dr. Petrie roughly kicked down the wood and barbed-wire barricade. Then he went back to the Delta 88, which he had decided to drive in preference to the Torino. Its air-conditioning worked, and it had nearly twice as much gas in its tank. He climbed in and started the engine. Adelaide tried to give him a small smile.

'I guess it's no use posting guards against diseases,' said Dr. Petrie. 'Not this disease, anyway.'

'No,' she replied.

Prickles said, 'Why do those men let flies walk on their faces?'

Dr. Petrie looked around. 'They're dead, honey. They're all dead, and because they're dead, they don't mind.'

'*I* won't let flies walk on my face, even when I'm dead.'

Dr. Petrie lowered his head. He said nothing.

They drove into Georgia in the early hours of Thursday morning, and it was only then that they saw how rapidly the plague had spread. Leonard Petrie kept on 75 towards Atlanta, but even as they drove north-west, away from the polluted eastern shores, they saw suburbs where dead housewives lay on the sidewalks, towns where fires burned untended, abandoned cars and trucks, looted stores, blazing farmland, rotting bodies.

Throughout the long hours of the morning, Adelaide sat silently, her head resting against the car window, saying nothing. Dr. Petrie didn't press her. He could guess what had happened, even if she hadn't told him. He had seen rape victims before, and knew that what she needed now, more than anything, was reassurance.

Dr. Petrie drove fast, and one by one they began to overtake other cars. Most of the stragglers were old family Chevvys and Fords, stacked high with belongings. It was almost bizarre what people felt they desperately needed to keep – even to the extent of hampering their flight away from danger. Dr. Petrie saw a Rambler groaning under the weight of an upright piano, and a new Cadillac bearing, with frayed ropes and great indignity, a green-painted dog kennel.

The plague survivors were heading north, heading west. They drove with their car windows closed tight, and they hardly looked at each other. Pale, tense faces in locked vehicles. As Dr. Petrie overtook more and more cars, the traffic became denser, and the jams became worse. At last, twenty or thirty miles outside of Atlanta, they were slowed down to a crawl, and way ahead of them, glittering in the fumy sunlight like an endless necklace that had been laid across the Georgia landscape, they saw a six-lane jam that obviously stretched the whole distance into the city.

'Oh God,' said Adelaide hoarsely. 'What are we going to do?'

Dr. Petrie stretched his aching back, and shrugged. 'There's nothing we can do. Maybe there's a turnoff someplace up ahead, and we can try to make it across country.'

The jam was made even more hideous as drivers died from plague at the wheels of their cars. Dr. Petrie saw wives and children mouthing frantic appeals for help through the windows of their cars, but the vehicles were now locked so solidly together that no one could open a car door. Anyway, every family was keeping itself strictly quarantined inside its own cell, and no one would risk infecting himself by going to assist anyone else.

It was the ultimate experience in American hostility, but perhaps it was also the ultimate experience in American togetherness, too, for the drivers and families who died inside their cars were not left behind or abandoned, but irresistibly pushed forward by the crushing metallic weight of the living refugees behind them.

Adelaide slept for two hours, and when she woke up she looked a little better. As they bumped and rolled gradually northwards, she made them a lunch of franks and canned mixed vegetables, and they drank Coke and orange juice. Police helicopters flackered noisily overhead, warning drivers who felt unwell to try and pull off the highway. There was no way they were going to be able to halt the exodus of plague survivors, and they didn't even try.

Inside the chilled confines of their air-conditioned car, Dr. Petrie and Adelaide and Prickles were shunted northwards in a curious dream. Trees and road signs went past so slowly and gradually that they grew tired of looking at them, tired of reading them. As far as they could see ahead, there was nothing but a wide river of car rooftops, wavering in the afternoon heat. Behind them, the same endless press.

The convoy's progress was further hampered by cars that had broken down or run out of gas, and had no way of filling up again. Only the slow-boiling fear of plague kept the immense and agonized jam inching forward. Dr. Petrie saw an old Buick that had immovably seized up being deliberately shunted off the highway by the cars around it. It overturned and rolled down a dusty embankment, with its family trapped inside it. And there was nothing anyone could do to help.

They began to pick up radio broadcasts. They were faint and crackly at first, and it was plain they were coming from a long distance. Adelaide identified them first. They were news programs from Washington D.C., distorted and faded by the intervening peaks of the Appalachians.

Eventually, though, they began to gain altitude, and as they did so the radio bulletins became clearer.

'... so far, there have been no reported outbreaks of disease any further north than Wildwood, on Cape May, New Jersey, but more than seventy miles of beaches on Long Island's south shore were closed just before noon this morning because of sewage that has been washing ashore for the past week. Bathing has been prohibited from Long Beach, practically next door to the Rockaways in Queens, all the way east to the western edge of the Hamptons in Suffolk County.

'Inland, two cases of plague have been reported in Baltimore, and further south the disease has taken a serious grip on Georgia, South Carolina, North Carolina, Virginia and parts of Maryland. The President is remaining in Washington against the advice of his aides, but it is understood that he is strictly quarantined, and that a helicopter waits on the White House lawn for possible evacuation measures...

'The Special Epidemic Commission set up yesterday by the President at a moment's notice has declared New York City a primary quarantine zone, on account of the density of its population and the seriousness of a possible outbreak of plague there... Accordingly, all access to Manhattan

Island will be filtered and controlled by paramedic teams, and if necessary the entire island will be sealed off from outside contact...'

Dr. Petrie switched off. He wiggled his fingers to ease the cramp in them, and said, 'It looks bad. Maybe we ought to head west. Once we're through Atlanta, we could head for Birmingham or Chattanooga.'

Adelaide said nothing. Dr. Petrie swore as the car behind them, a big bronze Mercury, nudged their Delta 88 in the rear bumper for the twentieth time.

Prickles, who had been dozing on the back seat, opened her eyes sleepily and said, 'Is it time for Batman?'

Dr. Petrie shook his head. 'No Batman tonight, honey. We're still stuck in all these cars.'

Prickles stared out of the window, disappointed. 'Can't we go home now?' she asked him.

Dr. Petrie reached over and took her hand. 'We can't go home for a long time, darling. But what we're going to do is find ourselves a *new* home. You and me and Adelaide. Isn't that right, Adelaide?'

Adelaide turned and looked at him listlessly. 'Whatever you say, Leonard.'

Prickles was satisfied by that answer, but Dr. Petrie wasn't. As Adelaide turned away again, he said, 'Adelaide, love, that's not like you. Not like you at all.'

She kept her face away. Outside, the afternoon shadows were beginning to lengthen.

'What's not like me?' she said, as if her mind were on something else altogether.

'Agreeing with me, just like that. You normally refuse to do what I want, on principle.'

She stared at the floor of the car. 'Well,' she whispered. 'Things change, don't they?'

'Like what?'

'Sometimes you find that refusing doesn't make any real difference.'

He didn't try to touch her. That would come later. Right now, he was intent on getting her to say what had happened. Just explaining it would start the long painful process of exorcism.

'How did it happen?' he asked her, so softly that his words were scarcely louder than breathing.

She raised her head.

'Was it back at the restaurant? At McDonald's?'

Slowly, she turned to stare at him. Her eyes were glistening with tears.

'You *know*,' she said, shaking her head. 'How did you *know*?'

'I am a doctor, Adelaide; and more important I'm a man who loves you, and knows you well.'

The tears rolled freely down her cheeks now. She couldn't say any more, and right now she didn't need to. She leaned her head forward and rested it against Dr. Petrie's shoulder, and cried.

Prickles looked at her with some interest, and said, 'Why is Adelaide crying, Daddy? Does she feel sick?'

Dr. Petrie smiled. 'No, darling, she doesn't. She doesn't feel sick. I hope she's feeling better.'

They saw the huge smudge of black smoke hanging over Atlanta before they saw the city itself. The evening was warm and still, and the smoke was suspended above in spectral stillness. Eventually, as the painful traffic jam edged nearer, they could make out the sparkle of fires in the city's downtown buildings, and they knew that Atlanta was destroyed.

Dr. Petrie turned the radio dial to see if he could pick up any stray news bulletins, but all he could get was howling and static.

'Maybe we could get off the main highway here and try the back roads,' suggested Adelaide. 'This is getting insane.'

Dr. Petrie said, 'I'll try. It looks like there's a turnoff just up there on the left.'

Forcing their way across two solid lanes of blocked-solid traffic was the worst part. It meant holding up other cars, and after a day of inching forward in heat and fumes and sickness, there weren't many drivers who had the patience or the inclination to let them past. Dr. Petrie rolled down his window and made a hand signal, and then just turned the wheel left and crunched into the car beside his.

The driver, a fat redneck with a fat family to match, mouthed obscenities at him. The man didn't open his window, though. He was too frightened of catching the plague.

The redneck gunned his engine and tried to force Dr. Petrie back into his own lane. There was a grinding of wheel hubs and fenders.

'*Let us through!*' screamed Adelaide. 'We only want to get through!'

The man wouldn't budge. He sat stolidly in the driving seat, refusing to look in their direction. For five minutes, the two cars crawled along side by side, their fenders scraping and screeching.

After a while, Dr. Petrie sighed impatiently and reached over for his automatic weapon. He lifted it up, and took a bead through his open window at the redneck's head. Then he waited. The man, who was making a point of ignoring him, didn't see what was happening at first. Then his podgy wife nudged him, and he turned and saw the rifle's muzzle fixed on his cranium. He jammed on his brakes so quickly that the car behind shunted into the back of him.

Dr. Petrie, steering-wheel in one hand and rifle in the other, crossed the two lanes of traffic in a couple of minutes. Then he sped the Delta 88 up alongside the main highway in a cloud of white dust, and took the small rutted turnoff to the left. The car bounced and banged on its suspension, but soon they were clear of the traffic jam and driving up the side of a gradual incline, into trees and scattered housing plots and fields.

Below them, they now saw in the reddish light of the seven o'clock sun, clouded in fumes and smoke, the endless glittering chain of the congested highway, and in the distance, five or six miles to the north-west, the immense shadow that drifted over Atlanta. They opened the car windows, and there was a rubbery smell of burning mingled with the fresher smell of the evening woods.

Dr. Petrie didn't know if the dirt-track they were following led anywhere, but he was prepared to drive across fields and streams if he had to. The most urgent need was to head west, and outstrip the plague. As far as he could make out, they were still well inside the infected area, and until they escaped it, they were still at high risk from National Guardsmen, looters, panicking drivers, and the bacillus itself.

It wasn't long before he had to switch on the car's

headlights. The sky was darkening into rich blue through the treetops, and moths were tapping softly against the car's windshield. Prickles was fast asleep in the back, covered with a plaid blanket, and Adelaide was beginning to settle down to doze.

'Leonard,' she said. 'I was just wondering.'

'Hmm?'

'It's about the plague. I was just wondering why you didn't catch it yourself.'

He shook his head. 'I've been wondering that myself.

I was exposed to so many plague patients down at the hospital, and I've been tired and vulnerable, too. But I *still* haven't caught it. And neither have you.'

'Oh, with me, I think it's just luck,' said Adelaide. 'But *you*, I don't understand. Dr. Selmer didn't catch it either, did he? Least, not as far as we know. I mean, you both touched that boy who had it, didn't you? That boy you treated on Monday morning? Surely you would have caught it from him.'

Dr. Petrie shifted in his seat. The track was getting narrower now, and he was beginning to suspect it would turn out to be a dead end. Tree branches were scraping and flickering against the sides of the car, and he was having trouble making out which was track and which wasn't.

'I've thought about it over and over,' he said. 'First of all, I wondered if the boy had a mild strain of plague that acted as an antidote to the main strain. But then why did he *die*? And why did his parents die? And what about all the other people that Anton and I were looking after? Why didn't we pick up plague from them? The only possibility that seems to make any sense is that Anton and I both did something that immunized us. Some part of our work, something to do with hospital or medical treatment, made us safe. But don't ask me what it was, because I couldn't guess.'

Adelaide said, 'I couldn't guess, either. But whatever it was, or is, thank God for it.'

She reached over and touched his thigh. 'Leonard,' she said. 'I do love you, you know.'

He didn't answer.

'I know it doesn't seem like it sometimes, but I do.'

He turned briefly and smiled at her. 'It *does* seem like it, always. Now why don't you get yourself some rest?'

She kissed his cheek, and then released the switch on her reclining seat and lay back to sleep. Dr. Petrie decided to drive on as far as he reasonably could, and then snatch a couple of hours himself. The track was still just about visible, and he wanted to put as many miles between the plague and them as possible.

As he drove, he thought some more about the curious question of his immunity from plague. It wasn't even an ordinary plague, but a fast-incubating breed that attacked the human system with such speed and ferocity that even a serum would have to be administered within half-an-hour of infection to have any chance of saving a patient's life. Not that any kind of effective serum existed. So how and why had he and Dr. Selmer escaped it? Maybe if he understood that, he would understand how the whole epidemic could be slowed down and stopped. And that would be some medical coup...

Was there another disease which he and Dr. Selmer might have both had in innocuous forms, and whose bacilli might have resisted the bacilli of super-plague? Was there any kind of airborne infection they might have picked up, or some airborne medication within the hospital? There had to be some common factor between Dr. Selmer and himself which would provide a clue. But he needed more facts before he could form a workable theory.

Outside, in the Georgia woods, it was now pitch-dark. The insistent sawing of insects was loud and steady, and Dr. Petrie seemed to have driven way out from any kind of civilization. He didn't even know if he was going east or west any more. He decided to stop for the night, and sleep.

He finally pulled the Delta 88 to a stop under a large sheltering tree. The car's engine and hood cooled down with a relieved ticking sound. He switched off the lights, and climbed out of the car to stretch his legs. The woods seemed very deep and silent and dark, although far away he could hear the distant rumble of a passenger aircraft. It was strange to think that, outside the plague zone, life was still going on as before, and that maybe in New York and Chicago and St. Louis, people were getting up and going to bed as if nothing had happened.

He opened the back door of the car and made sure that Prickles was tucked in properly. Then he took off his shoes and got ready to climb back behind the wheel and spend another uncomfortable night as a guest of General Motors.

There was a sudden sharp cracking noise, and something zipped through the car's windshield and out through the passenger window. Dr. Petrie instantly dropped to the leafy ground, and groped inside the car for his automatic rifle. Adelaide sat up and said, 'Leonard? What's happened?'

'*Down*,' he hissed, waving his hand. 'Get your head down. There's someone out there.'

He reached up to the steering column and switched on the car's electrics so that he could lower the driver's window. Then, using the driver's door as a shield, like the policemen he had seen in TV programs, he lifted his rifle and peered out into the dark.

There was a long silence. He heard tree rats scuffling in the darkness, and birds chirping nervously as they protected their young.

Dr. Petrie cocked his rifle and strained his eyes. He thought the shot had come from a large shadowy bush, but he couldn't be sure. Just to liven things up, he fired two shots in the general direction of the bush, and then listened.

There was an even longer silence. Then a voice quite close behind him said, 'Lay your gun down real slow, and raise your hands.'

Dr. Petrie cursed himself. All the time he had been protecting himself with his car door and firing into bushes, his attacker had been softly circling around him. He put down the automatic rifle and slowly stood up with his hands above his head.

He couldn't see his attacker at all. The night was too dark, and the man didn't move.

'You come from th' east?' asked the man, in a Georgia twang.

Dr. Petrie said, 'We don't have disease, if that's what you mean.'

The man sniffed. 'Maybe you do, maybe you don't. You can't *see* disease, can you? Not in the night, nor neither in the day.'

Dr. Petrie said, 'We're not doing any harm. We just want to pass right through.'

'I know you do,' said the man. 'And I aint gonna let you.'

'Why not? What's it to you?'

The man sniffed again. It's a lot to me, mister, and it's a lot to my family and my relatives and everyone else west of here. This here's the plague line, right here. Me and everyone else around here, we formed this vigilante committee, and if'n anyone tries to cross this plague line, I can tell you that they're taking their life into their own hands, because our agreement is that we shoot to kill. All you have to do is turn around, and go back where you come from.'

'Supposing I won't?'

'You will.'

'But just supposing I won't?'

'Well,' said the man patiently, 'supposing you won't, then I'll have to drop you.'

'And if I drop you first?'

'You won't.'

'But just supposing I do?'

There was a pause. Then, out of the darkness from another direction altogether, a thicker voice said, 'Mister, if you drop Harry first, I'll make damn sure I drop you second.'

Dr. Petrie lowered his hands. 'Okay,' he said. 'I think you win. Can we just spend the night here? I have a little girl, and I don't want to wake her up.'

'Just get the hell out,' said Harry.

'And if I refuse? No, don't answer that. You'll drop me. Okay, we're going.'

Dr. Petrie bent down to pick up his rifle. 'Leave the gun,' Harry said.

'Now wait a minute,' Dr. Petrie protested. 'If I'm going to go back into the plague zone, I'm not going without this.'

'Leave it!'

Dr. Petrie remained where he was for five or six frozen seconds, half-bending towards the rifle. He screwed up his eyes and peered into the night for the slightest giveaway of Harry's whereabouts. The other vigilante didn't matter so much, because if Dr. Petrie ducked down behind the car he would be out of his firing line.

Harry said, 'Come on, mister. Leave the gun and get your ass out of here. I aint won no medals for patience, and I aint going to win one now.'

Dr. Petrie saw a glint. It could have been the side of a pair of spectacles, or the buckle of a pair of dungarees. Whatever it was, it was enough. He dropped to the ground, snatched his rifle, rolled over in a flurry of leaves and fired a burst of three shots exactly where he had seen the glint.

A scatter-gun went off with a deep boom, and one side of the Delta was torn and spattered with pellets. Dr. Petrie wriggled under the car on his elbows, and fired again – a random arc of bullets that may or may not have hit something.

There was silence again. He quickly elbowed his way out from under the car, tossed the rifle inside, and climbed in himself.

Adelaide said, 'Are you all right? Did you hit them?'

He started the engine, backed the car wildly into the woods, swung it around and put his foot down. The scatter-gun went off again, and the Delta 88's rear window was turned to milky ice. Dr. Petrie drove fast and wild, and thumped heavily into two or three roadside trees before he considered it safe to switch on his lights.

Adelaide sat up. Only her reclining seat had saved her

from the first bullet, which had passed through the car in a diagonal line. Prickles was awake, but she was so tired that she wasn't even crying. She, too, was unhurt. The scatter-gun had ripped the car's outside skin, but hadn't penetrated the soundproofing inside the doors, or the vinyl upholstery.

'Did you hear what he said?' asked Dr. Petrie tersely.

'About the vigilantes?'

'Exactly. It looks like they've drawn a plague line down the Appalachians, and anyone who tries to cross it gets killed. Maybe they've even got themselves federal backing. The way this situation's been handled, who can tell?'

'What are we going to do?'

'I guess we could try to cross someplace else, but the chances of getting through in a car must be pretty remote. Maybe we ought to try our luck in the north. Try and get into New York City. If we stick to the back roads, it could take us two or three days, but if they're going to make it a secure quarantine area, it's worth a try.'

Adelaide rubbed her eyes tiredly. 'Let's do it then. Let's just get someplace where we can stop and have a bath and eat a decent hot meal. If I don't get out of these clothes soon, I'm going to stink like a skunk!'

Dr. Petrie grinned at her through the darkness. 'Me too. But then, skunks seem to fall in love just like the rest of us, don't they, so what's wrong with smelling like one?'

Adelaide settled down to sleep again, trying to make herself comfortable in the jolting car.

'Leonard,' she said, 'I'll give you a hundred good reasons. But not right now. Tomorrow.'

When it was scarcely dawn, and the car was still silvered with the cold breath of the night, they drove quietly out of the Georgia woods and back towards the main highway. They were low on gas, and Dr. Petrie's first priority was to find a filling station. Then, tanked up and refreshed with sleep, they would make the long and complicated back-road haul to New York City.

Adelaide was yawning. 'Do you think we'll make it?' she asked him.

Dr. Petrie pulled a face. 'Maybe, maybe not. It depends how far the plague has spread. Half of the time, though, I feel more frightened of the people than I do of the plague.'

She looked serious for a long while. Then she said, 'Yes. I know what you mean.'

Two

Esmeralda was arranging the last paintings in her Marek Bronowski exhibition when Charles Thurston III strolled into the gallery. He was looking very Fifth Avenue, in a lightweight suit of cream-colored mohair and a big floppy hat. He took off his sunglasses and stood back from the wall, ostentatiously admiring the pictures.

'Well, well, well,' said Esmeralda. 'If it isn't Charles Thirsty the Third.'

Charles gave a strictly regulated smile. 'Thurston, actually. If we're going to be friends, we ought to get it right.'

Esmeralda, in a dark red smock, was tapping the last hook into the green hessian-covered gallery wall. 'Who said who was going to be friends?' she said, through a mouthful of nails.

'I hoped that *we* were. You and I.'

Esmeralda straightened the painting. It was a vivid gouache of reds and yellows. Charles Thurston stepped forward and peered closely at the label underneath.

'This is a painting of Coney Island?' he said. 'It looks more like Hell on a warm day.'

'Same thing,' said Esmeralda.

She picked up her hammer and toolkit, and walked back

towards her elegant white-painted office at the back of the gallery. Charles Thurston followed her, and perched himself on the edge of her desk.

'You're very sure we're going to get along,' said Esmeralda.

'Of course I'm sure. Here's me, the famous art writer, and there's you, the beautiful gallery lady. It's a match made in Heaven, or someplace quite close. Perhaps a suburb of Heaven.'

'Heaven has suburbs?'

'Of course it does. Where do you think the people from Queens go when they die?'

Esmeralda laughed. She found Charles Thurston an inch too elegant for his own good, and an obviously incurable smartass, but there was something about him she really liked. He was, after all, very good-looking, and he gave the impression that when he got a woman into bed, he would lavish a great deal of time and athletic energy on exotic forms of stimulation. Esmeralda liked that.

'Well?' she said, reaching for her chrome cigarette box. 'Have you come to buy a painting? Bronowski is young and vital and, most important of all, he's still quite cheap.'

'Is that because nobody's discovered him yet, or because he's been discovered and nobody wants him?'

'Don't be so cynical. He's the new wave in gouache. Go on – buy one.'

'If I buy one, will you come out to lunch with me?'

Esmeralda lowered her eyelashes provocatively. 'Is that a condition of sale?' she asked him.

Charles Thurston laughed. 'How much is this young and vital and cheap artist of yours?'

'To you, five hundred.'

Esmeralda didn't look up. This was a favorite test of hers. It immediately weeded out the unsuitable suitors from the genuinely enthusiastic, because if a man wasn't prepared to toss away five hundred bucks for the sake of getting to know her better, then in Esmeralda's opinion he couldn't be really sincere.

Charles Thurston III flipped open his checkbook and scribbled a check with a handmade gold pen. He blew it dry, and passed it over with a flourish. It was for one thousand dollars.

'This is too much,' said Esmeralda, raising an eyebrow.

Charles Thurston shrugged. 'What's the use of buying just *one* painting? I have a couple of blank spaces either side of my living-room door, and Mr. Bronowski will liven them up nicely.'

He stood up, and tucked his pen back in his pocket. 'Perhaps you could show me some more sometime,' he said. 'My bedroom could do with livening up, too.'

Esmeralda smiled. 'I'm afraid Marek Bronowski is into landscapes – not erotica.'

'We can't all be perfect,' said Charles. 'Now why don't we find ourselves a bite to eat?'

She took off her smock. Underneath she was wearing a simple but beautifully cut blue dress, with a Victorian pendant and lots of bracelets. She brushed her hair, and then pronounced herself ready.

'Have you heard any more about the plague?' asked Charles Thurston, as they rode across town in a taxi.

'Nothing very much. Father's furious about it.'

'Oh?'

'Haven't you read the case of the plagiarized bacteria?

Father's suing some Finnish character in the Federal District Court, but the Finnish character's got himself a sneaky adjournment, on the grounds that all public-spirited bacteriologists should be off fighting the plague.'

Charles Thurston nodded. 'I see. I wondered what you were doing in that district. This plague's pretty serious, though, isn't it? They've got cops on the Lincoln Tunnel and the 59th Street Bridge, and they're turning back everyone with a southern license plate.'

'You're kidding.'

'No, it's true. I saw it myself this morning. They had some guy in a pick-up with a Maryland plate, and they were making him turn right around and go back to Maryland. They said on the news that there's a contingency plan for sealing off the whole of Manhattan.'

Esmeralda crossed her legs. 'Well, I don't know. It sounds to me like they're exaggerating the whole thing.'

Charles Thurston laughed. 'I'm glad someone's optimistic. Especially the daughter of the nation's leading bacteriologist.'

'Stepdaughter.'

'Does it make any difference?'

'You bet it makes a difference. Where are you taking me for lunch?'

'There's a unique little bistro I know. The prices are astronomic, but the food's terrible.'

'What's it called?'

'Chez-moi.'

'You mean the same chez-moi that has a couple of blank spaces either side of the living-room door, and has a bedroom that also needs livening up?'

'You guessed,' said Charles Thurston, with a winning smile.

Esmeralda didn't look amused. 'In that case,' she said, 'you'd better get this hack to turn itself around and take me right back to the gallery. I've heard of fast workers, but this is ridiculous.'

'What you're really saying is that you haven't even had time to clear my check.'

'I'm saying, Mr. Thurston, that I'm not a painting. I can't be conveniently bought with a paltry thousand dollars to fill a blank space on one side of your bed.'

'Don't you like me?'

'*Like* you? I don't even *know* you.'

Charles Thurston sighed. 'Well, if you want to skip lunch, you can. But at least come and look at it. I've prepared it myself – cold soup, smoked fish, salad, and chilled vintage champagne.'

Esmeralda looked at him curiously. He was very self-assured, and very handsome, and somehow she couldn't imagine him going to the trouble of spending the morning in the kitchen, just to make lunch for a girl he hardly knew. He was either very innocent or very devious, and right now she wasn't quite sure which. But he was intriguing.

'Okay,' she said slowly. 'I'll come and look at it. But that's all.'

The cab dropped them on the corner of a faded but still-elegant street. It was one of those tired enclaves of wealthy old widows who were too set in their ways to move away from encroaching slumdom, and there was a mingled smell of decay and expensive perfume in every lobby.

'This is a strange place to live,' she said, looking around the street.

'I like it,' said Charles Thurston. 'It reminds me every day that style is never permanent, and that today's lounge lizards are tomorrow's drawing-room dinosaurs.'

They ascended five floors in a dingy wrought-iron elevator that shuddered and groaned at every floor.

'You speak in riddles,' she told him. He smiled.

Charles Thurston's apartment was expensively decorated in a clean and rigid Scandinavian style that surprised her. There was plenty of natural stone, plain wood, and glass. Everything was in whites and browns and grays, and the fabrics were all woven wool or leather.

'This doesn't look like you,' she said, sitting down on a soft tan cowhide settee.

'Drink?' he asked her.

'Vodka martini on the rocks, please.'

He mixed the cocktails and brought hers over. She sipped it, and it was as cold and uncompromising as everything else in Charles Thurston's apartment.

'Why don't you think it's me?' he asked her.

'You're warm, and this place is chilly. I imagined you living with good Indian carpets and a few well-chosen antiques.'

He walked across to the window. 'I like my backgrounds neutral. The most important things that happen in a room are the people who live and love in it. I don't like to interfere with human beauty by cluttering my living-space with inanimate objects that keep crying out for attention.

'I think you just made that up. I don't believe a word of it.'

He turned back from the window and smiled at her. 'Would you like to see the lunch that you're not going to eat?'

'I'd be delighted.'

He took her hand, and led her into the dining-room. He had been telling the truth. The table was set for two with stainless-steel cutlery and hand-made Swedish glass and pottery.

'Well,' she said. 'I have to confess I'm convinced.'

Charles Thurston ran his hand through his dark curly hair. 'Won't you just sit and watch me eating mine?' he asked, with a mock-plaintiveness that, for all its obvious artificiality, still appealed to her.

She couldn't help giggling. 'All right,' she said. 'And since I don't like to be rude, you might as well give me just a teensy piece of fish, and maybe a tiny bowl of soup.'

'And just a thimbleful of champagne?'

She smiled. 'That will do, yes.'

Charles Thurston rang a small bell on the table. Esmeralda hadn't expected that, but then she supposed that a young man of his means would naturally have a servant.

Charles Thurston pulled her chair out for her, and she sat down. He himself sat at the opposite end of the table, shook out his napkin, and grinned at her.

The servant was no ordinary servant. When she walked in with the soup, Esmeralda took one look at her, and then shot a quick quizzical look at Charles to see if his face showed any signs of mockery or amusement. But there was nothing.

She was black, with close-cropped hair and a thin silver headband. She was exquisitely beautiful. Her eyes were deep and vivid, and her mouth ran in sultry curves. She was also extremely tall – at least six feet – despite the fact that her feet were bare. She wore a flowing kaftan that clung, as she walked into the dining-room, around huge firm breasts.

'This is Kalimba,' smiled Charles Thurston, off-handedly. 'Kalimba is what you would call a *treasure*.'

Esmeralda watched the black girl with widened eyes as she padded out of the room, her bare rounded bottom plainly visible through the diaphanous kaftan. In a small voice, she said, 'I suppose you would, yes.'

They sipped consommé in silence for a moment. Then Esmeralda laid down her spoon.

'Are you trying to tell me,' she said, 'that Kalimba is really your servant? And nothing else?'

Charles Thurston paused with a spoonful of soup half-lifted from his plate. 'I'm not trying to tell you anything.'

'Well, she intrigues me. I mean, she's very beautiful, and very sexy. Are you friends?'

'One has to be friends with one's servants.'

'Don't mock me, Charles.'

'I'm not. Kalimba is everything you say she is. She's beautiful and she's very sexy. She's also a very good cook, she makes beds, she cleans and dusts. Okay?'

Esmeralda frowned. 'I don't know. You baffle me.'

'Why do I do that?'

'Because you're after something and I don't know what it is. Up until I saw Kalimba, I thought it was my body.'

He finished his soup and laid his spoon down. 'You're reacting just like every girl does when she first sees Kalimba. She thinks: Why the hell have I been playing hard-to-get when he's got a woman like that around the place? It throws them off their usual game.'

Esmeralda raised an eyebrow. 'Is that why she's here? As an aid to seduction?'

Charles stood up and poured her a glass of Moet & Chandon 1966. It was well-chilled, and ferociously dry.

'Kalimba is here to serve lunch,' he said simply, with a faint suggestion of a smile.

A few minutes later, Kalimba came back for the plates. There was something about the black girl, silently serving and collecting up food, that was disturbingly erotic. She looked like a fantasy slave girl, with her sullenly pouting mouth and her lowered eyes. Esmeralda couldn't help noticing the way her charcoal-black nipples stood stiff under the flimsy fabric of the kaftan, and somehow it made her feel both aroused and inadequate. She often liked to play the slave girl bit herself with her stepfather, but in the presence of the dark and musky and mysterious Kalimba, she felt pale and plain.

The lunch continued. By three, two bottles of champagne were empty, and they were well into their third. Kalimba softly came and went, with coffee and sweets. Esmeralda felt light-headed and unreal, and somehow everything about Charles Thurston and Kalimba was no longer puzzling or threatening, but funny. She laughed at almost every story he told, and when he suggested they go into the living-room, and he put his arm around her, she didn't object in the least.

They drank more champagne, and Charles put on some soft drumming record that mesmerized her with its endless complicated rhythms. They sat on big embroidered cushions on the thick rug, and shared a cigarette, and laughed even more.

'You still confuse me,' she said, taking another sip of her drink. 'I mean – you're a very confusing person.'

'I think I'm very straightforward,' said Charles.

'That's what's confusing about you. You're straightforward, but you're not deep. You're like a rubber tunnel.'

He laughed. 'I'm like a – *what*? I was never called that before.'

Esmeralda was giggling so much she could hardly explain what she meant. 'Well,' she said, 'just imagine you're driving along and you see a tunnel ahead of you. Very straightforward. But supposing you drive into it, well, you just bounce back out again, because it's rubber. That's what you're like. I think I'm getting someplace with you, but I just bounce back out again. You're a rubber tunnel.'

They laughed and laughed until Esmeralda thought she was going to cry. Then, when they had quietened down, Charles reached over and took her arm and said, 'Esmeralda – do you mind if I lay something on you?'

She was bright-eyed. 'What?'

'Do you dig massage?'

'M-massage?' The idea of it seemed hilarious.

'No, listen, I'm serious. Massage can do fantastic things for your inner being. It calms you down, it brings you closer to yourself. I don't mean your massage parlor stuff. I mean real meditative massage.'

'Who's going to massage me?' she giggled. 'You?'

Charles shook his head. 'No – Kalimba. She's an absolute expert. I mean she's really into it. She's done it for me, and she's given me a whole new slant on myself.'

'Well,' said Esmeralda. 'I don't quite know what to say.'

'Try it. That's all you have to do.'

'I'm not sure.'

Charles checked his expensive wristwatch. 'Look,' he said, 'I have to make a phone call to the coast, and tidy up a few papers. That means that you and Kalimba can have a half-hour to yourselves. You can be totally private.'

'I don't know, Charles. I mean, Kalimba's kind of threatening, don't you think?'

'You only feel she's threatening because you don't know her. She's very warm and understanding. Just let her give you a massage session, and you'll understand.'

The idea of being massaged by Charles Thurston's tall and sultry black lady was quirky, but in the mood she was in, it seemed exciting as well. She giggled, and sipped some more champagne, and then finally said, 'Okay. I've done kinkier things.'

Charles Thurston leaned forward and kissed her on the forehead. 'That's terrific,' he said. 'I'll go call Kalimba, and I'll see you later.'

As he stood up, she tugged his hand. 'Charles,' she said. 'If I tell her to stop, she won't be offended or anything, will she?'

'Kalimba? Not on your life. She's a totally sympathetic person. Now, have fun, you hear?'

Esmeralda sat on a cushion cross-legged while Charles left the room. She heard him talking to Kalimba in the kitchen, but the black girl didn't speak once. Maybe she was deaf-and-dumb, or maybe she was just the silent type. Whichever it was, it didn't seem very warm, understanding or sympathetic. Esmeralda drank more champagne, and found she was laughing to herself as she drank.

She sensed Kalimba's presence in the room even before she turned around and saw her. The black girl had a kind of smoldering charisma that she couldn't ignore. Now, the kaftan had gone, and she was nude, except for a thin gold chain around her loins, and gold anklets around her legs.

Kalimba came softly across the room and squatted down beside her. Esmeralda felt odd tingles of sensation trickling up and down her spine, and suddenly she didn't feel like laughing any more. Kalimba's body was inky black, shining and perfumed. It had a sexual warmth that radiated from it and somehow warmed Esmeralda as well.

Without a word, Kalimba opened a jar of scented oil. Then she pointed to Esmeralda's dress, and indicated that she should pull it down over her shoulders. When Esmeralda fumbled, Kalimba took over, and unbuttoned the front of the dress for her, all the way down. Then she gently tugged it down around Esmeralda's waist.

Kalimba knelt down behind her, and Esmeralda could hear her smothering her hands in the scented oil. Then she felt the black girl's long supple fingers around her neck and shoulders, slippery with oil, beginning to flex and caress and soothe her.

Esmeralda, head bowed, felt the gradual warmth and relaxation flow through her shoulders, and closed her eyes. It was the most delicious sensation she had ever experienced, and she couldn't think why the idea of massage had repelled her so much.

She felt Kalimba reach for the clasp of her bra. At first

she raised her hands to resist, but the black girl gently held her wrists, and lowered her arms again, and she thought: *Why not? She's another woman – an experienced masseuse.*

Kalimba's slippery hands kneaded and massaged her back muscles, and all the tension poured away. Then she felt the girl's hands around her breasts, fondling and stroking them. She sleepily opened her eyes, and looked down. The long black fingers were pressing rhythmically into the gleaming white flesh of her breasts stimulating them, coaxing and arousing the wide pink nipples into stiffness.

She closed her eyes again. The feeling was so good that she wished it would last forever. She felt Kalimba's own rigid nipples brushing against her bare back as the black girl swayed from side to side, and had a strange urge to massage Kalimba's breasts in return.

Kalimba tugged Esmeralda's dress even further down. Her oily hands massaged the white girl's bottom, her fingertips occasionally brushing her sensitive sphincter. Esmeralda said: 'Mmmm... that's beautiful...' and she reached down between her own thighs to draw Kalimba's hand against the moist flesh of her vulva.

She never knew how long the massage lasted. It might have been ten minutes, it might have been an hour. She was more than high on champagne, and all the images of that afternoon were crystal-bright, but disjointed.

She remembered Kalimba's tongue lapping insistently between her legs. She remembered holding the black girl's tight-curled head, and kissing her full sensual lips. She remembered seeing a dark glistening flower, with petals that stickily parted to reveal a moist interior. Music, drumming, lips, eyes, fingers, and magical sensations.

She was lying on the floor, wrapped in an Indian blanket, when she woke up. Her mouth felt like used glasspaper, and her eyes were stuck together with sleep.

She lifted her head. Her neck ached. She tried to focus, but the room was dim, and outside, the New York sky was murky metallic green. It felt as if an electric storm was imminent. She looked at her wristwatch and saw it was seven-fifteen in the evening.

Gradually, unsteadily, she managed to stand up. Her head pounded with pain. Still wrapped in the Indian blanket, she padded across the apartment and called, 'Charles? Are you there, Charles?'

There didn't seem to be anyone around. She crossed the dining-room, with a table that was now cleared of all dishes and decorations, and peered into the main bedroom. The bed was neat and unslept in. It was covered in grayish-brown reindeer skin, and on the wall was a painting of snow in Lapland.

She went back into the living-room. She called out again, and at that moment the front door of the apartment opened and Charles walked in, beaming and confident.

'Esmeralda!' he said. 'You're awake!'

She nodded. 'I just woke up. I feel like hell. Why didn't you wake me earlier? I have to be home at seven-thirty. Daddy and I are going out to dinner tonight, and he's going to go crazy if I'm late.'

Charles kissed her. 'That's nothing,' he said. 'So you're fifteen minutes late. That's nothing.'

'What do you mean – "that's nothing"?'

Charles reached in his pocket and produced a small black something, a couple of inches long. Esmeralda tried to focus on it, but couldn't.

'What's that?' she said.

Charles tossed the black something in the air and smartly caught it again.

'This, my lovely gallery lady, is a roll of film. I have just come back from the photo laboratories, where even at this minute they are printing me up sufficient copies for my needs.'

She stood there and stared at him for a long, long time.

'Kalimba and me,' she said dryly.

'You guessed it.'

She dropped the blanket. She didn't care that she was naked. She picked her clothes up from the floor and slowly dressed. Charles Thurston bobbed and fidgeted around, tossing the film from one hand to the other, and saying, 'Well, that's it, isn't it? That's life.'

Esmeralda finished dressing and tugged a brush through her tangled hair. She collected her pocketbook and got ready to leave.

Charles Thurston said, 'Aren't you going to ask what I want? I mean, us blackmailers always *want* something.'

She paused. 'All right,' she said tiredly, 'what do you want?'

'Isn't it obvious?'

'It might be, but I'd prefer you to spell it out.'

He looked at her almost coyly. 'What I want, in return for these highly diverting negatives, is for your father to drop his patent action.'

That was when the reality of the whole day's work fell into place. She looked around the sparse, Nordic apartment and said, 'This is Sergei Forward's place, isn't it? I didn't think it was your style. And what about Kalimba?'

'Not her real name, I'm afraid. A hired gun, so to speak.'

She stared at his handsome, disgusting face.

'You won't take money?' she asked, softly. 'Five thousand to say the film didn't quite come out?'

Charles Thurston shook his head. 'A job's a job, lovely gallery lady. I have a reputation to maintain.'

'I see. How long do I have?'

Thurston looked at his watch. 'It's now seven-thirty. We would like to know how your father feels about the matter in twenty-four hours. Otherwise, every porn magazine in town gets these, along with *Scientific American* and every journal your father ever wrote for in his whole life.'

Esmeralda ran her hand through her hair. 'Now I understand the adjournment,' she said. 'If Sergei Forward had gone into court today, he would have lost the whole case outright. So he decided to get a little help from his friends.'

'I'm not his friend,' protested Charles Thurston III, as Esmeralda waited for the elevator. 'I just work for him. As far as I'm concerned, he's a cheap Finnish fuck.'

Esmeralda slammed the concertina gates of the elevator and glared at Thurston through the bars. 'Anything's better than being a cheap American fuck,' she snapped, as the elevator took her down.

By Friday afternoon – the same afternoon that Esmeralda spent in Sergei Forward's West 81st Street apartment – the plague zone had officially extended to New Orleans in the south, and with the help of police, National Guardsmen, vigilantes and cadets from summer colleges, it was being held back on a ragged line that stretched northwards to Jackson, Mississippi, Tuscaloosa, Chattanooga, Charleston and Cumberland.

The President had appeared on television at lunchtime and had said 'solemnly, and with a heavy heart' that he had to instruct every American to take up arms to protect the disease-free parts of the nation. That meant anyone from within the plague zone must be shot dead if they attempted to leave it.

'At all costs,' said the President, 'we must contain this threat to our national health and heritage, and urgently seek to find some kind of cure. At the present speed of plague within six weeks.'

A reporter from NBC News asked the President if some people were more susceptible to the plague than others. The President reported that interim figures indicated that adults succumbed more rapidly than children, and that certain groups of workers within the community appeared to be partially or wholly immune. These included *some* hospital workers, *some* employees of ConEd, *some* military and naval personnel, *some* merchant seamen, *some* dentists and doctors, and one or two assorted minor professions.

Was there any clue why these people might be less prone to plague? The President said no, but 'our best scientists are working on it.'

The Medical Workers' Union were still on strike, although in some of the worst devastated parts of Georgia, Alabama and South Carolina, there was radio, TV and telephone blackout, and it was impossible to discover what was happening. Even police helicopters were forbidden to take reconnaissance pictures in case the bacillus was airborne to operational height. The nation was locked now in a terrible paralysis of fear, and in spite of strict highway controls and the banning of westward airline flights, thousands of panicking refugees, in cars and pick-ups and motor-homes, streamed towards the west.

By five o'clock on Friday afternoon, the official estimate of plague dead was seventeen million. Every Atlantic beach was closed from Key West, Florida, to Portland, Maine. The most explosive story of the day, though, was where the plague-infected sewage had originated. It was being suggested by NBC and CBS, and strenuously denied by the New York Department of Sanitation, that the sewage was polluting the Eastern seaboard from an area twelve miles off the Long Island shore.

According to official sources, sanitation barges had left Pier 70 every day for longer than anyone could remember, and dumped untreated sewage into the Atlantic. It was supposed to sink to the ocean floor, and slide, in the form of black viscous ooze, down the shelving incline that would take it out towards the mid-Atlantic.

The New York Department of Sanitation, in a joint statement with the U.S. Environmental Protection Agency, agreed that the sludge was highly infectious, but that it could not have been a breeding-ground for the plague that had ravaged the southern states.

'Ordinary plague, *Pasteurella pestis*, is one thing,' said a spokesman for the department. 'But there is no scientific way in which ordinary plague could have mutated under the ocean into this particularly virulent and fast-growing form of super-plague.'

The department also denied that the raw sewage on the beaches of Florida and Georgia was anything to do with them. Yes – there had been eccentric winds and tides. But it stretched the credulity to suggest that tides had borne the sewage as far south as Miami.

A CBS reporter asked if it were possible for a message in a bottle, dropped off Long Island at the sewage-dumping spot, to float south as far as Miami. An oceanographer said that, with climatic conditions as they had been, yes. The CBS reporter then asked why, in that case, a lump of human feces couldn't do the same.

The spokesman for the Department of Sanitation gave an answer that became the morbidly popular catchphrase of the day. 'What you're suggesting,' he snapped, 'is crap.'

Herbert Gaines walked into the conference room at the Summit Hotel with his hands raised like a successful candidate for the New York presidential primary. Flashguns blinked in the crowded entrance, and he had more pictures taken for the press in the space of twenty seconds than he had in the last twenty years. He was wearing orangey panstick make-up to make himself look healthier on color TV, and his white hair was combed into a flowing mane.

'Welcome back, Herbert,' said a fat reporter in a creased blue suit. 'It's nice to have a hero around for a change.'

Beside Herbert Gaines, sticking close, was Jack Gross – all glossy suit and carnivorous teeth. He piloted his figurehead through the throng of pressmen and television cameras, and up towards a red-white-and-blue platform. More flashguns flickered, and Herbert tried hard to keep smiling.

Jack Gross waved his hands for silence.

'Ladies and gentlemen, my name is Jack Gross and I'm the agent for what we call the FTT. Now, does anyone here know what FTT stands for?'

It was meant to be a rhetorical question, but a *New York Post* reporter said, 'Fart Tunefully Tonight?' There was a general guffaw of laughter.

Jack Gross, his smile a little strained, waved his hands for silence again.

'FTT,' he said, quickly, 'stands for Face The Truth. And Face The Truth is what we call our particular group of dedicated Republican senators and congressmen, all of whom are totally committed to the revival of honest, no-nonsense, straight-down-the-middle politics.'

'Isn't that a contradiction in terms?' asked the lady from *Time*, sardonically.

'It has been up until now,' said Jack Gross. 'But let's think *why* American politics has gotten such a bad name. It's gotten a bad name because it's been the province of men who won't Face The Truth. That's what our group is all about. We've decided that no matter how unpalatable or unpleasant the true facts are, we're going to have to face up to them, and speak our minds no matter how unpopular our voice might be.'

He lowered his voice, and spoke with intense sincerity.

'Maybe, in the past, refusing to Face The Truth didn't matter so much. But today – right this very evening – America faces a disaster of hideous and unprecedented proportions. The plague has already laid waste our southern states, and the last we heard it was infecting parts of Jersey. We are right up against the wall, ladies and gentlemen, and we can't keep our eyes blinkered any longer.

'The crisis is so serious that an American hero has returned to speak the truth about it. A man whose voice once spoke out on the movie screen for honesty and purity and the preservation of the American way, and who has now emerged from honorable retirement to take up our cause. Ladies and gentlemen – Captain Dashfoot, better known as Herbert Gaines.'

There was a light smattering of applause. Herbert's movies were still doing the rounds of art houses and late-night TV channels, and most of the pressmen there had seen at least one of them.

Herbert Gaines stood up. With the TV lights on him, he hardly seemed to have aged. He could have dismounted from his Civil War horse just a few moments ago, flushed with success from his famous ride in *Incident at Vicksburg*. He raised his hand for silence.

'Ladies and gentlemen,' he said, in his rich, deep *timbre*. 'I never thought the time would come when I would feel it my bounden duty to ride once again in defense of the American people.'

There was clapping, and someone said, 'Dashfoot to the rescue!'

Herbert Gaines smiled ruefully. 'I wish Captain Dashfoot *could* come to the rescue, but we're shooting from a different script today. Our nation is being scythed to the ground by a foul and terrible disease, and what we need is not lone heroes on horses but quick and effective federal action.

'What we need, ladies and gentlemen, is someone who will speak the truth about this plague. Someone who will tell us where it really originated. They say sewage. All right

– but *whose* sewage? Are any of *you* infected with plague and hepatitis? Is *your* sewage infected?'

Herbert grasped the lectern in front of him, and lowered his leonine head.

'What we are saying here today, friends, is unpopular. It's unpopular,' he repeated, raising a rigid finger, 'but it's *true. I* know it's true, and *you* know it's true, and I dare any man in the continental United States to prove it aint so. That sewage – that infected sewage – has come from the bowels of the black man, from the bowels of the Puerto Rican, from the bowels of the shiftless vagrant and the unwashed hippie. Not only have they poisoned our society with their subversive politics and their revolutionary mania, they have actually physically poisoned our American sons and daughters with their excremental filth!'

The sound that went up from the press when Herbert said that was extraordinary. It was a kind of surprised moan, like a dog crushed under a car. A black reporter from *The New York Times* walked out and slammed both double doors of the conference room, and a young girl from the *Village Voice* shrieked out, 'You're not a hero, you're a fascist!'

Herbert Gaines, his eyes hard, his hands white, turned in the direction of the girl's voice.

'A fascist?' he said softly. 'Is it the mark of a fascist, to speak the truth? It's true, isn't it, that diseases communicated from the bowels are rife among black and Spanish peoples in America? It's true, isn't it, that the sewage dumped off Long Island contains the infections of diseased negroes? Because it's no longer inside them, this sewage, does that mean negroes no longer bear the responsibility for the disgusting plague it has caused?'

A television reporter said in a quiet but penetrating voice, 'Mr. Gaines, if you're blaming the colored elements in our society for this plague, what do you suggest we do about it?'

Herbert Gaines turned on him fiercely. 'I suggest this. I suggest we cast out our ineffectual political leaders at the first opportunity, and re-elect men who will keep the black man in his place, and the immigrants where they belong. Out of America.'

Another reporter said, 'Mr. Gaines, this is kind of extreme, all this stuff.'

Herbert Gaines turned his best profile to the cameras. 'Of course it's extreme. This is an extreme situation. It requires quick, decisive and urgent treatment. Face The Truth is the only political group that has faced up to that fact so far, and the only political group who could possibly save this nation from ruination and downfall at the hands of the black man.'

The same reporter said, 'What do you suggest we do? Ship 'em all back to the Gold Coast?'

Herbert Gaines smiled patiently and shook his head. 'Of course not. That would be ridiculous. But I have several suggestions that would finally overcome America's race problem once and for all. First – only black medics and doctors should be assigned to plague hospitals. They started it – they can take the risk of treating it. Second – when the plague has finally been contained, arrangements should be made over a ten-year period for the gradual rehousing of blacks in areas where their unsanitary personal habits do not threaten decent Americans.

'Every American citizen, under the Constitution, has the right to life, liberty and the pursuit of happiness. How can we truly say that we are upholding these rights if we jeopardize the first of them from the word go. An American is entitled to *life*, ladies and gentlemen, and if the diseased black man is allowed to walk beside him, work beside him, eat from the same plates, sit on the same seats and defecate in the same public toilets, then we have failed to protect his Constitutional rights. We have abdicated our responsibilities as leaders of this great nation.'

A reporter from the *Christian Science Monitor* said, 'Mr. Gaines, you're not a leader of this great nation. You're an out-of-work actor.'

Herbert Gaines, lit by a flurry of photographers' flashguns, said, 'I am a leader because I speak the truth. You, because you question the truth, are less than a patriot.'

In normal times, Herbert Gaines would have won fifteen seconds' attention on the early evening news. But these were not normal times, and the fact that press and television crews even stayed to listen showed that. As the conference continued, a strange disturbed buzzing filled the room, as if the newspapermen had just discovered some unsettling secret that had been deliberately hidden away from them.

By half-past five, the *New York Post* was on the street with a headline that ran: BLACKS TO BLAME FOR PLAGUE, *claims 'Captain Dashfoot'*, and that was only the beginning. Herbert Gaines was interviewed seven times that evening on New York and network television, and an almost tangible wave of resentment against the black population made itself felt across the breadth of the American continent. What Jack Gross had calculated exactly right, of course, was that everyone in America, including the President, was looking for someone to blame. Just as Adolf Hitler had successfully blamed the Jews for the financial depression of the 1930s, Herbert Gaines had laid the blame for the plague on the shoulders of the American blacks.

As night fell on New York City, fires broke out in Harlem, and the windows of black stores and restaurants were smashed by marauding gangs of white youths. Friday ended in Manhattan to the *wow-wow-wow* of fire trucks and the bitter smell of smoke. By midnight, thirty-six cases of arson had been reported, fifty-two cases of wilful damage, and more than a hundred injuries, varying from fractured skulls to knife wounds. Other crimes noticeably decreased, as black whores and muggers played it safe and made a point of staying home.

In the early hours of Saturday, Herbert Gaines was driven back to Concorde Tower in the back of Jack Gross' Cadillac. He was exhausted, and he was looking forward to a large brandy and a long sleep.

'You did beautiful,' said Jack Gross. 'In one day, you made more of a hit than Gerry Ford made in three years.'

Herbert rubbed his eyes. 'It seems to me that I've caused nothing but distress and confusion. Even if this whole thing about the blacks *were* found to be true, there are times when it's kinder not to tell the truth at all.'

Jack Gross grinned. 'Herbert, you're a man of conscience and no mistake. Can I pick you up at three?'

'You mean there's more?'

'Of course there's more. This is just the beginning.'

'Mr. Gross, I tell you quite plainly, I don't want to do any more.'

Jack Gross waved his hand deprecatingly. 'Don't even think that, Herbert. You're just tired. Have a nice rest, freshen yourself up, and then we're off to make a speech to the New York Republicans.'

Herbert Gaines stared at him gloomily. 'And if I refuse?'

Jack Gross smirked. 'You know very well. If you refuse, young Nicky starts singing in the girls' choir.'

Herbert looked out of the car window at the deserted wastes of 43rd Street. He felt desolated and old.

'Very well,' he said, after a while. 'If I have to do it, I suppose I might as well enjoy it. I'll see you at three.'

Kenneth Garunisch, as Friday dwindled into Saturday, was still talking with the officials of Bellevue Hospital. He had chosen Bellevue as his last discussion of the day, because he could walk home up First Avenue afterwards, and he usually felt like a short stroll at the end of a day's work to clear his head.

The cream-painted conference room was thick with cigarette smoke, and the table was strewn with overflowing ashtrays, newspapers, files, gnawed pencils and unbent paperclips. Talks had started at six o'clock on Friday evening, and they were still chasing the same points of principle around and around at midnight, like dogs chasing their own tails.

Garunisch, his tie loosened and his nylon shirt stained with sweat, was lighting one cigarette from the butt of the last, and he had dark circles under his eyes. Dick Bortolotti sat beside him looking waxy and strained. They had both been under tremendous pressure since they had called the strike, and every available hour of every day had been spent in talks and negotiations and organization. But the Medical Workers were still out, and intended to stay out until they were given a substantial package of pay guarantees and fringe benefits.

Ernest Seidelberger, the thin bespectacled Bellevue spokesman, was sitting mournfully at the other end of the table, struggling to light his pipe. He looked more suited for lectures on medieval manuscripts to bored housewives than union negotiations with hard nuts like Kenneth Garunisch, but he had a tedious pedantic way of refusing to give in, ever.

'Mr. Garunisch,' he said wanly, 'I can't repeat often enough that this hospital administration has nothing more to offer your members in the way of pay, bonuses or incentives, unless you can guarantee something special in return. At the moment, all you're offering us is work that they should be doing anyway under our last agreement with you.'

Kenneth Garunisch blew smoke. 'The plague was not mentioned in the last agreement,' he said hoarsely.

Seidelberger nodded his head patiently. 'My dear Mr. Garunisch, *no* disease is specified in the agreement, and so one can hardly make out a special case for this plague. I urge you to think again. Your members' action has already accelerated the spread of the plague by two days at least, according to my expert informants, and if you hold out any longer, and the plague reaches Manhattan, we here at Bellevue will be totally unable to cope with it.'

Garunisch was about to answer when there was a rapping at the conference door. A pale-faced young hospital executive walked in, smiled nervously at everyone, and leaned over to whisper something in Ernest Seidelberger's ear. Seidelberger listened for a few moments, his face expressionless, and then waved the young executive away.

Garunisch ground out his latest cigarette. 'Is it something we should hear?' he asked bluntly. 'Or is it privileged information for hospital bigwigs only?'

Seidelberger shook his head. 'It's not privileged, Mr. Garunisch. It's just been on the news. The plague has infected so many people in New Jersey that the state has been declared a quarantine area. Nobody is allowed to enter or leave, and anyone attempting to do so will be forcibly detained by the National Guard.'

One of the hospital negotiators, shocked, said, 'My *wife*'s in Trenton today, visiting her mother! And my *children*! They're all there! What am I going to do?'

Ernest Seidelberger said, 'I suggest you go home, Rootes. See if you can call your family from there. Meanwhile, I have a last word to say to Mr. Garunisch before we close this meeting.'

Rootes, shaking, gathered up his papers, crammed them into his briefcase, and left. When he had gone, Seidelberger looked steadily at Kenneth Garunisch, and said, 'You know what I'm going to say, don't you, Mr. Garunisch?'

Kenneth Garunisch shrugged. 'I haven't a notion, Mr. Seidelberger.'

'I'm going to demand that you send your members back to work. New Jersey is in quarantine, and that means the plague could be with us in Manhattan by tomorrow morning. This city is going to catch it, Mr. Garunisch, and thousands will die, and it will all be your fault.'

Garunisch's mouth went taut and hard.

'Mr. Seidelberger,' he grated, 'just because you work for a hospital and you wear a white coat, that doesn't mean that you are automatically on the side of the angels. My members, if they deal with plague victims, are going to be doing the next best thing to committing suicide. They *will* do it, just as they have always done it, but I'm damned if I'm going to allow them to do it without some recognition from the federal government and the hospital authorities. In Japan they paid *kamikaze* pilots a little bit extra, and gave them a few more privileges, and they did it because they recognized courage and they recognized human sacrifice. My members will give you their courage, Mr. Seidelberger, and they will give you their sacrifice, but they won't give it for nothing.'

Ernest Seidelberger sniffed. 'Fine words, Mr. Garunisch. But not quite accurate. Your members are not prepared to *give* courage; they're not prepared to *give* their lives. They're only prepared to *sell* them, at a price. I suggest to you, Mr. Garunisch, that your medical workers are whores, and that you are their whoremaster.'

Kenneth Garunisch stared at Seidelberger with bulging eyes for a moment, and then laughed loudly.

'In that case, Mr. Seidelberger, we're *all* whores. We're all getting paid for sitting here. All I can say is, when *you* get out on the street and strut your stuff, I hope you get picked up by some sex-starved matelot who fucks some sense into that impervious skull of yours. Come on, Dick, let's call it a night.'

Seidelberger sat silent while Garunisch and Bortolotti packed up their cases and made ready to leave. But as they opened the door of the conference room, he turned his clerical profile in their direction and said, 'Mr. Garunisch!'

Kenneth Garunisch paused. 'What is it? Did you finally see sense?'

Seidelberger shook his head. 'No, I have not seen what you so inaccurately call "sense". I just wanted to wish you a happy Saturday, and a long life, because the longer your members stay out on strike, the more urgently you will need it.'

Kenneth Garunisch bit his lip, saying nothing. Then he turned on his heel and slammed the door behind him.

Outside the hospital, on First Avenue, a warm and grimy summer breeze was blowing from the south-west. The glittering spires of Manhattan were reflected in the oily depths of the East River, and a lone barge chugged upriver towards Roosevelt Island. From the north, they heard the sound of sirens, and there was a strange amber glow in the sky.

A Medical Workers' picket was standing by the hospital entrance, smoking a cigarette. Kenneth Garunisch recognized him – a tough onetime stevedore called Tipanski. He had shoulders as wide as a taxi-cab, and a blue baseball cap.

He slapped Tipanski on the back. 'How you doing?'

Tipanski nodded. 'Okay, thanks, Mr. Garunisch.'

'What time are they relieving you?'

'Two-thirty. Then Foster comes on.'

'Any trouble?'

'Naw. But look at them fires uptown.'

'Fires? Is that what they are?'

'Sure. This Gaines guy says on the tube that the niggers is all to blame for the plague, so the white gangs have been cruisin' up to Harlem and puttin' a torch to everythin' that burns, and a few things that don't.'

Even as they spoke, a fire chief's car came howling past them.

'Mr. Garunisch,' said Tipanski. 'Is it true what they say about the plague? That it's comin' here? It says on the news there aint no way they can stop it.'

Kenneth Garunisch looked at the man for a long while, saying nothing. For the first time in his life, he was beginning to feel unable to protect his members. His instincts had always been those of a tough mother hen, scooping her brood into her wings at the first sign of trouble. But now, just across the Hudson, a different type of peril was growing, a peril that could be carried invisibly in the warm night wind, and could infect them all without any chance of saving themselves.

Kenneth Garunisch felt frightened.

'I guess they'll find some way of stopping it okay,' he said, unconvincingly. 'After all, they can seal Manhattan off like a lifeboat, right? Just close all the tunnels and all the bridges, and presto, we're all safe.'

Tipanski frowned. 'They seem pretty worried on the news, Mr. Garunisch. They even said what to do if you thought you had it.'

'Don't you worry, brother. When the time comes, we can deal with it.'

'Okay, Mr. Garunisch.'

Kenneth Garunisch was about to say goodnight, when he heard footsteps clattering up the sidewalk behind him. Dick Bortolotti said, 'Ken,' in a nervous kind of way, and tugged his sleeve. Kenneth Garunisch turned around.

There were five of them. They were hard-faced and big, and they could only have been off-duty cops. No mugger cuts his hair so neat, nor wears such a well-trimmed mustache. They wore black leather jackets, and they stood around Kenneth Garunisch and Dick Bortolotti so that there was no possible way to escape.

'Are you Garunisch?' said one of them gruffly.

Kenneth Garunisch looked from one cop to the other. He was trying to memorize their faces. He kept his arms down beside him, and said, 'What of it?'

'Kenneth Garunisch, the Medical Workers' boss?'

'What of it?'

'Yes or no?'

'Yes. What of it?'

Garunisch had once been a physically hard man but he was too old and slow these days. The leading cop slopped up to him, pulled back his arm, and punched him straight in the face. Garunisch felt his bridge-work break, and he was banged back against the hospital wall behind him. Another punch caught him across the side of the face and fractured his jaw, and then he was kicked in the wrist and the hip.

Tipanski, shouting with rage, tried to attack the cops, but they were too quick and too well-trained. One of them twisted his arm around behind his back, and another one thumped him in the stomach. Tipanski dropped to his knees on the sidewalk, gasping.

Dick Bortolotti got away. He ran down the length of the hospital as fast as he could, crossed 34th Street, and didn't stop running until he reached Second Avenue. He leaned against a building panting for breath, and then slowly and cautiously made his way back to Bellevue. As he crossed back towards the hospital, he had the strangest sensation that everything had changed now, and that life was never going to be the same again. The laws of the jungle had returned, and he was going to have to learn them.

Edgar Paston was lying on his uncomfortable bunk in the jailhouse, reading the weekly *Supermarket Report* which Tammy had brought him that lunchtime. It appeared that the spread of the plague was hiking up the price of oranges and other citrus fruits, although California growers – in the light of the plague's disastrous effects on the Florida crop – were predicting their most profitable year ever.

Edgar laid down his paper and checked the time from the clock on the flaking wall outside his cell. It was a few minutes past midnight, Saturday morning. He shifted uncomfortably, and yawned. He was exhausted, but he had never been able to get to sleep with the light on, and the cop in charge had refused to switch it off.

He wondered briefly what Tammy was thinking about. She was probably awake, too, lying alone in their quilted double bed under the painting of Yellowstone River in spring, listening to the children breathing in their separate bedrooms and feeling lonesome. The thought of it almost choked him up, and he had to think about something else to stop himself from crying.

He thought, too, about the dead Boy Scout. The cops had questioned him for four hours solid, and they still didn't believe him. The shooting happened again and again in his mind, like a loop of film. He saw himself stepping out of the supermarket door. He saw himself raising the gun. They were *laughing* – that was the trouble. If they hadn't been laughing, he wouldn't have fired. He saw the dead boy lying on the concrete car park, and someone said, 'Is he dead?'

Edgar was almost dozing off when he heard footsteps. He blinked. The cops were bringing in a new prisoner – he could distinguish voices. Edgar rolled over on his bunk and pretended to be sleeping, in case he got involved in any more pointless conversations.

He heard the cop say, 'In here.'

Another voice, younger, said, 'You mean I don't get a cell to myself? What is this?'

'This aint the Ramada Inn,' said the cop. The cell door unlocked, squeaked open, and then banged shut again. There was a jingle of keys. Edgar kept his eyes shut and faced the wall.

For a while, he heard the new prisoner shuffling around. Then he heard the lower bunk complain as the prisoner sat down on it. Eventually the newcomer stood up again, leaned over him, and shook him by the shoulder.

'Hey man – are you awake?'

Edgar Paston opened one eye. 'I wasn't,' he said blearily, 'but it looks like I am now.'

'I'm sorry, man. I just thought you might be awake.' Edgar rubbed his face, and sat up painfully. Then he swung his legs over the side of the bunk, and looked at his new cellmate for the first time.

At first, he couldn't believe it. But then he felt his throat tighten, constrict. Just a foot or two away from him, pale and foxy-faced, still methodically chewing gum, was Shark McManus.

Edgar stared at him.

Shark McManus said, 'Do they bring you coffee in this joint?'

Edgar said hoarsely, 'I don't understand.'

'You don't understand what, man?'

'Don't you know who I am,' said Edgar, in a tight voice. 'Don't you recognize me?'

Shark McManus shrugged. 'Sorry, man.'

Edgar said, 'Last night, you and your gang of hoodlums broke into a supermarket out at the crossroads, and wrecked it.'

McManus looked surprised. He screwed up his eyes and said, 'Not me, man. You must've gotten the wrong dude.'

Edgar climbed unsteadily down from his bunk. He faced McManus from only six inches away.

'I don't have the wrong dude, McManus. That store you wrecked was mine.'

McManus chewed steadily for a while, but his chewing became slower and slower, and he finally stopped altogether. He stared at Edgar as if he couldn't grasp what was going on, and he nervously rubbed at the side of his neck.

'You and your kind, you make me *sick*,' said Edgar, plucking off his spectacles and pacing the floor. He turned on McManus again, 'You're like wild beasts!'

McManus looked uncomfortable. But then he said, in an unexpectedly quiet voice, 'Well, man, you may be right.'

'*Right?*' snapped Edgar. 'Of course I'm right. You smash, you destroy – you'd kill if you had to. What the hell do you think the world is out there? Some kind of jungle?'

McManus sat down. 'Yes, man,' he nodded. 'You're right.'

Edgar bent over him. 'Don't think you're going to appease me like that. Oh, don't you think you're going to get away with it that easy! If I have anything to do with it, I'm going to make sure that hoodlums like you are torn out of Elizabeth, root and branch. You hear?'

McManus nodded. 'I hear you. I hear you loud and cuh-lear.'

Edgar put his spectacles back on and peered at McManus close and hard. 'Is that all you can say?' he asked. 'After all that you've done, and all the trouble you've caused, is that all you can say?'

McManus frowned, as if he was thinking, and then gave a small smirk.

'I do have one thing to say,' he said quietly.

'And what's that?'

'It's a question, really. And the question is, if you're so respectable and upright, and if you're going to tear us all out root and whatsitsname, then what are you doing in the slammer along with me?'

Edgar stood straight. He took a deep breath. 'Last night,' he said, 'after you wrecked my store, I went after you with a gun.'

'Don't tell me it was unlicensed.'

Edgar shook his head. 'It was licensed, all right. I was going out to find you and I was going to teach you a lesson! The trouble was—'

McManus looked up. 'Yeah?'

'The trouble was—'

Edgar could hardly get the words out. The reality of last night's killing suddenly stuck in his throat like a terrible knotted obstruction.

'You can tell *me*, man,' said McManus, mock-sympathetically. 'After all, it was *me* you wanted to shoot.'

Edgar looked grim. 'I went out, and I shot and killed someone I thought was you. It wasn't you at all, and that's what I'm doing here.'

McManus stared at him in disbelief. Then, gradually, a smile began to twitch at the corners of his mouth. He guffawed once, then again, and then he laughed out loud. A sour voice in the next cell said, 'For Christ's sake, can't we get any fucking sleep around here?'

McManus, wide-eyed with amusement, said, 'You wasted someone you thought was me? You really did that? Oh, man, you're beautiful! Tell me who it was!'

Edgar lowered his eyes. 'It was a Boy Scout. I don't know his name.'

'A Boy Scout! Oh, man, you're incredible! Don't you know that? You're just too fucking *much*! He blows away a Boy Scout, instead of me!'

Edgar thumped his fist against the wall of the cell and roared, 'It's not funny! Damn you – it's not funny!' McManus stopped laughing and frowned. 'I'm sorry, man. I didn't mean to upset you. But you have to admit it's beautiful.'

'Beautiful?' said Edgar disgustedly.

'Yeah. You know – poetic justice.'

Edgar turned his head away. 'If there was any kind of justice in this world, *you'd* be lying in that morgue, instead of that innocent kid.'

McManus shrugged. 'Come on, man. Don't be so mad. There isn't nothing you can say that's going to bring him back – now is there?'

Edgar didn't answer. He felt as if he had rubbed his face in a bucket of wet grit. Tired, dispirited, and anxious.

'I mean – death comes to all of us, in time, doesn't it?' said McManus. 'Especially now.'

He got up off his bunk and walked around the confines of the cell. 'I mean – you and me, we're lucky we're inside here, instead of outside there on the streets. Out there – well, I mean, *wow*. It could *be per-il-usss*!'

Edgar looked up. 'What do you mean by that?'

Shark McManus chewed his gum equably. 'It's the *plague*, man. How long have you *been* in here?'

'The plague?'

'It's all over Jersey. Everybody's supposed to lock themselves at home, man, and not go out. They got the National Guard patrolling the state line, and if you try to leave, you get blasted. It's true! I was out there ripping off a short, and that's why they pulled me in.'

Edgar Paston stared at Shark McManus for a moment, and then said, 'No – that's nonsense. My wife was here just a few hours ago. She didn't say anything about it. And why haven't the police told me?'

McManus shrugged. 'I don't know. It all happened real quick. They knew they had a couple of sick people in Atlantic City, but then I guess a few people panicked, and kind of brought the plague up this way.'

'But – Tammy!' said Edgar. 'My kids! They're out there!'

Shark McManus didn't look at all fazed. 'Don't worry about it, man. *Everybody's* out there, excepting us.'

Edgar Paston went to the bars and shouted for the guard.

'Forget it, man,' said McManus. 'This whole joint is practically empty. They got all their guys out on the street, picking up the stiffs. I aint joking, man. I saw a couple of stiffs myself, out by the crossroads.'

Edgar Paston turned on McManus. 'Kid,' he said, 'if you're fooling me, so help me I'll tear your head off.'

Shark McManus simply smiled. 'I aint fooling.'

'In that case, we have to get out of here.'

'Why? This is the safest place.'

'What you seem to forget is that my wife and kids are out there.'

'Man – there's nothing you can do. Even if you get back home, they won't let you out of the state.'

Edgar Paston thumped on the bars of the cell. 'That's not the point. The point is that I'm a father, and my family's at risk. I have to *be* there!'

Shark McManus lay back on his bunk and thought for a while. Edgar shouted a few times, but when the prisoner in the next-door cell finally told him to keep his fucking yapper shut, he went back to his bunk and sat there with a gray, worried face, and kept silent.

An hour passed. Edgar Paston lay on his side for twenty minutes and dozed, but the light still glared in his eyes, and he had the added irritation of Shark McManus' endless whistling. He sat up and scratched his head.

'Are you awake, man?' said McManus.

'Yes, I'm awake.'

'Listen, man – do you really want to get out of here?'

'What do you suggest I do? Tear the cell door down with my bare hands?'

'It doesn't have to be that complicated. If you want to get out of here, I can get you out. But you have to make me a promise.'

Edgar eased himself down off his bunk, and looked at Shark McManus like a man who's found a dead cat under his bed.

'A promise?' he said. 'To *you*?'

Shark McManus pulled a face. 'It's the only way, man. Either you make the promise, or you stay here.'

'But the whole reason I'm in here is because of you!'

'That's the deal. No ifs or buts or maybes.'

Edgar lowered his head, and sighed. 'What's the promise?'

'All you have to do is take me with you. I need wheels and I need some respectable support. With your image and my know-how, we can get out of Jersey and into Manhattan, and the way they say it on the news, it looks like Manhattan's a kind of a plague-free zone, and they aint letting anyone catch it.'

'You can really get me out?'

'Sure. Do you promise?'

'Well…'

'It's up to you, man. Me, I don't have no family at all. I could sit here for ever and it wouldn't bug me.'

Edgar Paston looked serious. 'What you're asking me to do is to go back on everything I think about people like you,' he said quietly. 'I think I'd rather get help from a snake.'

Shark McManus grinned. 'That's settled, then. Now, all you have to do is lie on your bunk and start shaking and sweating and moaning.'

'What the hell are you talking about?'

'Just do it, man. Shake and sweat and moan.' Reluctantly, Edgar Paston climbed up on to his bunk again, and lay back. He made his hands tremble, and started to wail feebly.

Shark McManus looked at him in exasperation. 'I said

shake and sweat and moan, man. You're supposed to be *sick*. You're supposed to be *dying*. You sound like you didn't do nothing worse than walk into a smelly public toilet.'

Edgar, more convincingly, shouted, 'Ohhh! Oh, *God*, I'm dying, oh God! *Ohhh…!*'

That was when Shark McManus yelled for the guard. He didn't call politely like Edgar had done. He screamed '*Guuuaaarrrddd!!*' at the highest pitch of his lungs, and straight away the duty cop came running down the corridor with his keys jangling.

'What's all the goddamned noise?'

'Guard,' panted McManus. 'You have to get me outta here! This guy's got *plague*! Look at him – he's dying!' The guard peered anxiously through the bars. Edgar was twisting and groaning and clutching the bedclothes, trying to sound as if he was making his last struggle to fight off a virulent, fast-breeding disease.

His performance was convincing enough to make the guard unlock the cell door, and walk over to take a suspicious look at him. Edgar redoubled his cries and moans, and rolled his eyes up into his head so that only the whites were exposed.

Shark McManus softly stepped up behind the guard and hooked his revolver, pickpocket-style, out of his holster. Then he called, 'Okay, man, the plague's over for now!'

The guard swung around, reaching for a revolver that wasn't there. McManus was holding the gun in both hands, and there was a wan grin on his foxy face.

'Throw your keys down,' he said. 'On the floor, man, and no shit!'

The guard did as he was told. Edgar got down off his

bunk, and stood uncertainly beside Shark – a reluctant lawbreaker who found himself increasingly committed to evading justice. He tried to smile reassuringly at the cop, but the cop just glared at him, and said nothing.

They locked the guard in their own cell, and walked swiftly and quietly along the corridor to the stairs.

Upstairs, treading as silently as they could, they found that McManus was right. The police station was almost deserted, except for a switchboard operator who was sitting behind a glass division with his back to them, busily dealing with emergency calls. They crossed the polished lobby, and they were out through the swing doors and into the night before anyone could notice.

'You see,' said McManus, 'it's a piece of cake.'

Edgar said nothing. Now he was out of jail, he felt less inclined to keep McManus with him. But a promise was a promise – and even more persuasive than Edgar's honor was the fact that McManus was now armed. Edgar said, 'This way,' and they began to walk through the night towards the crossroads.

They kept as close as they could to buildings and shadows, but even Edgar doubted if anyone was out looking for them. The night was different – there was a curious atmosphere about it that made him both excited and fearful. He could hear ambulance sirens warbling along the highway to Newark, and there was hardly any traffic around at all. A couple of police cars passed them by, and they squeezed themselves in the doorway of a delicatessen, but the cars were silently speeding on a more important errand, their red lights flashing urgently through the dark.

'How far is your house now?' asked Shark McManus.

'You know that when they start looking, that's the first place they're gonna check up on.'

'Just around the next corner,' panted Edgar. 'That's it – the one with the hacienda ironwork.'

McManus nodded. 'Nice residence, man. Looks like it pays to run a supermarket.'

Edgar glanced at him and said nothing. McManus added, edgily, 'Well, I guess you have to make allowances for accidental damage.'

Edgar rang the door-chimes. There was a long pause, and for a moment he thought that Tammy had gone away, or was lying upstairs dead. But then the light went on in the hall, and she came to the door in her pink dressing-gown and curlers.

'Edgar! What's happened? Did they let you out?'

Edgar stepped quickly inside the house, hurried Shark McManus in after him, and closed the door. He kissed Tammy, and held her close to him, for a moment too overwhelmed to speak.

'Er— Tammy, this is someone who helped me.'

'Someone who *helped* you? What do you mean?'

'We just broke out of the jail. The plague is everywhere, Tammy, and they're not even looking for us. We have to get away.'

Tammy was incredulous. 'You broke *out*? But *why*?'

'Tammy, we have to get away. Shark says there are bodies in the streets – out at the crossroads. The plague is everywhere. There are people dying like flies.'

'That's true, ma'am,' nodded McManus. 'Flies.'

Tammy looked from Shark to Edgar and back again. 'It said on the news it was okay. They said the state was in quarantine, and that nobody was supposed to leave, but it was all right if you stayed indoors.'

Shark shook his head. 'Baloney. I been out on the street and I seen it. This thing kills you like you wouldn't believe. I saw four stiffs on main street alone. I rolled a couple of 'em for jewelry. They must have died instant.' Tammy frowned anxiously at Shark, and said, 'Edgar – is this boy a criminal?'

Shark held out his hand. 'Oh, don't you worry about me, ma'am. I'm strictly from petty larceny. You know – phone booths, that kind of stuff. I just came along with your husband here to *help*.'

Edgar took Tammy's arm, and gripped it firmly to communicate his tension and his seriousness. 'Darling – this is our only chance. Shark knows the streets, and how to avoid the law. He got me out of jail in about five minutes. I swear it. Apart from that, he has a gun.'

Shark waved his heavy black police .38. 'You see? Fully loaded, too!'

Tammy looked at Shark and she saw in his eyes the cold concealed threat that even Edgar hadn't detected yet. 'I see,' she said quietly. 'In that case, I suppose I'd better get the children ready.'

Edgar could see she was upset. He reached for her hand again as she turned to go upstairs. 'Tammy,' he said, 'you have to see that this is the only way.'

Tammy didn't turn around. 'If you say so, Edgar.'

She went upstairs, and Edgar watched her go, biting his lip.

Shark, tucking his revolver back in his pants, said, 'Hey, man, I hope I haven't caused you any domestic whatsitsname.

You know? I may rip off a few stores now and then, but I aint no homebreaker.'

Edgar shook his head. 'I don't think you could break us up if you tried, Shark. Tammy and me – well, people say we're inseparable.'

Shark grinned. 'That's cute, man. I love a story with a happy ending.'

It didn't take Tammy long to get everything packed. She loaded the Mercury wagon with canned food, blankets, medical supplies, water, soft drinks and spare clothes. Shark McManus kept a lookout for police cars, but the streets of Edgar Paston's tidy suburb were silent under the early-morning stars, and the only sign of life was a neighbor's curtain, twitching suspiciously as they prepared to leave.

At three-fifteen, they locked up the house. Chrissie and Marvin, yawning, climbed into the back of the car with Tammy, while Edgar drove and Shark McManus sat next to him. Shark kept his revolver resting on his lap. He was behaving amiably, but he was also making it clear that any interference or argument would not particularly amuse him. They kept the radio playing in case there was any news of National Guard blockades or possible escape routes from Jersey.

Every half-hour, there was a plague bulletin, and a repeated message telling people what to do if they thought they had plague. The message was sober, but it was also absurdly optimistic, and if you didn't know how terrifyingly quickly the plague had spread across the Eastern seaboard, you could have been forgiven for thinking that your pallor, your pains and your chronic diarrhea were nothing worse than a severe tummy bug.

The Pastons and Shark McManus drove through the pallid night into the early dawn. They were flagged down once by a motorcycle cop just outside Jersey City, but he seemed more interested in checking Edgar's driver's license than questioning their destination. He looked around the station wagon a couple of times, and then waved them on. He was obviously tired out after a night's duty.

The radio said, 'Now, it's important not to let your anxiety about this epidemic prompt you into ill-considered action. The federal authorities in charge of this situation say that the best thing you can do – safer for your family and safer for your neighbors – is to stay home. If you do not have sufficient foodstuffs to last you – well, simply wave a makeshift flag or banner from your windows, and your local police department will bring you supplies. Stay at home, folks – it's the sensible way, and it's the safest way.'

Tammy said, 'They're bound to stop us and send us back home. Edgar, why don't we just turn back? Please!'

Shark McManus turned in his seat. 'Of course they'll stop us. But if we use our noodles, they won't turn us back. Now relax, will ya? I have some brainwork to do.'

Tammy said, 'Edgar – tell him we're turning back!'

But Edgar said nothing, and kept on driving through the outskirts of dreary Jersey City – through the silent, deserted suburbs – with the emasculated obedience of a man who knows he will never have the courage to argue against a gun.

Shark McManus, chewing gum noisily and repetitively, directed Edgar through the streets of Jersey with laconic expertise. It was a dead city of parked cars and wind-blown garbage, and the gradually-brightening sky only made its shabbiness look worse.

Tammy sat there, pale-faced, with dark rings under her eyes, and the two children silently dozed, with heads lolling against the seat. Tammy was coming along because Edgar was her husband and she was Edgar's wife, but – with a strange kind of internal tension that she had never felt before – she was beginning to suspect that Edgar was not the man she had once thought him to be.

She even wondered if he had shot that Boy Scout out of something more than the righteous defense of property and the American way – out of violence, even, and calculated hatred. A bond of some sort – an understanding – seemed to have grown up between Edgar and this hoodlum Shark McManus. She looked at the back of her husband's neck as he drove and it looked like the back of a stranger, someone she didn't love very much at all.

At five-thirty in the morning they stopped. She opened her eyes and realized she'd been sleeping. They were third or fourth in a line of cars that was being checked by police and National Guardsmen by the entrance to the Lincoln Tunnel.

'Edgar,' she said. 'What's happening?'

Edgar didn't turn around. 'Lincoln Tunnel,' he said flatly. 'We got as far as here, and we didn't get stopped by the cops once. We can thank Shark for that.'

'That's right, ma'am,' grinned Shark McManus. 'Right through them back-streets like rabbits through a warren. Any time you want to get yourself out of a jam, just call on Shark McManus, and you're saved. Service with a smile.'

Tammy said, 'They won't let us through here, whatever happens.'

Shark pointed across the gray ruffled waters of the

Hudson, to the gray spectral spires of Manhattan. This morning, the city looked like a ghostly mirage of itself – an oasis of purity in a desert of disease.

'You see that?' he said, smiling lopsidedly. 'That's where we're headed, ma'am, and aint nobody going to stand in our way.'

Two cops in amber sunglasses strode up to their car and signaled for Edgar to roll down his window. They looked tired, but tough, and they had four or five armed National Guardsmen backing them up.

'Hi, folks,' said the cop, checking the inside of the car. 'Can I ask where you come from, and where you believe you're headed?'

'We came from Elizabeth, New Jersey,' said Edgar, in a dry voice.

'And we're headed for *there*,' put in Shark, nodding towards Manhattan.

The cop looked thoughtful. Behind him, one of the Guardsmen was yawning.

'I'm sorry, folks,' said the cop, 'but we have emergency regulations in force right now. Nobody is permitted to leave the state of New Jersey, and nobody is permitted to enter Manhattan.'

Edgar Paston lowered his head tiredly. 'What you're saying is, we have to turn around and go home?'

'I'm afraid that's the message, folks,' said the cop.

Edgar turned to Shark. 'Looks like we don't have any option,' he said.

Shark shook his head. 'Life is full of options, man.'

He produced the police .38 from under the seat, cocked it, and pointed it straight at Edgar's head, a half-inch from his right ear. The two cops quickly stepped back, and drew their pistols.

One of them called, 'Hey, George! Trouble!' to the National Guardsmen. The men lifted their rifles, and two of them ran across to the other side of the road to keep the Pastons covered.

'Okay, kid!' yelled one of the cops, in a rough voice. 'Don't be a dead wise guy! Throw the gun out, and come out of there with your hands up!'

'Start the engine, Edgar,' hissed McManus.

'What?' said Edgar faintly.

'Start the fucking engine. Get this heap moving.'

'They'll kill us.'

'No, they won't. They're good guys. Now get moving.'

Edgar hesitantly reached for the ignition keys, and started the engine. Shark screamed, '*If any of you guys fires a single shot, this dummy gets it in the brain! Just one shot, you hear!*'

Tammy said, 'Please – you don't know what you're doing!'

'Of course I know what I'm doing,' said Shark. 'I'm getting us into Manhattan. Now move your ass, Edgar, or I'll blow your head off!'

Slowly, the Mercury wagon rolled down the gradient towards the tunnel. Two or three police and National Guardsmen jogged along beside it, while the rest of them ran back to their patrol cars, started them up, and tailed the Pastons at a circumspect distance.

As they entered the tunnel, a police bullhorn gave them a raucous message, weirdly distorted by echoes and half-drowned by the draft that blew through the tunnel from the Manhattan shore.

'Listen, kid! Throw out the gun! You don't have a chance! We have both ends of the tunnel sealed! You'll never get away with it! Throw out your gun and you won't get hurt!'

Tammy was sobbing. Chrissie and Marvin sat white and frightened. Only Shark was relaxed. He held the .38 steadily against Edgar's head, and chewed gum as casually as if he were propping up a street corner.

'Come on, Edgar,' he coaxed. 'Drive a little faster, man.'

Edgar speeded up. He could see the black and white police car, fifteen or twenty yards behind him, with all its lights on. They were going too fast now for the jogging cops and guardsmen to keep alongside, and McManus even found time to wave to them.

'So long, suckers! See you in the city!'

The drive through the Lincoln Tunnel seemed endless. As they went deeper under the Hudson, it seemed to Tammy that it was more like the end of the world than ever. There were tears running down her face, and her hands were tightly clenched in her lap.

Gradually, they perceived the gray light of morning ahead of them, washing wanly down the tunnel gradient. They also saw the police cars pulled across the roadway, and the armed officers waiting for them.

'Okay,' said Shark, 'this is the difficult part. Stay cool and everyone is going to be fine.'

'What do you want us to do?' asked Edgar, in a numb voice.

Shark peered along the tunnel towards the roadblock.

'There aint no way we're going to *smash* our way through there, so we're going to have to *walk*. Just before you get to the roadblock, pull up sharp. Then we all get out of the car at once, and we stroll in a bunch towards the cops, and through. I want *you* in front, Edgar, and I'm going to have this piece right up against your skull. Then I want the missis and the kids all around me, so none of those police marksmen starts taking pot-shots. You understand?'

Edgar nodded. They were only seventy yards away from the roadblock now. He could see the police squatting down behind their cars, gripping their guns in readiness. The patrol car that had been tailing them all the way through the tunnel edged closer, and its headlights dazzled Edgar in his rear-view mirror.

They rolled nearer and nearer the roadblock. The patrol car behind them was almost touching their rear bumper.

'Stop,' said Shark McManus, and opened his door.

There was an echoing silence. Shark beckoned Edgar to shift himself across the front seat, and pulled him out through the passenger door. Then he gripped the back of Edgar's shirt-collar with one hand, and pressed the .38 against his skull with the other.

'*Don't anyone move!*' he yelled. '*One move and this guy gets it!*'

Then he snapped at Tammy, 'Come on, ma'am. Get your butt out of that car and stand here.'

Tammy opened her door. It was never recorded what the New York police thought she was going to do, or whether they had any reason to believe she might be armed. But there was a sudden echoing crackle of shots, and the rear windows of the Mercury were smashed into milk and blood. Edgar yelped, and tried to reach the car, but McManus fiercely tugged him away, and kept the gun pressed to his head.

'*Don't shoot!*' screamed McManus. '*One more shot and I kill him!*'

The police held their fire. Awkward, crab-like, holding Edgar tight against him, Shark McManus shuffled towards them. One of the cops raised his gun, but the lieutenant in charge waved him back.

There was silence as Shark McManus and Edgar Paston made their way slowly up the Lincoln Tunnel towards daylight. They were covered every foot of the way, but the police had not yet been given instructions to fire on potential plague carriers, and they let them pass.

'Have them followed,' said the lieutenant impatiently. 'They can't walk around like Siamese twins for the rest of their lives. The minute that kid drops his guard, I want him hit.'

He turned back to the Mercury wagon. A young paramedic was opening the doors, and easing Tammy and the children out. There was blood everywhere. Tammy had been hit in the left breast and left shoulder. Chrissie had been hit in the ear, and Marvin had been hit twice in the chest. They were all still alive, but the doctor was shaking his head and looking pessimistic.

'Do I *have* to take them back to Jersey?' he asked the lieutenant. 'Those few extra minutes are going to make all the difference.'

The lieutenant shrugged. 'It's the rules, Jack. Nobody gets into Manhattan, alive or dead. I'm sorry.'

'Christ,' said the doctor. 'You shot 'em.'

The lieutenant grunted. 'Sure. But I didn't infect 'em.' The doctor nodded towards the slowly-disappearing figures of Shark McManus and Edgar. 'What about those two?'

'We'll get 'em. Just stick to what you're good at. Band-Aids and lint.'

Long after Shark McManus and his hostage had disappeared from sight, the police could hear Edgar weeping, his sobs echoing and distorted down the empty tunnel, like the cries of a lonesome seal.

One of the four people who had died of plague on the main street of Elizabeth, New Jersey, on Friday night, was a 52-year-old insurance salesman from Hoboken named Henry Casarotto. The pain of his dying had been so intense that he had bitten his own left hand, and his infected sputum had dribbled on to his fingers and his red signet ring. His signet ring, New Jersey police discovered, had been removed by a looter sometime after his death.

They had no way of knowing that it was now on the right hand of Shark McManus, and so they had no way of warning the detectives and patrolmen who followed McManus along West 39th Street on Saturday morning that their only possible hope of survival was to shoot first, and worry about police procedure later.

It was six minutes after six o'clock, and the plague had arrived in Manhattan.

Three

O n Sunday afternoon, it began to rain. The temperature
dropped six or seven degrees, and there was a heavy,
cloudy wind from the sea. Dr. Petrie drove northwards up
the Atlantic Coast of New Jersey with Adelaide fast asleep
beside him, and Prickles singing softly to herself in the back.

The plague had stricken New Jersey swiftly and
relentlessly, as if the living breath had been stolen from the
whole seven thousand square miles of it in one night. Bodies
lay prone on the rain-slicked roads, just where they had
fallen. Cars and trucks were abandoned in the middle of
the highway, with their drivers sitting like pallid waxworks
behind the wheel. They passed a few other cars, driving
aimlessly through the wet afternoon, but almost every town
they came to was deserted, silent and strewn with bodies.

Leonard Petrie drove through Perth Amboy at five-
forty-five, and calculated on reaching Manhattan before
it grew too dark. The rain lashed against the windshield,
and the tires made a sizzling noise on the concrete highway.
He sucked a peppermint, and watched the wipers flopping
backwards and forwards – trying to think of diseases and
diagnoses he should have remembered from medical school,
just to keep himself from closing his eyes and dropping off

to sleep. Prickles sang, 'There was an old woman tossed up in a blanket... Seventeen times as high as the moon.'

The radio, strangely, was silent – except for whoops and squeaks and whistles and the occasional burst of Morse. He had picked up regular broadcasts from New York stations until about lunchtime, when they had suddenly faded. He had had no news of the plague now for almost six hours, and no idea if Manhattan Island had been sealed off, or if it was still possible for refugees to cross the Hudson and seek sanctuary.

He felt as if the whole world had died around them – as if they were consigned to drive for the rest of their lives down dull, rainy streets of empty cities, searching for an America that had gone for ever, and could never be found again.

Every now and then, he saw helicopters beating across the windy sky, and he tried flashing his headlights at them. One of them had seen him, and had circled noisily overhead for a few minutes, but then it had heeled away and headed westwards like all of the others. The plague had made people even more suspicious and violent and remote than ever before.

Whenever he had visited New York before, Dr. Petrie had always flown into LaGuardia. He remembered the glittering spires of the Empire State and the Chrysler Building, and the sparkle of traffic along Roosevelt Drive and the Triborough Bridge approaches. But now, as the World Trade Towers loomed out of the murky dusk, and the skyline of Wall Street and downtown Manhattan emerged from the rain behind them, he realized with a sensation of eerie apprehension that the city was in darkness. As far as he could see across the choppy black waters of the Hudson, Manhattan Island was a sinister castle in the sea, with buildings that stood like pale and ancient ramparts, gleaming dimly through the low clouds and the teeming rain. Not a light winked anywhere.

He pulled the car to the side of the street and switched off the engine. The sound of rain pattering on the vinyl roof was the only sound there was in the whole world. Dr. Petrie rubbed grit from his eyes and leaned his head forward in exhausted resignation. For the first time in days, he didn't know what to do, or which way to turn.

Adelaide stirred, and opened her eyes. 'Leonard?' she said. 'What is it? Why have you stopped?'

Dr. Petrie looked up. Then he nodded towards the distant skyline. Adelaide blinked her eyes and peered into the gloom.

'Leonard...' she said. 'That's New York! Leonard, we've made it!'

She reached over happily and kissed him. But he gently pushed her away, and pointed out into the dusk.

'Look again.'

She frowned. 'What's happened?' she said. 'Where are the lights?'

He shook his head. 'They could have had a power failure. It's happened before.'

Adelaide stared at him. There was an uncomfortable silence between them that was prolonged by their mutual refusal to acknowledge what had happened. Finally Adelaide said, 'It's the plague, isn't it? They've caught it here.'

Dr. Petrie nodded. 'Yes,' he said huskily. 'I expect they have.'

'What are we going to *do*?' she asked. 'Oh God, Leonard,

we can't go on running away for ever. The plague seems to spread faster than we can move.'

Dr. Petrie coughed. 'I don't know. I just don't know what to do. I suppose in the end we'll catch it like everybody else.'

'We haven't caught it yet.'

Dr. Petrie stared at the dribbles of rain coursing down the windshield. 'I don't know whether that's a blessing or not. What's the use of staying alive when there's nobody else around to make it worthwhile? What does a doctor do when all his patients are six feet underground?'

Adelaide leaned over and kissed him. 'Leonard, you're tired. You've been driving for days. Don't get depressed.'

Quite unexpectedly, Dr. Petrie found himself weeping. It was years since he'd last cried. Adelaide watched him tenderly and said nothing.

'I'm sorry,' he said, blowing his nose. 'That was ridiculous.'

Adelaide shook her head. 'No, it wasn't. You have a lot of things to cry for.'

'It doesn't help solve our problem.'

'It might do. It might stop you from bottling all your feelings up, and turning yourself into a nervous wreck. You've had so much to contend with.'

'I'm a doctor. Doctors don't get sick.'

Adelaide smiled. 'Don't you believe it.'

Prickles, who had been sleeping on the back seat, stirred and yawned. 'Is it time for *Star Trek* yet?' she said, sitting up.

Adelaide pulled a face at her. 'How can you watch *Star Trek* in a car?'

'I forgot,' said Prickles, rubbing her eyes. 'I was having a dream I wasn't in a car.'

'Anyway,' said Adelaide, 'having no television is probably the best thing that ever happened to you. All that garbage they put on for kids. And think of your health. Think of all that radiation you get from sitting in front of color TVs. Not to mention the eyestrain.'

Dr. Petrie was just about to start up the car again, but he paused. He turned to Adelaide and said, 'What?'

She was confused. 'What do you mean?'

'What was that you just said?'

'I don't know. Eyestrain, something like that.'

'Before that.'

'Oh, you mean radiation?'

'That's right. Radiation! Radiation from color TVs!'

Adelaide said brusquely, 'I wish you'd kindly explain what radiation has got to do with anything.'

'I don't know precisely,' said Dr. Petrie. 'But do you remember what they said on the radio about certain people being less prone to plague than others? Children was one category, and so were ConEd power workers, and doctors.'

'You've lost me.'

'No, it's very simple. That was what I was trying to work out before. I was trying to think why Anton Selmer and I should both escape the plague, even though we were heavily exposed to it. There were one or two other doctors at the hospital, too, who seemed to be immune. Now you mention *children*, sitting in front of color TVs. How many hours of television does the average American kid watch per day?'

'Don't ask me. Six or seven?'

Dr. Petrie nodded. 'Right – that's a lot of television, and a lot of radiation. And that's what Dr. Selmer and I had in common, and what we've all got in common with certain types of power workers, and others. We were supervising X-Rays, and we must have picked up a mild dose of radioactivity.'

Adelaide thought about it. 'It's a *theory*, isn't it?' she said. 'I mean, it's better than no theory at all.'

Dr. Petrie started up the car, and they pulled away from the curbside.

'It could be nonsense, but it's the only thing that seems to fit. I mean, if the plague has been mutated into a super-plague, maybe it was mutated by radioactivity. In which case, radioactivity seems to be the only thing that can ward it off.'

They drove through the rain towards the Holland Tunnel entrance.

'Are you going into Manhattan?' Adelaide asked.

Dr. Petrie nodded. 'I guess we have to. They can't have had the plague for very long, and if I've got some kind of theory about curing it, I think I really have to tell someone.'

'But Leonard—'

'What's the matter? Don't you want to go?'

'Leonard, it's not a *question* of wanting to go. Look at it – it's dark and it's getting darker. That city's bad enough when it has lights. It's going to be a jungle in there. You can't take Prickles into that.'

Dr. Petrie slowed the car and took a long left-hand curve. The rain fell through the light of their headlamps in a careless pattern.

'Adelaide,' he said quietly, 'I don't see that we have any choice. All we have to do is find someplace secure to stay for the night, and then tomorrow we can get in touch with the hospitals. As long as I can tell someone about this radiation theory, we're okay. Then we can leave.'

'Leonard,' said Adelaide, 'I'm *frightened*. Can't you understand that?'

He glanced at her. 'Don't you think I'm frightened, too?'

'Then why go? We could skirt around New York altogether, and drive up to the Catskills. We could be safe there. You said before that we were going to find ourselves a place to stay until the plague was all over.'

Dr. Petrie nodded. 'I know.'

'Then *please*, Leonard.'

They had almost reached the tunnel entrance. For a moment he was tempted to turn around, and escape from the plague for good. They could drive upstate, and into Canada, and leave America to the ravages of fast-breeding bacilli and whatever fate was in store for her. But then he shook his head.

'Adelaide,' he said, 'I've only got a theory, but maybe nobody else has put two and two together in quite the same way. Maybe this could help to cure the plague, or slow it down, and if it does that, how can I leave Manhattan with a clear conscience? There are seven million people in this city, Adelaide, and if I only saved a seventh of them, that would be a million people. Can you imagine saving the lives of one million people?'

Adelaide lowered her head. 'Do you think, Leonard, that even *one* of those million people would stick their neck out to save *you*?'

'I don't know. That's irrelevant.'

'It's not irrelevant! You're risking your life to save people you don't even know, and who would probably leave you to die in the gutter if it meant putting themselves out. Leonard, you're not a miracle worker, you're not a *saint*! I know you want to be famous – but not this way! What's the use of being famous when you're dead?'

Dr. Petrie was straining his eyes, trying to see the tunnel entrance. He stopped the car and shifted it into Park.

'It's nothing to do with fame, Adelaide. If anything, it's to do with shame. I ran out on Anton Selmer, and left him to cope with the plague alone. If you really want to know the truth, I'm ashamed of myself. I feel I've betrayed something.'

She looked at him carefully. 'Is that why you tried to shoot that security guard in the car park? Because you were ashamed of yourself?'

'Probably, I don't know.'

'Oh, Leonard.'

They sat in silence for a while, and then Dr. Petrie said, 'If you want to stay behind, darling, you'd better stay. But I've got to go into the city, and that's all there is to it. I love you, you know.'

'Do you?'

He nodded.

'I don't know whether to believe you or not,' she said. She paused, and her eyes were glistening in the darkness. 'But I'll come. If that's what you want, I'll come.'

Prickles interrupted. 'Have we got to that place yet?'

'What place, honey?'

'Unork.'

Adelaide laughed. 'It's *New York*, not Unork. Yes, honey, we're almost there. Daddy's just going to take a look-see, and make sure this tunnel's okay. Aren't you, Daddy?'

Dr. Petrie grinned. 'Sure. I won't be long. Just hang on in there.'

He took his rifle and climbed cautiously out of the car.

It was so wet and gloomy as he walked up to the entrance to Holland Tunnel that he couldn't see what had happened at first. A large armored police van was parked diagonally across the road, and two black and white police cars were parked on the curb. A torch was shining dimly somewhere behind the cars, but Dr. Petrie couldn't see anyone around. Rain spattered into his face and seeped into his shoes.

'Hallo!' he called. 'Is there anyone there?'

There was a long rainswept silence. Across the river, in the murky graveyard of Manhattan, he thought he heard the brief echoing wail of a siren, but he couldn't be sure.

He walked up to the van, and peered into its rain-beaded window. Inside, huddled on the seats, were five or six policemen, and they were all dead. Dr. Petrie circled around the cars, holding his rifle at the ready and found a seventh cop, hunched-up and pale, with his face in a puddle. In his hand was an electric torch which was still shining. Dr. Petrie stood there in the rain staring at him for a while, and then he turned around and went back to Adelaide and Prickles.

'The plague is here too. They're all dead.'

'Oh, God,' Adelaide sighed.

Prickles said, 'Is this Unork, Daddy? Can we go there?' He looked back at her and smiled. 'We're on our way, honey.'

Dr. Petrie started up the car, and drove around the police van, down the rain-streaked entranceway to the tunnel. All the lights were out, and it was pitch-black, hot, and stifling.

The journey through the tunnel was like a miserable and terrifying ride on a ghost train. The sound of their car made an uncanny roar, and their headlights cast weird shapes and shadows. Dr. Petrie had to drive slowly, because of derelict cars lying wrecked and abandoned, and bodies sprawled on the ground. He had a horror of driving over a corpse by mistake.

It took almost half-an-hour of slow driving to get through the tunnel. He was worried that the car wouldn't make it. It was now caked with dust and grime and dented from countless collisions and rough detours. During the long haul north, Dr. Petrie had begun to wonder if life wasn't anything but narrow back-roads and rutted tracks, and the Delta 88's creaking rear suspension agreed with him.

At last, they were climbing the tunnel gradient towards Manhattan. They emerged on Canal Street in steady rain and darkness. Slowing down to five or six miles an hour, they crept cautiously east towards the Bowery, headlights probing the streets, looking for any sign of life, or death. The dark city enclosed them like a nightmarish maze, hideous, threatening and unfamiliar.

They saw the first bodies on the Bowery. There weren't many, but they lay on the sidewalks and in the road with their clothes sodden and their eyes staring sightlessly at the ground.

'Isn't there anyone around *anywhere*?' asked Adelaide, looking out into the night. 'The whole place seems deserted.'

As they turned uptown, they began to see a few lights – dim candles burning high up in apartment-block windows and hotels. They also saw living people for the first time. Every building's entrance seemed to be locked and patroled by security guards and vigilantes with torches and guns. On Second Avenue, Dr. Petrie pulled the Delta 88 into the curb and shouted to a man standing outside an office block with a rifle and a guard dog.

'Hey! Can you tell me what's happening?'

The man raised his rifle. 'Scram!' he snapped back.

'I just came in from Jersey!' shouted Dr. Petrie. 'I want to find out what's happening!'

The man waved his rifle again. 'If you don't get the fuck out of here, I'm going to blow your head off!'

Dr. Petrie said, 'Listen—'

The man fired one rifle shot into the air. It made a booming sound that echoed all the way down the avenue. Dr. Petrie closed his window, and swung the car away from the curb as quickly as he could.

As they drove further uptown, they drove slowly into hell. In the distance, up beyond 110th Street, there was the rising glow of burning buildings, as white youths ransacked Harlem and the Spanish ghetto. Even through the rain, there was an acrid smell of smoke and burning rubber. All around them, white and colored looters were running wildly through the darkened streets, breaking windows and raiding stores.

Bodies lay everywhere – infected by the plague or killed by muggers. Dr. Petrie saw a black girl lying dead on the sidewalk, her green dress up under her arms. He saw a young boy of fifteen or sixteen who had fallen face-first on to a broken store window.

It was the noise that was the worst. All through the dark canyons of Manhattan there was the screeching and wailing of sirens, the endless smashing of windows, the report of gunfire, and a kind of grating roar, like a demonic beast crunching glass between its teeth, as the panicking population screamed and howled in a frenzy of destruction and despair.

'Do you know where it is? The nearest hospital?' asked

Adelaide tensely, her eyes wide with fear, as they drove across 23rd Street.

Dr. Petrie nodded. 'I want to get to Bellevue, on First Avenue. I visited there once before, and I know one or two of the staff. I just hope to God they're still alive.'

Across the street, they saw a gang of black youths pushing over a Lincoln and setting fire to it. The fuel tank exploded in a hideous glare, and one of the youths was drenched in fiery gasoline. The others stood around and laughed as the boy shrieked and stumbled and tried to beat the fire away from his blazing face.

Adelaide raised her hand to her mouth and retched. 'Oh my God, Leonard, it's unbearable.'

Dr. Petrie reached over and briefly squeezed her shoulder. 'Please, darling. We're nearly there now.'

Suddenly, he heard a siren whooping behind him. He looked in his mirror, and a blue and white police car came flashing and howling down 26th Street, flagging him down in a tire-slithering curve. Dr. Petrie stopped the car and waited.

Two cops, guns drawn, climbed out of the police car and walked towards them. Both men wore respirators and gloves. They stood a few feet away from the Delta 88, and one of them called out in a muffled voice, 'Get out of the car!'

Dr. Petrie opened the door and did as he was told.

'Hands against the roof!' called the cop. Dr. Petrie laid his hands on the wet vinyl. The rain was easing off now, but it was still enough to make him feel uncomfortable.

'Don't you know there's a curfew?' asked the cop. 'What are you doing on the streets?'

'I just came in from Jersey. I didn't know about the curfew.'

'From Jersey?'

'That's right. But we're not infected. None of us has plague.'

'What makes you so sure?'

'We came from Miami originally. We've been exposed to plague for five or six days, and none of us have caught it. I'm a doctor. Would you like to see my ID?'

'Just hold it up.'

Dr. Petrie did as he was told. One of the cops shone a torch on the papers, and leaned forward to read them. 'Seems okay,' he told his buddy.

'Have you had the plague here long?' asked Dr. Petrie. 'I thought you were going to try to seal the whole city off.'

The cop shook his head. 'That's what *we* thought, too, but it seems like some nut managed to get through. Real neighborly, huh? We had the first calls yesterday evening, and it's been total panic ever since.'

'Does everybody have to stay off the streets?'

'It's for your own protection, doctor. Ever since the power went out, we've had every psycho and madman out on the streets like bugs crawling out of a drain.'

'What about the federal government? Are they helping?'

The cop shrugged. 'Who knows? The last I heard, the city of New York was told by the President to act brave, and go down with all flags flying. Jesus – you can't cure it, so what's the use?'

Dr. Petrie said, 'Maybe it can be cured. I'm on my way to Bellevue right now, to talk about it.'

The cop holstered his gun. 'Well, if you can cure it, you deserve to be called a saint.'

Dr. Petrie climbed back into his car, and the cop called

out, 'Watch your step around Bellevue. The medical workers are still out on strike, and it aint exactly a ladies' coffee morning. You got a gun?'

Dr. Petrie nodded.

'Well, take my advice, and use it. The wild animals are out tonight, and I don't like to see innocent people getting themselves torn apart.'

The cop was right about Bellevue. In the dim and unsteady light of emergency generators, a sullen group of medical workers was picketing the casualty department, and there was an angry crowd of relatives and parents trying to force their way through with plague-sick people on makeshift stretchers. Twenty or thirty ambulances were jammed in the street, and more arrived every moment, in a deafening moan of sirens.

Dr. Petrie parked the Delta 88, and helped Adelaide and Prickles out. He collected his automatic rifle and a couple of clips of ammunition, too, and then locked the car. No doubt some marauding gang would break into it and steal what few possessions they had left, but they might be lucky.

With Adelaide carrying Prickles behind him, he pushed his way through the shouting crowds towards the hospital entrance. One woman with disheveled hair and torn tights was shrieking at a picket, 'Bastards! Murderers! You're all going to hell!'

The picket was yelling back, 'That aint true! That aint the truth! You want your sick looked after so much, you do it yourself!'

Another man bellowed, 'What would Jesus have done! Tell me that! What would Jesus have done!'

Dr. Petrie found himself wedged between a burly picket

and a tall black man in a bloodstained alpaca suit. He pushed, but they wouldn't give way. Finally, he lifted his rifle and prodded the picket in the back with it.

The man turned around, sweaty and aggressive, and said, 'Who the fuck are you pushing, Charlie?'

'Out of my way!' Dr. Petrie shouted. 'Just get out of my way!'

'What are you going to do? Shoot?' roared the man. 'You wouldn't have the fucking nerve!'

Dr. Petrie, afraid and angry, fired the rifle at the man's legs. The picket yelled in pain, and dropped to the ground on one knee.

'My foot! *Christ!* You've hit my fucking foot!'

There was blood spattered all over the ground. The crowds heaved back – swaying away from Dr. Petrie and the sound of the shot. He roughly pushed Adelaide and Prickles around the fallen picket, and shoved them in through the cracked glass doors of the casualty department. A security guard, trying too late to keep them out, slammed the doors behind them, and bolted them.

'I'm a doctor,' said Dr. Petrie breathlessly, holding up his papers.

The security guard glared at him. 'A doctor?' he said. 'With a gun?'

'Have you *been* out there?' snapped Dr. Petrie. 'Have you seen what it's like?'

'What do you want?' said the guard. 'Was that shooting out there?'

Prickles was crying. Dr. Petrie said firmly, 'I want to speak to the doctor in charge of the plague. I have some very important information. Can you call him for me, please?'

The security guard looked uncertain. Outside, the pickets were hammering on the door. One of them smashed the glass with a pick-ax handle, and reached in to try and open the locks.

'Seems like you're in *trouble*,' said the security guard. 'I'm sorry, friend, but I can't let you stay here. It's more than my job's worth.'

Dr. Petrie lifted his rifle.

Adelaide said, 'Oh, God, Leonard – no more shooting.'

He didn't listen. Still panting for breath, he told the security guard to lay his revolver on the floor. 'Now call the doctor in charge of the plague,' he said coldly, 'and make it goddamned quick.'

The security guard lifted the phone and pushed buttons. Dr. Petrie kept an anxious eye on the doors while the guard asked the switchboard to connect him with Dr. Murray. The pickets were systematically thumping their shoulders against the frame, and one of the top bolts was already hanging loose from its screws.

Eventually, with a sour face, the guard passed the phone to Dr. Petrie.

'Dr. Murray?' said Dr. Petrie. 'I have to be quick because we have a kind of disturbance down here. My name's Dr. Leonard Petrie, and I'm a physician from Miami, Florida. I know a great deal about the plague from experience, and I also have a theory about treating it. Can I come up and see you?'

Dr. Murray sounded elderly and cautious.

'You say you come from *Miami*? I though they were all wiped out down there.'

'I managed to escape, with my daughter and a friend. I just arrived in New York, and I really have to see you.'

'I'm a busy man, Dr. Petrie.'

'I know that, Dr. Murray. But this could save hundreds of lives. Maybe millions.'

The casualty department doors were almost off their hinges. The pickets were shouting and kicking at the wood and glass. Adelaide was clutching Prickles close, and retreating as far back down the corridor as she could.

'Dr. Murray?' asked Dr. Petrie.

There was a pause. Finally, Dr. Murray said, 'Oh, very well. But I can only spare you five minutes. Come up and see me on the fifth floor, room 532.'

Dr. Petrie put back the phone. Almost at the same moment, the angry pickets burst open the casualty department doors, and scrambled inside with their makeshift weapons.

Dr. Petrie lifted his rifle. The pickets held back, but they watched him intently and closely, and as he stepped away from them down the corridor, following Adelaide, they stalked after him with hard and humorless faces.

'Leonard,' said Adelaide nervously. 'Leonard, they'll kill us.'

Dr. Petrie stopped retreating. He raised the rifle to his shoulder and took a bead on the nearest picket. The men stayed where they were, silent and threatening, but he could sense that they were uncertain.

He said, slowly and loudly, 'You have ten seconds to turn around and get out of here. Then I start shooting, and I don't care what I hit.'

The pickets stayed where they were. For one terrible moment, he thought they were going to call his bluff, and make him open fire. He could feel the sweat running down inside his collar, and his hands were shaking.

'*Do you hear me!*' he shouted. '*Ten seconds!*'

A man with a fire-ax took a pace nearer. Dr. Petrie swung the rifle around and aimed at his head, and the man stopped.

'*Eight seconds!*'

The pickets looked at each other. One of them said, 'Aw fuck it, we'll get him later,' and threw down his chair-leg. One by one, the others did the same.

Quickly, Dr. Petrie took Adelaide by the arm, and led her down the corridor to the stairs. He didn't trust elevators, with the power the way it was.

'Can you climb four flights?' he asked Prickles. Prickles, white-faced and frightened, gave a nod.

They found Dr. Murray in a cluttered office on the fifth floor, talking on the internal telephone, and drinking black coffee out of a plastic cup. He was a gray-haired, intense-looking man, with big fleshy ears and heavy horn-rimmed spectacles.

'Dr. Murray?' said Petrie, putting out his hand. Dr. Murray shook it limply.

'You'd better take a seat,' said Dr. Murray mournfully. 'Just move those papers – there's a chair under there someplace.'

They sat down. Dr. Petrie self-consciously propped his rifle against the side of Dr. Murray's desk, but Dr. Murray didn't register surprise or concern.

'Now,' said Dr. Murray, 'what is it you wanted to see me about?'

'It's the plague,' explained Dr. Petrie. 'It started in Miami, and I saw some of the earliest cases myself, and treated them.'

'With any success?' asked Dr. Murray, dourly.

'None at all. The only thing we discovered was that it

was related to *Pasteurella pestis*, but that it didn't respond to the usual antibiotics or serums.'

'I know that,' said Dr. Murray. 'So what are you trying to tell me?'

Dr. Petrie coughed. 'I'm trying to tell you, Dr. Murray, that even though it's a fast-breeding bacillus with no known antidote – a bacillus that has wiped out almost the entire population of the Eastern seaboard in one week – I haven't caught it.'

'I can see that.'

'You don't understand,' insisted Dr. Petrie. 'I haven't caught it for a *reason*. My daughter hasn't caught it for a reason. My girlfriend hasn't caught it because she has stayed almost exclusively with us, and we're never going to get it.'

Dr. Murray opened a drawer in his desk, took out a pack of stale Larks, and unsteadily lit one up. He kept the cigarette in his mouth, puffing smoke out sideways like a poker player.

'What you're trying to tell me, Dr. Petrie, is that you know why you haven't caught it? Is that it?'

'Exactly. We haven't caught it because we've been exposed to radiation. In my case, it's X-Rays. In my daughter's case, color television. I believe now that my daughter did get a mild dose of plague, but because she was kept away from other carriers, she recovered.'

Dr. Murray took off his spectacles. 'I don't understand you, Dr. Petrie. How can radiation possibly have any effect on a plague bacillus?'

'It can have an enormous effect. It's my supposition that, somehow, radiation reached the raw sewage that was dumped off the Long Island coast, and that *within* the radioactive sewage, the common plague bacillus mutated into a fast-growing and very virulent super-plague. Perhaps further doses of radiation can mutate it further into a harmless form, or slow down its incubation. I don't yet know. I was hoping that you and some of your doctors here could help me find out.'

Dr. Murray thought this over. Then he said, 'Dr. Petrie, I think you have a very interesting notion, there. But what I am *not* is a research bacteriologist. I am trying to run a metropolitan casualty department here, and at the moment, what with the strike and the plague, I'm not making much of a go of it. What you need is a man who can turn your theory into scientific facts – if it's a theory that's any good.'

'Can you suggest anyone?'

Dr. Murray reached for his desk diary, and leafed through the pages.

'There are two very good men,' he said. 'At the moment, they're both fighting each other in court, as I understand it, over some new technique of theirs. But they both have good reputations, and they're both interested in radioactive mutation of bacilli. Here we are – Professor Ivor Glantz – and Professor Sergei Forward.'

'I've heard of Glantz,' said Dr. Petrie. 'A bit of a lone wolf, if I remember.'

'Brilliant, though,' said Dr. Murray. 'If there's any foundation to your theory at all, he can find it.'

'Where do I find *him*?'

'You're very fortunate. He lives on First Avenue, in Concorde Tower. He's a rich man.'

'I didn't know research bacteriologists got rich.'

'They do if their fathers are bankers, and they take out a

patent on self-aborting bacilli for the brewing industry. Ivor Glantz devised the bacillus that made Milwaukee not only *famous* but extremely *profitable*.'

'I see. Perhaps you and I are in the wrong branch of science, Dr. Murray.'

Dr. Murray ignored him. 'I can let you have a note to take to Glantz, on hospital paper. They won't let you into the tower otherwise. Right now, they won't let you into any place at *all* unless you're known.'

'Thank you,' said Dr. Petrie, as the older man unscrewed his pen and scribbled a letter. 'I just hope that we can do something to make your job easier.'

Dr. Murray grimaced. 'There *is* one thing. When you're up at Concorde Tower, you can take that rifle of yours and make a large hole in Kenneth Garunisch.'

'That reminds me,' said Dr. Petrie. 'Is there another way out of this place? I kind of unsettled the medical workers' pickets on the way in.'

Dr. Murray nodded. 'We'll get you out. Would you care for some coffee before you go? My secretary will make you some next door. Right now, I have to get back to the wards.'

When Dr. Murray had left, they sat for half an hour by the window of his secretary's office, sipping hot coffee and staring out over the darkened city. The windows were soundproofed, but they couldn't keep out the endless howling of sirens, and the crackle of shots. The city was black and shadowy, lit here and there by sparkling orange fires. It looked like a medieval vision of the devil's kingdom; a place where demons and beasts roamed in echoing darkness. Not even the stars looked down on the twentieth-century city that had become, at last, the realization of a fifteenth-century nightmare.

Ivor Glantz had just come out of the shower. He was wrapped up in a white toweling bathrobe, and he dabbed his perspiring forehead with a succession of tissues pulled from a Kleenex box.

'Dr. Petrie,' he said, assiduously gathering up sweat, 'I have to say that I admire your courage. You and your lady, *and* your little girl.'

Dr. Petrie, shaved and smelling of Braggi, was sitting on the wide cream-colored 1930s settee, with a large Scotch in his hand. For the first time this week, he felt clean and civilized. Prickles had been dressed up in one of Ivor Glantz's pajama jackets and put to bed in the small bedroom, while Adelaide and Esmeralda were talking in the kitchen, and making supper.

'It wasn't courage,' said Dr. Petrie, smiling tiredly. 'Far from it. It was survival. They burned down Miami, and we had to get out.'

'You think they did that deliberately?' asked Glantz.

'Set fire to the city? I don't know. I don't understand the way the federal government have handled this thing from the very beginning. Down in Miami, we were all beginning to feel like sacrificial lambs.'

Glantz smiled. 'You did well to get out of it, anyway. If you want to stay here for a few days, you're welcome. We have our own power in this building, and we're very secure. This block was designed as a maximum-security project. You saw how tight they've got it defended downstairs.'

Dr. Petrie sipped his Scotch. He was suddenly beginning to realize how utterly exhausted he was. He didn't even know if he was going to be able to stay awake for supper.

'Have you thought about my theory?' he asked.

Ivor Glantz nodded. 'Sure. I was thinking about it in the shower.'

'And how does it grab you?'

Glantz tapped ash off his cigarette. 'It grabs me pretty well, if you want to know the truth. It's one of those theories that's wacky enough to work. You see, most epidemic diseases are sparked off by a particular combination of historical and environmental circumstances. Sometimes the circumstances are so absurd and unusual that you could never predict they were going to happen. But we've had all the ingredients for this epidemic in American society for years, and it only took a couple of odd happenstances to get the whole thing going.'

Glantz got up, walked across to the drinks cabinet, and poured himself a large whiskey.

'Ingredient *one* is plague itself,' he said. 'We have had plague in the United States throughout the twentieth century, and every single year – particularly in the Western states – we suffer plague fatalities. It's endemic in squirrels and rats in the West, and there have been cases reported in Florida, as you probably know.

'Ingredient *two* is the raw sewage – the medium in which plague bacilli were incubating beneath the ocean. The sewage, if you like, was the laboratory in which the bacilli was mutated.

'Ingredient *three* is the radioactivity. Well – we don't have any proof where the radioactivity comes from, but I can guess that radioactive waste might well be dumped into the ocean from industrial processes, or maybe atomic-powered ships and submarines have offloaded uranium fuel in the area where the raw sewage was lying.

'Given those three ingredients, all it took was an unusual climatic situation, with reverse currents and changeable winds, and the epidemic was served up to us on a plate.'

Glantz sat down again, and puffed his cigarette. 'It's a classic epidemic situation, Dr. Petrie, and that's why I believe your theory is right.'

Dr. Petrie nodded wearily.

'The problem is,' said Ivor Glantz, 'that even if it's right, we have to *prove* it's right, and even when we've done that, we still have to find a way to communicate our information to the federal government, and make sure they act on it.'

'Is Manhattan completely cut off?'

'As long as the power is out, yes. They were flying helicopters out of here for most of the day, but I should think they've all been commandeered by now. The same goes for boats. And as long as we've got plague in the city, there isn't anyone who's going to fly in here to bring us out.'

'What are we going to do, then?' asked Dr. Petrie. 'It looks like I wasted my time.'

Glantz shrugged. 'I don't think so, Dr. Petrie. I don't have any test facilities here at home, but I can work out the probability graphs and all the mathematics. I guess we can check your theory to the point where we're sixty-five percent sure about it, and I think that should be enough to convince the government. What we need to discover is the critical level of radioactivity which renders the plague harmless, and then we're all set. Anyone who hasn't caught it already could be given a dose of X-Rays, and they'd be protected.'

'What about pregnant women?' asked Petrie. 'We couldn't give X-Rays to them. The last thing we want to do is cure the plague and wind up with a whole generation of deformed children.'

Ivor Glantz shook his head. 'I don't think the dosage is sufficiently high to make it a problem. But we'll check. Once we're reasonably sure, we can get a message to Washington, or wherever the President is hiding himself, and they can do the basic practical research outside of the plague zone.'

'You seem very confident,' said Dr. Petrie.

'I'm not in the least confident,' Glantz replied. 'But it's the only theory we've got, and we might as well make the best of it.'

'Do you think there's a chance?'

'Oh, sure. Of course there's a chance. There is no bacillus in my long and varied experience that can't be destroyed or mutated into complete harmlessness by the correct application of radioactivity. The same goes for humans, if you must know.'

Dr. Petrie finished his Scotch. 'How long will it take?' he asked. 'The mathematics, I mean.'

Ivor Glantz shook his head. 'Hard to say. Two or three days. Maybe less, maybe more.'

'And meanwhile, the whole of New York just dies?'

'I can't help it, Dr. Petrie. As soon as I've eaten, I'm going to sit right down there and start work, and that's a promise. But I can't work miracles.'

Dr. Petrie stood up and walked over to the window. Sixteen floors below, the streets were dark, blind and chaotic.

He saw red flashing police lights and ambulances, and the smoke from a smoldering store rising almost invisibly into the rainy night sky.

'I sometimes wish it were true,' he said quietly.

'You sometimes wish *what* were true?' asked Glantz.

Dr. Petrie let the drapes fall, and turned back into the room. 'In Miami,' he said, 'they used to joke about me and call me *Saint* Leonard. I just sometimes wish it were true.'

Glantz looked at him oddly.

'Don't worry,' said Dr. Petrie. 'I'm not a religious maniac, and I'm not going out of my mind. But I've spent most of my medical life nursing rich old widows, and now I've suddenly seen that there's so much more to medicine than dishing out placebos to dried-up geriatrics with more money than sense.'

Glantz sniffed. 'Don't knock money,' he said. 'Money makes it easier to have scruples.'

Dr. Petrie rubbed his face exhaustedly. 'I don't know whether I want scruples right now.'

'Have another drink instead.'

Ivor Glantz was pouring Dr. Petrie another large dose of Scotch when Adelaide and Esmeralda came in with a hot egg-and-bacon quiche and a fresh salad. The girls laid knives and forks on the glass coffee table, and they all sat down to eat informally.

'Usually,' said Glantz, 'Esmeralda insists that we eat in the dining-room, with starched napkins tucked under our chins. But tonight we'll make an exception.'

Adelaide said, 'I don't know how we're ever going to thank you for this. It's so bad out on the streets, I thought we'd never get out of it alive.'

'It doesn't take people long to revert to the jungle, does

it?' Ivor Glantz remarked. 'You only have to pour a few drinks down most people, and they start behaving like apes. That's how alcohol works. Layer by layer, it anesthetizes your civilized mind, until you're nothing but a caveman. Or cave-*woman*.'

Esmeralda was slicing quiche. She didn't look up, but handed Dr. Petrie a plateful of food. He smiled at her, because he found her attractive. Her long black curly hair was tied with ribbons, and she was wearing a dark brown satin negligee trimmed with lace and bows. She looked a little pale, but it suited her fine profile. He found himself glancing at the soft mobile way her breasts moved underneath the satin, and her long bare legs.

Adelaide was too tired and hungry to notice. She was looking scrubbed and plain, with no make-up at all, and her brunette hair was tied back in a headscarf. She'd borrowed a pink dressing-gown from Esmeralda, and the color didn't suit her at all. Sexual attraction, thought Dr. Petrie, as he ate his flan, is the unfairest urge ever.

Ivor Glantz washed a mouthful of food down with whiskey. 'To some people,' he said, 'this plague is a blessing.'

Dr. Petrie frowned. 'What do you mean by that? I mean – who could ever benefit from a disaster like this?'

'Oh, you'd be surprised. Our next-door neighbor is Kenneth Garunisch from the Medical Workers' Union. He's been pressing for more pay for his members, because of the dangers of treating plague victims. Then there's Herbert Gaines. You remember Herbert Gaines – the actor? Well, he lives upstairs. He's gotten himself into politics now, and his main plank is that blacks and immigrants have caused the plague, and we ought to vote a right-wing Republican into the White House to get rid of them. Then, of course, there's Sergei Forward.'

Dr. Petrie was puzzled. The way that Ivor Glantz had spoken that name – loudly and vehemently – it had seemed that he was speaking to Esmeralda. But Esmeralda still didn't look up, and carried on eating in silence.

Dr. Petrie said, 'Dr. Murray mentioned him. Isn't he the guy you're—'

'Yes,' said Ivor Glantz. He was still looking at Esmeralda, and not at Dr. Petrie at all. 'He's the guy I'm suing for infringement of patent. Or at least, I *was* suing him for infringement of patent. The plague, among other things, has let him off the hook.'

'You must be pretty galled.'

Glantz turned to Dr. Petrie at last. 'Galled?' he said. 'You bet your ass I'm galled. It's a life's work, right down the river. But that's not the worst part.'

Dr. Petrie glanced from Ivor Glantz to Esmeralda. There was some indefinable tension between them. Esmeralda was still holding her knife and fork, but she wasn't actually eating. Her knuckles were white, and she was staring at her plate as if willing it to disappear into the sixth dimension. Adelaide caught the atmosphere, too, and looked up with a frown.

'The worst part,' said Ivor Glantz, 'was losing a life's loyalty, and a life's love.'

There was a long silence. Then Esmeralda stood up, and took her plate out of the sitting-room and into the kitchen. They heard her scraping her supper down the sink-disposal unit.

'Es!' Ivor Glantz called.

She didn't answer.

'*Es!*' he called again.

She appeared at the kitchen door. 'I'm not very hungry,' she said. 'I think I'll go to bed.'

Ivor Glantz took a deep breath as if he was about to shout something, but then he changed his mind and breathed out again. Esmeralda went off to her bedroom, and, turning to Dr. Petrie, Glantz said, 'How about one more Scotch, doctor? I'm sure you can justify it on medicinal grounds.'

Dr. Petrie passed his glass. He watched Ivor Glantz unstopper the crystal decanter, and pour the drink out.

'Listen, Professor Glantz,' he said gently. 'I don't mean to be personal, but…'

'But what, Dr. Petrie?'

Dr. Petrie shook his head. 'I'm sorry,' he said. 'It's none of my business.'

Glantz handed over his Scotch. 'Of course it's your business. You're a guest here.'

'I didn't mean to pry. It just seemed that, well—'

'I know what it seemed like. Well, it's the truth. I've decided to withdraw my action against Sergei Forward. The reason I've decided to do so is because my stepdaughter is being blackmailed. It appears she was rather *indiscreet*. That's if you want to put it mildly.'

Dr. Petrie sat back. 'Is that the price? Is that what the blackmailers are asking for? Your withdrawal from the case?'

Ivor Glantz nodded. 'Of course. That's why my stepdaughter was set up in the first place. It was a deliberate ploy by Forward to hit me below the belt. I can tell you something, Dr. Petrie – if ever I lay my hands on that Finnish bastard, so help me I'll tear his lungs out and use them for water wings.'

'Surely it wasn't Esmeralda's *fault*?' said Adelaide. 'If she was set up, how can you blame her?'

Glantz swigged whiskey. 'I blame her because she got herself drunk and she let them do what they wanted. Not *once* did she think about me, and what could happen if she got involved in something like that. She lives under my roof, I pay for everything she wears, eats, and wipes her ass with. I bought her an art gallery and two hundred paintings to stock it with. I'm a stepfather in a million, and all she can do is get herself squiffy on two glasses of champagne. Do you know, Dr. Petrie, how much that bacteriological process means to me?'

'What do you mean? Financially?'

'Of course, financially! What do you think this is – the Alexander Fleming Home for needy bacteriologists? Dr. Petrie – over twenty years, that process could have brought me, in royalties and dues and industrial licenses, something in the region of thirty million dollars.'

Adelaide's eyes widened. 'I see what you're talking about. I think *I'd* be sore, too.'

Ivor Glantz shook his head. 'I'm not sore, my dear. I'm out of my goddamned mind with rage.'

Shark McManus started moaning again. He was lying curled-up on the cold plastic tiles of a travel agency's second-floor office on Third Avenue, shivering and sweating in the darkness. From where he lay, he could see the legs of a desk, and a waste-paper basket, and a half-open door. He still clutched his .38, but his sight kept blurring, and he was hurting so bad that he didn't even know if he could pull the trigger or not. Pains like red-hot rakes stabbed into his groin and his stomach, and every now and then a scalding squirt of diarrhea soaked into his jeans.

'*Paston*,' he whispered. 'You still there?'

Edgar Paston stood by the window, pale-faced and perspiring. In the street below he could see gangs of black youths running and shouting and smashing windows.

'I'm here,' he said quietly. He came across the office and bent over McManus with a serious face. 'How do you feel?'

McManus winced. 'Oh, terrific.'

Edgar said, 'Shark, I have to find you a doctor.'

McManus moaned again, and shook his head. 'Where do you think you're going to find a doctor – out *there*? I know you, Paston – you're going to go – straight to the cops – and tell them it was me.'

'Shark, you'll *die*!'

'What the fuck – do you care? I used you – you used me – and your family got wasted.'

Edgar stood straight again.

'I still think I ought to try and find you a doctor. There have to be doctors who wouldn't ask questions.'

McManus almost laughed. But his laughter turned to coughing, and his coughing became gasps of pain.

'Paston – you're such a stupid shit!'

'Don't say that, Shark.'

'Aah… why should you care?' whispered McManus.

Edgar clenched and unclenched his fists. He seemed to be trying to say something that wouldn't quite form itself into coherent words. He wiped his perspiring forehead with his shirt-sleeve, and then he said, 'Shark—'

McManus was moaning. Edgar knelt down beside him, as close as he could, and took his hand.

'Shark, I *do* care.'

Shark's breath smelled bad, and his face, in the gloomy darkness of the office, looked like a white wax death-mask.

'Shark, I don't want you to die.'

Shark slowly moved his head from side to side.

'Thass... bullshit.'

Edgar Paston leaned over the dying boy and held his face in his hands. Shark's eyes were almost closed, and he was breathing thickly and slowly through his parted lips.

'Shark, listen, I have to tell you this. Please, listen, will you? I have to tell you.'

McManus opened his eyes a little wider and stared at Edgar as if he had never seen him before in his whole life.

'I don't suppose you'll understand,' said Edgar. 'But I have to tell you anyway. I know Tammy and the kids were killed, but you have to believe that I don't blame *you*. You were trying to help us, Shark, I know that. It was the cops who killed them. You have to understand that I don't blame *you*.'

The office was so dark that it was impossible to tell if Shark McManus was listening or not. He quivered from time to time, and whimpered, but he didn't answer.

Edgar Paston was crying now. 'Shark,' he said, 'I got it all wrong. I didn't understand. Don't you see? I got it all wrong because *I* was dead and *you* were alive. I didn't recognize you for what you really were. Shark, you've got your *youth*. Look at me. How old do you think I am? Shark, I've never had a youth! It was school, and then it was college, and then it was Tammy and the kids and work. Christ, Shark, you've got freedom and love and confidence and everything, and all I've got is a useless dreary stupid supermarket!'

Shark McManus, after a few moments, seemed to smile. He managed to raise one limp hand and touch Edgar's tears.

'Paston,' he croaked. 'You're such a stupid shit.'

'For Christ's sake, don't *say* that.'

'I *have* to say it, man. It's true.'

Edgar Paston sat up. His voice was unnaturally high, and in an odd way he was almost hysterical.

'*God!*' he shrieked. '*Can't you see how much I envy you?*'

McManus was in less pain now. He gave a few breathy chuckles, and rolled his head to one side.

'Paston,' he whispered. 'I don't want to be envied by you. I think I'd prefer to die.'

Edgar got to his feet, and automatically brushed the dust from the knees of his pants.

'Well, that's too bad,' he said impatiently. 'That's just too bad because I'm going to go right out there and find you a doctor. You're going to get well again and then we'll see. Give me the gun.'

'Paston,' said Shark, 'you're out of your head. You can't go out there.'

'Give me the gun, Shark.'

Edgar bent over and caught hold of McManus' wrist. Shark was too weak to resist him, and he gave up the .38 without a struggle.

'Okay now,' said Edgar, forcefully. 'I'm going out there and I'm going to find you a doctor. Give me an hour. If I'm not back after that time – well...'

'Can I die then?' asked Shark McManus. 'Am I allowed to?'

Edgar leaned over and patted him on the cheek.

'You are not to die,' he said tenderly.

Shark nodded. 'Okay, then. I won't.'

Edgar took the gun and left the office. He walked along the landing to the concrete staircase that led down to the street. As he reached the top step, he heard an unexpected scuffling noise, and he paused. He peered into the darkness, and he could have sworn that he saw something moving. He wished he had a torch.

Feeling his way down step by step, with his hand against the rough concrete wall, he came to the next turn in the stairs. He heard the noise again. There was a high-pitched squeaking, and the patter of feet.

'*Rats*,' he said to himself. 'Oh, Jesus!'

He descended the next few stairs cautiously. The rats scuttled down ahead of him, and he could see their eyes reflecting the dim light from the open street door. He managed to reach the sidewalk, kicking a couple of rats aside, and it was only then that he realized how many there were. The office building was teeming with rats, and so were the streets. Disturbed by the chaotic violence and looting, frightened by fires, aroused by the smell of dead bodies, they were rising from the sewers and electrical conduits of Manhattan in a gray tide.

Edgar ran across Third Avenue and turned down 52nd Street. Now he was out in the open, his confidence was shaken. It was menacing and strange, and the fires that burned through the drizzling rain cast enormous shadows. He had no idea where he could find a doctor, and he peered hopelessly at all the signs and nameplates he saw.

From Third Avenue, he reached Lexington Avenue.

Uptown, he could see immense fires blazing. Whole blocks were alight. Downtown, it was all darkness and savagery. He crossed the street and walked quickly towards Park Avenue, panting hard and clutching his pistol tight.

He didn't see them until he had turned the corner. There were eight or nine of them – marauding black teenagers with clubs and knives and razors. They had raided three hotel bars on the East Side, and they were fiercely drunk. The day before, white hoodlums had come up to Harlem and thrown gasoline bombs in their neighborhood stores and their houses, and they were out to fix honkies and nothing else.

Edgar raised the .38.

'Don't you come a step nearer, or I'll shoot!'

The black kids jeered and laughed. Edgar, holding the pistol in both hands, aimed directly at a silhouetted head.

It went through his mind like an action replay. The supermarket doorway. The laughter in the car park. The shot. One of the kids fell to the ground, without a sound. The rest of them scattered. 'He's dead all right. I got him in the head.'

And while his finger froze on the trigger, a tall black boy in green jeans ducked under his line of fire and stabbed him straight in the face with a broken gin bottle. The glass sliced into his cheeks and mouth, and he dropped the gun on to the sidewalk in a slow-motion twist of agony.

They cut his face up first. He felt knives in his eyes. Then one of them grappled his wet, petrified tongue, and they sliced it off with a razor. The last thing he felt before he died, in a hideous burst of agony, was the broken bottle they forced, laughing, into his rectum.

Shark McManus died that night, too. As he lay on the floor of the office, helpless and weak and soaked in diarrhea, the rats came scampering in. He was so close to death that he scarcely felt them running over him, and at one moment he thought of the kitten his father had given him when he was six, and he opened his arms to embrace the scuttling gray tribe that bit at his flesh and turned his hands into raw bloody strings.

'Paston?' he said hoarsely.

There was no answer. He heard a squeaking, pattering noise that he didn't understand.

'Paston?' he said again.

No answer.

'Paston?'

After the hideous chaos of the night, the morning was gray and silent. The rain stopped, and a smeary sunlight filtered across the East River and into the broken streets. Uptown, fires still burned in Harlem, and the black carcasses of buses and cars were littered all over the streets of the midtown hotel district, smoldering and smashed. The sidewalks were glittering with powdered glass, and amongst it, like frozen explorers caught in a strange kind of snow, were the bodies of plague victims and riot casualties.

One or two police cars patroled the streets slowly and cautiously, driving over rubble and bricks and debris. The cops all wore respirators and goggles, and were heavily armed. There were still a few stray looters around, and they had orders to shoot to kill.

The rats were still in evidence – swarming into abandoned delicatessens and restaurants, and over the corpses that lay huddled up in every street.

Every office block and apartment building was locked and guarded and under siege. But even if the residents were able to keep out the looters and most of the rats, they couldn't protect themselves from the plague. During Monday morning, the fast-breeding bacilli brought painful death to thousands of New Yorkers, transmitted by minute specks of infected saliva. It only took a word of encouragement to pass the plague on, or the touch of a hand in friendship.

Some people died slowly, in prolonged agony, while others succumbed in two or three hours. By midday, almost seventeen thousand people were dead, and several apartment buildings had become silent, pestilent mortuaries. As the people collapsed, the rats scurried in, devouring food and flesh in a suffocating orgy of self-indulgence.

Other people, trapped in elevators since Sunday by the power failure, began to collapse from exhaustion, thirst and lack of air. There was no one to rescue them, and they died in a squalid confusion of darkness and urine.

In the subways, imprisoned in darkened trains, people moaned and cried and waited for the help that would never arrive. Old people and invalids sat in their apartments in front of dead televisions, waiting for nurses who didn't dare take to the streets. Drug addicts, shivering and sweating, haunted the Lower West Side looking for fixes.

Dr. Petrie, up on the sixteenth floor of Concorde Tower, stared down at the city for almost an hour. Adelaide and Esmeralda had taken Prickles to meet the Kavanagh children on the floor below, and Ivor Glantz was locked in his study, laboriously working out the mathematical probability of destroying the plague with radioactive rays. Dr. Petrie drank coffee and tried to relax. He had slept badly, with nightmares of travelling and suffering and violence, but he felt better than yesterday. He was just wondering how long they could survive on the sixteenth floor, without food supplies, or any guarantee that their water or power would hold out.

He was going to pour himself another cup of coffee when there was a rap at the door. He walked across the sitting-room and switched on Ivor Glantz's closed-circuit TV. The building super was standing outside, looking agitated. Dr. Petrie opened the door.

'Hi,' said the super. He remembered Dr. Petrie from the night before, when they had banged on the glass doors of Concorde Tower and shouted to be let in. He was a thin, nervous man with greasy hair and a neatly-clipped mustache. 'Can I come in?'

'Sure. Professor Glantz is working right now, but if it's urgent—'

The super worriedly chewed at his lip. 'It's getting pretty serious, to tell you the truth. I got assistants going round the whole building, informing everyone.'

'What's the problem?'

'Well,' said the super, 'we got quite a crowd outside. You know – people who were caught on the streets when the power went off. They want us to let them in, and they've started cracking the front doors already.'

'How many are there?'

'Well, it's hard to tell, maybe a couple of dozen. I took a look off the roof, and the same thing's happening to other condos, too. I guess quite a few people got caught out last night, and now they want to get back inside.'

'You can't let them in – you know that, don't you?'

Dr. Petrie said. Even if they're residents, they may have plague. This whole apartment building could be wiped out in an afternoon.'

'Well, yes, sir, I know that. But I was trying to figure how to keep them out. They're smashing down the doors, and some of them have guns.'

There was another knock at the door. Dr. Petrie turned around, to see a stocky, bristle-headed man standing in the doorway, wearing a turtle-neck sweater, plaid pants and bedroom slippers. His face was bruised, and he had a magnificent black eye.

'I hope I'm not interrupting you people,' said the man. 'But I was thinking we ought to get together and have ourselves a pow-wow.'

'Good morning, Mr. Garunisch,' said the super.

'My name's Kenneth Garunisch,' said the new arrival, walking in and holding out his hand to Dr. Petrie.

'How do you do. I'm Leonard Petrie. Dr. Murray at Bellevue said I should blow a hole in your head.'

Kenneth Garunisch chuckled. 'That sounds like Murray, all right. Are you a doctor, too? I guess I'm not too popular with doctors. What's the matter, Jack? You look like you ate something that disagreed with you.'

The super nodded. 'I was telling this gentleman here, Mr. Garunisch. We got a pretty mean crowd of people down on the street, and they're trying to break their way in.'

Kenneth Garunisch took out a cigarette and lit it. 'You got top security locks and doors down there, haven't you? That should keep 'em out.'

'For a while, I guess. But they look like they want to get in real bad.'

'Do you want some help?' asked Kenneth Garunisch. 'I have an automatic, and some rounds.'

'I've got this rifle here,' said Dr. Petrie, pointing to the automatic weapon he had left in Ivor Glantz's umbrella stand.

Kenneth Garunisch said, 'I think we ought to get ourselves together and form a defense plan. Is Professor Glantz around? Maybe we can rope him in, too.'

'Wait there,' said Dr. Petrie. 'I'll go see.'

He walked across to Ivor Glantz's study and rapped gently on the door. There was a pause, then Glantz said, 'Come in!'

The study was dense with cigarette smoke. The walls, papered in dark brown art-deco wallpaper, were covered in graphs and diagrams and illustrations of radiography equipment. Ivor Glantz was bent over a large walnut desk, with a slide-rule, log tables, dividers and a cramful ashtray. His shirt was crumpled and stained with sweat, and he was frowning at columns of figures through a thick pair of reading glasses.

'How's it going?' asked Dr. Petrie.

'Slow,' said Glantz. 'This problem has to have fifteen million permutations. Without a computer, it's like trying to write the Bible in two days.'

'Do you think it's going to take you that long?'

Ivor Glantz took off his spectacles. 'Two days, you mean? Not a chance. It's going to take *longer*. The trouble is, I don't have any expert help. I need someone to double-check these figures, and give me some different angles and ideas. This could take months.'

'Then do you think we ought to take the theory straight to Washington, and let *them* work it out?'

Ivor Glantz shook his head. 'It wouldn't wash. If we turned up in Washington with that kind of theory, they'd laugh in our faces. They don't have any bacteriologists on the government payroll with any imagination or style, and this theory would sink into the swamp of professional jealousy like a goddamned brick.'

'But there are lives at stake, for Christ's sake! We have people dying in thousands!'

Ivor Glantz stood up. 'Dr. Petrie,' he said, 'I know people are dying but it's no use. What you forget is that Washington, right at this moment, is being inundated with theories and ideas and schemes for stopping the plague. Some of them good, some of them mediocre, and some of them totally crazy. Unless we can substantiate this theory with figures, it's going to wind up in some minor scientist's in-basket, and it probably won't see the light of day until the tricentennial, if there's anybody left alive to dig it up.'

'You sound pretty cynical,' Dr. Petrie said.

Ivor Glantz nodded. 'I *am* cynical. If you think that big business is a cut-throat game, you ought to try science. It's a second-rate scramble for recognition, and honors, and as much money as you can milk out of as many foundations as possible. That's why we have to waste our time here working out thousands of figures, and letting millions of Americans die.'

Kenneth Garunisch poked his head around the door. 'Is this a private harangue or can anyone join in?'

Ivor Glantz grinned tiredly. 'Hi, Mr. Garunisch. I was just sounding off about scientific ethics. You've met Dr. Petrie?'

'Sure. Listen, Professor – do you think we can get some of our neighbors together for a council of war? Jack the super says there are people outside on the streets, trying to break their way in. I think we ought to work out some plan of defense.'

Ivor Glantz sighed. 'Mr. Garunisch,' he said, 'I have to do a month's work in a couple of days. I don't think I have time for councils of war. I don't need defense, I need a first-class assistant bacteriologist.'

Kenneth Garunisch pulled a face. 'I don't think I'm going to be able to oblige you there, Professor. But let's say you're busy. I'll ask Herbert Gaines and that Bloofer guy. If I need your help – can I call on you?'

'Surely. Now, if you gentlemen will excuse me, it's back to the slide-rule.'

Four

At five that afternoon, in Kenneth Garunisch's mock-Colonial apartment, the residents of the sixteenth and seventeenth floors of Concorde Tower held a council of war. They were going to talk about self-protection, food and survival, and then their elected representative was going to speak to a meeting of representatives from all the other occupied floors. Mrs. Garunisch had made some rather clumsy cold-beef sandwiches, because her cook Beth had been out on the streets last night, and although Mrs. Garunisch didn't know it, Beth was lying dead and posthumously raped in a side doorway of Macy's.

Herbert Gaines was there, incongruously dressed in a yellow safari suit, and looking nervous. Nicholas sat beside him, in a sailor sweater and jeans and rope sandals, as sullen as ever. Adelaide sat possessively close to Dr. Petrie on the big floral settee, and Esmeralda sat by herself, elegant and cool in a white pleated 1930's suit. Prickles was allowed to sit in the corner, drinking coke and reading a picture book. Mr. and Mrs. Blaufoot hadn't shown up, and it didn't look as if they were going to.

Kenneth Garunisch had appointed himself chairman. He had a louder and harsher voice than anyone else. He sat in his biggest armchair, with a beer and a pack of cigarettes, and he formally declared the meeting open.

Herbert Gaines immediately raised his hand to speak.

'Mr. Garunisch,' he said, 'I do believe we're all wasting our time. The time we should have acted was *days* ago, when we were first threatened by this epidemic. Instead – in spite of my own personal warnings – everybody sat back and let it happen.'

Kenneth Garunisch sucked at his cigarette. 'With all respect, Mr. Gaines, I don't think that two or three racialist speeches on television could have done anybody any good. In fact, I contend that last night's looting and rioting can be pretty largely laid at your door. You, and your right-wing pressure group. Preaching intolerance isn't going to get us any place at all.'

'I don't think that locking ourselves away in this ivory tower is particularly tolerant,' retorted Gaines. 'Perhaps we ought to be more democratic about it, and invite all those plague-ridden people in.'

'Plague is nothing to do with democracy!' snapped Garunisch. 'The only thing we can afford to consider here is our own survival!'

'I'm afraid I agree with that,' said Dr. Petrie. 'I've seen what the plague has done, all the way from Florida, through Georgia and Alabama and the Carolinas, and there is no way that any of us can let ourselves come into contact with people who might have contracted it. We have to keep those street-level doors closed at all costs, and if we can't do that, we're going to have to build second-line defenses on the stairs.'

'This is absurd,' said Herbert Gaines. 'We're making the

same mistake we made last week. We sat on our butts and let it happen. If you ask me, the only possible answer is to get *out* there and drive those people away. If necessary, kill them.'

Nicholas looked up. 'Herbert,' he said quietly. 'You can't *mean* that.'

Herbert Gaines turned on his youthful lover with a set, angry face. 'Maybe I wouldn't have meant it before, but what the hell does it matter? If you preach speeches at people, they go off mindlessly and slaughter each other. If you *don't* preach speeches, they're so careless and stupid that they might smother themselves in their own excrement and die of disease.'

Dr. Petrie said, 'Mr. Gaines—'

Herbert Gaines waved him into silence. 'Just listen to me for a moment,' he said hotly. 'When I made those political speeches last week, I didn't believe a single word I was saying. Not one word. I stood up there and I mouthed whatever my political friends told me to mouth. I did it because they were threatening me – or rather, they were threatening Nicholas. I suppose you could call me a physical coward, and a moral coward as well, but I did it, and I'd like to know how many people wouldn't have done the same.

'The insane thing was that people actually paid attention to what I was saying. The television and the newspaper reporters actually took me seriously. People actually went up to Harlem and burned down stores and houses. My God, they say that people get the politicians they deserve, and they do. If I can stand up and speak poisonous crap like that, and the American people are prepared to believe me, then I can only say that they must have *won* this plague in some kind of celestial competition. This plague is America's prize for stupidity, crassness, arrogance, prejudice and intolerance.'

Herbert Gaines sat down. There was a long uncomfortable silence. Nicholas reached out and took Gaines' hand, and gave it a slight, almost imperceptible squeeze.

'Okay, Mr. Gaines,' said Kenneth Garunisch at last. 'You've made your point. But what we need to talk about now is survival, not divine retribution.'

'What do we have in the way of guns?' asked Esmeralda. 'If these people do break in, we're going to need them.'

Dr. Petrie said, 'We have a rifle and two handguns. Not much ammunition. We can't rely on them for long. We have a baseball bat and plenty of kitchen knives if it comes to hand-to-hand stuff.'

Adelaide asked, 'If these people have got the plague, won't they die anyway, after a few hours? Surely if we can hold out for a day or two, they'll all be dead?'

'The girl's right,' said Garunisch. 'The only problem is, that's a pretty fierce mob out there, according to what the super says. The plague may get *them* before they get *us*, but we ought to be prepared in case things work out different.'

'I vote we go down and take a look at them,' said Esmeralda. 'At least we'll know what we're up against.'

'I second that,' said Dr. Petrie, raising his hand. Esmeralda looked across and smiled at him.

Herbert Gaines said, 'I vote we go down there and shoot them while there's still time.'

Garunisch stared at Gaines heavily. 'Mr. Gaines,' he said, 'let's just take this thing one step at a time, shall we?'

'I think Papa would like to come,' put in Esmeralda. 'If you can wait a couple of minutes, I'll go and fetch him.'

Eventually, armed with Dr. Petrie's rifle, two automatics, and Nicholas' baseball bat, they all, with the exception of Prickles, collected at the top of the service stairs and began the long descent to the street. The power was still working, but none of them wanted to trust the elevators. Ivor Glantz, who had reluctantly left his mathematics for half-an-hour, was puffing and gasping by the time they had reached the thirteenth floor.

'Don't you worry, Professor Glantz,' said Dr. Petrie. 'The return journey is even more fun.'

'Fun my ass,' growled Glantz. 'I'll be lucky to come out of this alive.'

It took them twenty minutes to reach street level. The lobby was wide, spacious and glossy, with a veined black marble floor and walls clad in smokey mirrors. There were luxuriant potted palms, and a lingering scent of expensive perfumes.

The front doors of Concorde Tower were of thick tinted glass, and almost fifty feet wide. The initials CT were engraved in the glass in elegant Palace script. There was a set of inner doors of the same heavy glass, but they hadn't been fitted with the same security locks as the outer ones, and they probably weren't capable of holding an angry mob back for very long.

Dr. Petrie held Adelaide's arm. Outside the front doors, pressed against the glass like distorted creatures in a gloomy vivarium, was a crowd of almost a hundred people. They screamed soundlessly at the building super and his five uniformed security men, who stood nervous but unmoving with billy-clubs in their hands. The crowd's fists pounded against the armoured windows. They were trying to break them with bricks and hammers and chunks of loose rubble, but so far they had only succeeded in cracking two of the doors, and badly scratching a third.

Kenneth Garunisch went over to Jack, the superintendent, 'How long do you think those doors can keep 'em out?'

'It's hard to tell,' said the super. He tried to keep his eyes averted from the men and women who were shrieking insults and obscenities at them from only inches away, their faces and hands squashed white and flat against the glass.

'A couple of hours? A day? How long?' prodded Garunisch.

The super shrugged. 'It depends. I've seen a few of 'em go down. I guess they got the plague out there pretty bad. But there's always more. What I'm worried about is if they find a tow-truck, and get a chain through those door-handles.'

'All right, Jack,' said Garunisch. 'If it looks like they *are* going to get in, don't hang around to fight 'em off. They won't be feeling very friendly towards you, so high-tail it to the stairs and lock the fire door. Then keep climbing those stairs until you reach the first occupied floor – that's seven, isn't it? – and lock the fire doors all the way.'

'Okay, sir. I got you.'

Ivor Glantz came across to Dr. Petrie and touched his arm. For some reason, he was looking pale.

'Are you okay?' asked Dr. Petrie. 'You look a little sick. Is your heart all right?'

'I thought I saw someone,' whispered Ivor Glantz. 'Someone I know – out there.'

'Out there?' said Adelaide. 'Maybe it was someone who usually lives here, and they've been trying to get back in.'

Ivor Glantz shook his head. He left Dr. Petrie and Adelaide and walked towards the glass doors of Concorde Tower like a man who has seen a vision. Only a foot away from him, the silently-shrieking crowd were thumping harder and harder at the windows, and knocking chips of glass away with hammers and bricks.

Dr. Petrie was horrified and fascinated at the same time. Ivor Glantz stood there staring at the crowd, his arms hanging limply by his side, while the crowd were furiously howling and shrieking and battering at the glass.

Esmeralda suddenly said, 'Oh, my God.'

Dr. Petrie turned. 'What is it?' he asked her. 'What's wrong?'

'Oh, my God,' breathed Esmeralda. 'Just look.'

Right in the forefront of the shrieking crowd was a tall pale man with a bandage around his arm. He was staring at Ivor Glantz wild-eyed, and shaking his head from side to side in almost epileptic fear. The sight of this man had transfixed Ivor Glantz, and he seemed incapable of moving.

'*It's Sergei Forward!*' said Esmeralda. 'It's the Finnish man that father's been fighting in court! Oh, my God, they've got to let him in!'

Dr. Petrie took her arm, 'They can't. If they open those doors just an inch, then we won't stand a chance. They'll all get in. They'll kill us.'

'But don't you *see*,' said Esmeralda. 'If we let Sergei Forward in, he can help Papa with his work! We could finish it in *days* instead of *weeks*! Papa desperately needs help – and look, Sergei Forward could do it!'

Esmeralda ran over to her stepfather, but Ivor Glantz turned away as if he hadn't even seen her. He walked unsteadily back to Dr. Petrie, and held out his hand. 'Professor Glantz?' said Dr. Petrie.

Ivor Glantz said, 'Give me a rifle.'

Dr. Petrie held back. 'I'm sorry, Professor.'

Glantz reached out and twisted the automatic weapon out of Dr. Petrie's grasp. His eyes were bright and feverish, and he almost seemed to be snuffling in rage.

'Professor Glantz – you can't do that! Professor Glantz!'

Dr. Petrie tried to snatch Ivor Glantz's sleeve, but Glantz pulled away, and he waved the rifle towards him.

'*Get away!*' he said harshly. '*Just get away!*'

He turned back towards the window, and raised the rifle in his hands. The people who were pressed against the glass could see what he was going to do, but there was such a crush of people behind them that they couldn't escape. They simply opened their mouths in fear and screamed soundless screams. Sergei Forward appeared to be paralyzed with terror, and he could only stand there and watch, his hands pressed against the glass, as Ivor Glantz aimed at his face from only two or three inches away.

'*Christ!*' bellowed Garunisch. '*Stop him! Someone stop him!*'

Jack the super made a half-hearted attempt at a football tackle, but Glantz stepped back and smacked him away. Before anyone else could move, he had lifted the rifle again and fired into the glass.

The whole door collapsed outwards in huge slices. Nearly quarter of a ton of reinforced glass sheared into hands, faces, upraised arms, and broke on the ground outside with a horrific flat ringing sound.

The shrieking of the crowd filled the lobby with hideous noise – cries of pain and terror, and cries of frustrated fury. They flooded into the reception area trampling over dead and dying bodies, and Ivor Glantz was swept away like a man carried out to sea.

'*Back to the stairs!*' bellowed Kenneth Garunisch. '*Back to the stairs!*'

Dr. Petrie seized Adelaide and Esmeralda by the hand, and pulled them towards the emergency stairs. Kenneth Garunisch pushed them hurriedly through, and Herbert Gaines, whimpering in fright, followed after. Nicholas was hitting at a bloody-faced vagrant with his baseball bat, and just managed to push him away and duck through the door to the stairs before a mob of screaming men reached him, waving clubs and knives. Kenneth Garunisch slammed the door, locked it, and dropped the bolt across it. They heard the crowd bang up against the other side like an avalanche.

'*Papa!*' cried Esmeralda. '*Where's Papa?*'

Kenneth Garunisch reached out and held her arm. 'Miss Baxter, it was no good. I couldn't keep the door open any longer.'

'You mean he's still—'

'He wouldn't have felt very much, believe me.'

'He's still *out* there? You mean he's still *out* there?'

'Miss Baxter, it was his own fault! If he hadn't fired that shot!'

'*They'll kill him!*' screamed Esmeralda, in an almost unbearably high-pitched voice. '*They'll kill him!*'

Kenneth Garunisch said to Adelaide, 'Please – take her upstairs will you? We have to get out of here and lock all these fire doors.'

'You have to let me through!' said Esmeralda. 'I have to get him out of there!'

Garunisch stood firm. 'Miss Baxter, it's impossible.'

'I demand that you let me through!' insisted Esmeralda, suddenly haughty.

Kenneth Garunisch shook his head. 'Come on, Miss Baxter, let's just get out of here.'

Esmeralda glared furiously for a moment, but then her face softened and collapsed with anguish.

'Oh, God!' she sobbed. 'It's my fault! Oh God, it's all my fault! He was so good, you don't even understand!'

'We understand,' said Herbert Gaines, consolingly.

'You *don't*!' shrieked Esmeralda, off-key and hysterical. 'He was my lover!'

They locked and bolted every fire exit up to the ninth floor, and when they were there they took the added precaution of levering open the elevator doors and wedging them with a long gilt settee. The elevators had been switched off by now, but they just wanted to make sure that the furious mob downstairs didn't get them working again.

'Listen to that,' said Kenneth Garunisch, leaning over the open elevator shaft.

Dr. Petrie listened. From the first floor, there was a sound like strange trolls at the bottom of an echoing drain – screams and hoots and cries.

'Did you ever see *The Third Man*?' said Garunisch.

'You remember the scene at the top of the Ferris Wheel? When they looked down at the people below, like dots, and Harry Lime says something like – "would you feel any pity if one of those dots stopped moving for ever?" Well, what would you say if one of those animals down there stopped screaming? Maybe Gaines was right. When it comes down to it, just show me one American who gives a fuck about any other American.'

Dr. Petrie said, 'I'm a doctor, Mr. Garunisch. I try to give at least half a fuck.'

Kenneth Garunisch looked at Dr. Petrie narrowly. 'You think I'm wrong, don't you? For the strike, and all that?'

'Does it matter?'

Garunisch looked down into the depths of the elevator shaft. The distorted screams and groans continued.

'It matters to me, Dr. Petrie. I stood up for a principle I believe in. If the whole of America has to die for that principle, then I still believe it's worth it.'

'Even if the principle kills the very people it's supposed to protect?'

Kenneth Garunisch turned away. 'Principles are everything, Dr. Petrie. Without principles, we cease to be living beings.'

Herbert Gaines came up. His yellow safari suit was smudged with dust, and his leonine hair was sticking up like fuse wire.

'I'm sorry to interrupt this debating society, but I think we ought to start barricading our apartments. Maybe we ought to see what food we have available, too, and share it out.'

Esmeralda, who was calmer now, almost uncannily calm,

was sitting at the opposite end of the ninth-floor landing smoking a cigarette.

'We have a whole freezer full,' she said. 'Lamb, beef, hamburger, chickens, turkeys, vegetables. I guess we can hold out for months.'

'So have we,' nodded Garunisch. 'How about you, Mr. Gaines?'

Nicholas spoke for him. 'Oh, we're fine, too, aren't we, Herbert? I think our supplies lean a little heavily on ready-made goulasch, but I suppose my digestion can just about stand it. Herbert had one of his cooking jags last month, and goulasch is the only damned thing he can do.'

Herbert Gaines turned around angrily: 'What's the matter with my sole veronique? Or my couscous?'

Nicholas sighed. 'Oh, Herbert, they're lovely. Can't you ever take a goddamned joke?'

Dr. Petrie took Adelaide by the hand. 'I suggest we all stay in one apartment. You can lock all your valuables up in your own apartments, but if we all stay in separate places, we've lost any means of communication. Supposing the mob gets up here and breaks open your door, Mr. Gaines, or yours, Mr. Garunisch, and you've got no way of calling out for help from the rest of us?'

'I think Dr. Petrie has a point,' said Kenneth Garunisch. 'We can move beds and food into one condo, and defend it together.'

Esmeralda stood up. She was white-faced and her eyes were smudges of shadow. She looked like Ophelia, drowning in the weeds.

'If we're going to do that,' she said, 'we'd better use my

place. We have a closed-circuit TV on the door – and apart from that, the settee in the den turns into a double bed.'

'Is that agreed then?' said Garunisch.

'What about Mr. and Mrs. Blaufoot?' asked Herbert Gaines. 'Don't you think we ought to have a word with them?'

While the rest of the survivors shifted beds into Esmeralda's apartment, and carried in food and belongings, Kenneth Garunisch went up to Mr. and Mrs. Blaufoot's door and rang the bell.

There was a long pause. Then Mr. Blaufoot said, 'Who is it?'

'It's me, Mr. Bloofer. Mr. Garunisch from downstairs. Can you open the door?'

There was another long pause. Then Mr. Blaufoot said, 'Leave us alone. We're all right.'

Kenneth Garunisch sighed. 'Mr. Bloofer,' he said leaning against the door, 'you have to know that a mob of people have broken into the tower. They could be coming upstairs to make trouble. Apart from that, they've probably got plague. Now, can you open the door?'

He heard the locks and bolts being drawn back, and the solid mahogany door was opened an inch. Mr. Blaufoot's glittering eyes looked out from the darkness.

'Mr. Bloofer? Please?' said Garunisch.

Mr. Blaufoot opened the door all the way, and stepped back. Kenneth Garunisch walked into the thick-carpeted condominium, and was surprised to find that it was in darkness. Across the room, sitting in a tall carved chair, Mrs. Blaufoot sat in a black dress, pale and red-eyed.

'Are you folks all right?' said Garunisch. 'Is there anything wrong?'

The Blaufoots were silent. Mr. Blaufoot walked over and stood next to his wife.

Kenneth Garunisch looked at them uneasily. Then he saw the framed photograph on the small polished Regency table, just in front of Mrs. Blaufoot. He stepped over and carefully picked it up. She looked very much like Mrs. Blaufoot.

Mrs. Blaufoot said coldly, 'Put it down, please.'

Garunisch frowned, but he laid the photograph back on the table. He said huskily, 'Is this your daughter?'

Mr. Blaufoot nodded. 'Yes, Mr. Garunisch, it is. We heard about her on Sunday morning, shortly before the telephone system went dead. A relative of ours had managed to escape from Florida early in the plague, and he was able to get to St. Louis. This relative had seen her.'

'And is she all right?' said Garunisch. Then he looked around at the closely-drawn drapes and Mrs. Blaufoot's black dress, and said, 'Well no, I guess she's not. I'm sorry. That was clumsy of me.'

'She's dead, Mr. Garunisch,' said Mrs. Blaufoot. 'She died of lack of medical attention, with bronchial pneumonia. She didn't even have *plague*. The medical workers were out on strike, and my daughter died.'

Mr. Blaufoot added, as if it made any difference, 'She was going to be a concert pianist.'

Kenneth Garunisch coughed. He hardly knew what to say. In the end, he muttered, 'Listen, I'm really very sorry.'

Mrs. Blaufoot stared at the screwed-up handkerchief between her bony hands. 'Sorry isn't really enough, is it?'

Garunisch shrugged. 'No, I guess it isn't. But I *am* sorry, and there is nothing more I can say. I acted, when I called that strike, according to my lights.'

Mrs. Blaufoot looked up. 'In that case, Mr. Garunisch, I hope that your lights soon go out, like ours did.'

During the night, most of the sixty or seventy people who were huddled together in the lobby of Concorde Tower died of plague. The black floor and the polished mirrors on the walls reflected their painful, grotesque faces as the bacilli swelled their joints and clogged their lungs. Their groaning and whimpering echoed like a terrible chorus of damned souls, but it wasn't the worst noise. The worst noise was the rustle and scamper of rats – big gray sewer rats – as they scuttled over the sleeping and dying bodies, and gnawed at dead and living flesh alike. Some of the rats sniffed at the locked fire door, which even the angriest rioters hadn't been able to break down, and some of them poured into the open elevator doors and dropped, with the soft thud of furry bodies down to the basement.

They scented warmth and they scented food and they began to climb, twisting their way up the elevator cables. The empty shaft echoed with their twittering and squeaking, and the scratching of their claws on the steel wires. Eventually, they reached the ninth floor, where the doors were wedged open by the gilt settee, and they ran out of the elevator shaft and on to the landing. The upper fire doors had been left open, and they wriggled and pattered up the stairs, sniffing at locked apartment doors and over-running floor after floor.

In three hours, the stairs and landings of Concorde

Tower, right up to the roof level, were a scampering mass of ravenous rats.

Dr. Petrie was deeply asleep when someone touched his forehead. He stirred, and unconsciously tried to brush the hand away. He had been dreaming about Miami, and he thought he had been eating a picnic lunch on the beach with Prickles and Anton Selmer. He opened his eyes, and found himself in the den of Ivor Glantz's condominium, lying on the settee now converted into a double bed.

Esmeralda whispered, 'Sssh.'

He could see her in the gloom, her face pale and sculptured. She was wearing her black curly hair tied back with a ribbon, and she smelled warmly of Arpège.

'What is it?' he whispered back.

'Sssh,' she repeated.

He looked quickly to one side, and saw that he was now alone in the bed. He had been sleeping with Kenneth Garunisch, while Adelaide and Prickles and Mrs. Garunisch shared the master bed in the main bedroom.

Esmeralda said, 'Garunisch couldn't sleep. He's in the kitchen, having a smoke and reading a book.'

'He reads *books*?' joked Dr. Petrie. 'You amaze me.'

'Don't talk,' said Esmeralda, laying a finger across his lips. 'Even walls have ears.'

Without another word, she lifted the bedsheets and climbed in beside him. The bed creaked, and she suppressed a giggle. Then she curled her arms around him, and she was all soft and warm and slithery in her pure silk nightdress.

'We can't do this,' hissed Dr. Petrie, in spite of the fact that his body was all too obviously saying he could.

'Don't talk,' said Esmeralda. 'Just remember what I've been through and give me a chance.'

He sat up, and held her wrists. He could see her moist lips gleaming in the dim light of the den.

'Esmeralda, we can't do this.'

'You're a doctor, aren't you?'

'Sure, but—'

'But nothing! If you're a doctor, you know the importance of therapy after a psychological shock. I don't want love, Leonard, I just need a few moments' oblivion!'

He didn't release her wrists. 'Thanks for the compliment,' he whispered. 'Now I'm only good for a few moments' oblivion!'

'You know I didn't mean that.'

'Well, what did you mean?'

'I mean that this is an emergency. A medical and psychological and romantic emergency. For Christ's sake, Leonard, we could all be dead tomorrow. Don't you believe in final grand gestures?'

'If I believed in final grand gestures, I'd be lying dead as a door-nail in Miami, Florida.'

'What's that got to do with us making love?'

'I don't know.'

'Well, kiss me,' she said, 'and I'll show you.'

He could have resisted. He could have said no. But her long warm thigh moved against his bare leg, and her hand reached down and cupped his tightened balls, and her sexuality washed over him like a wave of drunkenness. He leaned forward and kissed her, and their tongues touched, and their teeth bit.

They didn't say a word. She pushed him back against the bed, and sat astride him, lifting her glossy silk nightdress around her hips. He reached up and felt her hardened nipples through the slippery material, and she sighed, and kissed his forehead, and raised herself up so that he could socket himself between her thighs. Then she slowly sat down on him, squirming her hips as she did so, so that he felt a massaging warmth rising up him.

The door of the den was still ajar. They knew that anyone could walk in at any moment. But they made love slowly and relished every sensation it brought, until they couldn't suppress their urgency any more, and they were panting at each other with bright eyes and expressions of something like pain.

Esmeralda twitched and shook violently. Leonard Petrie felt something grip him between the legs, and they both achieved the few moments of oblivion they were looking for. Then they were lying side by side, quiet and wet, and even if it wasn't a final grand gesture it was at least a kind of temporary therapy for traumatized minds that had been through more emotions and horrors than it was possible to take.

Dr. Petrie kissed her. 'You'd better go now,' he said gently. 'Mr. Garunisch is a fast smoker.'

Esmeralda cuddled him close, and pressed her lips against his side.

Kenneth Garunisch, in blue-striped pyjamas, put his head around the door and said, 'Hey, you two. Don't hurry on my account. I'm just going to finish this chapter.'

He was wakened by the sound of a helicopter. He sat

up, listening. Esmeralda had long since gone, and Kenneth Garunisch was lying next to him with his face buried in the pillow, snoring. The helicopter noise came and went, as if it was circling around somewhere in the vicinity. He climbed out of bed, tugged on his pants, and went to the window.

At first, he couldn't see where it was. The noise of the rotors was bounced off buildings in all directions, and the sky was gray with cloud. But then he saw it turning around the 38-story United Nations Plaza building, and circling towards Concorde Tower with its blades flickering and its navigation lights shining through the murk.

Kenneth Garunisch sat up, rubbing his eyes. 'What's going on?' he grunted.

'It's a helicopter,' said Dr. Petrie. 'It's been circling around here for a couple of minutes. Maybe it's the cavalry.'

Garunisch swung his legs out of bed and came to take a look. 'Some hopes,' he said. 'They've probably just come for a snoop at the doomed survivors.'

'Do you think we ought to wave?' said Dr. Petrie. 'There's always a chance they're looking for people to rescue.'

'Do what you like,' said Garunisch.

The helicopter was really close to the tower now, circling slowly around and shining a powerful light in their direction. It was a small two-seater Bell, with a perspex bubble cockpit. Dr. Petrie waved both hands.

At that moment, Herbert Gaines pushed into the room, hastily tying his Japanese bathrobe around his waist.

'Is that a helicopter?' he asked.

'It aint a June bug,' said Kenneth Garunisch.

'They've come!' said Gaines. 'They said they'd come, and they have!'

Adelaide came into the room and took Dr. Petrie's arm. 'Leonard – what is it?'

Herbert Gaines was elated. 'It's the people from Washington! They called me on Saturday when the first news of the plague leaked out. They said they'd bring in a helicopter to rescue me! And here they are!'

'Well,' said Dr. Petrie, looking at Kenneth Garunisch. 'It looks like politics pay and principles poop out.'

Garunisch shrugged.

Herbert Gaines went to the window and flapped his arms about frantically. For a while it didn't look as if the helicopter pilot had seen him, but then the dazzling searchlight probed into the apartment window, and Herbert Gaines was lit up like an actor on a stage.

'*I'm here!*' he shrieked. '*I'm here! I'm here!*'

They saw the helicopter pilot pointing towards the roof, and then the machine turned a half-circle and rose out of sight. Herbert Gaines, whimpering with excitement, rushed into the sitting-room and pulled on his yellow safari suit. The rest of them watched him in tense silence.

'Well,' said Herbert, lacing his shoes, 'I think I'm ready to go!'

Nicholas, scruffy from sleep and wearing nothing but a dark brown bath-towel, said, 'Is that it? You're just going?'

Gaines stopped lacing his shoe and looked up. Then he cast his eyes around at everybody else, and saw their expressionless, unsympathetic faces, and bit his lip.

'Well... yes. I mean, *yes!*'

'What about me?' said Nicholas. 'You're just leaving me here? And what about all these other people?'

Herbert Gaines lowered his eyes. 'Nicky,' he said, 'the helicopter only has room for one. You saw that. It's a two-seater. I can't take anybody with me.'

Garunisch coughed. 'Couldn't we draw lots?' he said gruffly. 'Or maybe one of the ladies should go instead?'

'Listen,' said Gaines, almost desperate, 'it's up there *now*! It's *waiting*! It won't wait for ever!'

Garunisch examined the floor. 'You're an old man, Mr. Gaines,' he said harshly. 'You're an old man and you've had a long life. Now, supposing one of these young ladies went instead of you. Or what about Nicholas here? He's a good friend of yours. Don't you think enough of Nicholas to give up your place in that chopper, and let him live?'

Herbert Gaines stood up.

'They sent the helicopter for *me*,' he insisted. 'The only reason it's *here* is because of me. The party needs me, and that's why they've taken the risk. What do you think they're going to say if that thing flies all the way back to Washington with Nicky aboard? Do you think they've spent all that money, and wasted all that energy, just to educate a half-educated faggot who can't even cook?'

Nicholas stared open-mouthed at Herbert as if he couldn't believe what he was hearing.

Garunisch grunted. 'If that's how you feel, Mr. Gaines, perhaps you'd better just get the hell out. I don't think any of the rest of us would like to stand in the way of your cowardice, seeing as how it's so pressing.'

Gaines said, 'Look – as soon as I get to Washington – I'll make sure they send another helicopter back – a *bigger* one – for all of you—'

Garunisch flapped a hand at him. 'Don't bother. You

might strain your brain trying to remember to do it, and we'd hate to see that happen.'

Adelaide said, 'Mr. Gaines?'

Herbert Gaines was buttoning up his safari suit and making for the door. 'Yes?' he said.

Adelaide didn't answer at once. Not until Herbert Gaines had turned around and looked at her.

'I saw your movie once, Mr. Gaines.'

Herbert Gaines' mouth twitched. 'My dear, the helicopter's waiting – I really can't—'

Adelaide said, 'I like the line when Hannah Carson says to Captain Dashfoot: "Oh, you brave, brave, honorable man, would the world were all like you."'

Gaines paused. In a quiet voice he said, 'My dear, you've got a regrettably good memory.'

He stood at the door, his hand on the latch, so obviously striking a tragic theatrical pose that Nicholas said, 'For Christ's sake, Herbert, just fuck off.'

Herbert Gaines lifted his lion-like head. 'I will send more helicopters,' he said, in his richest voice. 'I promise you that upon my life.'

He opened the door.

He was so involved in his melodramatic pose that when the rats rushed at him, their heavy bodies thumping against the half-open door, he was taken completely by surprise. The rats leaped and jumped at him, and more of them scuttled into the apartment and disappeared under the makeshift beds and into the drapes.

Dr. Petrie ran across the sitting-room and banged himself against the door so that it slammed shut. He crunched four or five rats in the doorjamb, and they squealed and writhed, with blood running out of their narrow noses. Adelaide and Esmeralda and Mrs. Garunisch, panting with fright, picked up cushions and brooms and chased after the rats that had managed to get into the apartment.

Herbert Gaines had a rat swinging from his sleeve. He flapped at it uselessly until Kenneth Garunisch picked up a heavy cigarette lighter from the table and knocked the rat away. Then he stepped on its head and killed it.

'Oh, Mother of God,' gasped Gaines. 'Oh, Mother of God!'

'Well, darling,' said Nicholas, turning to Herbert Gaines. 'So much for your helicopter now.'

Herbert Gaines was shaking. 'I'm still going!' he said. 'Don't think that a few rats can stop me!'

'A few?' said Dr. Petrie. 'Did you see how many there were? The whole building must be thick with them!'

Herbert Gaines said, 'It won't wait, you know! The helicopter won't wait!'

Kenneth Garunisch was helping his wife to corner the last stray rat and beat it to death. He came over to Herbert Gaines with blood on his hands. Behind him, Mrs. Garunisch had suddenly gone into a burst of hysterical weeping, and Esmeralda was trying to soothe her.

'Mr. Gaines,' he said, 'you're crazy. If you go out there, you won't last two minutes. Those rats are fierce and they're hungry. I've come up against them before, when I was a kid, and I've seen a man have half his nose bitten off. That was just one. There must be *hundreds* out there.'

Dr. Petrie looked at the old actor and said, 'It's no use, you know, Mr. Gaines. You might as well admit it.'

Herbert Gaines looked up at the ceiling. Just a few stories

above him, perched impatiently on the roof, was his means of escape, his way to a glittering political destiny.

Kenneth Garunisch said, 'Power's an attractive thing, Mr. Gaines, aint it? You've tasted it now, haven't you, and wasn't that taste good?'

Herbert Gaines stared at him. 'I don't know what you mean. I have to *go*, that's all. They sent the helicopter and I have to *go*.'

He paced urgently across the room. Then he said, 'Fire! That's it! They don't like fire!'

'Mr. Gaines,' said Garunisch, 'what the hell are you talking about?'

'It's true!' said Gaines. 'You can always fight them with fire! It's in that movie – *River Boat*! Now, where's that *Variety* we brought down with us? Nicky – where is it?'

Nicholas, sulking, didn't even answer. Herbert Gaines fumbled around in his touzled bed until he found the paper. He rolled it up, and brandished it around.

'This, my friends, will be my salvation!'

He picked up the table lighter that Garunisch had used to kill the rat, and he flicked it. Then he carefully applied the flame to the edge of *Variety*, until the paper was burning like a torch.

Dr. Petrie stepped forward, but Kenneth Garunisch reached out and held his arm.

'Let him go, doctor. Just help me make sure that no more rats get into the place. You can't stand between a man and his destiny, even if you think he's a shit.'

Dr. Petrie said, 'But it's insane! He won't last a minute out there!'

'That's his problem. He wants to go.'

Nicholas, standing next to them, nodded his head. 'You're right, Mr. Garunisch. Herbert's a born martyr. You'd have to kill him to stop him killing himself.'

Herbert Gaines was making sure that the copy of *Variety* was well alight. Then he went to the door, and held it in front of him.

'You wait till they see this!' he said triumphantly. 'This'll sort them out!'

Dr. Petrie and Kenneth Garunisch positioned themselves behind the door so that they could slam it shut the second that Herbert Gaines had gone through. The room was already smokey and filled with black wisps of ash, but Herbert had his paper burning well now, and was ready to go.

He opened the door, waving the blazing *Variety* in a wide fluttering arc. The rats went for his legs like gray greasy torpedoes, but the flames were enough to keep them from jumping at his face and throat.

Kicking three or four rats away, Dr. Petrie shut the door again, and locked it.

Herbert had three flights of stairs to go to reach the roof. The first flight wasn't too bad, because he managed to knock most of the rats away from his legs, and his paper was still burning. Halfway up the second flight, with his heart pounding and his sixty-year-old lungs beginning to feel the strain, he started to falter. The flames abruptly went out, and he was left with nothing but a half-burned *Variety* to beat off the most vicious animals he had ever seen.

The third flight was the beginning of his Calvary. The rats were hanging on to his arms now, and biting into his back and his sides. His legs were thick with them, and he could feel their teeth in his thighs. He kept his hands over his face and stumbled up blindly, but they still leaped up at him and bit into his fingers, until his hands were gloved in rats.

The agony of it was enormous. He couldn't even cry out, unless they bit into his mouth, and there was already a huge brown sewer rat dangling from the soft flesh under his chin. He tried to keep his mind above the pain, above this dreadful cloak of biting, squeaking creatures, and firmly concentrated on the roof – the *roof* – and his wonderful helicopter.

He had to take one hand away from his face to open the door to the roof. His arm seemed to weigh hundreds of pounds, and it was swinging with rats like the fence round a trapper's cabin. One of the beasts launched itself at his cheek, and he lost precious seconds hitting it away.

The helicopter pilot was a 36-year-old veteran called Andy Folger. He was checking his watch impatiently when the roof door opened, and the first thing he did was start up his engine and get his rotors turning. He cast a quick eye over the fuel reading, and then reached over to open the opposite door of the cockpit. The quicker he got this mission over, the better he was going to like it.

He heard a muffled screaming noise, and he turned. He had a feeling in his stomach like an elevator dropping thirty floors in ten seconds. Folger stared at the hunched heap of wriggling gray fur that was moving towards him. He couldn't understand what he was seeing at first, and when he did, his mind almost blanked out.

He didn't see the rats that ran out of the open door to the stairs, and scuttled across to his helicopter. He reached over to close the cockpit door again, and one of them leaped up and bit his hand. He banged the rat against the side of the cockpit, but it clung on, and while it clung on, another rat jumped into the helicopter, and another.

He beat the animal away from his hand, revved the engine, and pulled back the stick. The helicopter's rotors whistled faster and faster, and the Bell lifted off from the rooftop and circled away towards the north.

Three rats scurried around the cockpit, and one of them jumped at Folger's face. He tried to smack it away, but then another rat nipped at his arm.

The helicopter went out of control. Wrestling against twisting rats and a bucking control stick, Andy Folger saw the horizon turn upside down, and the buildings of First Avenue swivel all around him. He saw streets – sky – buildings – streets – and then the helicopter fluttered and twisted and plummeted eighteen stories. It fell on to the glass roof of a supermarket and exploded in a hot spray of fire that rolled upwards and burned itself out.

On the top of Concorde Tower, Herbert Gaines neither saw nor heard. His mind was still somewhere inside that costume of rats, but it was dwindling very quickly, and was soon to be gone. Sometime during the afternoon, the power from their generator died. They were sitting quietly around the apartment, and the lights suddenly dimmed and went out. They heard the freezer motor in the kitchen shudder and stop.

Dr. Petrie, who had been sitting on the settee with Prickles, reading her a story, looked up.

'Daddy,' said Prickles, wide-eyed, 'it's gone dark.'

Kenneth Garunisch got out of his armchair and went to try the lights. There was no doubt that they were dead.

He shrugged and said, 'It's the generator. The goddamned thing's probably clogged up with rats.'

Esmeralda, sitting cross-legged on the floor, said, 'What are we going to do now? All our food's going to spoil. I doubt if we've got enough canned stuff to last us a week. There are six of us, right? – seven including Prickles – and I don't think we've got more than nine or ten cans of meat, and a few dozen cans of fruit. Maybe I should check.'

'Jesus,' said Nicholas. 'That's all we need.'

Kenneth Garunisch lit a cigarette. 'I thought you'd be pleased. Now you won't have to force yourself to eat Herbert's goulasch.'

'Ken – I don't think you ought to speak ill of the dead,' said his wife worriedly.

'Why not?' said Garunisch, blowing smoke. 'That was what he wanted, wasn't it? A glorious fiery plunge from the top of the city's ritziest apartment.'

Nicholas lowered his head and sighed. 'I don't know what he wanted, Mr. Garunisch. He was actually very kind. Except to himself, that is.'

Dr. Petrie put down the story-book and stood up. 'I think the most important thing now is to work out how we're going to survive. What is it – Tuesday? I guess anyone who was left on the streets on Sunday will be dead of plague by now. It should be pretty safe outside as far as looters and muggers are concerned.'

'What about rats?' asked Adelaide.

Dr. Petrie ran his hand through his hair. 'I'm not sure about rats. If anything, the rats will probably have gotten worse.'

'So what are we going to *do*?' asked Mrs. Garunisch.

'I mean – those rats are so *fierce*. I can't bear the thought of them.'

'The water's off,' called Esmeralda from the kitchen. 'That means we don't even have anything to drink.'

'Plenty of whiskey,' said Garunisch wryly, holding up Ivor Glantz's crystal decanter.

'Does anyone here have a car?' Dr. Petrie asked.

'A car?' frowned Garunisch. 'What the hell do you want with a car?'

'Well,' said Dr. Petrie, 'if the rats are really bad, then it's going to be too dangerous for all of us to get out of here at one time. It only needs one person to trip or fall, and the whole party could be put at risk. But if one or two could wrap themselves up in blankets or something, and make protective helmets to cover our faces, then maybe we could make it to the basement car park.'

'Then what happens?' said Garunisch. 'This is a dead city. Where do you think you're going to get help?'

'You have enough food for two or three days. That's all it should take to drive out of the plague zone and organize some kind of airborne rescue. Let's not kid ourselves – you're all wealthy people, and if anyone can get rescued, you can.'

Mrs. Garunisch furrowed her brow. 'Supposing we *don't* get rescued?' she said anxiously. 'What then?'

Kenneth Garunisch reached over and took her hand. 'Gay,' he said gently, 'we've never talked like that and we never will. The doctor's right – we've got as good a chance as anyone.'

Dr. Petrie went to the walnut sideboard and picked up

a heavy sheaf of papers. 'More important than any of us, though,' he said, 'is this.'

Mrs. Garunisch peered at the sheaf suspiciously. 'What's that?' she asked sharply.

'This is the mathematical work on the plague that Ivor Glantz left unfinished,' explained Dr. Petrie. 'I'm not a research scientist, but I've looked through it, and as far as I'm able to understand, it's sound. I think that if we can get these papers to the federal government, we can persuade them to investigate the idea further, and with any luck at all we could help to stamp out the plague. Whoever gets out of here will not only have the task of sending help to the rest, but they'll have the vital responsibility of delivering these papers to the department of health.'

'How do we know the whole country hasn't been wiped out?' said Nicholas. 'I mean – Jesus – the whole of New York in three days!'

Dr. Petrie riffled through the papers of equations and formulae. 'We don't know. The last we heard, they'd managed to hold the plague at the Alleghenies. Maybe the situation's worse by now. It probably is. But if we can get these papers to Washington in time... Well, who knows? We might be able to save the mid-West and the West Coast.'

Kenneth Garunisch said, 'Well... that sounds impressive enough. You could have had my car, but I left the keys in my apartment.'

'Esmeralda?' asked Dr. Petrie. 'How about you?'

'I left mine parked on the street,' said Esmeralda. 'I expect it's a total wreck by now.'

Nicholas said, 'I should think that Herbert's Mercedes is

okay. It's in the basement. I have the keys here – he always left them with me.'

Kenneth Garunisch looked at him appreciatively. 'Looks like Captain Dashfoot did us a good turn after all.'

'It's only a two-seater,' said Nicholas. 'There's a kind of small contingency seat at the back, but you couldn't travel for very far in that.'

Kenneth Garunisch opened the cigarette box on the table and took out the last of Ivor Glantz's cigarettes. 'In that case,' he said, striking a light, 'I suggest that Dr. Petrie goes, and takes his daughter along with him. Prickles would fit in the back – wouldn't you, Prickles?'

Prickles nodded shyly.

Dr. Petrie said, 'No – this has to be fair. I suggest we draw straws, and give everybody a chance.'

Garunisch pulled a face. 'Don't talk dumb. Supposing *Gay* draws it. How's she going to get out of this goddamned rat-infested building, drive all the way to Washington, and then convince the federal department of health that she's found a way to cure the plague? Gay couldn't convince the Mother's Union that fish paste sandwiches are better value than bagels and lox.'

'*Ken*,' said Mrs. Garunisch, hurt.

Garunisch put his arm around her. 'Don't take it the wrong way, Gay, but it's true. Dr. Petrie has to go. It's his idea, anyway. Can you imagine *me* trying to sell it? You know what they think of me in Washington right now. Or Nicholas here, in his sailor suit?'

'There's still a spare seat,' said Dr. Petrie.

Adelaide, sitting next to him, looked up. She frowned, and said, 'But surely—'

'That's true,' said Garunisch, interrupting her. 'We can draw lots for that. Esmeralda – do you have any drinking straws?'

'Of course,' said Esmeralda, and went into the kitchen to fetch them.

Adelaide tugged gently at Dr. Petrie's sleeve. He turned around.

'*Leonard,*' she whispered. 'I thought that—'

He put his finger to his lips. 'Don't worry. Whatever happens, you'll be okay.'

'But I want to go with *you*!'

He laid his hand over hers. 'Darling – we're all in this together. We all have to take the same risks. Trying to get out of here is going to be far more dangerous than staying. If you ask me, Herbert Gaines didn't even make it upstairs.'

'That's not the point!'

'Sshh,' he said. Esmeralda had come back with the straws. She handed them to Dr. Petrie along with a pair of kitchen scissors.

'Okay,' said Garunisch. 'Cut them to different lengths, and whoever draws the longest straw gets to go. Agreed?'

Dr. Petrie trimmed the straws. Keeping his back turned, he arranged them in his hand. Then he walked over and offered them to Nicholas.

Nicholas plucked one out quickly, with his eyes shut. 'It's a short one,' he said, 'I know it is.'

He held it up. It was.

Dr. Petrie moved across to Kenneth Garunisch. The old union leader thought for a while, rubbing his chin, and then he carefully picked the straw in the middle. It was longer than Nicholas' straw, but it was still short. He shrugged, and twisted it up.

Mrs. Garunisch was next. She was dithering and anxious. She didn't actually want to pick the longest straw, because she preferred to stay with her husband, but she knew how insistent he was on playing by the rules. If she picked it, he would make her go.

She pulled one out. It was short. She let out a big puff of relief.

Adelaide looked across at Esmeralda. 'Her first,' she said to Dr. Petrie.

Dr. Petrie shook his head. 'I'm going around the room clockwise,' he said.

Adelaide lifted her eyes and stared at Dr. Petrie for a long moment. He stared back, sadly. They say that a woman can always sense when a man no longer wants her, and he wondered how it showed. He wondered, too, when he had stopped wanting her. It hadn't happened all at once, and it was nothing to do with Esmeralda. What had happened last night had been no more than a human attempt to feel *something* after so much misery.

Maybe the whole experience since the beginning of the plague had changed him, and made him come to terms with what he really was and what he wanted to be. It seemed to him now that Adelaide was part of a life that had become remote and irrelevant. Like tennis, and swimming, and Normandy Shores Golf Club.

'Pick,' he said softly, holding out the two remaining straws.

Adelaide picked.

Dr. Petrie held out the last straw to Esmeralda. She didn't look at him – simply took it, and held it up.

Esmeralda's straw was fractionally longer than Adelaide's.

'There you go, then,' said Kenneth Garunisch loudly. 'That settles that!'

Esmeralda stood up. She kept her eyes downcast, and she said simply, 'I'll get my things together.'

Adelaide shrieked out, 'You *won't*!'

Dr. Petrie held Adelaide's shoulder. 'Darling, it was a fair draw. I can't do anything about it. We had to decide somehow.'

'I'm left behind while you're going,' said Adelaide. There were angry tears running down her cheeks. '*You* didn't have to pick a stupid straw!'

'Come on, now,' put in Kenneth Garunisch, 'I thought we'd decided all that!'

'Well, decide again,' snapped Adelaide, the tension of all she had been through giving her a note of desperation. 'Leonard is my fiancé and that's all there is to it. Would *you* go without *your* wife?'

'Adelaide, you'll be safer here.'

'I don't care! I want to go with you!' she shrieked.

Dr. Petrie turned around angrily, and was about to rebuke her, but he checked his tongue.

Esmeralda said, in a quiet voice, 'It's all right. Let her go. I'd rather stay here anyway.'

Dr. Petrie said, 'Esmeralda—' But she shook her head and wouldn't look at him.

'Take her,' she said. 'Go on.'

Adelaide was mopping her eyes with a handkerchief. Dr. Petrie felt irritated at her outburst, but at the same time he was almost relieved. Leaving Adelaide behind would have given him the familiar tangles of guilt that he had felt about Margaret.

The trouble with being a doctor, he thought, is that even your lovers become your patients. How can I cause Adelaide the same kind of anguish for which other women come to me to be treated? I'm supposed to cure diseases, not spread them.

Dr. Petrie sighed. 'All right, then,' he said, almost inaudibly. 'If that's what you want.'

It took them almost two hours to get themselves ready, and by the time they'd finished, they looked like fat and scruffy astronauts, all wrapped up in quilts and blankets, and tied up with strings and cords.

Dr. Petrie had bagged Prickles up completely in a duvet, and he was going to carry her on his back. He and Adelaide were both padded all over, with their thick blanket leggings tucked into three pairs of Ivor Glantz's walking socks, and their hands wrapped in gloves and bandages. They had made themselves hoods out of their quilts, covering their faces up completely except for their eyes, which were protected with pieces of nylon mesh cut from a vegetable strainer and safety-pinned into place.

Dr. Petrie had Kenneth Garunisch's automatic pistol tucked into his belt in case of emergencies, and he carried the precious car keys inside his glove.

'I'm going to lose pounds,' he said, in a muffled voice. 'It's like a goddamned Turkish bath in this outfit.'

Kenneth Garunisch handed him the Glantz statistics, securely buckled up in a canvas map case, and shook him by the hand.

'Don't forget to send back the choppers,' he said with a grin. 'I wouldn't like to think I was going to spend the rest of my life in this dump.'

Dr. Petrie nodded his quilted head. He was already sweating like a mule inside the blankets, and he wanted to get their escape over as quickly as possible.

He said goodbye to Nicholas, and to Mrs. Garunisch, and then he padded over to Esmeralda's room.

She was sitting by the window, looking out over the gray light of later afternoon. Through his mesh facemask, she took on a new softness, and he hardly knew what to say to her.

She turned, and gave a small smile. 'You look as if you're off to the North Pole,' she said. She came over and took his hand.

'As soon as I get to someplace safe, I'll have a helicopter back here straight away,' he said.

Esmeralda put her hands to her face and looked at him gently.

'Don't worry about me,' she said. 'You have other things to think about. You know, I believe you could do something really great, Leonard, if you ever gave yourself half a chance.'

He nodded. 'That's what Margaret used to say.'

'Margaret?'

'My ex-wife. She's dead now. She died of the plague.'

'I'm sorry.'

'Well – I think the only reason she wanted me to realize my potential was so that she could bask in reflected glory.'

Esmeralda smiled. He couldn't be sure, because his vision was so blurred, but she might have been crying.

'There's only one sort of glory that counts, Leonard,' she

said. 'And that's the glory of survival. You'd better go now. They're waiting for you.'

He held out his huge swaddled arms, and held her close, then he turned around and padded back into the sitting-room. Adelaide was waiting for him, all wrapped up, and Prickles was nothing more than a big blue bundle on the settee.

'All right, everybody,' said Dr. Petrie. 'This is it!'

Kenneth Garunisch and Nicholas helped him to get Prickles on his back. She clung around his shoulders, and they tied her firmly in position with a long leather belt from an old suitcase.

Nicholas prepared to open the door to let them out. Garunisch and his wife held broom-handles in case the rats rushed in.

'Are you ready?' said Nicholas. Dr. Petrie nodded.

'Okay then – *now*!'

The front door was flung open. The rats scrambled at them like a tide of filthy water, squealing with ravenous hunger. As Dr. Petrie stumbled forward with Prickles on his back, urgently pushing Adelaide in front of him, he could see nothing through his facemask but a torrential swarm of furry bodies, filling the hallway and writhing on the stairs.

They made the first flight down to the fifteenth floor with rats suspended from their quilted shins and hanging from their shoulders. Dr. Petrie kicked the rats around his legs with every other step, and tried to smash them against the walls, but even when they were dead they clung on, until their bodies were pulled away and devoured by more clamoring rats.

Adelaide, her arms heavy with the rodents, tripped and

fell against the stairs. Dr. Petrie, with Prickles on his back, could do nothing more than nudge her. She managed to struggle up to her feet again, turning and twisting herself to try and shake some of the rats off, but all they did was sway on her arms like over-heavy tassels from a curtain.

They made it down to the twelfth floor with rats all over them, gnawing and tearing at their quilts and blankets, and turning them into shambling man-sized beasts of wriggling brown fur. Adelaide fell again, and Dr. Petrie had to tear rats away from her back to try and reduce their disgusting weight. He was now so overwhelmed by the creatures that he was literally tearing them in half to pull them off.

It took them a further ten minutes to reach the ninth floor. Dr. Petrie was smothered in sweat, and panting for breath in the foul air. The building's air-conditioning had stopped with the power failure, and the corridors were so soaked in the acrid urine of rats that his eyes smarted and he could hardly make his lungs work. Prickles, clinging to his back, was a muscle-tearing load that he could barely even think about.

He waded knee-deep through squirming rats towards the fire door to the next flight of stairs. The door was locked – and jammed. Beating rats away from his quilted hood, he forced his way over to Adelaide and shouted, '*It's stuck! I can't get it open!*'

Adelaide stumbled against him. 'You have to!' she screamed. 'I can't take any more! You have to!'

Dr. Petrie peered around the hallway through his face-mask. The gilt settee was still wedged in the open elevator doors, and he grabbed Adelaide's shoulder and pointed towards the shaft.

'Can you climb?' he yelled. 'Can you slide down the wires?'

She shook her rat-decorated head, making their tails swing. 'Leonard – it's nine stories! I can't!'

'You'll have to! If you don't, you'll have to go back! Just do what I do!'

Shifting Prickles higher on his back, Dr. Petrie battled his way through the clinging, tearing rats to reach the elevator doors. He climbed laboriously up on to the settee, and then reached over towards the elevator cables. At the first try, he missed, and for a moment he thought he was going to overbalance. Through his facemask, he could see the dark shaft dropping over 130 feet to the ground.

Adjusting Prickles' weight, he reached out again. This time, his gloved hand reached the cable. It was slippery with grease, and difficult to cling on to. He reached over with the other hand. His weight made the settee slip a few inches, and he had to pause, stock-still, in case it tipped down the shaft completely.

Adelaide shrieked, '*Hurry! I can't bear it!*'

Tentatively, Dr. Petrie reached out once more, and this time he managed to grasp the cable with both hands. Sweating and gasping, he pushed himself off the settee, and let his legs dangle in space. He then slid awkwardly down beside the settee, until he was able to curl his legs around the cable below it, and climb down further.

'Adelaide!' he shouted. 'Adelaide – come on!'

He couldn't wait too long for her. He was barely able to keep his grip on the slippery elevator cables as it was, and Prickles was now an agonizing burden of pain. He tried to kick a few rats from his legs, and two or three of them plummeted down the breezy elevator shaft to the basement, turning over and over as they fell.

At last, he saw Adelaide, alive with rats, crawling out on to the settee. He saw her peer down the depth of the shaft, and hesitate.

'It's all right!' he yelled. 'Just keep your head, and it's all right!'

Adelaide put her hand out and tried to reach the cable. The settee groaned and shifted downward again, and she held back. Then she tried to reach out once more, her arms heavy with clinging rats.

She caught hold of the wire and gripped it.

'Now the other one!' shouted Dr. Petrie.

Adelaide paused, then lunged forward to seize the cable. There was a scraping sound, and the gilt settee tilted under her weight. It slid downwards against the wall for a few feet, and then dropped, with a hideous crashing and banging, nine stories down to the ground. They heard it hit the bottom, and smash.

Adelaide was clinging tightly to the wires. She was sobbing out loud, and it took Dr. Petrie several minutes to make her hear.

'Slide down slowly!' he said. 'Hand over hand! Don't go too fast or the wire will burn through your gloves!'

'I can't!' she wept. 'I'm too frightened! I can't!'

'For Christ's sake, you'll have to! There's no other way!'

Burdened with rats, Dr. Petrie began his cautious descent. Every few moments he rested, gripping on to the wire until he felt as if his hands were painfully locked. His face was running with sweat, and his heart felt as if it was grating against his ribcage. He could hear Prickles saying something muffled, and shifting about in her duvet, but there was nothing he could do. He just prayed to God she would try and stay still.

They reached the eighth floor. Dr. Petrie paused for another rest. He was breathing in coarse whines, and he was beginning to shake and tremble all over. He was just about to start climbing down again when Adelaide said, '*Leonard!*'

'What is it?'

'*I can't – feel my hands!*'

He tried to look up. 'What?'

'*I can't feel my hands!*'

He blinked sweat out of his eyes. 'Try wriggling your fingers!'

There was a pause. Then she screamed, '*I can't feel them!*'

She must have let go. She dropped past him without a sound, knocking him a glancing blow on the shoulder. He didn't hear anything, not even when she hit the ground. He clung on as tightly as he could, a tattered quilted figure hanging to a wire, and he wept silently as he climbed down floor by floor, one after the other, with his hands bleeding and his body raw with pain.

It had just been raining. A flat watery sunlight glossed over the wet streets, and reflected from windows and spires. Dr. Petrie drove slowly through the broken debris of downtown Manhattan towards the Holland Tunnel, his hands roughly bandaged on the steering-wheel, his face strained and exhausted. Prickles, her hair damp with sweat, lay on the seat beside him, fast asleep.

On the back shelf of the car, in its canvas map bag, was Ivor Glantz's work on plague control by irradiation.

As he drove, Dr. Petrie sang softly, under his breath. The day faded into early evening, and early evening faded into night. He drove through the Holland Tunnel and into Jersey. He drove south-west, across a derelict and deserted continent, towards the distant end of the plague zone, if there was one. It seemed, for a while, that the whole of America was his, and that he and Prickles were the only people left alive.

It was when he stopped singing that Prickles woke up. She looked at him, in the dim green light of the instrument panel, and he was sweating and pale.

'Daddy?' she said.

He didn't answer.

'Daddy? What's the matter?'

Dr. Petrie smiled as much as he could. There was a sharp pain in his groin, and he wasn't sure how much longer he could drive. He gradually slowed the Mercedes down, and pulled it in towards the side of the highway.

He stopped the car and switched off the engine. They were in Delaware, just outside of Wilmington. The night was dark, and there was the sound of insects from the highway verge.

Prickles said, 'Daddy – are you sick?'

Dr. Petrie shook his head. He touched her honey-colored hair, and her serious, beautiful, unpretty face.

'Do you know something?' he whispered. She looked at him attentively. The pains were worse, and he was beginning to feel nauseous.

'What, Daddy?' she asked, when he didn't say anything more.

Things seemed to be advancing and receding. Leonard Petrie felt sharp tearing pains start up in his bowels.

He stared at Prickles and said quietly, 'You will never forgive us for this.'